LORDS OF PAIN

WE *KEEP* WHAT'S *OURS*

SAMANTHA RUE
ANGEL LAWSON

Copyright © 2022 by Angel Lawson & Samantha Rue
All rights reserved.

No portion of this book may be reproduced in any form without written permission from the publisher or author, except as permitted by U.S. copyright law.

Printed in China

LORDS
OF
PAIN

WE *KEEP*
WHAT'S *OURS*

SAMANTHA RUE
ANGEL LAWSON

Copyright © 2022 by Angel Lawson & Samantha Rue
All rights reserved.

No portion of this book may be reproduced in any form without written permission from the publisher or author, except as permitted by U.S. copyright law.

Printed in China

THE ROYAL HOUSES OF
FORSYTH

To late nights, getting lost in messy stories with your best friends.

PROLOGUE

ROYALTY

Gnawing at my fingernail, I ask, "What about this one?"

Mary frowns through my screen. "Not enough tits, sis."

"Seriously?" I look down at my cleavage. I won't pretend like I've got the biggest tits in the world, but I'm not totally flat, either. Things might be a lot easier for me if I were. "I'm completely hanging out."

"Pfft," she says. "Show some nipple or something, Story. The Daddies cream themselves over a hint of nipple." I tug at the top of my tank and rub my thumb over my nipple. It hardens. Mary, who I'm talking to over video chat, gives me a thumbs up. "Perfect."

"What should I ask for?" I snap a few test pictures, trying to look sexy and far happier than I feel. "I keep getting gift cards to Starbucks, but I have to sell them to get the cash."

"Then start going for straight cash," she says, smacking on a stick of gum. "He's obviously on the line."

I didn't mean to get into being a Sugar Baby, but after posting a photo of myself on the beach in my bikini over spring break, the requests kept coming in on my ChattySnap account. I was curious at the time, but not enough to really follow through with anything.

Not until things got bad enough.

Three months later and I've got quite a following. Apparently, virgins aren't a social embarrassment in the world of Sugar Daddies the way it is at my high school.

"Five bucks for a tank without a bra," Mary lists off, "ten for full cleavage with a little nipple. Twenty for topless, but I think if you change into the pale pink tank, you'll get more money."

I do the math. If I send out five topless pics, that's a quick hundred bucks. That's a bus ticket and a meal. It's not enough to really set me up for The Plan, but it's a nice start. Just holding the ticket in my hand will be enough to make this all bearable, for just a little while longer.

"Okay," I say, pushing back the nerves that have started building in my stomach. The deeper I get into this, the scarier it is. Scary because it involves exposing myself to strangers. Scary because they'll have a part of me—the same part of me I've been trying so hard to keep to myself. Scary because I need it, and if there's one thing I've learned this past year, it's that needing something means giving in to someone else's power.

"My tank is down in the laundry room," I explain, antsy. "Let me grab it and just get this over with."

Mary hangs up and I leave my phone on the bed. The laundry room is downstairs, off of the kitchen. Even though it's been a year, I'm still not used to the size of this house—my stepfather's house. Before my mom married Daniel, we were living in a two-bedroom apartment that overlooked the railroad tracks. Now we're in a cozy seven-thousand square foot McMansion with a pool and an entertainment room downstairs. For a long time, it felt more like a hotel than home.

Now it feels like something else.

I sneak through the kitchen and eye the discarded pizza boxes on the island. That and the trash talk coming from the basement are a sure sign that my stepbrother and his friends are downstairs.

I pause at the realization, feeling stupid.

Laughter bounces up the stairs, like a sharp warning. Killian and his best friends, Dimitri Rathbone and Tristian Mercer, are inseparable, spending all their time together as the reigning kings of our high school. The three of them comprise the complete royalty of the senior class. I don't need to be living with one of them to really *know* them—everyone just does.

I shouldn't be surprised they're over. It's all around school that Tristian got dumped by his girlfriend the other day. If petty high school drama didn't look like juvenile bullshit from my vantage, I'd probably call it a huge scandal. Being a girlfriend to one of these three is like winning the damn lottery. You get the infamy, the expensive gifts, and what basically amounts to three round-the-clock bodyguards. These three share everything, and they protect what's theirs.

She's obviously smart, though. She probably discovered what all those other girls never will: that it's not worth it. They're cold boys, eyes always watching. There's a certain cast to their faces when I'm around that makes the hair on the back of my neck rise. Luckily, I'm a junior and it's been made very clear that I'm never to look at or address them, and under no circumstances should anyone consider my stepbrother and I family.

Not that I'd ever want to be associated with an asshole like him, anyway. There for a minute, right at the start, Killian had been fine. Not kind, nor warm, nor even cordial, but a lot like a prisoner might treat his cell-mate. It was an acceptance, an acknowledgment, that neither of us had a choice in this. He'd been almost sympathetic, bordering on friendly. Briefly, I'd thought of us as allies.

It didn't last long.

I'm not sure exactly when it stopped, but these days, my stepbrother goes out of his way to make it perfectly clear that he loathes me. His friends alternate between ignoring me and sending me vicious, mocking barbs as their eyes track me, waiting, hoping to get a rise out of me. I used to wonder why, trying to figure out what I'd done to make them so mean to me. Killian and his friends are the kind of boys who are blessed with it all; looks, brains, money, athleticism. They're gods around campus and the attitude doesn't stop when they're at home, especially down in Killian's lair.

I know now that they never needed a reason.

Hearing them is just a reminder of how exhausting it all is, tiptoeing around this house, avoiding all the landmines. There's one at every step, it seems. The whole thing has made me paranoid. I feel like I'm constantly being watched. Or that someone has been in my room. I could handle that, though. For my mom. For security. But once things escalated…

I take a deep breath to settle my nerves. I have The Plan, right? I just need to get the money and then I'm home free. I'll get my shirt, flee back to my room, lock my door, and get my business over with.

There are three baskets of clean clothes in the laundry room—mostly Killian's football gear. The whole room smells faintly of sour sweat and lingering body spray. No matter how many times my mom bleaches his uniform, the stench never really goes away. I bend over and sort through one of the baskets for my blush-colored tank.

"Thank god," I sigh, snagging the cotton shirt in my fingers. "Found you."

"Nope, looks like *we* found *you*."

My heart leaps up my throat and I spin, hand clutched to my throat. Tristian and Dimitri—Rath, as everyone calls him—stand in the doorway.

"God, you scared me." I exhale, darting my eyes between them. "You shouldn't sneak around like that."

"Why not?" Tristian says, a sharp, lopsided grin tugging at his mouth. From the glassy look in his eyes and the way he reeks of beer, he's clearly been drowning his sorrows down there. I'm not dumb enough to imagine he's broken-hearted from getting dumped. Probably just nursing his bruised ego. "You're the one sneaking around up here like a frightened little mouse."

Tristian is insanely good-looking. He's all blond hair, tan skin, and lean, hard muscle. I know that, out of the three of them, he does best with the girls.

Much like Killian and Rath, he's also enormous. Intimidating not just because of his size, wealth, and popularity, but mostly because of *something else*.

His smile never quite reaches his eyes.

They're ice blue and carry a glint of cool detachment. Just looking into them makes me want to wrap my arms around myself.

Rath is the opposite of Tristian, with his inky-black hair, lip piercings, pale skin, and dark eyes. He's quieter than the other two, those intense eyes always watching, tracking. We had a class together for a single semester last year, and it was enough to make me hate even being in the same room with him. A long stare from him always gives me a hind-brain impulse to hide. "Check it out," Rath says, jerking his chin at me. "Story's not wearing a bra."

Just the mention of it makes my nipples hard, doubling my embarrassment.

"Perky little nipples, eh?" Tristian says, taking a step into the small room. My eyes flick to his hand, wrapping around the door jamb, caging me in. His lips part and he wets them with his tongue. "Are they sensitive? Did they get hard just from me talking about them? Or do I need to touch them?"

My jaw drops and I cross my arms over my chest. "You're a pig." I start toward the door prepared to squeeze past them, but they block the exit completely. I jerk back, nostrils flaring angrily. "Get out of my way."

"Answer one question for us, Story, and then we'll let you go," Rath says, propping his shoulder against the jamb. He's wearing a lazy smirk and I can smell the beer wafting off him, too. I try to peer over his broad shoulders, hoping to see Killian somewhere. He can't stand it when I'm around his friends. He'll get them to back off.

Finding no sign of him, I release a frustrated sigh. "What do you want to know?"

Rath's head tilts, eyes taking me in. "Are you a virgin?"

"What?" My cheeks are blistering before the word is even out of my mouth. "That's none of your business!"

They both laugh, the tone deep and mocking. Tristian shakes his head, eyes flashing in something menacing and delighted. "Oh Story, only virgins say it's no one's business. You just gave yourself away."

My mouth forms around a weak denial, but I clamp it shut. "Well, who cares?" I snap. "So what? I'm a virgin. Big deal!"

"Nothing we didn't already know," Tristian says, taking another step forward. I move back and bump into the hard edge of the washing machine. "You have that look. All innocent and clean and pure. The kind of thing that just makes you want to..." He reaches out, ignoring the way I bat his hand away when he tries to stroke my collarbone. "Mess it all up."

He has no idea just how hard his words hit.

Rath rakes his bottom lip through his teeth and I don't like the look in his eyes—hungry and heavy. "There's something about virgins, you know?"

"That nervous energy," Tristian agrees. "It gets my dick hard."

"I like the begging." Rath adds, his deep voice shifting into a falsetto, *"Please don't, it hurts!"*

The anxious butterflies in my stomach turn to stone.

"But my favorite part," Tristian says, blue eyes pulsing and dilating, "is breaking them in. Feeling that tight pussy wrapped around my cock?" He reaches down to...*shift* himself. "There's nothing better than that. Damn, what I'd give to break you in right."

"You guys are disgusting," I say, lifting my chin. "I'm not scared of you, you know. You're just a bunch of socially-stunted shitheads. That's probably the only way you can get it, isn't it? Bullying girls into giving it up? No wonder your sorry ass got dumped."

Tristian's demeanor shifts on a dime, all traces of joking washed away. "What did you just say to me?"

I shrug, shifting my glare to Rath. "Guess *someone* in the senior class has more than two brain cells to rub together." I know from the way his eyes sharpen that he's remembering the class we shared. Looking back to Tristian, I say, "It's not like it's a secret that Genevieve tossed you to the curb. Too bad money can't buy you a personality to go with your micro dick."

I'm trying to hold my ground and look tough, but I can't stop the embarrassing shudder of fear at the way their faces harden, eyes sparking in anger. I sense what's going to happen a beat too late. Tristian moves quickly, darting forward and clamping his hand around my throat. My chest hitches on a panicked inhale, hands grabbing his wrist, but his arm is like steel.

He's not squeezing my throat, but he flexes his fingers, and I read the message loud and clear. *He could*. Roughly, he says, "Pretty shitty way to treat someone who was just giving you some compliments. Isn't that right, Rath?"

"Rude as fuck," Rath agrees.

"Maybe," Tristian says, prying my fingers from his wrist, "we should show her just how small our dicks *aren't*." He yanks my hand down until it's pressed to the bulge at the front of his jeans. "As you so obnoxiously just pointed out, I seem to be finding myself short of a steady fuck these days. Maybe I'll take you, after all."

I fight to pull my hand away, mouth screwing up in disgust, but he holds my palm there for a long moment, grinding against it. "Fighting will only make it hurt more, baby. I know that's not what you want…or is it?" He tilts his head, like he's assessing me. All he gets is the feel of a hard, involuntary swallow beneath his palm. "Maybe you would, huh? You like it rough? Because we're good with that."

Rath stonily adds, "Crazy good."

I try to speak, but my voice is trapped somewhere in my chest, caught in the irony of the moment. Here I've been keeping my eye on one threat only to walk into another.

This can't happen. Not now. Not like this. Not with these guys. Not when I've managed to dodge worse—so much worse since moving in here. My eyes drop down to Tristian's wrist. The corded muscles in his forearm as he holds me by the throat flex and shift beneath the skin. I test my strength against his other hand, yanking it sharply away from his crotch. I do, but I'm not fooled. He just let me. Even one of these guys would be impossible to fight off, but two? My heart goes from racing to thunderous as I realize how entirely overpowered I am here. I could fight. I could kick, scream, lash out.

Or I could reason with them.

They can't be as bad as all that, can they?

"Come on, let me go." My voice comes out in a whisper. "I just want to go back to my room."

Tristian's lips curl into a sinister grin. "But the fun's just beginning, isn't it?"

A shadow moves in the doorway and my heart leaps. Killian's broad shoulders fill the space. He looks between his friends and me, face blank.

"Killian," I say, eyes pleading, "tell them to let me go."

"What's going on?" he asks casually, like his friend doesn't have me by the throat, pinned to the washing machine. "I thought you were bringing down more beer."

Rath's dark eyes remain fixed to me as he explains, "Story was just telling us how she's a virgin."

My stepbrother's face remains eerily blank. "Was she, now."

Tristian's looking straight into my eyes when he adds, "We were saying how we'd be happy to help her fix that pesky problem."

From the expression on his face, you'd think Killian was being asked whether or not he wanted pepperoni on his pizza. So casual and aloof. Unaffected.

I swallow to remove the dry lump from my throat. "Killian, I don't know why you don't like me, but—"

"You don't know why I don't like you?" He barks a caustic, scoffing laugh. "Your white-trash slut of a mother wrecks my family, and brings her little whoreling with her, and you can't figure out why I don't like you." His eyes slither down my body, lip curling. "I don't give a shit what these two do to you. They could both fuck you at the same time, and you know what I'd do?" His eyes spark and blaze, and there's no mistaking the surety of his words. "I'd *laugh.*"

He means it, and for some reason, I'm surprised. I always knew he hated me, but this?

This is fucking evil.

Killian is never going to be my saving grace.

"I'll tell your dad," I blurt, panicking. Normally I'm not a narc. Snitches get stitches and all that. I've never told on Killian for the other things he's done; the weed, the porn, the party he threw a few months ago where two girls left crying. Secretly, I hoped that keeping my mouth shut might make him warm to me, at least a little. Clearly, I was wrong. But the thing about Killian's dad is that he *likes* me. "I'll tell him that you let them do it."

Killian's face shutters, his brown eyes staring blankly back at me. "Just because my dad has some idiotic weakness for sluts doesn't mean he'd choose you over me."

The way he says it, the emphasis on the word slut, makes me wonder if he knows what his father is doing, what he tried to do, but I'm desperate so I continue, "If you let me go, we can pretend this never happened, okay? I won't—I will never say a thing, Killian, I swear."

Abruptly, he barks out a harsh laugh. "You're such a fucking idiot. I really hope your tits get bigger, because that's clearly all you've got going for you. You really think I'd let trash like you live under my roof and not come up with some leverage of my own?"

"Leverage?"

He reaches into his pocket and pulls out his phone. Tristian's still holding my neck and his thumb keeps sweeping up to my jaw, stroking little circles into it. Each caress sends a tremor across my limbs. Nausea rolls in my belly as my stepbrother holds up his phone. I only have to see a glimpse of the screen to know what he's talking about. He smirks when he sees the recognition on my face.

"That's right, *Sweet Cherry*. You say a word about me and my friends, and

I'll show my idiot dad, who thinks you're the most innocent little snowflake, exactly what you've been doing online." He flips through the Sugar Baby account I made, including the photos I've posted. I look far from innocent. "Quite the little lucrative business you've got going on, Cherry. You may be a virgin but you're far from innocent. I mean, who's to say anyone would even believe you after seeing this? You, slutting it up just like your gold-digging mother? Tsk tsk." He taps the phone on his chin, eyes full of amusement. "Nah, I think you'll give my boys exactly what they want."

Fuck.

The Plan. I need quick money, and that's the only way I'm going to get it, but worse is the threat of Killian's dad finding out.

"I'll give you a cut of the money," I say, breath coming in frantic gasps when Tristian's grip tightens around my throat. "Whatever I make, I'll give you a quarter. *No.* Half of it!"

Killian barks a dark laugh. "That's fucking rich. You giving me money? You two hearing this shit?"

Tristian smiles and it lights up his whole face. "Oh, Sweet Cherry, we don't want your money. I thought we made that clear." His face tips down into mine and he runs his nose down my cheek. His breath is hot, reeking of beer, and my skin crawls. He looks back at Rath. "How do we want to do this? Who gets to pop this delicious little cherry?"

Do this?

Rath wagers, "You fuckers owe me for last month."

Tristian scoffs. "Eat shit, that's nowhere near equal value. You still owe me for Sophomore year."

"You're still on about that?" Rath complains, face hardening. "Fine. Three thousand and my guitar."

Hot tears spring to my eyes. This can't be happening. They're negotiating over me like a piece of meat. "Please don't do this," I beg. "Don't hurt me. I'll give you whatever you want, just don't…take *that*."

"Ah, the begging," Rath groans, hand coming down to cup his crotch. "Fine, four thousand."

My knees buckle, but Tristian's hands move to my arms, holding me up. Rath slides behind me, hands cinching around my waist. I make eye contact with Killian again, silently pleading with him. His gaze is cold. Uncaring. It's more than obvious he doesn't give a damn about what happens to me. That's why it shocks me when he says, "Neither of you are fucking her."

Tristian and Rath both freeze, turning to look at him.

"Do whatever else you want to, I don't care, but..." He rakes his fingers through his hair, looking away, jaw tight. "The last thing I need is for her to bleed out all over the laundry room floor. I'm not cleaning that shit up, and I'm sure as hell not explaining it to my dad."

"The biggest value a girl has is her innocence," Daniel told me that night in his office. His words, his hands, made my stomach twist painfully. *"Who you give that gift to, Story, will be the most important decision you make."*

Did Killian get that same lecture? Something tells me he did.

Rath mutters a curse of disappointment in my ear, but Tristian's eyes sweep over me, undeterred. He takes a step back and says, "Fine. Let's see your tits."

It's a demand, and although I should fight back and say no, I'm scared that Killian will tell my mom and Daniel about my Sugar Baby account.

Rath doesn't give me more time to think about it anyway, grabbing the straps of my tank top and shoving them down my arms. He grunts behind me and I feel his gaze over my shoulder. Tristian licks his lips and reaches for me, his fingers grazing the underneath of my breast. "A little small, but soft. Am I the first one to touch them?"

I clamp my mouth shut and glare defiantly, refusing to let them take anything else personal away from me. He grins wickedly and pinches my nipple. I yelp in response and try to twist away. Rath doesn't let me move far, holding me against his solid body. The proximity makes it impossible not to feel the hard bulge in his pants.

"I asked you a question, Sweet Cherry." Tristian's fingers circle lazily around my other nipple, waiting.

"Yes," I grind out, lying. "You're the first."

"Thank you." He tweaks me softly, sending a flare of traitorous sparks down my body.

"Dude," Killian says, "I know you're having a bad week and working some shit out here, but my dad will be home soon. Whatever you're going to do, just get on with it."

Tristian runs his thumb over my mouth, eyes fixed to the movement. "Get on your knees."

There's no mistaking what he wants me to do, and after Killian told him to hurry, he picks up his pace. There's no time to process as he unbuckles his belt and pulls down his jeans. He's not wearing underwear and his penis is just as hard as it'd felt under my palm before. It's big, straining at the skin and pointing right at me. I stare down at it, frozen in shock until Rath's hands bear down on my shoulders, forcing me to my knees.

To my horror, Rath comes down with me, still aligned with my back. I hear his zipper lower while one hand snakes around to grope my breast.

"What are you doing?" I ask, barely recognizing the sound of my own voice.

"Watching," he says, nipping at my earlobe. "Feeling. Getting off. There's more than one way to enjoy a girl."

I take one last look at my stepbrother, one last chance to hope he's come to his senses. There has to be something human inside of him. I refuse to believe otherwise. But I don't find any sympathy there. God, no. I find him in the process of shoving his hand down his shorts and pulling his own cock out. He leans back against the door jamb and takes two long strokes as he watches. The movement is obscene and strangely hostile. It looks like a warning.

Tristian's fingers touch me under the chin, and he redirects my gaze upward, toward his icy eyes. "Open up, Sweet Cherry. I want your eyes on me the whole time. I want to see those pretty lips wrapped around my cock. I want to see it when I come and you swallow it down. I want you to watch me while it happens." He licks his lips, thumbing my mouth open. "Understood?"

I nod, understanding everything. Understanding that no one, not even family, is going to save me. Understanding that this is all life is for me now, one sicko after another, lining up to take something from me. Someone a little more naïve might think it was bad luck.

I know better.

I open my mouth and take him in.

I close my eyes and try to shut everything out, to curl into the back of my brain the way I've learned. It isn't me doing this. This is just automatic. Something else has taken over my body and I'm watching it, locked away somewhere safe.

I can't quite get to that place this time, though.

Tristian makes a low sound, hand fisting in my hair as my lips slide up his shaft. Rath's breaths are loud against my ear and his touch is inescapable, hand cupping my breast, rolling my nipple between forefinger and thumb.

"Never sucked a dick before, have you Cherry?" Tristian's thumb prods at my cheek, and despite his disapproving words, his voice emerges in a pained rasp. "You realize that's where the real money is, don't you? Daddies would pay a sweet penny for some head if you can do it right." He tightens his grip on my hair and thrusts into my mouth.

I sputter angrily around his cock, jerking back.

He holds me still. "I thought I told you to look at me. Not very good at following instructions, are you?"

My hands curl into tight fists against my side, but I do it. I pry my eyes open and wrench them up, meeting Tristian's glazed eyes.

"That's a girl," he says, patting my head like I'm a dog. "I'll make this easy on you."

It's laughable. *Easy*. Nothing about this is easy. I'm trying so hard to ignore the sight of Killian in my periphery, of Rath's hand skating down my ribs, that I'm taken by surprise when Tristian starts thrusting in and out of my mouth. My hands shoot up to his hips, holding him back, but his eyes narrow, grip tightening in my hair.

"Either I fuck your mouth or you get better at this. Your choice, Story."

I hold his hips, glaring up at him even though my eyes are welling with tears. And then I start bobbing my head. I'm pretty sure blow jobs aren't supposed to be like this—bitter and angry in the way I work my tongue against him. I look into his eyes as I do it, watch them dilate, jaw slackening. Now, it's more of a promise than a blow job.

A promise that these boys aren't going to break me.

"Fuck," Tristian breathes, feet shifting. "Yeah, that's it. Shit, she's really doing it."

I can feel Rath behind me, the bounce of his arm as he jerks himself. His hand snakes down my stomach, shoving into the waistband of my shorts, and I know better now than to fight.

Doesn't mean I don't try.

"Shh," he says into my ear. "Relax." Despite what's happening here, his fingers are slow and teasing when they push into my panties, shoulders curling around me. I already know what he's going to find down there, but it doesn't make it any less humiliating when he pauses. He whispers low into my ear, "Should I tell them how wet you are for this?"

My fingers are digging bruises into Tristian's hips, but he doesn't even seem fazed.

"I don't think I will," Rath decides, fingers rubbing tight circles around my clit. "Now we can both have a secret. Keep your mouth shut about mine and maybe I won't tell everyone how much of a slut you are for all three of us. You are, aren't you?" His chuckle is warm and damp against my ear. Loud enough for the others to hear, he adds, "You could be ours, you know. We could take turns. We don't mind sharing if it's with each other."

PROLOGUE | STORY

My angry tears spill over, making hot tracks down my face. Tristian keeps his eyes locked on mine, but brings his hand to my cheek, thumbing them away. "Don't cry, now. We're just having a good time. You want us to have a good time, don't you?" My only response is the way I stare at him, wet-eyed and full of hate. He sighs as I suck him. "I don't get it, Killer," he says, talking to my stepbrother. "Used to be, we could show a girl a little attention and she'd trip over her own feet to be ours. Nowadays, all these bitches do is fuck around."

He fists a hand in my hair, yanking me deeper onto his dick, glazed eyes flashing. It makes me cry harder, because that, combined with what Rath is doing to me, is making my hips want to grind into Rath's hand, and *god*.

It's the worst part of all of this, knowing that Rath could be right.

Maybe this is what I am.

A magnet for creeps, something to be used, and a slut for all of it.

Tristian's head falls back, eyes falling closed, and I'm grateful for the reprieve when the sharp, building ache between my legs reaches a full crescendo, clenching as Rath moves with the movement of my hips. The reprieve doesn't last long. Tristian thickens and pulses in my mouth, his thick, salty release surging against my tongue. He cups the back of my head and presses me close, holding me there as he empties himself between my lips.

Behind me, Rath grunts, yanking me against his chest, and I'm caught in the middle of them, being pulled two different ways. I hear more than see Killian finish, his rough, breathless groan startling me.

Tristian pulls out of my mouth, but not before he grabs my hair and rasps out, "You know what to do now, don't you?"

Rath takes his hands out of my shorts and grabs my jaw, forcing my chin up. "Swallow him down, pretty girl."

It takes me three tries to do it without gagging, but I hold Tristian's gaze as I obey, swallowing his release. I hope it looks like how Killian had before—hostile—a warning—instead of showing this lost, aching thing in my chest.

"Good," he says, stroking my cheek. "You're so good for us, aren't you,

Cherry?"

I don't know how I manage to get my feet under me, but I do. I clamp my hand over my mouth as I bolt away, the sound of their breathless chuckles following in my wake.

KILLIAN PAYNE

1

A NEW LADY

Three Years Later

There's a knock at the door.

"Yo, Killian, time for our first interview."

"Yeah, give me five minutes." I grimace. "Maybe ten."

"Martin isn't going to wait ten." It's Tristian's voice. He must have just returned from the job on the South Side. "And neither am I."

I look into my dresser mirror, taking in the rippling hard muscles I've spent the last three years refining as starting quarterback on the Forsyth University football team. My body is a work of well-crafted art, and I'm not even talking about the ink covering my arms and chest. It's designed to dominate. My eyes then shift down to the girl in front of me, bent over the flat surface. Between her big, possibly fake tits, the gold charm from her sorority necklace bounces with every thrust of my hips. Her teeth bare down on her bottom lip.

"Five minutes," I say again, but it comes out in a grunt that Tristian may not have heard. I don't give a fuck, slamming into her harder. The mirror bangs against the wall, and the girl—I think her name is Cheryl, possibly Sherry—lets out this sharp, pained whimper. I smirk at her reflection. "That hurt, honey?"

"Y-yes," she squeaks, brows squeezing together. "A little."

I grab a bunch of her bleach-blonde hair in my fist and yank it back, growling, "Good."

It's getting harder and harder for me to come without a little pain added to the mix. I've been pounding into this girl for forty minutes and only now do I feel the tingle in my balls that lets me know that my orgasm is finally building. That whimper, the pinch of pained upset on her face, is swiftly getting me there.

I close my eyes and set my rhythm. Despite the blonde under me, my mind conjures up long dark hair, pale creamy skin, and blue eyes filled with just as much hatred as fear. The ache in my cock builds, tension coiling tighter with every thrust. I reach around to—maybe Shanna's—chest and grab her tits, pinching her nipples between my fingers.

"Killian, stop," she begs, trying to pry my hands from her flesh. She squirms, twisting in an attempt to get away, and that finally triggers the orgasm. I pump into her hips, slamming hard and violent into her from behind. Her cunt squeezes around me. Well, as tight as her well-fucked pussy can manage. I'm in the middle of my final thrust when the door opens, Tristian's head popping inside. His eyes go to the girl's tits first, then up to my face.

"Killer, all the applicants are downstairs. We've put this off long enough. We have to find our Lady before the semester starts tomorrow, so stop fucking around."

Placing a hand on the sorority girl's back, I pull out roughly, leaving her bent and breathless across the dresser. My dick feels nearly raw from taking so long. Maybe if her cunt wasn't so worn out, I could've come faster.

But probably not.

Blondes stopped doing anything for me years ago.

Four years ago, to be exact.

She looks back at me and scowls. "Jesus Christ, Killian. You're such a fucking asshole."

1 | KILLIAN

"Yep," I say, wiping off my dick. I bend and toss her the clothes in a pile on the floor. "You heard Tristian. I have a meeting. Go."

She gapes and looks at my buddy. Tristian. One of my best friends since as far back as I can imagine. He and Rath and I have been through thick and thin, bad and worse. He's seen way more sordid shit than my spunk running down some slut's thighs. He just gives her a sharp grin and shrugs. If she's looking for sympathy, he's the wrong one to ask.

A moment later she's out in the hall, trying to get her panties over her skinny hips and futilely covering tits. Like every LDZ hasn't seen her naked and spread-eagled already.

Rath squeezes past her in the hall, saying, "You guys need to hurry up, Martin is about to lose it."

I pull up my jeans and remind him, "Martin works for us. We're the Lords, not him. He can chill the fuck out for a minute."

"It's not just Martin," Tristian says, clearly annoyed with me. "The Dukes have their Duchess. The Counts have their Countess. Even the Princes have their Princess. We're dragging ass with finding a Lady. Makes us look weak, Killer." He says this even as he pulls the pistol from the waist of his jeans, shutting it in the drawer of my dresser. "I did not just spend three hours on the South Side negotiating with two people named Nick and Pretty Nick to have this be our downfall."

I pull on a shirt, guessing, "Pretty Nick give you trouble?" He usually does. Despite the name, nothing about him is pretty.

"Nothing more than the usual," he answers, folding his arms.

I rub my chin. "Do I need to have my dad talk to him?"

Rath cuts in, "What you need to do is *not* be fucking last year's Lady."

"He's right." Tristian nods. "That won't fly once we have our own Lady."

I roll my eyes at this, not needing them to tell me the rules here. Fidelity when it comes to a house's girl is a joke. The Dukes, the Counts, the Lords… we fuck who we want, when we want, how we want. The Princes might get off on treating their girl like a princess, but that's not us.

Either way you shake it, though, fucking a previous Lady is a huge affront—not just to the current Lady, but to the whole system itself. It says she's worth having outside the context of The Game. It tells her she's special. Better than the rest of the Ladies. Someone to keep around.

No Lady is any of those things.

"Relax," I assure them both. "I just wanted to approach this with some post-nut clarity. You two will be panting over the first big-tittied whore who walks into this place, but I'll be level-headed. We need some new blood. I'm sick of the same, tired pussy."

Tristian stresses, "We have to choose someone good—someone interesting. I saw the Duchess last week, and she is fucking *stacked*."

I scoff at this. "Big tits are nothing." All the girls are pretty and slutty. It takes something special to really set one apart in this place.

"Choosing a Lady is the worst part of winning The Game," Rath complains once again.

"Yeah," Tristian agrees, mouth twisting into a devious smile, "but *having* one is the best part of winning The Game."

The Game. The fuel that runs the Lambda Delta Zetas, or Lords, as everyone calls us. Despite the titles, the Lords are the highest tier frat on campus, and the most notorious due to the cutthroat Game played every year. It's pretty simple, all the frats on campus compete for who gets the most points by participating in a variety of challenges.

Lords always win.

As a result of our long history of owning this town, the Lords reside in our fancy as hell brownstone, complete with custom, individual rooms, a cook, a personal assistant, and of course—the very best-worst part—our own Lady, hand-selected by the previous year's winners.

Years ago, Tristian, Rath, and I made a pledge to own the Lords by senior year. We made it by our junior year instead. We didn't even have to work for

1 | KILLIAN

it—our names were enough to get us to the top—but we did anyway.

The Game isn't the garden-variety university shenanigans. There's a lot riding on the line. Reputation. Stacks of money. Careers. Mostly, it's about proving that you're the most ruthless, the most heartless, the worst of the worst, the cream of the creep crop. Some frats don't even bother with it. The Princes treat their Princess like a pampered little show wife. But we know what this Game is all about.

It's a competition that was practically made for us.

We moved in at the end of the summer, each of us taking a room in the house. Martin is our personal assistant who handles the logistics of the frat. Ms. Crane is the housekeeper and cook. They both come with the brownstone.

But the Lady? Well, that's a special job, created by Lords decades before. A female college student is hand-picked to live in the house and provide for our needs—*all* of our needs—as we see fit. In return, she gets special status on campus, free room and board, and the badge of honor of surviving a year with the most merciless guys on campus. It takes a special kind of woman to handle a Lord. It takes even more to handle three of them—especially when those Lords are me, Tristian, and Rath.

Two weeks ago, an announcement was made for this year's Lady. Martin collected the applications and set up the interviews. All we have to do is sit through them and make a selection, which, according to last year's residents, is supposed to be a fucking blast.

For them, it probably was. But for us? Well, let's just say the three of us haven't had the best luck when it comes to branding a girl as our own. We've always fucked discriminately, but these days it's one-and-done, and it's easier like that.

Look at what happened our senior year of high school, Tristian finally falling for someone he deemed worthy of the title only to find out she'd been fucking the softball coach behind his back. He plays it off pretty well these days, but Rath and I know how deep that cut goes. Rath has never let any girl close enough to deduce the scent of his deodorant, let alone live under the same roof. And then there's me, still obsessing about the one who got away. Instinctively, my gaze moves down to the inside of my bicep, to the tattoo I'd gotten Freshman year; a girl with dark hair and big eyes.

If we find a good Lady, it'll be hard to set her free. If we pick a bad one, then we'll have to live with substandard pussy for the next nine months. There's no great outcome here.

"At least we can make them do anything we want," Rath says, echoing my thoughts as we enter the parlor. That'd be a silver lining if it weren't already our usual MO. "Whittaker made every applicant give him a blow job last year."

Tristian and I nod, knowing all too well. The ones who didn't get on their knees were instantly cut.

"Yes," Martin says, looking relieved to see us ready for interviews. "They've all signed waivers. They're well aware of the position they're applying for."

We each take our seats and Martin escorts the first girl in. She's blonde, sexy, and wearing six-inch fuck me heels.

I barely glance up before saying, "Next."

STORY

2
THE INTERVIEW

I STAND IN FRONT of the brownstone, checking and rechecking the address. It's unnecessary. Everyone knows this place. For a house that's indistinguishable from the others on first glance, it only takes a moment of scrutiny to feel that this one has a strange presence. Regal. Looming. A little colder. It's hard not to think about what's behind this door. Right this second, they're in there, waiting, so close that my pulse is racing against the truth of it.

I know from my research that the house has four stories in all, including the basement, with the fourth floor probably overlooking the park. The location is perfect for students, coveted, a quick walk or bike ride to the University half a mile away. It's not a surprise that the most powerful club at the school has this for their residence.

After reconfirming the address one last time, I climb the front steps and approach the door. The brass knocker is a huge, heavy skull with Greek letters carved into the forehead. The Lambda Delta Zetas, or Lords, are a century-old exclusive club that has dominated Forsyth University for just as long. There's no doubt I'm in the right place.

After taking one last look over my shoulder, I wrench open the door and let myself in. Three other girls are already waiting in the front room—a formal parlor. Each, I assume, is here to apply for the same position. My stomach twists in anxiety as I look around, half expecting one of the guys to appear in a doorway.

I give a tight smile to the girl closest to me and take a seat in one of the armchairs. It doesn't matter how long I've prepared to be here, under the same roof as *them*. It still feels like I'm jabbing a knife into a light socket, waiting to get zapped.

I try not to compare myself to the other applicants, but it's hard. It's obvious from their hair, clothes, and physical beauty that a certain type of girl is expected here, one that doesn't surprise me in the least. I know instantly that I don't fit the mold. The pitying looks they give me in return confirms that they know it, too.

Save it, I think bitterly. I'm not here to be some show poodle for a bunch of frat boys. I wouldn't be here at all if I had other options, but desperate times call for desperate measures.

And that's exactly what I am.

Desperate.

Why else would I come here, to these three men who have already hurt me, shamed me, violated me? It'd have to be bad, to seek them out, to put myself beneath their heels again, but willingly this time. Once again, my stomach turns at the thought. Even though I've faced it down and accepted what must be done, it doesn't make it easy.

I never told on Killian and his friends for what they did to me, which is funny, in a horrific sort of way. I'd ended up shutting down my sugar baby account anyway. Obeying their disgusting orders was all for nothing, in the end. I didn't leave my room for a week, faking sick, and falling into a deep depression. Something about the three of them knowing about my sugar baby account bothered me almost as much as what'd happened in the laundry room. As a result, I'd deleted all traces of my online activities.

The Plan was dead in the water. There'd be no getting out—not on my own, not without help. After a week of hiding in my room and cleaning up my past, I begged my mother to let me apply to boarding school. She and Daniel argued about it for days, until eventually the word came. He'd agreed to pay for me to go to an all-girls school across the country. It wasn't ideal. My plan had been to run away. To be on my own and *free*. But sometimes you have to make compromises.

I packed my things and never looked back.

The first year away was about getting my shit together. I focused on my studies, joined activities and groups, tried my best to adapt to this idea of a normal, safe life. Things were even going smoothly.

Until the first letter from Ted arrived.

He was one of the first sugar daddies I'd spoken to. The letters were terrifying at first, the constant panic of having been found, even clear across the country, infecting every aspect of my new life. But really, the letters were nothing, not in comparison to what came next. The gifts. The messages on my personal social media. The emails. The photos. The videos. They grew more and more threatening, possessive, bitter at my lack of response. Even when I finally did get my wish—when I finally ran away from it all—he still found me again.

It was the biggest escalation that finally drove me here, to this awful place, with these terrible, heartless people.

The click-clack of heels on the marble floor echo down the hallway and another girl appears from the back of the house. Her blonde hair is in a sleek ponytail, her dress bright blue and cinched at the waist with a belt. Her shoes match and have sharp, pointed heels. Although she looks put together, her cheeks are red and she's rubbing at something on her skirt with a handkerchief.

"Fucker came on my dress," she says to the room. "This thing is silk!"

If anyone is shocked by what she says, they don't show it. I'm grossed out but unsurprised. There's nothing I'd put past these guys. They already proved that to me in spades.

A youngish, serious-faced guy appears in the hallway and calls out in a wobbly voice, "Bridget Walker?"

The brunette next to me stands and smooths out her skirt. She appears confident but I see the falter in her step. She's smart to be nervous. She's walking into a goddamn lion's den, a sweet little lamb for the slaughter.

The door clicks shut down the hall. I stare at my nails, wondering for the millionth time if I'm doing the right thing. Then I remember that this isn't about the right thing. It's about survival.

"So," the redhead across from me says. I glance up and see her addressing the other girl in the room. She's curvy with smooth brown skin. A chain hangs around her neck with an elegant, cursive 'D' settling in the dip of her cleavage. "A friend of mine had her interview yesterday."

"Oh yeah? Any advice?" D asks, as though we're not competing for the same position.

"They're all good looking and sexy. Intimidating. But you know that, I'm sure. It's obvious when they're walking around campus. But she said one of them seems really nice, at least. Sweet and charming, all smiles."

Tristian Mercer. I'd know that description anywhere. People are so easily taken by it, even though he's mean as a snake beneath the façade.

"Then there's the quiet one with the piercings. Hot as hell, but super intense. Stared at her the whole time and totally gave her the creeps."

Dimitri Rathbone—Rath.

"And then there's the psychopath."

"The what?" D asks, frowning.

"Killian, you know? Killer. He's like ridiculously, panty-melting hot. Got a full ride for football, but…I don't know. She said something is just off about him. It's like he's more than just a jerk. Like maybe he's dangerous."

D seems to consider this. "Dangerous can be sexy."

"Yeah," the redhead says, flipping her hair over her shoulder, "I know, but this is like another level. She said he's completely in control at all times, to the point that when she blew him, he lasted so long her knees were rubbed raw and her jaw had totally locked up by the time he finally came."

And that would be Killian Payne. My stepbrother. They have no idea just how much of a psycho he really is.

D just rolls her eyes. "That's nothing special. I auditioned to be Countess last month and you wouldn't believe some of the stuff they made me do."

Red holds up a hand, head shaking. "No, I mean…obviously, any house is going to put their girl through the wringer—"

"Except the Princes," I cut in, trying not to wilt under their gazes. I've done my homework. I know all about the rival frats and their respective girls.

Red snorts. "The Princes don't even count. They're total pussies." Despite this, I see the way her eyes flick away, the spark of resentment there. She'd interviewed to be their Princess, no doubt about it. "But the Lords take it to another level. They're more than just controlling. It extends to everything. What you wear, when you eat, where you sleep. They completely rule your life. They own you."

"And in return, you're the most powerful girl at school. No one can touch you. Well," she laughs, "except them. Are you trying to scare me off? Because I know what I'm getting into. I've done my research."

"Same," Red replies. "Being the Lady on campus is the highest position you can have on the social scale at FU. I'll do whatever it takes to get there." Her gaze shifts to me. In a moment of clarity, I realize that this little gossip session was meant specifically to frighten me. "What about you, sweetie? Are you willing to do what it takes to be their Lady?"

Down the hall, the door swings open and the brunette, Bridget, emerges. She stumbles for a couple steps before finding her footing, eyes rimmed with red. Her shirt is wrinkled, skirt all twisted sideways, lipstick slashed into a dark smear over her mouth. She glances at the three of us, declaring, "Fucking pigs," and storms out of the house.

When we're alone again, I look at Red and D, smiling sweetly back at them. "Oh, I'm willing to do what it takes."

I know what I look like compared to these girls. They're all in heels and tight skirts, low-cut tops, breasts hanging out, hair teased and shiny, lips stained a whole palette of glossy reds. They look ready. Prepared. *Eager*.

By contrast, I'm wearing a simple sundress and flats, my hair up in a clean ponytail. Just a touch of foundation and blush, nothing more. I must look cute and innocent next to them, like someone who doesn't know what she's agreeing to. I look like someone who'll be scared away. Someone who'll have to be chased. Someone who'd say no.

"Better than that," I add, looking away. "I know exactly *what* it takes."

"Mary McBeth…"

It takes me a minute to realize the man is talking to me, even though I'm the only one left in the room. The two other girls had both gone in and left—each looking a little numb on their way out the door. I'd given a false name. I couldn't tip them off that I'm coming in for the interview.

"That's me," I say, standing up. He gestures for me to follow him down the hall, stopping before a pair of closed wooden doors. I take a deep, steeling breath. He gives me a final sympathetic look before turning the knob.

They pay us no attention as he crosses the threshold, each too caught up in themselves to notice who's entering. I peer around him, getting a good look at the guys who nearly destroyed me. It's been over three years since I laid an eye on any of them.

All three look a little older. Rath has a leather journal in his lap, scribbling notes inside. Wireless headphones are plugged in his ears. The lines of his jaw are sharper than before, more defined by the dark scruff of his beard, and he has a new nose piercing to go with the two in his bottom lip. His hair is a bit longer, shaggier around the ears, and his body is long, taking up the entire leather loveseat. He still has the same presence I remember from high school, like the

light bends around him, making his aura just a touch darker than everything else.

Tristian sits across from him, and time has served him just as well. His cheekbones are sharper than I remember, hair still an immaculate sweep of pale gold. He has a man's face, now. Full lips and long, dark eyelashes that oppose his fair hair. He's scrolling through his phone, smirking at whatever he's perusing. He almost looks nice.

Almost.

If it weren't for the red handprint blooming across his cheek.

Either Red or D must have slapped him. Internally, I'm impressed. They'd both seemed completely down for this. It's good to know that even these boys'—these *Lords'*—biggest fans still have their limits.

I shift my gaze to the third man in the room. Killian, my stepbrother. I almost don't recognize him. His eyes are cast down at the floor, jaw flexing around something that looks frustrated and impatient. He's bigger than before, probably a half a foot taller, wider across the shoulders and chest. His shirt looks handmade, fitted perfectly to accentuate the bulging muscles in his arms and chest. Below that is the sprawling canvas of ink that his skin has become. His arms are absolutely covered in tattoos. No single one stands out more than the others, but I can clearly see the word 'KILL' spelled out across his rough knuckles. If the boy I once knew looked strong and intimidating, then I don't even have words for the man standing before me right now.

Killian looks like a gangster.

When his eyes first find mine, it feels like my heart wants to beat itself from my own chest. His body might be different, but that face and those eyes…

I'd know them anywhere. I've seen them in my nightmares for years now. Always watching, looming, observing me.

Despite that, I can't help but notice the similarity between his face and his father's. This sharper, harder, more mature version of Killian is still devoid of any sort of emotion. Even as he takes me in—even as his eyes flash in realization—that doesn't change.

"Your final appointment is here," the guy says. "Is there anything else you need me to do?"

"Shut the door," is all Killian says, eyes still pinning me in place, and their lackey steps back, encouraging me to enter. I step into the room and feel their gazes on me all at once. Now it's my stomach's turn to feel like it wants to exit my body. Every hair on my body stands on end, and for a moment, I feel like I might run.

I'd practiced what I wanted to say a million times over the last week, but now that I'm here facing them down, it's caught in my throat like a boulder. The way they all stare at me, silent and still, makes me wonder if they're feeling the same thing. Maybe they're not used to being confronted with their past crimes. Maybe they expect their trash to stay gone once they've thrown it away.

It's Tristian who shakes out of it first. "Well, well, well. If it isn't Sweet Cherry," he drawls, my nickname like honey on his tongue. He leans back, throwing his arms over the back of the seats. His gaze fixes itself to my mouth. "This is an unexpected surprise."

Rath pulls the buds from his ears slowly, one by one, dark eyes assessing me. Apart from the tight line of his lips, his face is expressionless, that cold gaze making me shiver under its inspection.

With the two of them looking at me, it's like I'm back in that laundry room all over again. They're the predators. I'm the prey. I have to curl my hands into fists to stop them from trembling under the intensity of the memory. The sharp taste of semen. Fingers sliding through my folds. The sound of their harsh, excited breaths as they used me like a cheap toy. No. I won't tremble and cower before these men.

I'm not that girl anymore.

Tristian jerks his chin at me. "You never said your little sister was in town, Killer."

Killian's still staring at me, but now his face is set into a hard scowl, lip peeled back. He's looking at me like he just scraped me off the bottom of his shoe. "She's not my sister."

"Not so little anymore, either," Tristian says, eyes sweeping over me before once again settling on my mouth. I get this humiliating flash of memory—the way his penis felt as it slid between my lips, the warmth of his fingertip as he swept my tears away. I feel the heat bubbling on my cheeks and it makes his lips tip up into a smirk. "Look at you, all grown up."

He's right. I've matured. Physically, emotionally. A year of boarding school, a few months on the street, and a year and a half working and living and *surviving* has a way of doing that to a person. It's already obvious that these three are exactly the same as they were that night. There's no remorse here.

"What are you doing here, Story?" Killian asks, voice deep and rough. "Last I heard, you'd skipped out on boarding school and fucked off to parts unknown. Now you show up on my doorstep? If you're looking to even the score, you're a little late. If we were untouchable before, then we're practically Teflon now. Should have stuck around if you wanted to take a shot."

I push my shoulders back, chin up. "I'm here to interview for the position. I'm applying to be your Lady."

There's a long stretch of silence, their eyes unblinking as they absorb my words.

"You're applying to be our Lady," Killian says, voice hard and flat. He leans forward, shoulders shifting, and rests his inked elbows on his knees. "Are you even fucking aware of what the job entails?"

Unflinchingly, I answer, "To serve the needs of the Lords that live in the household." It's a bit of a copout. They're the only Lords living here.

"You know, maybe I'm misremembering," Rath says, head cocked to the side, "but the last time we talked, you weren't very compliant about serving others."

"Not willingly, anyway," Tristian adds, flashing me a sharp, lopsided grin. "Although that didn't bother me very much."

"It's like you said," I insist, voice like stone. "I've changed."

"Does my father know you're here?" Killian asks, knitting his fingers tightly together.

"Since June. He's the one who helped me get into Forsyth." The hatred in Killian's eyes turns a shade darker. "But I'd rather do this on my own. I figured that a job that took care of my room and board would be the right step."

"This isn't just cleaning bathrooms and making us meals, you understand that, right?" Tristian drops the mocking smile for something more condescending. "We already have a housekeeper, sweetheart."

I nod once. "Yes, I know."

"Tell us, Sweet Cherry, what does being our Lady entail?" he prompts, the wicked curve of smile tugging at his lips.

"It means you're in charge."

"Of?"

"Everything." I swallow, well aware of what I'm about to do. What they don't know is why I'm so willing to do it.

Tristian watches me. He's still got that charming ease. That same disarming, sexy demeanor. Facing him is worse than the others, because even for me—even after what he did to me, after how he treated me—it's so easy to fall into it. To let it lull you. To believe that he's not as bad as the rest.

Right up until he strikes.

"There's a contract," he says, eyes darkening. "We're perfectly solid here, Story. But for our own benefit, I think I want to hear you say what you're willing to do. Be specific."

My stomach sinks, palms growing clammy as I fight to remain composed. My voice nearly sounds mechanical. "I'll…pleasure you. I'll let you do things to me."

Tristian raises an eyebrow, clearly not having expected this level of bluntness. "And? The contract gives us unilateral rights to control every move you make for the next year."

"What you wear," Rath adds, staring at my chest. I can still feel the ghost of his hands on them. His cock rubbing against my backside. His harsh whispers into my ear.

Tristian nods. "When and what you eat."

"When you sleep."

"Who you fuck," Killian says, suddenly joining in.

"*How* you fuck."

I steel myself. "I can handle that."

The guys glance at one another. Rath stands and walks toward me. I'm still standing near the door. I never got very far into the room. "You didn't handle it last time, Story. We waited for you and you never came. Killer sat outside your room, but it was locked. Then you ran and erased every trace that you existed."

"That was different. I wasn't ready then. I am now."

Rath's tongue darts out and he raises his eyebrow. "Take off your dress, then. I want to see how much you've changed."

It's a test. A test to see if I'll comply. But I also know that they don't like easy. Whoever slapped Tristian probably has the best shot at this job. It's a fine line, knowing what they want, and I have to tread carefully here. I also have to get control of my fears before I blow it.

"Take off your dress, Sweet Cherry, or this is over before it starts." Tristian leans back against the couch, leather creaking. He makes this movement with his hips and I see the bulge in his pants. I can still taste the phantom sourness of him, even after all this time.

My fingers shake as I reach up to finger the strap of my dress. I refuse to look at Killian. I know damn well he's not going to put a stop to this. My stomach whirls, bile climbing the back of my throat.

It's not worth it, it's not worth it.

"Cherry, we don't have all day. We interviewed ten other girls, and every single one of them was willing to do anything I asked," Rath says, annoyed by my hesitation. "I don't know what game you're playing, but being a Lady is serious business. Maybe you should take this as an opportunity to run. You're so good at it, after all."

I swallow my nerves and hook my fingers beneath the straps of my dress, tugging them from my shoulders, dragging them down my arms. The dress flutters to the floor at my feet, and suddenly, I'm bare, standing in nothing but panties and a pale blue, lace bra. Their eyes suspiciously watch my every move, and I know as much as they might hate me, they want me just as badly.

Tristian shifts forward in his seat, like maybe he's about to reach out for me. He never does, though. His tongue darts out to wet his bottom lip. "She's bigger," he tells the others. "Do you remember how big her nipples were?"

Rath nods at my chest. "Size of a half dollar. Are they bigger now, too?"

I dart down to grab my dress, shimmying it back up my torso. Once I'm covered, I send them a hot glare. "If you give me the job, then maybe you'll find out."

A wide grin splits Tristian's face. "Still feisty. Maybe even more than before."

"Tell me something," Killian says, eyes dilated. "What exactly do you have that the other girls don't?"

I play the card I'd been holding onto for years. The same card I'd thought nothing of until that night with them. That's when I realized how much importance it has. How much power.

"Easy," I say, righting my dress. "I'm still a virgin."

KILLIAN PAYNE

3
THE GAME

No one speaks for a long moment after Story has been dismissed. There's a tension in the air that's so palpable, it's making my leg jitter, knee jumping up and down.

It's only when I look up and see them both staring at me that I bite out, "She's obviously bullshitting us."

Rath lifts an eyebrow. "How do you know?"

"Any slut can say they're a virgin," I point out. "She probably sold her cherry to some geriatric fuck ages ago."

Tristian starts, "But what if—"

"Am I the only one here not thinking with my dick?"

"No, you're the only one here thinking with your grudge," Tristian answers, tucking his hands behind his head. "I know you think she jilted you or whatever, but let's face it. Story is the one."

Thankfully, Rath has some sense. "Sure, let's just invite her into our lives, give her access to everything she needs to completely fucking destroy us."

I gesture to Rath. "Exactly. There's no way she isn't chomping at the bit to take us down after what we did to her."

Tristian just shrugs. "What did we do to her? She had choices."

Rath smirks. "No *good* choices."

"When are choices ever good, anyway?" Tristian rolls his eyes, gaze landing on me. "If she wants to take a shot, I say we let her." His eyes spark with the same malicious glee I'm used to seeing on him. Tristian's always preferred the struggle over easy pickings.

"It's a risk," I point out, hands forming tight fists. "She'll never be loyal. Take it from someone who knows: you let that girl live under your roof, you're going to regret thinking she's yours."

Seeing her walk through our door was like being confronted with the ghost of disappointments past. My poker face is damn near flawless, but I was still shocked to see her standing there, looking every bit the pretty, innocent little piece of ass she always did.

It reminds me of the first time I saw her; the night at the restaurant when my dad introduced us all. I knew that he'd intended her for me. He had to have. She was just too perfect, too pure, too sweet and cute. The first time I smiled at her, she squirmed in her seat, red blooming over her pale cheeks, ducking her head to hide a grin. I knew then that she'd be mine.

I was wrong.

Only now do I allow myself to really feel the tornado of emotions seeing her brought out in me. There's anger, like always. Too many layers of fury to really inventory. Anger that my dad made her and that gold-digging slut part of our family. Anger that she was supposed to be mine, but never was. Anger that she chose someone else. Anger that the night in the laundry room should have sealed the deal, but all three of us were too drunk and pissed off to do it properly. Anger that she just up and left.

The worst part of it, though—the part that makes me want to fling this coffee table through the fucking window—is that even through all that rage and resentment, I still want her.

"Think about it. A *virgin*, Killer," Tristian says. "None of the other houses have anything close."

"And neither will we," I grind out. "She's lying."

He seems unbothered by this, lounging back. "So we make it a part of the contract. If we find out she's lying, we bump her for an alternate."

Rath asks, "And what about the sign?"

"What sign?"

He gives Tristian a long look. "The one that's all red and flashing 'hey, this is clearly a trap'?"

Tristian scoffs. "Like we said. We're Teflon. Let her try."

Rath rolls his eyes, but I see the gears turning. "She still does have that air about her."

"All innocent and nervous. Fuck." Tristian reaches down to squeeze his boner. "The Counts are going to lose their shit when they see what we've got."

They aren't getting anything, they're just too dick-brained to see it. "It's not happening."

The two of them look at me, expressions hard.

"This isn't just your decision, fuckwad. We decide this democratically." Tristian raises a palm. "All in favor?"

Before Rath can raise a hand, I add, "He's right, you know. Showing up on our doorstep three years later? That doesn't sound like Story. Something's going down here."

"Maybe she got a taste of my cock and finally came back for more," Tristian says, shrugging. "She wouldn't be the first one."

"You're deluded."

"And you're too wrapped up in your bad blood to see this for what it is." Tristian leans forward, leveling me with his gaze. "You can finally have her, Killer. We do this, and she's ours—for real, this time. This isn't some drunken high school fuck-around in your laundry room. Isn't that why you've always hated her so much?" He shakes his head, looking both sympathetic and annoyed. "You always hate what you can't have."

"Who says I want her? I could have any girl in this whole fucking town.

She's nothing special." I know instantly that they see through my bullshit.

Rath is the only one with balls to say it, though. "Give me a break. Find you a brunette to fuck from behind, and you come in like five minutes flat. I bet you still think of her when you jerk off, too."

Tristian laughs. "He's got a point."

I flip him off. "Maybe I just don't like blondes."

Rath leans forward to flick that space on my bicep—the tattoo of the dark-haired girl. "Or maybe you're just an obsessive psycho." His words don't have any bite to them. As if he's in any position to throw stones here. "But look at it like this, right? If she's our Lady, she'll be right down the hall. Every night. *Sleeping*."

Tristian immediately catches on, pitching forward to add, "We can take the lock away. Or, even better, we can give you the only key."

I glower at them, but internally, I'm already imagining it. Sneaking into her room, looking at her there, all tucked into her bed. I remember the way her lips always looked, puckered in concentration as she dreamed. The way they felt around the hard tip of my dick, so soft and wet. The way I'd leave some of my come on them, spreading it around, marking her as my own. Story was always a hard sleeper. Barely anything could wake her. I was careful back then—too careful, moved too slow. But now?

Now, I could do anything to her.

Just like that, my dick is rock hard.

Fuckers. Complete, insufferable fuckers, the both of them.

Rath lifts a hand, saying, "I'm in," and looks at me expectantly.

I thought she was mine the first time we met. I thought she was mine again that night in our old house, when I finally let myself have a piece of her, however small it might have seemed.

But that's the thing about Story that these guys don't realize. She's like sand slipping through your fingers. Water through a sieve.

You can't keep what you can never grasp.

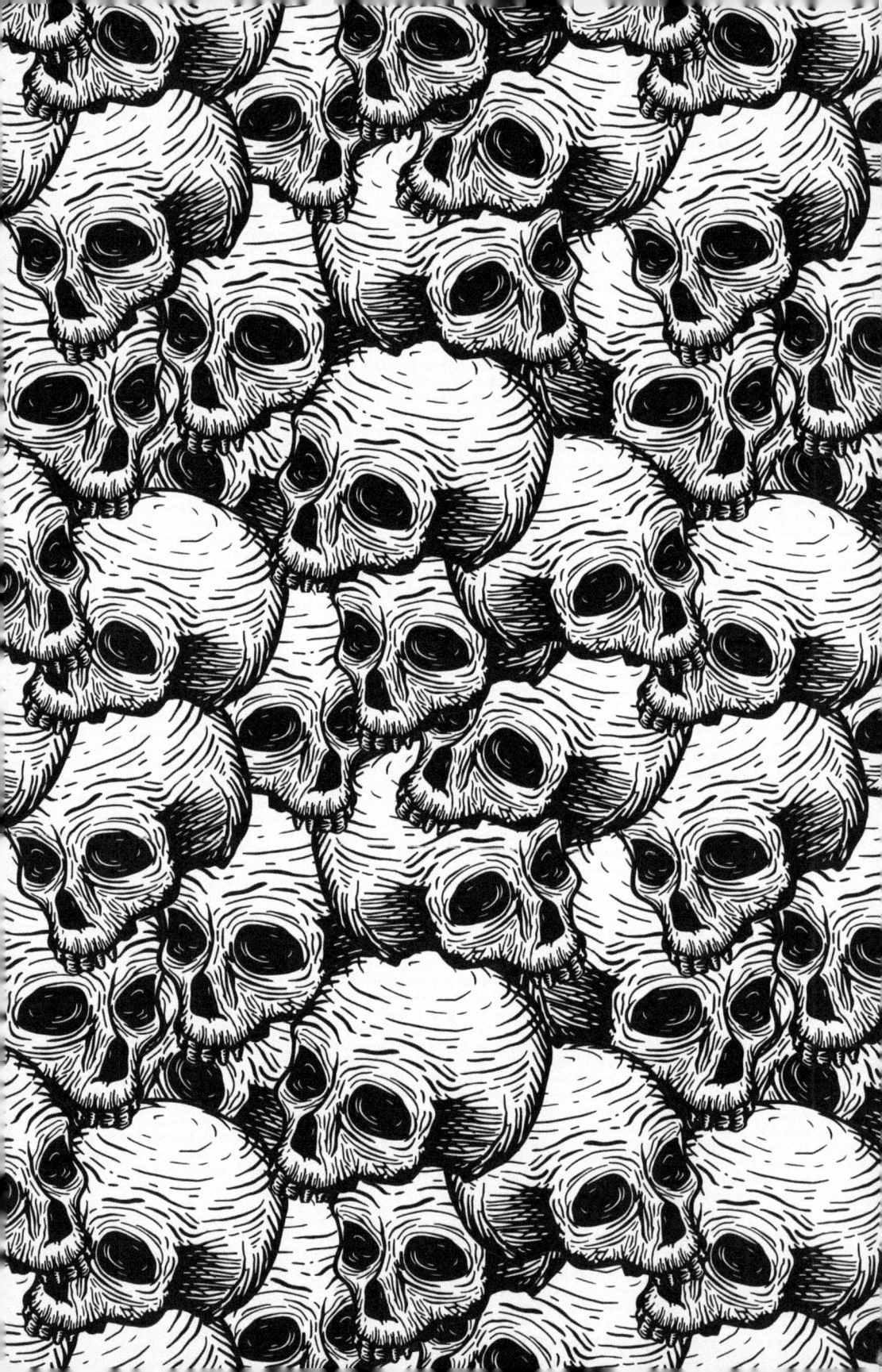

STORY

4

THE WAGER

As much as I knew it was a long shot to become Lady, I'm still disappointed when I don't hear anything by the next morning. Ideally, I wouldn't have had to return to the room I've been renting under my mom's name, other than to get my belongings.

If I can't move into the Lords' house, I'm going to have to make a decision quickly about what to do and where to go next. I can't live by myself, and I can't put just anyone in the position of living with me, either.

Not with Ted out there.

I walk over to the small desk in the corner of the room I'm renting and pull the envelope out of my suitcase. It's plain and white, with my name typed across the front. I'd walked into my room at my boarding school and found it on my pillow.

Dear Sweet Cherry,

When you shut down your account, I was very disappointed. The connection we developed, your sexy words and photos…it's all I think about. It's all I dream about. But I know what your stepbrother and his friends did to you. I understand why you had to run. What I don't understand is why you had to leave me, too. Did he find out? That must be it. We were perfect for one another. There has to be a reason you left.

Tell me? Are you still a virgin? I hope that by being at the all-girls school, you're able to stay pure. I want to be the one that claims you. Now that I know where you are, I'll be waiting and watching for my opportunity. I can be patient, for a bit...

Yours,

Ted

A photograph had also been stuffed in the envelope, a compromising picture that I sent to a few of the Sugar Daddies for money. Ted had been one of those Daddies. He was no one special. Just someone to earn some quick cash off of until I could get out of dodge. Back then, I hadn't really been paying much attention to the people on the screen. They were barely even real people to me. Just a means to an end.

It wasn't until that first letter, the mention of my stepbrother, that it hit me.

Ted must have been Killian.

Who else would know? Who else would chase me across the country like this just to torment me?

It would have been easier if it *were* Killian. It'd mean that he and the others were the only ones who knew about what they did to me. Nothing could ever be so simple, though. I quickly realized that this was someone else.

Dear Sweet Cherry,

Did you get my gifts? Did you like the flowers? I know orange is your favorite color.

I must admit that it's very upsetting that you ran away. I had so many plans for the two of us. Do you not want to see me? Did you give the one thing I asked you to save to someone else? Are you nothing but a common whore?

No. I refuse to believe that. You made a promise and I know you'll keep it.

That's why I sent you the gifts, to let you know I still believe in you. In us. One day soon I'll find you and I'll make you mine.

Until then,

Ted

It, too, was accompanied by photos of me. In class. In my dorm room. Standing in line at the canteen. Laying down in the nurse's office when I'd come down with the flu. Each photo was progressively more alarming. This wasn't someone across the country. This was someone local, someone horrifyingly present and persistent. He knew where I slept, what I ate, when I went to class.

That's when I began doing some of my own stalking.

Killian's social media is a tribute to narcissism. Back then, he posted up to a dozen times a day. He was easy to keep track of, and among all the photos of him posing with girls, it became obvious that it wasn't his MO. Killian took girls and tossed them aside. He didn't chase them. He tormented them, yes, but the letters, the gifts, the teasing, weren't his style at all. They weren't nearly interactive enough to be. This isn't how Killian prefers to hurt people.

Still, I couldn't stop tracking his profile—*all* of their profiles. At first it became a sick fascination, watching these guys who'd hurt me so badly. Wondering what makes them tick. Wondering if they felt bad. Wondering if they were doing it to other girls.

But the fascination wasn't so sick. I realize that now. After what they did to me, there was some comfort in knowing where they were. I couldn't shake them, even after a year. Even after three years, even from across the country, I could feel their eyes on me, their deep breaths and fingertips. I constantly woke, drenched in sweat, caught in feverish dreams of being choked by a thick cock shoved down my throat, the bitter taste of semen on my tongue. The only thing that made it go away was watching them. Ironic, the stalked became the stalker. I watched their successes, their failures. Much like in high school, they dominated college. Killian has become a superstar in football, Rath is deeply involved in the music scene, and Tristian seems to have a different girl on his arm every night. I knew when they got into Forsyth University, and I knew when they became Lambda Delta Zetas—Lords.

That's how I heard about the position of Lady.

I shove the letter and photos back in the envelope and hide it back in the pocket of my suitcase. Grabbing my backpack, I exit the room. It's the first day of classes, and I can't be late. Daniel probably went out of his way to help me register and get through the admissions process, even though the deadlines had already passed. He has a lot of sway at the University, and getting on the wrong side of it will put a wrench in my plans of avoiding him at all costs.

I close and lock my door, double checking that it's secure. It's not a great apartment. When Ted finds me—and I have no doubt that he will—it'll take almost nothing to get inside.

As I walk toward campus, I'm once again caught with the question: Would he? Would he break in and hurt me? The letters aren't so sweet anymore. They're impatient, edged with angry desperation, uncaring. What happened in Colorado is proof enough that he has no limits.

If I don't make the position of Lady, then I'm not sure what I'll do. I have no plan B.

Yet again, I check my phone, hoping to see a text from the Lords. There's nothing. Being on a college campus is both a positive and negative. There are a lot of people around, so it's easy to blend. But knowing the guys are so close has me on a razor's edge, shoulders tucked up to my ears, eyes scanning the distance.

I enter the psychology building, anxiously searching for my first class—room 202, second floor. I find the stairwell and head up, traveling with a handful of other students. I've only just stepped onto the landing when I jolt to an abrupt stop. Killian leans against the wall, tattooed arms crossed over his chest, dark eyes zeroed in on me.

The other students pass without sensing that anything's off. Even though I shouldn't be surprised he knows exactly where to find me, a tingling, alarmed sensation rolls up my spine. His presence is like a startling ache in the universe, something that throbs unavoidably in my awareness. It's yet another reminder that this thing I'm doing here is dangerous. Trading in one evil for another was never going to be ideal.

His face is completely void of emotion. No expression. He jerks his chin to the side, gesturing for me to follow him. Forcing my legs to move toward him is like moving through molasses. Every molecule in my body screams for me to run, but I don't. I walk two feet behind him, aware that everyone we pass notices him and gives him the same wide berth I feel compelled to give him. He pushes a door open and walks through.

I take a long, unsteady breath before following him in.

The door closes behind us with a click that's as loud as a gunshot. A glance around reveals that we're in an empty, dimly lit classroom.

Alone.

I swallow thickly, hand tightening around the strap of my bag. "I have class in ten minutes."

Eyes tracking the way I remain by the door, the muscle in Killian's jaw tics. "I came to formally offer you the position of Lady."

"Oh." A conflicted shudder runs through me, dread warring with relief. "I figured after I didn't hear from you…"

Despite this having been his decision, he doesn't look happy about it, eyebrows drawn low and angry over his eyes. "We had to discuss it and come up with a few…compromises."

I shift uncomfortably. "…compromises?"

"Guidelines," he bites out. "Parameters. It's our business, not yours."

I nod, practically feeling the hatred rolling off him in waves. "I understand."

He makes a low, mocking sound. "You're not as slick as you think, Story." He leans against the desk at his back, strong arms folded against his chest. "Rath and Tristian might not see the forest for the trees, but I've got a pretty nice view. I don't know what game you're playing here, but I'm going to tell you now, it won't fucking fly."

My voice is weak when I argue, "There's no game."

"Of course not. You just came here to submit yourself to our complete control for the hell of it." He licks his bottom lip, gaze roaming down my body. "It doesn't matter. You have no idea what you're getting yourself into. I tried to tell the others you'd run, first opportunity you got. They're laboring under the delusion you have any sense of follow-through."

I meet his gaze, trying to make my voice sound as steely as I feel. "I'm not going to run."

His eyes narrow. "You did last time."

"That was different," I start, but I know it's useless. Killian doesn't care what it did to me. He doesn't care that I'd already been trying to find a way out. He doesn't care that I'm agreeing this time—that's what makes it different. Instead, I say, "You made it very clear that you hated me living in your house. I figured I was doing you a favor by leaving."

His eyes flash in anger and I stiffen, already backing toward the door when he rears forward. "Doing me a favor?" he growls. My back hits the door just as his palm makes contact with the wood, slamming into the space beside my head. His low, angry hiss is like venom against my ear. "I wasn't done with you, Story. *We* weren't done with you. If you take this position, there's no running away. You'll belong to us and no one else. Not until we get tired of you."

He means it as a threat, and that's exactly what it is. If I agree to this, I'm giving myself to them, wholly. What he doesn't realize is just how comforting that promise is—not belonging to anyone else.

Heart pounding, still cringing away from the hard chest in front of me, I breathe, "I know."

From my periphery, I can see the muscles in his arm shift and flex. "You'd fucking better know, because this is your choice. Not mine."

Nodding, I stare at my feet, unable to look him in the eye, not without thinking about that night and how he looked pleasuring himself. "I won't run away again." I feel his fingertips under my chin. His touch isn't gentle, and he forces me to look up at him.

"I want to make one thing perfectly clear," he begins, the lines of his face sharp and hard. "The only reason Rath and Tristian didn't fuck you raw that night is because I told them not to."

"I know." I ask the question I've wanted to know the answer to for three years. "Why did you stop them?"

He pins me with his stare, something dark and strangely reluctant lurking there. "Because I could."

My stomach twists itself in a disgusted knot at my next words. "Thank you."

His low, raspy chuckle sends an icy chill up my spine. "Oh, Sweet Cherry. Don't thank me. I'm not your savior, then or now. You need to get that through your pretty little head. I'm not going to stop them from doing what they want to you. Tell me you understand." The words are a direct command, full of an oddly business-like authority.

I swallow loudly. "I understand."

He's so close that it's getting hard to breathe anything that isn't the masculine scent of him. "And no more lying. All that shit about you being a virgin? Just how stupid do you think I am?"

My eyebrows pull together. "I *am* a virgin," I insist, even as his jaw hardens.

He steps forward, his huge frame towering over me. "You expect me to believe that? On your word alone?"

My mouth falters around several aborted replies. "How else can I prove it?"

Suddenly, his hand is on my thigh, yanking the bottom of my dress up. "You can stand still, keep your mouth shut, and let me judge for myself." I jerk back, away from the feel of his hand forcing its way up my dress, but the door stops me. Regardless, I can see the flicker of irritation on his face at my flinch. "Look at that, you're already terrible at taking direction. I don't think this bodes well for you."

At his words, I force myself to still, even as his fingers find the edge of my panties and pull them roughly aside. Even when he shoves his fingers between my legs, invading my most private area, I try to remain like stone, closing my eyes against the coming intrusion.

I inhale sharply at the way he prods, the tip of his finger burying itself inside me. I can't hold back the wince, the way my cheeks blaze in humiliation, the sting of tears behind my eyes as he mechanically inserts his finger to the knuckle. I squeeze my eyes shut, hands forming fists in the fabric of my skirt.

"Relax," he says, his deep voice full of annoyance. "If you stopped being such a frigid bitch for five seconds, it might even feel good." Teeth gnashed, I shake my head, willing it to be over before anything like that can happen. With a rough sound, he thrusts his finger, pulling it out just to push it back inside. After a moment, he pauses there, the warmth of his exhale washing across my face.

When he remains frozen, I hesitantly open my eyes.

His dark gaze is fixed on my lips, mouth parted, watching me as his finger remains there, deep inside my core, warming itself in my heat. His finger moves and he blinks, a slow, heavy motion as he pumps it into me, canting forward.

He's going to kiss me.

The realization hits me like a sledgehammer.

I suck in a panicked breath just as he stiffens, yanking his hand roughly from my skirt. His face is shuttered now, all harsh lines and stony glare. Any trace of…whatever that was—fixation, curiosity, want—is wiped away.

"Be at the house tonight by six. Bring your shit. You'll be living there for the duration of the school year."

I nod, squeezing my thighs together against the phantom pang of his invading touch, willing the tears not to fall. I won't let him see me cry again. My trembling hand is already wrapped around the knob of the door when his voice rings out.

"We don't like hairy cunts," he says. "Come shaved."

I find the courage to turn the knob, to turn my back to him, moving so quickly I almost trip over my feet. My heart pounds as I burst into the hall, still feeling the malice of his presence against my spine, watching, waiting. Nevertheless, he doesn't chase me.

That's why it has to be him.

That's why it has to be *them*.

TRISTIAN
MERCER

5

THE CONTRACT

Rath is ruled by his emotions.

He's always been a moody little bitch, quick to hold a grudge, slow to cool his head. On anyone else, it'd be juvenile, but Rath is also ruthless and filled with conviction. It just makes him a scary son of a bitch. I used to think it put him at a disadvantage, always so quick to lose his shit about something, but now I know better. Despite being hotheaded and vicious, he's also calculating and patient. Always spicy.

By contrast, most people think Killian is a robot.

He's a pro when it comes to hiding a weakness, a little too good at coming off unaffected. His ability to set aside all emotion, to get a job done, is a big part of what makes him dominate on the field. It's also why we're so good at what we do down in South Side, able to hold this town in the palm of our hands. People are scared of him precisely because they can't tell what's going on under that hard, blank exterior.

I'm better at harnessing both.

I might be pissed, but you'll never know it. Not unless I want you to. The ability to read people—to understand their desires, their fears—and use it to my advantage is a classic Mercer trait. My dad is a master at it, owning any room he enters. Manipulative, my mom would always call it. But to us, people are putty, easily out-maneuvered. All it takes is some good, old-fashioned bullshitting.

It rarely works on Killer and Rath. They know me too well, for one. But mostly, their personalities are just the worst for it. Neither of them bend. Everyone knows it. If you took one of us away, the whole pyramid would probably crumble. It's not easy being Lords of the school, and even less easy being three north side elites. There are responsibilities, obligations.

That's why, despite his perfectly still expression, I know the instant Killian walks through the door that he's in a tangle.

"What'd she say?" I ask, knowing he'd gone to talk to Story.

To the other houses, having a girl is probably nothing but fun. That's how it was always meant to be—a display of mastery to the campus and alumni, a way to let off steam, having a little pet to come home to, to bring to parties, to parade around like a prize. There's a lot more riding on it for the three of us. We can't afford to just let anyone in, and it takes a special kind of girl to handle our brand of ownership.

Killian strides across the library, straight to the bar to pour a drink. Rath and I share a look. Killer isn't a huge drinker—especially not during the playing season—but it's not unexpected. Story showing back up was a shock to all of us, but it's hit him harder than us.

His voice is rough from the whiskey when he answers, "She seems to understand."

Rath snorts, a biography of Jimi Hendrix fanned open in his lap. He thinks we don't know, but he's not reading it. "Somehow I doubt that."

I disagree, "She knows what she's getting into better than most." And it's true. Story's been under our heel before. She's felt our anger, our praise, the brutality of our appetite for her. It was only once, but it was more than enough. Story knows us in a way all these other bitches never could. These two underestimate her. "So she's agreeable?"

Killian scoffs. "A little too agreeable."

"She wants something," Rath guesses.

"Wrong," I say, slipping my phone into my pocket. "She *needs* something. Her showing up like this could only be out of complete desperation." Both of them meet my grin with blank faces and I roll my eyes. Fuck, these two have zero imagination sometimes. "Desperation makes a person do just about anything. Don't you get it? We're holding all the cards here. Lighten up."

Martin appears in the doorway, holding a stack of papers. "I have the contracts you requested."

Martin is a little older than us, but most people couldn't even tell. He's a scrawny nerd. He's also wicked smart. As a junior lawyer with Jackson & Wolfe, he's been assigned to work with the Lords. *Exclusively*. It's part of the legacy—having a connection with the firm. Each set of Lords had one before us, and the ones who follow will, too. The Jackson and Wolfe families were Lord-bred long before the three of us were born.

Killian swallows the rest of his drink and walks over, taking the papers from Martin. He skims the information while handing a set to me and Rath. The top section is a copy of the contract that Story will need to sign before she steps foot in the house. It outlines the expectations very clearly. It's a lot of legalese, but I'd made sure the language was plain enough to a layperson. It'd be easy to rope this girl into something she doesn't expect, but that's the wrong play here. Better to let her see just how much we're going to own her—every move, every moment, every strand of hair on her pretty little head. Her agreement will seal what I already know.

Story is in some dire-ass straits.

"You got all the conditions down?" Killian asks, eyebrows raised as he moves to the second part of the paperwork. "Including the additions to The Game that we made last night?"

"Yes, sir," Martin says. "They're added to the bottom of the current list."

The Game is a long-standing tradition with the Lords. Having a Lady who's obligated to meet our every whim is a bit too easy for men like us. We need a challenge, a difficult pursuit, which is why none of the other girls passed. They were too fucking easy, chomping at the bit for a pat on the head, ready to service us however we saw fit.

Yawn.

But not Story. Maybe she's changed—matured—but even though she's obviously desperate, I could smell the fear rolling off her body. The nervousness. The dread. It's going to be tooth and nail with her. It got my dick instantly hard.

The three of us sit quietly for a moment reading over the points system of The Game. The idea is simple. Each item gets a point. Since we won the game last year and are already living in the brownstone, we needed another prize. We'll no longer be a team, because for this, we'll be competing against each other. The Lord with the highest number of points by the end of the year wins. The prize?

Sweet Cherry's *cherry*.

Each of us want it, but only one can take it. It's probably Killian's, by rights, which is something that was brought up *with feeling* during the discussion. He's not wrong. We just don't give a shit. Killer had his chance with her. They lived under the same roof for a year. Whatever drama was going on between him and his dad has fuck-all to do with us.

So that's the endgame. One of us is going to take her virginity, and these two dumbasses don't know it yet, but it's going to be *me*.

The problem with a house having a girl is that it's a delicate balance. Just look at the Princes and their Princess. It's too easy to humanize them, to make them seem like…girlfriends. They're not. They're owned. Subservient. For the Lords, the prize isn't in the Lady herself. It's in the possession of her.

5 | TRISTIAN

Our history with Story complicates matters.

We've already had a taste of her, for one. Plus, Killer's got all his baggage. Rath and her seem to have a brief history, too. I've got none of that. To me, Story's just some girl who gave me a really thrilling blowjob once upon a time. But I'd be lying if I said her ability to get my boys all tangled up didn't bother me.

That's why we had to revise The Game—to keep us on task. We agreed to a few changes this year because of our history with her, mostly because Killian has massive control issues and is obsessed with his stepsister. Everything is put on a point scale. The way we won last year was by the three of us accomplishing every task on the list. There's nothing we won't do. No degradation too small. No female we can't convince or manipulate into our beds. For Story, that has to shift a little. It'll be about the small things; how often she wears an outfit we picked out, if we provide 'correction' for insubordinate behavior, how, when, and where she sucks our cocks. There are more points for voyeurism or exhibitionism, and humiliation. There's less for willing cooperation, unless it's explicit, enthusiastic consent, but more for tactical coercion. The art of the mindfuck will be my own personal specialty.

I suspect this will be a high-points game.

"You all need to sign the top copy," Martin says, holding out a pen.

I read through it once more, since my position is a little more vulnerable here. Killer is all brute aggression, and Rath is all about the slow, simmering tension. Their own strategies are up-front. Mine are far more subtle.

It only takes me a moment to find the right clause; anyone who informs Story of The Game will be summarily disqualified from the competition for the prize.

"So," I say, once the paper is signed and Martin has left the room, "any particular plans on how to welcome Sweet Cherry into the house?"

"We don't," Killian says, pouring us each a glass of whiskey. "As a reminder that she's not special, we won't be here when she arrives. There's business we need to attend to in South Side. I say we take care of it and let her fucking stew."

Rath and I both take a glass and stand, holding our glasses out.

"Let the mind games begin," Rath says, smirking.

I thrust my glass out, clinking the crystal with the others and repeating Rath's words, "Let the mind games begin, indeed."

STORY

6
THE FIRST NIGHT

When I return to the brownstone that night, I've managed to get this wild, terrified feeling under control. At least sort of. It's not like I can ever feel relaxed around these three. On the contrary, I'm determined to keep my defenses up at all times. Something tells me that's exactly what they want. Killian in particular seems to enjoy terrorizing me. I still feel a twinge of soreness from his earlier 'inspection', not strong enough to be called pain, but just present enough that it can't be ignored.

This time, the door is locked. With a deep breath, I bang the brass skull knocker. It swings open a moment later, revealing the guy from the other day.

"Good evening," he says, gesturing for me to enter the front room. "We met before, but I didn't introduce myself. My name is Martin. I'm the Lords' assistant."

"I'm Story. Story Austin," I reply, giving him my real name as I peer around the foyer once again. When I turn to the man—Martin—I give him a onceover. I wonder if I'll be under his thumb, too. I wonder if he'll want to do things to me. He doesn't look like a ruthless sadist, but neither does Tristian. It's a dumb notion, anyway. The Lords don't share with anyone but each other. "You're their assistant? You don't look any older than me."

"I'm twenty-five actually," he says, shutting the door. I take note of him turning the lock, the click sounding final and grim. "The Lords have always had an assistant assigned to them by the firm. It's an honor to serve them, as I'm sure you're aware."

I only barely manage to hide the face I want to pull. Sadist or not, if this guy thinks being their 'Lady' is an honor, then he's a creep. Unfortunately, I'm not in the position to make my feelings on the matter known. "I see."

"I mostly manage things for the frat and house; maintenance, repairs, and legal advice."

I wonder if he signed a contract that gave over the rights to almost every freedom in his life like I did.

Doubtful.

Speaking of the contract, my eyes are drawn to the thick envelope waiting in Martin's hand. I nod toward it, asking, "Is that it?"

Martin's gaze follows mine. "Yes. Why don't you follow me?" He leads me to the same parlor I'd waited in the other day, still immaculate, and places the envelope on the table in front of the sofa. "I'll give you a few minutes to look it over. Let me know if you have any questions." Despite this, he doesn't leave, instead opting to fold himself down into a wing-backed chair near the fireplace.

Reluctantly, I take a seat on the sofa, gently sliding the papers from the envelope. The beginning is practically in Latin, but I get the gist. This contract seals my fate, yadda yadda, I'm agreeing to it of my own free will, blah blah. Going over the stipulations of being Lady is an exercise in humiliation, my face blooming hotter and hotter with each line, realizing that this Martin guy knows every single one.

Many of them are boring, such as always dressing presentably, always being available to the Lords, never speaking to males other than the Lords or their staff without permission, keeping up my figure, a promise that every encounter and exchange between me and the Lords will be strictly confidential.

Then there are other ones. Mostly sexual, completely vile. I'm giving my consent to a whole plethora of things, and they aren't even worded to sound nice. It's all blunt and completely unavoidable.

I must pleasure them each on their command.

I must submit myself to punishment when I don't.

I must never wear a bra while under their roof.

I must always remain waxed or shaved.

I must never masturbate unless I'm given permission to.

I must remain on birth control.

The list goes on and on, more and more vulgar with each line item. At one point, I glance up at Martin, half expecting him to look as uncomfortable as I feel.

He just smiles placidly back at me. "I'll give you a copy so you can remember it all."

Right.

Even worse than that is the non-disclosure agreement. According to the contract, I need to give collateral—something damaging they can hold over my head. I take it as the joke it was obviously meant to be. They already hold quite enough over my head.

Because of this, I don't think twice about pulling the two photos from my bag—the ones Ted had sent me, from the sugar baby site. In both of them, I'm in compromising positions. But Killian has no doubt already seen them. He probably already has them saved somewhere. This is just some macho bullshit to ensure that I know he has them.

"Before signing this," I say, tapping the paper. "Am I allowed to add my own stipulations?"

His eyebrows climb his forehead, but his responding grin is full of humor. "The Lords aren't exactly open to negotiations. But I suppose you're allowed to try."

I nod, already knowing this. I won't get much. I should choose one thing, big enough to put some power back into my hands, challenging enough that they might be put off, possibly enough leverage to negotiate some of their stipulations down.

After a few moments, I decide, jotting the words at the bottom of the list.

Martin takes the contract from my hand with another one of those sedate smiles, eyes flicking down to catch my amendment. He pauses for a moment, seeming to re-read, before meeting my gaze again. "I'll just need to check this with the others first."

"Of course," I answer, waiting as he pulls out his phone.

I watch as his thumbs fly over the screen, sending the message, and I almost regret them not being here—not being able to see the looks on their faces at my condition.

His phone pings with a response after only five minutes. "Well then," he says, staring down at the screen. "It seems the Lords are amenable to your condition."

I freeze. "What?"

"They agree to the change of terms," he says, passing the contract back. "All it needs is your signature."

No way.

No fucking way should they have agreed to that. They should have said no, and then had Martin agree to take something off their requests in concession.

I remain frozen for a long moment, wishing I had time to properly strategize here. Does this mean I can make *more* requests? Did I choose wrong? Should I have negotiated something else?

It doesn't matter.

Whether they agree or not, none of them will be capable of following through. When they fail, the contract will be null and void. Forcing myself not to think too hard on what I'm doing, I sign the bottom line.

Martin nods, stuffing everything back into the envelope. "If you're ready, I can show you to your room." After a beat, he adds, "*Lady.*"

The title makes a frisson of disgust roll up my spine.

He leads me up the narrow staircase to the first floor, where two doors lead off the hallway. He eyes my suitcase. "I'm not sure how much you'll need from your own belongings. Clothing and toiletries are provided. Each item has been cultivated to the Lords' particular tastes." He stops at a door and gestures to the handle. "This will be your room."

I turn the doorknob and step inside, taking in the space. It's not quite what I expected. The room is spacious and warm, with windows that overlook the front of the house. There's a double bed made of iron, with rose-colored bedding. A pale green couch sits against one wall. Another holds a fireplace. The décor is not modern, but comfortable. Feminine. I notice perfume bottles on the dressing table, one I notice as my preferred fragrance, and a scarf hanging on the back of the chair. Momentarily, I wonder what other women agreed to stay in this room before me? How were they treated? Did they get nice bedding, scarves, perfumes?

I'd half-expected to just be tossed in a squat cell with nothing but a bucket.

"Do you live here, too?" I ask Martin.

"No," he answers, lifting a hand to pick lint from his shoulder. "Although I am available to the Lords on a twenty-four-hour basis, seven days a week. I'm only here to make sure you settle in since the Lords couldn't be present to welcome you."

I frown. "Where are they?"

"They have business," he says vaguely, his tone making it clear that he won't elaborate.

"Oh." It seems odd that they wouldn't take the opportunity to make me feel even more uncomfortable. I've been on edge all day, anxious about what would await me. The reality is both a relief and a disappointment. I've put off their torment for just a little while longer. A part of me just wants to get it over with, though. "Well, thank you for showing me my room."

"You're welcome, Story. I left you some dinner in the kitchen, if you're hungry." A weirdly thoughtful gesture from the man who's helping to legally bind me into sexual serfdom.

I touch my stomach and realize I haven't eaten all day. I've been on edge since I got back in town, but now that I'm finally in this house, I feel some of that tension unwind. Ted isn't going to come after me here—not if he knows what's good for him. And if he does, then…

Well, then he'll be their problem.

Plus, it seems like I don't even have to worry about the guys tonight.

"Thank you," I answer, trying for a smile that probably escapes as a grimace. "I'll get something after I unpack."

Martin leaves the room, and a few minutes later, I hear him go out the front door, the latch snapping into place behind him. The first thing I do is check the locks on my bedroom's door.

"Thank God," I mutter, testing the knob. The lock works well.

I explore the rest of the room, looking into the large, nicely-sized bathroom. This door has a lock, too. There's a shower, a massive bathtub, and a large vanity. The cabinets and drawers are filled with toiletries and cosmetics—expensive, high-end brands. There's a box of tampons and three months of birth control pills—prescribed by the campus doctor. Soft towels are stacked on a shelf by the tub. I go back into the bedroom and place my suitcase on the bed, unzipping it to reveal my things. I left my old apartment in a hurry, leaving behind most of my belongings. I never made a lot of money or had much in the way of possessions, so my clothing options were already slim. I walk to the dresser with a handful of old cotton panties and open the top drawer. Inside, I discover that there are already clothes inside, just like Martin implied. I pick up one of the lacy scraps of fabric and see that the tags are still attached. Bras and panties, sheer tanks, and boy shorts. All in my size.

Did they buy all of this today?

I finger a black, strappy, lacy bralette. This isn't something I'd wear. Too revealing, not enough function. It's clear from the selection what the guys are expecting from me. Frilly underthings and very little else.

I finish unpacking, adding my own pathetic clothing to the drawers. My worn jeans are tucked in next to the crisp, designer denims folded in neat stacks. I hang a few things in the closet. There are outfits in there too, including stylish shirts and a few dresses. Some casual. A few for dressier occasions. Also brand new. In stark contrast to the lacy bras and panties, the clothes I must be intended to wear outside of the house are strangely modest instyle, if not in function. It takes me a while to understand, but eventually, I do.

I'm meant to look like every inch the sweet little virgin I've branded myself as. The clothes are cute, but revealing enough to be considered a tease. Skirts that are a little too short, pants and tops that are a little too tight. I suppose I should be thankful that I won't be forced into wearing stilettos and tube tops.

Instead, it just makes my stomach churn.

By the time I'm finished, I don't just need dinner, I need a drink as well.

In the kitchen, I find the plate of food in the refrigerator, and I familiarize myself with the room while it heats it up in the microwave. In the back of the pantry, I find a bottle of vodka. I'm not a big drinker, but I need something to calm my nerves. I pour a shot in a glass and knock it back. The burn down my throat licks like fire, but it eases the hard knot in my stomach.

I sit at the table, blessedly alone, and eat the meal that was left for me. It's a plate of roasted chicken and green vegetables. I'm hungry, but it's hard to force down, so I end up dryly swallowing half of it and picking at the rest. Unable to remember if a lack of cleanliness would result in 'correction', I clean everything diligently when I'm finished, making sure it's spotless.

Afterward, I refill my glass with another shot and take a self-guided tour of the first floor.

The house is undeniably historic, with period pieces scattered throughout. Stained glass windows, carved woodwork, antiquated built-in cabinets. The fixtures are a combination of old and new. A heavy glass chandelier hangs over the massive dining room table. An oil portrait of a man is mounted over the stone fireplace in the living room. Everything reeks of expensive old world taste. It's all frankly way too elegant for Killian, Tristian, and Rath. Where are the pizza boxes? The industrial-sized boxes of condoms? The video games and bongs?

I figure that stuff has to be somewhere, so I head up to the second floor, stopping at the door across from my bedroom, curious about what's inside.

I'm shocked to find the door unlocked, and I take a paranoid glance behind me before stepping inside. A familiar scent assaults my senses before I even turn on the light. It's a mixture of soap and masculinity, sweat, and spicy cologne. My fingers flip the switch, and I instantly know that I'm in Killian's room. Our rooms were adjacent when I lived at Daniel's house, too.

I shouldn't be surprised he placed my room so close to his.

His bed is a huge, king-sized monstrosity with a headboard of solid black wood. His bedding is a cool slate gray, the walls a lighter shade. The room is unsurprisingly tidy. Pizza boxes aside, Killian had always been a neat-freak. He hated things being haphazard, too much of a control freak to tolerate the smallest glimpse of chaos.

Every piece of clothing is put in its place, shirts lined up neatly in his closet, pants below. Every item on his dresser is neatly arranged, from his keys to his day planner. I walk by the dark piece of furniture and see a photo in a frame; him as a little boy with a woman I recognize as his mother.

It's not the first time I've seen this picture. Once, after we first moved in, the housekeeper mixed up our PE T-shirts. I carried it into his room and saw the picture sitting on his dresser. I was staring at her beautiful face when I heard, *"What the hell are you doing in here?"*

I jumped. "B-bringing your shirt." I held it out like a shield. "It got mixed in with my laundry."

"Stupid maid," he muttered, striding into the room. He was seventeen and already pushing the agro-jock persona. He grabbed the shirt and scowled. "Why are you still here?"

I glanced at the photo and his eyes followed. "Is that your—"

"Don't you fucking dare say her name. If you do, I'll..."

I didn't give him time to finish. I tried to find out more about Darla, Killian's mother, but she was never mentioned, at least never around me. Aside from the photo—clean, angled just-so, clearly treated with care—it was as if she didn't exist. I never knew what happened to her, just that any mention of her made Killian even chillier than usual—and that was saying a lot.

Much like back then, the frame is one of few personal items in the room. Everything else serves a purpose. Being here, smelling the scent of him, is making me remember being alone with him earlier in the day. The way he'd advanced on me, caged me in, the sight of his shoulder, muscles shifting beneath the fabric as his finger invaded me. The way his eyes looked, hooded and dark.

I'm not deluded enough to think he truly wants me.

No.

He's a cold-hearted sociopath. He wants to hurt me, humiliate me, control me. Whatever he feels, it's more about him feeling powerful than it is about me.

The urge to go through his drawers or the sleek laptop on his desk is overwhelming. He looks so different from back then. Harder. Rougher. I wonder how else he's changed. But even though some part of me is dying to figure him out before I'm completely at his mercy, I hold back. Killian is too smart to leave something out where I can easily find it, and he's paranoid enough to not only make it hard to find something incriminating, but to also set a trap that could get me in more trouble.

The room, his personality, everything about him makes me bristle. I leave quickly, eager to escape the specter of him that lingers there.

Turning away from my room, I head back to the staircase and climb to the next floor. There are two more rooms. I choose the one over mine. It doesn't take me very long to realize whose room this is.

Tristian's.

The massive black and white canvas print of himself over his bed is the only clue I need.

It's the most absurd thing I've ever seen. I stand at the end of the bed and gawk at the enlarged photograph. In it, he's shirtless, showing off his defined physique. He's leaner than Killian, not needing the bulk for the field, but still perfectly toned. The lighting expertly emphasizes the ladder of muscle on his abdomen and the cut V under his hips. He's strikingly attractive, always has been. The smile toying at his lips is that of a trickster. Kind, yet cruel. Sexy, but dark.

Against my will, my eyes drop the skin right above the waist of his pants. I think about that defined muscle, the texture of skin, and am struck by the startling, unwelcome awareness that I've been *right there*. I've had that bulge beneath his pants in my mouth. I've felt that skin below his belly against my forehead.

I turn away to avoid thinking about it.

The décor of the room is modern, sleek, and sterile. Despite this, it's not coldly impersonal like Killian's room. No, Tristian Mercer admires himself far too much for that. It's obvious that everything in the room has been carefully curated; books arranged by spine color, a gigantic, top-of-the-line flatscreen perched on the wall, and a closet full of expensive designer clothes. There are a few personal things, though. A framed photo of a little girl bearing a familial resemblance. Knick knacks, a mug that was handmade by a child—perhaps the one in the photo. They don't match anything else in the room. They're not put on display for the sake of appearances. This is something he cares about more than all that.

Could Tristian actually love something?

Does he have the capacity?

It's a curious thing, but it's also not long before that sharp face smirking down at me begins to make my skin itch. I put a mental pin in it and quickly exit the room, closing the door behind me.

I turn to the opposite door and open it, jaw going slack at what awaits me.

This is a surprise.

Dimitri Rathbone is the quietest of the three. Back in high school, he was also an athlete—goalie on the soccer team. He was known for his ruthless aggression on the field, but otherwise was a mystery. He was always so intense and broody, even when we partnered together that year in English. He barely spoke to me at all, instead opting to send me the occasional—and very effective—withering stare. That was alright. Withering stares, I could handle.

And then, during that same class, I found out his secret.

Once I knew, the intensity of his cold looks and hard glares ratcheted up to eleven. I can still hear him whispering in my ear that night at our house, his fingers discovering my own most humiliating secrets.

His size and demeanor have always been terrifying—the kind of guy a girl would rather not have look their way at all. Not like Killian, who, if a girl could catch his attention, she'd instantly become popular. Or Tristian, who could, if he wanted, bestow her with a sexy, secretive smile and have her eating out the palm of his hand. The Rath I'd known was an observer, watching quietly, and waiting for his moment to strike.

This room? It must belong to someone else.

I step into the cluttered mess, eyes drawn to the central focus of the room. *Not* his bed. That's pushed against the wall, bed sheets twisted and unkempt. No, the object dominating the room is a beautiful grand piano. Sheet music rests on the stand and I spot the leather journal he'd been writing in the day of my interview. I step forward, curious. Has he improved? What might I find inside; tales of his exploits, or just music notes, scribbles and diagrams?

I run my fingers down the soft front cover of the journal, but paranoia makes me stop short of opening it. What if the room is bugged? Maybe there are cameras. I'd put nothing past them.

I graze my fingertips over the uncovered keys instead. It's not the only instrument visible in the room; several guitars are propped against surfaces or hanging on the wall. I recognize the cases for a violin and a trumpet sitting on a far shelf. There's other stuff, strange equipment with dials and buttons, all hooked up to a huge, three-screen computer station. Perhaps this is for recording.

But that's not all I discover while walking across the room. There's a wall of shelves, cubes filled with old-school record albums. Hundreds of them. I look over and see the antique record player, an empty cover sitting on top. *Ella Fitzgerald*. I flip the switch and the black disk starts to spin. Carefully, I rest the needle in the groove.

The strains of music fill the room, and all of a sudden, the weight of the day—the last few months—just crashes right down on my shoulders. It could be the food in my belly, or maybe the vodka, maybe just the fact that Rath's room is warm and cozy, far more comfortable than it has any right to be.

Whatever it is, I'm exhausted, and I sink into the leather couch next to the record player, kicking off my sandals. It's early and I have no doubt the guys are at a party or something, likely to be gone all night. Picking up the sleeve of the album, I study the back and let myself relax.

I'm not sure how much time passes. There are the lilting, sweet yet powerful tones of Ella Fitzgerald, and then a slow, eventual change in the music.

That's what ultimately rouses me.

The room is dark, save for a lamp sitting atop the huge piano, and I can't help but sink into the sound washing over me. The record music was good, but this? The chords reverberate through the room, something slow and haunting, dark and yet alive. A little too alive.

It's *live*.

I bolt upright. The musician is only a few feet away, back straight, hands roaming over the keys, inky black hair falling into his eyes.

My heart hammers wildly at the realization Rath is right there. He doesn't look my way, seemingly enraptured in the music he's playing. Maybe I can get out of here and get back to my room without him noticing?

I stand, the album cover sliding to the ground. I wince, but the noise is quiet, soft. I carefully bend, picking it up quickly, then placing it on the couch. Rath doesn't turn my way, so I continue with my escape, grabbing my shoes and starting toward the door in a tip-toe.

"I feel like one of the three bears," he says suddenly, voice carrying over the music, "coming in here and finding a girl sleeping in my room."

Frozen, it takes me a moment to squeak out a weak, "I'm sorry." I keep my eye on the door, inwardly calculating how long it'll take me to reach it. "I turned on some music and must've fallen asleep. I won't bother you again."

The music stops, a tense silence falling over the room.

He turns, the soft light of the lamp casting his profile into sharp relief. "You know, in some versions of that story, the bears eat Goldilocks for invading their personal space." There isn't a hint of amusement on his face. "I wonder what kind of punishment is appropriate for this situation?"

The way he looks at me makes my throat twist itself into a tight knot. Rath is dangerous, but it's maybe the worst kind of danger—the kind that isn't obvious, isn't known yet. I've never been alone with him before, and I don't want to be right now.

Stupid.

It's the whole reason I moved in here. I couldn't think of three scarier people to live with. But now that I'm here, pinned under the weight of his gaze like an insect, I'm beginning to regret it.

"I didn't know you were a musician," I say, hoping to divert his attention. "Or that you were into music at all. You're very good."

He doesn't look appeased. If anything, it just makes his expression colder. "I'm a private person, which is why it was a bit disturbing to find you in here without permission."

"That was rude. I know." I look around at the mess, hands wringing. "It's just…comfortable. In here."

He tilts his head, the light from the lamp catching on the metal piercings on either side of his lip. Snake bites. He pats the top of the piano. "Sit."

I blink. "What?"

He sweeps a hand over the ebony top. "Come sit and listen as I play. I think that'll be your punishment."

My eyebrows furrow, some of my discomfort beginning to unwind. "I'm not sure that's the negative consequence you think it is."

He doesn't respond, but his expression tells me not to try his patience. I leave my sandals by the door and shuffle over to the piano. I'm trying to figure out how to get up on the top when his hands clamp around my waist and he lifts me up, placing me on the smooth surface.

His scent wafts over me, like the memory of that night. He'd grabbed my waist then as well, right before he pushed his fingers between my legs. I press my thighs together and smooth out my skirt, willing my knees not to tremble. His eyes dart from my face to my hands, then he sits on the bench and begins to play.

In high school, Rath was well known for his ability to catch anything on the soccer field. Jokes about his fast fingers echoed down the hallway. As I watch him now, I think I understand. They're long and slender, quick, and definitely skilled.

While playing, his gaze vacillates between the sheet music and my face, down to my knees, back to the music. The melody is angry, violent, but that's not what entrances me.

It's the way he's looking at me while he's playing it.

It's impossible to read, whatever's in his eyes. Anger, yes. Intensity, sure. Beneath it all lurks a promise, as if he's trying to tell me something without using the words. Whatever the message is, it's not good.

When the music slows, his fingers pause on the keys, his chest heaving.

I swallow loudly in the silence, heart banging wildly in my chest. "That—that was amazing, Rath. I didn't know you could read music." I watch the storm of fury build in his eyes, realizing my error a beat too late. I try futilely to scramble back. "No, I didn't mean—!"

But he's already bolting forward, boxing me in, two palms slamming down on the top of the piano. "You don't know anything about me," he hisses, nostrils flaring.

Nodding frantically, I agree, "I know, you're right, I don't know."

But the thing is, I do.

That semester we spent in English together made it very clear. Rath never read aloud like the rest of us. He made me do all the worksheets. When we had to journal, he'd copy mine without even asking. When we had to read separate short stories, he'd sit there and do absolutely nothing until I read it aloud. To him. I eventually worked it out for myself.

Dimitri Rathbone, although smart and talented, wasn't fully literate.

Scrambling for some morsel of saving grace, I blurt out, "I could help you, you know. I'm the only one who knows about it, right? I could…I'm under a non-disclosure. I can't tell anyone. So I could teach you how to read."

If anything, this just makes his flash hotter. "You think I can't read? You're wrong." Despite the feral look in his eyes, he backs off a bit and I exhale shakily. "I can read you just fucking fine. Look at your knees."

Without really meaning to, I do it, following his gaze down. My knees are pressed together so tightly that they're aching.

"You're afraid, Sweet Cherry." The feel of his hands clamping around my knees makes me flinch. "You think you can get through this without giving up a part of yourself. Right now, you're thinking that you'd like to pry my hands off your knees and slap me in the face." Closer, eyes cast in shadow, he whispers, "You're also not letting yourself think about how much you'd like it if you didn't."

"You're wrong," I answer, my voice quiet.

He chuckles, low and dark. "You should've run like Goldilocks." His thumbs press twin divots into the flesh above my knees. "Because this is one of those stories where the girl *is* punished for breaking into the bear's room. You know what I'm going to do, right? I'm gonna eat you up."

That fear, that feeling of being off balance, comes rushing back in a wave of paralyzing panic. "Wait, I thought…"

"I know what you thought. You thought you'd snoop around in here and see a different side of me. The artistic, creative, perhaps *gentle* side? Maybe then, you'd realize that I'm really just misunderstood. That I'd feel bad for what we did to you. Isn't that right?" His mouth curls into a slow, mean smile. "How's my reading so far?"

I suck in an alarmed breath. "Rath…"

"That person doesn't exist, Story. I'm still the guy from that night. The same one who felt you up and watched as you sucked Tristian off. The one who would have fucked you if your brother hadn't stopped it." He leans toward me, hands creeping up my thighs, and whispers in my ear. "I'm also the one who knows your secret. How hot you were for it all. How fucking *wet*. I think it's my turn to learn a little about you tonight. I'm going to find out if it still does it for you."

Instinct kicks in and I thrash against him, trying to leap off the piano. It's no use. Those quick hands secure me before I can even slide off the top. His fingers press painfully into my flesh as he forces my thighs apart. I struggle back, but I'm not strong enough.

His voice is harsh and ragged when he says, "This is what you agreed to, remember? Or do you not want to be our Lady? If you do, you're going to let me eat your pussy."

I still, chest heaving with the fight. "Can't I just…do it to you?" He's right. I agreed to this. But I'd been preparing to pleasure *them*, not the other way around. I won't know what to expect, how to react. "Like with Tristian?"

He shakes his head. "I can get any girl on this campus to suck me off. That's not what I want. I want to taste you. I want to feel you come apart on my tongue, and then I want you to go to bed thinking of how much you loved it."

Blood, even though I don't want it to, rushes down my body and pools into a warm heat between my legs.

"Now," he runs his hands more gently down my outer thighs, coaxing, "you can fight me, or you can sit back and enjoy it. Either way, I'm going to get what I want."

It's not a threat. It's a promise. I've been on the other side of it once before. I've seen that look in his eye and I know there's no choice here. Numbly, I relent, unclenching my legs, giving him the barest access.

His voice emerges smooth like velvet, "Good girl." His hands inch up my skirt until they vanish completely. He bends, breath hot on my knees. With Rath, I have no idea what to expect, but it's certainly not the soft, warm kiss on my inner knee, or the slick feel of his tongue as it inches higher, exploring the stretch of flesh up my leg. It's not the deep inhalation as he breathes me in, mouth parted, eyes closed. His hands run up my hips, fingers hooking over my panties. "Let's see how well you follow instruction. Lift up," he demands, eyebrow arched. I fight the tremor of nerves as I obey.

His impatience returns when he yanks off the panties, pulling them down my legs and over my knees. He holds them up and says, "These aren't the ones we bought you."

Now, I know my knees are trembling. "I-I didn't have time to change."

"Don't make that mistake again." I look down as he drops them on the piano bench, and I see the hard tenting in his pants. This isn't how I wanted it to go—losing my virginity on a piano just because I pissed someone off.

"Open up," he says, pushing my knees apart. "Show me your pussy."

It seems like it takes forever to will my body to give in to his command. I force my legs open in small, nervous jerks, trying to quell the fear in my stomach, the tremor in my muscles. When he flattens his palms to my thighs, pushing them open wider, I slam my eyes closed, shoulders seizing up.

There's a moment of silence, and then, "Good." He's staring hotly between my legs, tongue peeking out to wet his lips. "You shaved like a good girl." He touches my clit with his thumb and a current shoots through my body, hips bucking forward of their own accord. Rath's back straightens and he grins, licking his thumb. "Just as sweet as I remembered."

"And you're still a pig, like I remember." There's one thing that's different about me this time. I refuse to cry. I won't. I got myself into this, I asked for it. I have to accept it, but I don't have to like it.

He laughs, chest bouncing. "Still a mouthy little shit, too. That's okay. We like it."

My fingers are wrapped around the edge of the piano, clenched tight. Rath pries them off, rests them on his shoulders and dives back in. This time it's his tongue flicking across the bundle of nerves. My belly seizes and my hands, desperate for something to hold onto, thrust into his long, shaggy hair. He groans against me, mouth humming against my sensitive flesh. I fight against the overwhelming sensation, reminding myself that I don't want this. I don't like it. I don't like him.

I *hate* him.

But what he's doing, *god*.

I will my body not to react, not to succumb to his skilled tongue and warm breath. I bite my bottom lip, I stare at the ceiling, I recite the words to my favorite song. Anything to ward off the sweet sensations building at my core.

His tongue seems just as skilled as his fingers, though, rubbing and licking in ways that I wouldn't have even thought to conjure. I draw on the fear that I've carried for all these years, the nightmares that kept me up at night. Rath whispering in my ear. The feel of his hard cock against my back. The sound of him coming. The fact he knew my secret.

Because he was right.

I did get wet while Tristian forced his cock down my throat. My body wanted something my mind couldn't comprehend. I'd told myself over and over it wasn't true. That I hadn't really felt like that. That my mind was playing tricks on me.

That it was a lie, how some part of me, no matter how small, wanted *more*.

Yet here I am again; being forced against my will and *liking* it.

"Stop fighting it," he says, easing back to meet my wide gaze as his thumb makes circuits around my clit. His eyes are heavy-lidded and glazed, mouth shiny with my slickness. "I don't get you. You agreed to this. You like it. Why fight it? I'm going to make you come for me, Story."

Still, I try to remain like stone. Even as he dips down to lathe my clit with his tongue, one deft finger slipping into my entrance, I tell myself that it's not all that great—that I can beat this.

And then he uses his thumbs to spread my pussy apart and flattens his tongue against my clit. The ball of tension building in my center abruptly explodes, whether I want it to or not. Suddenly, I'm fisting two handfuls of his hair and grinding myself against his mouth, jaw agape as I gasp with the clench of orgasm.

I tell myself that it's not me. Not really. This is just my body, desperate for a release after a long, difficult week. I can't help it.

Rath kisses my clit and sits up, lips shiny and wet between the piercings. "Pretty good as far as first lessons go, don't you think?" he says, ignoring the fact that I'm staring sightlessly past his shoulder.

My eyes drop down to his pants where his erection bulges against the fabric. Now that he's done, I know he'll want more. He'll want to take the one thing that's still mine. The one thing I had to barter with in this sick, cruel world.

His eyes search mine for a moment, like he's wondering what I think. I scowl back, hoping to hide my shame behind disgust.

"Go," he says, surprisingly. "Get out of here." I gape for a minute, brain lost in the fog of my orgasm, trying to understand what's happening. He adjusts himself and grimaces. "Go!" he roars and I scramble off the piano. I don't stop for my panties or my shoes. I just bolt for the door.

I race down the stairs, almost tripping and catching myself on the banister, not stopping until I'm in my room. Shut tight inside, all alone.

Then I exhale, and allow myself the space to acknowledge the truth.

That was the best orgasm I've ever had. His mouth, his hands, this tongue.

They might be attached to a monster, but they were just…

So goddamn good.

I slide down the door and sink to the floor. Jesus. My pussy is still warm, still wet, practically vibrating from the remnants of the orgasm.

I can't let him know.

I won't.

I can barely accept it myself.

7
RATH'S REVENGE

IF IT WEREN'T FOR The Game, I would be bending Story over my piano right about now, fucking her senseless. The thought of it—the vision of my cock burying myself into her tight, wet pussy—is so vivid and alluring that I have to practically force her to leave.

She must sense it because she doesn't just leave. She runs like hell, scurrying down the hall like a scared little mouse.

Groaning in frustration, I walk across the room, my erection painful and stiff, intending to close my door. Instead, I find Tristian leaning against it, his arms crossed over his chest, eyebrow raised.

"That was quick."

I shrug a shoulder. "Didn't even have to work for it. She was curled up on my couch like a present, waiting to be unwrapped."

"Bet she doesn't make that mistake again."

I laugh, still tasting her on my mouth. "I wouldn't be so sure about that. I made that girl come so fucking hard, she's probably still all jelly-legged."

Tristian hums like he doesn't care, but I can see the jealousy lurking under the façade. "Three points, then?" he asks, eyes falling down to the tent in my pants. Sure, I could have made her suck me off, but barebones compliance is the smallest point-value for head. I'm biding my time with that, maximizing my point gain.

"Five," I correct. "The door was wide open."

He narrows his eyes, like he wants to protest an open door being an exhibition, but we'd already laid out just about every variation, and an open door is worth two points. If there's one thing Killian is good at, it's managing to break any possibility down into micro-granular opportunities.

"I still think three is too much." Tristian would. Exhibition is more his thing than mine.

I roll my eyes, but don't bother arguing this again. Three points for giving our Lady an orgasm was my own idea. I know Tristian and Killer. They're both too involved in their own dicks to give much thought to getting a girl off. Me? Hell, that's part of the thrill, making a girl shake apart under my hands, my tongue, my dick. The way she'll look at me after, half affronted, half awestruck. It's easy to give a girl a bad fuck. Giving her a good one is the better challenge.

"Maybe," I smirk back at him, "to those of us who only think of clits in a vague, abstract, purely theoretical kind of way."

He flips me off and I laugh, turning to shut the door behind me. Competition has always been fierce between us, and things escalated the prior year when we worked together against the rest of the Frat. But adding Story to the mix is going to be interesting. There's something about this girl, like just seeing her brings out something feral and wild inside. I know I'm not the only one who feels it.

When I step back in the room, I get hit by her scent, both the sweet floral smell of her shampoo and the tangy aroma of her pussy. My eyes drop to the faded gray cotton panties I'd left on the piano bench. I pick them up and press the soft, worn fabric against my nose. I close my eyes and inhale, thinking about what it was like to have her writhing against my tongue.

My cock twitches and I laugh. God, she fought so hard, yanking and pulling at my hair, pretending like she wasn't into it. But that's always been

Sweet Cherry's MO. I'd seen her sugar baby account back in the day. The girl is a tease. I saw the way she strung those old fuckers along. The way she acted *so* innocent. She's not. She's a horny bitch. Why the hell would she come into my room and curl up on my couch if she didn't want me to play with her? Considering her little addendum to the contract, there's no doubt the girl has an appetite.

I crash on the couch and unzip my pants, pulling out my cock with one hand and gripping her panties in the other.

I may have let Story get away without pleasuring me tonight, but the taste and feel of her are enough to spur my imagination. It's not the first time I've had to conjure up the memory of her to get off, and something tells me it won't be the last.

Still, the orgasm is lacking. Even as I catch my spunk in her panties, I'm thinking that next time is going to be different. Let her stew in the knowledge that I know my way around her body. Then, I'll make her return the favor.

Maybe it's the fading endorphins, but suddenly I'm dumped into the chilly reminder of Story mentioning my little…issue.

Scowling, I throw the panties in the trash—Ms. Crane will love that shit—and pick up my journal, flipping it open. It's not like I never tried to get better at reading. It was just easier, paying people off to take my tests, to let me copy. After so long, I didn't even have to pay at all. One nice, long stare was enough to make people compliant—teachers included. Do it to the right people at the right times, they won't even realize you *need* it. One day I realized it was too late, I was *too fucking old*, to have problems with this kind of shit. Might have flown in grade school, but in middle school? High school? Fucking college? No way.

But somehow Story figured it out.

It's late when I descend the stairs, pack of cigarettes in hand. I pass Killer's room, right across from Story's, and don't have to press my ear to the door to know he's probably already in there. Looks like I'm not the only one jacking it to Sweet Cherry tonight.

Just the only one feeling pissed off afterward.

"Heard you got a new toy," Ms. Crane says when I step out into the back garden. Not much light reaches back here, but I can still make out the lines of her ancient, worn face.

I light my post-nut cigarette and shrug. "I've barely taken it out of the package yet."

Her laugh is gravelly and harsh, a lot like her voice. Ms. Crane is in her late fifties, but she doesn't look a day under seventy. "You boys are gonna get it one of these days."

"Hell yeah, we are," I say, deliberately misreading her words. "How was bridge?"

She flicks her own cigarette. We're used to these little garden cigarette meetings, although Ms. Crane must smoke like three packs a day. She practically lives out here. "Nasty bitches. Can't suffer 'em."

"Because you're such a ray of fucking sunshine," I respond, exhaling a cloud of smoke into the night air.

"Only thing worse than bartering pills with a dozen bitter old hags is working for you three dickless cockroaches."

I put a hand to my chest. "You secretly love us like we're your own."

Her shrewd eyes land on mine. "If I'd given birth to someone like you, I would have blown my brains out."

"No, you wouldn't have."

Ms. Crane is the baddest bitch I know. She was married to the oldest, sickest crony in South Side up until three years ago. She's probably seen and lived through shit that would even make Killian shudder. We wouldn't let anyone talk shit to us like she does. Ms. Crane isn't just anybody.

"No," she agrees, blowing a plume of smoke. "Would have solved you with a coat hanger long before it got to that point."

I snort. "Tell me how you really feel, you old bat."

"Very well," she says, stubbing out her cigarette. "You know what happened to my husband, don't you?"

I raise an eyebrow. "Pretty sure everyone does."

She nods. "You keep playing your little games. One of these days you're gonna get the wrong girl. Just you watch your back. You hear?" She punctuates this with a pat to my cheek that could almost be called affectionate.

Except then she flips me off.

What I don't tell her is that I'm always watching my back. Story knows my secret—something that even Killer and Tristian don't even know.

If she knows what's good for her, she'll keep it.

STORY

8

POWER STRUGGLE

My sleep is filled with the hot, dreadful sensation of eyes, watching me, waiting. It's a silly instinct. Ted was never so obvious. I wouldn't even know he'd been watching me until a photo would arrive of me doing mundane things, completely unaware of his gaze on me. Eating at the table. Doing my homework over a cup of coffee. Pulling all-nighters in the library. Packing my duffle bag. Getting on the bus—any bus, I barely looked—in an attempt to run from him.

I'd been at the boarding school until the summer following my junior year. I knew that I couldn't go home, so I hopped that random bus and ended up in Colorado. It's hard getting started when you're lying about your name and age, but I just about managed. I was even able to live with some of my co-workers, a closet masquerading as a bedroom for three hundred a month. For a while there, things were…

Well, not nice. But as nice as they could be, considering.

And then Ted found me again.

This time, he was beyond angry. The letters I'd been used to getting—full of frustration, but also longing—had turned into nothing but postcards with obscenities and threats scribbled on the back. Eventually, there'd be photos of my roommates with big dark 'X' marks over their eyes. It was, quite frankly, almost too ridiculous to take seriously.

The last mail I'd received had been a photo with me and one of my roommates. A guy named Jack.

In the photo, Jack's hand was on my shoulder and I was smiling back at him. Perfectly innocent, just two casual acquaintances parting ways before conflicting shifts. I'd barely gotten to know Jack at all, in fact. It would have been a stretch to even call us friends. But the back of the photo was full of the same scrawled word, over and over.

Whore.

My first night at the Lords' house, I only wake once, confused about the pitch-dark room, heart pounding with some phantom awareness that I'm not alone. I lay silently for a long moment, breath caught in my throat, waiting for someone to appear out of the shadows. When it never happens, my pulse slows, the weight of sleep dragging me back into another disturbed slumber.

When I wake again, the sun is streaming through the curtains. I stretch, well aware that even with the memories and paranoia, I'm still probably more well rested than I have been in weeks. I know being in the Lords' house is a big factor.

As much as I don't want to admit it, maybe the orgasm didn't hurt either, unraveling something tense and unwelcome in the deepest parts of me.

A beeping sound catches my attention and I roll over, taking the phone off the bedside table. It's instantly obvious that it's not my phone. This one doesn't have the shattered screen in the right hand corner and is also a much newer model. I run my hand down the sleek sides and look at the screen. A memo from Martin fills the space:

Shower/Dress
(First Day Outfit is in the Closet—marked.)
Put on the wrist cuff
Downstairs by 8 a.m.

Inspection

Breakfast

School

Inspection? I think back to Rath when he saw my worn cotton panties. His displeasure with me not wearing the new lingerie they'd provided was evident. I walk over to the closet. Hanging on the inside of the door is an outfit I hadn't noticed the day before. There's a note pinned to the shoulder declaring, *"First day."*

It ascends absurdity. No human girl would knowingly wear something like this, I'm convinced. It's a tennis-style skirt, pleated and short enough that if I bend over, I'm pretty sure it'd show my panties. The fabric is white with black piping at the hem. There's a top to go with it, a soft-looking shirt that ties at the shoulders. The front drapes slightly in a way that I know will accentuate my breasts. A pair of pristine, white sneakers is on the floor, short socks tucked inside.

"The Lords take it to another level. They're more than just controlling. It extends to everything. What you wear, when you eat, where you sleep. They completely rule your life. They own you." The redhead's voice echoes in my ear from the day of the interview.

On my dresser is a wide leather wrist cuff. I pluck it up, thumbing the bronze skull in the middle. It's the same as the door knocker. Arranged around it in a triangle are the letters K, T, and D.

Killian, Tristian, Dimitri.

It takes me a moment to realize what this is. Their mark. Something to wear to show others that I belong to them, am owned by them.

The idea of being branded like cattle raises my hackles. I'm not dumb, though. They're not nearly as mysterious as they like to think they are. I know one reason they picked me is because I'm not like the other girls who wanted to be Lady. I'm not a doll they can dress up and play with. If they wanted someone like that, they should have picked another Lady.

They think they're the scariest thing in my tiny little world, is the thing. Scary, yes. But they aren't the worst.

One day, maybe soon, they're going to figure that out.

Feeling energized and determined, I step into the steaming shower and scrub my entire body. I can't help but notice my brand of shampoo is on the small shelf nestled in the tiles. Everything else I need, in a variety of product lines and brands, is neatly arranged; body scrubs, loofahs, shaving gel and razors. I take the time to test them all, spoiling myself. The bastards owe me that much.

It takes a little longer than expected to get ready, but I feel better once I'm in my soft jeans and worn hoodie. I ease my feet into my old sneakers and head down the stairs, twisting my hair into a knot as I get to the bottom step.

Martin's waiting for me at the landing, a clipboard in his hands. He looks up from his watch, eyes immediately assessing my outfit. A deep frown sets in his mouth.

"Did you not get my memo this morning, Lady?"

"I did." On a very new phone.

Which I think I'll keep.

"You're late." Again, he checks his watch, mouth slanted disapprovingly. "By six minutes. And your attire…"

"Is comfortable," I conclude.

He briskly corrects, "Is unacceptable."

"I have three classes today. This is what I would always wear."

He looks away, patience wearing visibly thin. "Yes, but you are no longer on your time. You made an agreement, signed a contract, to be a Lady with all that entails." His voice lowers and I hear a tinge of nervousness when he adds, "The Lords won't be happy."

"Well, that's nothing new. The Lords are never happy with me. I'd rather be comfortable."

"Miss Story…"

He's interrupted by the thunder of feet on the wooden steps. I turn, stomach dropping at the sight. The three of them are ridiculously gorgeous, each in casual but expensive clothes for a day of classes. But that's not what's making my stomach churn unhappily. It's the expressions on their faces. The instant Killian sees me, his face twists into hard disgust. Tristian's eyes narrow and calculate. Rath licks his pierced lips, presumably in memory of what happened between us the night before. His gaze bores through me, like he's envisioning me on that piano, struggling against his hold.

I fight the tingle in my belly, the raised hairs on my arms and the intense urge to flee. Killian had made that perfectly clear: No running.

"Martin," Killian says slowly, "did you not leave out the outfit we selected for Story today? And our bracelet?"

"Yes, I did, sir."

His steel gray eyes lock with mine. "So you just willfully disobeyed us."

I lift my chin, feeling my resolve begin to crumble. "I wanted to be comfortable for the long day ahead."

Tristian laughs. "Typical college girl. Thinking people care what you want."

"Martin," Killian says again, his voice in that same, even, terrifying tone. "Please go upstairs and bring down the approved outfit chosen for Story to wear on her first day as our Lady. And don't forget the bracelet."

"Yes, sir." The little man scurries up the stairs.

"Why does it matter what I wear?" I ask, trying to reason with them. "All you guys ever want is for me to take off my clothes anyway, right? Isn't that what this is about? Sex? Forcing yourself on me?"

It's Tristian who answers, his eyes narrowed. "You really like to flatter yourself, don't you? Today is your first official, public-facing day as *our Lady*. That means the second you step out that door, you're representing this house. You're representing *us*. It's about setting a standard."

Killian agrees, "Anyone can be a convenient hole, Sweet Cherry. We demand excellence." His gaze sweeps over me like I'm a piece of trash. "What you're wearing may be acceptable for a common student at Forsyth, but you aren't common. We aren't common. We're Lords and you're our Lady, and that's exactly how you're going to conduct yourself. Am I clear?"

Martin returns, holding the outfit in one hand and the shoes and bracelet in another. "Where shall I direct Miss Story to change," he asks. "The first floor powder room?"

"No," Killian replies, crossing his massive arms over his chest. "It's time for breakfast. Story can change in the dining room while we eat."

"What?" Surely he can't mean...

While I gape in disbelief, Martin is already moving, carrying my outfit down the hall toward the dining room. Killian follows him, apparently done with my feeble show of rebellion. Rath is close behind, tossing me a wink that makes a disgusted feeling slither up my spine.

I turn to Tristian, asking, "Is this for real? Are you really going to watch like I'm some sort of dinner theater?"

He grins, but it's not friendly. He steps forward and places his fingers under my chin, forcing my gaze to his. It's a move so similar to *that night* that it makes me stumble back a step, overcome with the sudden, intense sense of memory of him invading my mouth.

"It's going to be so much fun breaking you down, Sweet Cherry." He raises a thumb to tug at my bottom lip, pupils dilating at the sight. "Something I don't think you understand about us, is that although we're ready to do the hard work of molding you into the perfect girl, none of us are very patient. I suggest you get in that room and do as you're told."

I don't dare to respond, instead jerking my head away from his grasp. If this is the punishment for not dressing right, then I'd hate to see the punishment for back-talk. With heavy feet, I follow him down the hall toward the dining room, a lump rising into my throat with every step.

The instant I step inside, I'm struck by the delicious scent of breakfast foods—pancakes, bacon, toast, eggs. The plates are huge, fit for the large men sitting around the table. My stomach growls, but even though the only thing

I've eaten in days was half of the plate left for me last night, the three place settings make it clear that I haven't been invited to eat with them. And now that I'm being punished—in the form of being their morning entertainment—it's not even clear if I'll get to eat at all.

The outfit Martin brought down is laid out on the table; the skirt, the top, and a lacy pair of panties. I stare numbly at them, pushing down the nausea in my stomach, futilely trying to convince myself this isn't a big deal. It's just flesh. Some days, it feels like this body was never my own to begin with. Why start feeling possessive over it now?

"I suggest you get moving," Killian says, taking a sip of orange juice. "If you're not ready by the time we leave for campus, the consequences will be unfortunate."

My eyes dart to Tristian, who appears completely unfazed as he eats a huge forkful of something resembling fruit. I then give Rath one last look, hoping that something must have passed between us last night. Some connection. A fondness. Anything that would make him step in and stop this.

Instead, he's staring right at me, those dark eyes sparkling as if he can't wait. He even hums when he slathers his pancakes with butter.

Whatever. *I can do this,* I think, standing before the clothes. I agreed to this stupid shit-show and belittling me is one of their favorite games. I take a deep breath and turn to the side where I don't have to look at them. My fingers shake as I unzip my hoodie, revealing the free FU T-shirt I'd been giving upon registering. I drape it over one of the chairs, then unbutton my jeans, sliding them over my hips and down my legs. Balancing myself on the edge of the table, I kick them off my feet. The air in the room is chilly on my freshly shaved legs. I shiver and regretfully pull my shirt over my head. Glancing at the other end of the table, I see that while the guys continue to eat, they're still watching me closely. Rath's eyes are fixed on my chest, my nipples peaked, both from the exposure and the hot gaze of the guys. He slowly licks syrup off his fingers, one by one.

Tristian tilts his head and declares, "You know, I don't totally mind the ratty panties. Plays into my Cinderella fantasies."

Killian just peers at his watch and inhales two pieces of bacon. To be honest, I'm just glad he doesn't have his hands down his pants. That'd be the way to ruin breakfast for me forever.

Reaching for the bra clasp on my back, I start to turn, shielding myself. "Ah ah ah," Tristian sharply chides, "I don't think so. You know how much I love to look at your tits, Sweet Cherry."

Trying my best to ignore him, I take off my bra and quickly lower my panties. Every inch of my skin burns with heat and humiliation. If I thought this was going to be easy, I was mistaken. Their eyes wolfishly drink me in, and as usual, my body threatens to betray me, prickling with a confused tangle of dread and stimulation. Because it's not just hatred I see in their eyes. It's want. They want me despite everything, and I don't know how to handle that.

I want to make this moment of complete nakedness as brief as possible, so I dive for the bastard-approved panties.

"No." Killian's voice rings out loud and sharp, bringing my movements to a jerking halt. "Bracelet first." Gnashing my teeth against a wave of anger, I snatch the cuff from the table and loop it around my wrist. He adds, "Wearing that is a privilege. It means you belong to us."

"You can take it off to shower," Rath says, lazy eyes still roving my bare body. "But otherwise, we want it on you at all times."

"*All* times," Killian stresses.

"Fine," I grind out, snapping the cuff into place before once again going for the underwear.

This time, it's Tristian who stops me. "What's the rush, Lady? I think we should get a good look at you, wearing nothing but our mark." The smirk on his mouth is full of humor, knowing exactly how badly I want to cover up.

Fed up with the game, I give in, extending my arms, turning toward them, allowing them to look their fill. "Happy?" I spit, glaring daggers at them all.

The smirk fades from Tristian's face, replaced by something stonier. "No, I don't think I am. You're not treating this privilege with the respect it deserves. Come here so I can get a closer look." His tone is full of warning, possibly of a greater punishment.

"I thought we didn't have much time," I argue, glare shifting to my stepbrother.

Tristian replies, "The longer you take, the less time we'll have."

Killian raises an eyebrow, jerking his chin toward Tristian. I take it as the order it is. Taking a long, hard, steadying breath, I step around the table to Tristian's side, fixing my eyes to a point on the wall.

Tristian hums, turning to me. "Your tits really are pretty nice, you know? You shouldn't hide them under all those ugly, cheap things." He punctuates this by tipping forward and taking one into his mouth.

I inhale sharply, caught off guard, but the look in his eyes as he tongues my stiff nipple is full of a warning that he doesn't need to verbalize. I stay put, hands tightening into shaking fists as he assaults my nipple with long, sucking kisses, only pulling back to meet my gaze as the sharp point of his tongue dances around it. The feel of it sends hot sparks down my chest, straight into the pit of my stomach, settling like electricity between my legs.

I can't help my flinch when he wedges a hand between my thighs, climbing up, fingers grazing just below—

"We don't have time for that," Killian's sharp voice rings out.

Tristian holds my gaze as his hand slides away, mouth leaving me with a final parting kiss to my breast. "We'll finish this later," he promises in a ragged voice, but not before giving one of my ass cheeks a playful smack.

When they say nothing else, I dress, first pulling on the panties, then the shirt and skirt. I'm still shaky and furious, so embarrassed that every inch of my skin feels set ablaze with it. My nipple is damp and still tingling from the feeling of Tristian's hot mouth and the way he played with me.

Because that's exactly what this is. They're just toying with me. Hoping for my anger, my humiliation.

I won't give it to them.

Killian eats another plate of eggs while I slip on my socks and shoes. I stand and look at them expectantly. "Is this appropriate enough for you?"

"Go fix your hair," Killian says, waving me off. "It looks like a fucking rat's nest."

I only just manage not to sprint from the room, leaving my old clothes discarded on the dining room floor. Martin, who's waiting in the hallway with my bag, hands me a hairbrush and a protein bar. "You may use the powder room down the hall. Don't take long, they'll be leaving soon and will expect you to be ready."

I take them from him and enter the bathroom, taking a moment to stare at myself. My cheeks are flushed, the tip of my nose is red, and yeah, my hair is a mess. Underneath all that is the slowly fading buzz of…something. I'm not sure what it is, but it feels a lot like defeat.

It's hard to think all this degradation and humiliation could be worth it. Maybe, if Ted had been nothing but scary letters and creepy stalking, the answer would have been no.

Then I remember the last time I saw Jack. The way the light from the lamp had made his face look almost…*shiny*. How it'd taken me too long to realize it was blood. I remember the silence of his little room in Colorado and how I'd stood there for too long—stunned, checked-out—without noticing the word painted on the wall in his thick, darkening blood.

Whore.

It's all so much easier then.

I fix my hair up real nice for them, looking just as empty as I feel. Just as empty as they want me to be.

Because they might not know it yet, but eventually, Ted will come. He'll make these three his new target. And if I know Killian and his friends, they'll fight back harder than anyone else would.

Yes.

Being their toy will be easy.

The hard part will be deciding who I want to lose more.

STORY

9
THE RULES

It'd started out pretty basic with Ted. He'd slid into my DMs, giving me compliments on my photos, asking me about myself. I told him what all the men wanted to hear; that I was still in high school, that I liked to have fun, that I was a virgin. I mean, it was all the truth. I didn't even have to lie.

Ted was the first one to give me money. The first to ask me if I wanted to see a picture of his cock instead of just throwing one into my inbox whether I wanted to see it or not. He was the first to give me choices, talk to me like a real adult and not just a doll or some kind of plaything. He was nice. He said he liked my smile.

It didn't make much difference to me. I was there for the quick cash, however I could get it. Out of the men I was flirting with online, Ted was the most serious. But to me, there was nothing genuine or authentic about it. But I'd be lying if I said it didn't make me feel good. To feel wanted. To feel special. To feel these things from someone anonymous who couldn't hurt me.

Living with Daniel and Killian was difficult. They were like two sides of the same coin. Killian was on a mission to make sure I knew just how worthless he thought I was, and his father…

Well.

The way his father treated me was much more complicated than that.

When Ted asked me to save myself for him, to let him be the one to take my virginity, it was nothing to agree. What the hell, right? If that got me more money? Faster money? It's not like he'd ever know otherwise. It wasn't a promise I was ever committed to keeping. I never planned on meeting Ted at all. Ever. I planned to get out of Daniel's house and start over. Which is why I didn't even think about him when I shut down my account after Killian revealed he knew about it. It'd just been a temporary means to an end, nothing more.

Except Ted managed to find one of my emails, initially created just to collect spam. He wasn't ready to let me go and I got the feeling pretty damn quick it wasn't a game to him. He made it clear; I'd made a promise and he planned on me keeping it, whether he had to force it or not.

I deleted that email, talked my mom into boarding school, and then ran away and vanished. But Ted is a part of me now. A part of my life. He hangs over me like a toxic cloud, unpredictable, unshakable.

He could be watching the four of us right now.

That's what I think about as I walk across the campus at Forsyth, flanked on either side by Tristian and Rath. Killian walks a few feet ahead of us and I focus on his broad shoulders, wondering what these three would do. They've done horrible things to me—probably other girls, too—but that's easy. We can't fight back. But what about someone their own size? What about someone scarier than them? Would they, could they, take him down? Or will Ted roll in here and conquer them?

Maybe they'll all destroy each other and I can skip off into the sunset, finally free of it all.

Yeah, right.

"Hey," Tristian says, loping his arm over my shoulder and pulling me against his hard side. "How does it feel to have the most coveted position in school?"

I watch my feet against the pavement, not bothering to shrug his arm off. "I doubt anyone really cares," I reply, shifting my backpack. "This is college. Not high school."

His laugh is deep and soft in my ear. "You think that means the stakes are lower? It's the opposite, actually. We're not talking about who gets an invite to the head cheerleader's house on Friday night. This is about the future, power, and who wields it. Every single guy in this school, of a certain status, wants to be a Lord. And every girl wants to be our Lady." He leans in to whisper in my ear. "Trust me, they're jealous."

As ridiculous as he sounds, one glance around tells me that people actually are paying attention. The student body as a whole seems fully aware of the three of them, making space as Killian leads them down the quad. The girls look at them wistfully, their gazes raking over their handsome faces and fit bodies. Then they jump to me, the flirty smiles vanishing for a colder expression. If jealousy really was a color, their faces would be green.

This is made even more evident when another group—five guys and a girl—slow their steps as they pass us.

One of the guys says, "See you finally chose one. Took you long enough."

Tristian, eyes hidden behind sunglasses, sends him a cutting smile. "What can I say? Unlike you, we actually have standards."

The whole group freezes, turning to the four of us slowly. "At least we don't have ours dressed like Country Club Hooker Barbie," one of them says, tugging the girl to his side. She's prettier than me, without a doubt, with long blonde hair and stunning blue eyes. "Lords never did have taste."

Rath shrugs. "And Barons have never been able to see when something special is staring them in the face."

One of the Barons gives me a long head-to-toe look. "Two legs, two tits, and three losers attached to her? Doesn't seem very special to me."

"Look harder." Killian steps up, smiling meanly. "Because as I recall, I was fucking your Baroness over the arm of your couch last year. And I know each of my boys have had her. She's worn out pussy."

One of them steps closer, voice low, eyes sparking. "You need to mind your fucking mouth, Payne."

"And you need to mind your business," Tristian says. I cringe as he presses a kiss to my neck, lips spreading into a grin. "Don't be salty that our Lady hasn't been passed around like a cheap forty-ounce, like yours. Sucks to be you. We're still breaking ours in."

I close my eyes, face blooming hot at his words. "Jesus Christ."

A Baron gives me a skeptical look, scoffing. "I bet plenty of guys around here have had her."

"None of you have." Rath shrugs, grabbing my hand to lead me away. I obediently follow them, trying to bat down my embarrassment.

"Did you have to say that?" I hiss to Tristian.

He gives a simple, "Yes," as if that were the dumbest question he's ever heard. I shouldn't be surprised. Breaking me in? There was no way they weren't going to flaunt me being a virgin. It's the whole reason I'd bartered with it to begin with. I'm probably lucky he didn't just come out and say it.

It doesn't make me want to crawl into a hole any less.

Forsyth University has a central meeting spot in the quad; a magnificent fountain topped with an eagle taking flight. The water is noisy, splashing down into a blue, glossy pool. Students sit on the flat edges, talking, studying, gossiping. Killian stops in front of the structure and turns.

"I have practice all afternoon," he says, presumably to me, even though he doesn't make eye contact. "You'll meet back here?"

"My music class is over at four," Rath says, pulling his ear buds out one at a time and tucking them into his pocket.

"I'll be at the business school until then as well," Tristian turns to me, eyes falling to my mouth. "What about you, Sweet Cherry?"

I cringe again, not liking him using that name in public. It's bad enough that everyone's probably going to know I'm a virgin. What if my classmates knew my past? Or worse? What if Ted is somewhere nearby? "Don't call me that here, and I'm done at two."

"Then you'll wait in the library until they're finished, and they come pick you up. Oh," my stepbrother says, finally looking in my direction, "don't forget to check in. Every hour. Between every class. There's a group text programmed on your phone."

"I can't just go home?" I ask. The answer comes in the dark cut of his eyes in my direction. I shrivel up against it. "Fine."

He and Rath walk off. Tristian stands by me for a moment longer, arm still over my shoulder. "I know it seems extreme, but this is how it works, Story. You're to be available to us at all times. Loyal. Devoted. You go to and from school with us. You can leave when we do. And if you can manage to exemplify all of that, you might find yourself enjoying certain privileges. Being our Lady isn't all about punishment, you know."

I don't ask what those privileges might be. Something tells me they're probably more for their enjoyment than my own. "Sure," I answer dubiously.

"Good girl," he replies, leaning over and kissing me under the ear. His touch is gentle, sweet—purely for show. I've seen nothing to make me believe there's a kind bone in Tristian's body, but he more than anyone is aware that people are always watching. "See you in the library this afternoon."

He walks off, taking his delicious, masculine scent with him. Finally free of them all, I take a deep breath to settle my nerves. I have a whole day of classes ahead of me—a day without their orders and looks and touches.

I catch the eye of one of the girls sitting by the fountain, textbook open on her lap. She's watching me, eyes pinging from me, to my wrist cuff, to where Tristian is disappearing over the bridge to the business school. I open my mouth to explain. To say something about what she'd just witnessed. To justify the humiliation of being led around by three aggro cavemen.

Before I have the chance, she shuts her textbook, mutters a low, "Lucky bitch," and walks off.

THESE DAYS, PARANOIA has become my constant companion. Much like the night before, when I woke up thinking that someone was in the room with me, that same feeling follows me as I go from class to class. I can't shake the eerie feeling that someone is watching me as I crisscross around campus, going from building to building, class to class. I keep waiting for one of the guys to appear with opinions about my clothes or hair, but I never see them. What I do find are the eyes of the other students, carefully assessing the new Lady. I'm disappointed to find that word travels as fast in college as it did in high school.

Thankfully, my day is busy enough that I scarcely have the chance to hyper focus on the disaster my life has become. Remember all those PSAs about your online behavior following you for the rest of your life? Yeah, make me the poster child.

It's one of the reasons I've chosen social work as my major, with a focus on adolescents. Maybe I can help some other kid not make the worst decisions of her life before she graduates high school.

My final class, Child and Family Development, runs late, the teacher droning on and on, despite the fact we should have left ten minutes ago. A few other students shift anxiously in their seats, eyes darting to the door. I know their anxiety is nothing like my own. I doubt any of them have three impatient Lords monitoring their every move.

It'd taken me until the afternoon to realize the fancy new phone I'd been given was less of a gift and more of a Lo-Jack. I'd discovered the tracking device is on, allowing them to know my location at all times. I've had no desire to find out what happens if I don't check in on time, so I've been diligent—until now, which is why I'm not surprised when my phone vibrates on my desk.

Lord Rath: You're late checking in, Lady.

Lady: Sorry. Class ran over.

Lord Tristian: Next time excuse yourself and report in.

"Miss Austin," the Professor calls my name, staring at me over her thick glasses. "Am I boring you?"

"No ma'am," I reply, feeling every eye in the room shift my direction. My cheeks heat. "I'm late to an appointment. That was the reminder."

The professor looks at her watch and frowns. "Very well. I can see you all twitching to leave. We'll stop here, but from now on, please keep your phones in your bags."

Lord Killian: Story…

Everyone around me packs up their belongings. I furiously type out a reply.

Lady: My class ran late and my prof is strict about devices.

I shove everything into my bag and start across campus toward the library. My stomach grumbles, a reminder I never had breakfast or lunch. And aside from the paltry dinner the previous night, I've barely had a chance to eat in days.

I reach into my bag for the protein bar Martin had so helpfully supplied me with. It's smushed down in the bottom, buried under my laptop. I've got my head half shoved into my bag when I run into someone.

"Oh, I'm so sorry!" I say, pushing my hair out of my face. A ripple of panic rolls down my spine when I realize who I've bumped into. "Daniel?"

"The one and only," he replies, smiling tightly.

It takes me a long moment to untangle my discomfort. Surely, most of that is due to our strained relationship. But some of it is because his hair, eyes, and jawline were inherited by the very man hell bent on tormenting me. It's hard to look at Daniel and not think of his son.

"What are you doing here?" I blurt, instantly regretting the curt tone. "I mean…Killian didn't mention you'd be here."

Daniel raises an eyebrow. "You've seen Killian, then?"

I realize that Daniel doesn't know I'm living with the Lords. And come to think of it, I'd really rather he never did. "I saw him earlier, in the parking lot."

"I see." Daniel shifts, sliding a hand into a pocket. Much like his son, Daniel isn't very expressive. "I've come to see you, actually."

I swallow. "M-me?"

He nods, smile pulling at the aged corners of his cool eyes. "Just wanted to make sure everything was going okay for you. I went to the room you've been renting, but you weren't there."

"Oh." I blink, scrambling to find an excuse. "I'm actually just rooming with some friends for now. It's free, so I won't have to put you out any more than I already have."

He waves dismissively. "Please, it's no trouble at all. You're family, Story."

We keep a polite distance, both shifting our eyes awkwardly. Something tells me this isn't how family is supposed to act around one another.

"Well, everything is going fine. Great, in fact."

"So you're all settled in?" he asks, watching me.

"Yep."

He hums, shifting his gaze somewhere in the distance. "It's just that you haven't come by the house yet. Your mother's been upset about it." At my frown, he hastily adds, "Not that she'd say anything. You know how she can be."

I nod in agreement. "Yeah, she does tend to do that."

"I hope..." he starts, forehead pinching as he starts over. "I hope we can move past all that...unsavory business from before you left."

Unsavory business.

It's odd to hear it spoken of so casually, as if it weren't the very catalyst that drove me to earn quick money to escape the entire fucking situation. It's even odder to look back on it, and to realize that out of all the terrible, greedy, entitled, toxic men currently ruining my life, that what happened with Daniel was practically nothing in comparison. Briefly, I get the sense that my reaction to it all had been *silly*.

Daniel is every bit his son's father. He might not be as upfront about it. He might even understand the word 'no'. But at the end of the day, they're cut from the same cloth. I've never forgotten that.

And I won't start now.

I smile prettily. "Water under the bridge, Daniel."

Some of the tightness in his eyes eases at this. "Glad to hear it. And you should come by sometime. If you'd like, I can arrange a day, just for the two of you. We really are very happy to have you home and safe."

I nearly laugh at the word. *Safe.* Oh, Daniel. You idiot. "I'm glad to be back," I lie. "I'll give Mom a call later."

Nodding, he pulls his keys from his pocket, giving them an idle jiggle. "If you need anything, please don't hesitate to contact me. College is tough and I know you've had a rough couple of years. Your mother and I are always here for you." Before departing, he adds, "If you see my son around, be sure to tell him his old man came sniffing about, would you?" He taps his temple. "Gotta keep that one on his toes."

I stare at his retreating figure, wondering if that's how Killian will end up. Handsome and gray-haired, rich, powerful, and *almost* capable of sincerity. Somehow, I can't imagine it.

Unwrapping the protein bar, I take a bite, but find my appetite for it is gone. I chuck it, uneaten, into the nearest garbage bin before climbing the stone steps to the library entrance. This building was one of my favorite sights during my orientation tour. The entry has a marble floor and statues of the founding members of the university tucked into alcoves. Crossing into the main area, the scent of old paper clings to the air and I inhale deeply, feeling a sense of stability here. No matter what kind of upheaval is going on in my life, libraries stay the same.

After confirming the location of the study rooms, I take the curving marble stairs, running my hand over the black, wrought iron bannister. I pass the second floor for the third, and pause at the landing to catch my breath. There's a small balcony overlooking the space below, just off the main walkway. I settle here, enjoying the view, catching my breath.

"You're late."

Before I can turn, two hands clamp down on the railing on either side of my body, trapping me between strong arms. Tristian's warm scent envelops me. I take a deep breath and reply, "You're early."

"That's not how this works, Story." I feel his nose nudge my hair, almost like he's pulling in my scent, too. "I'd say you're confused about our expectations, but I think you're smarter than that. Are you intentionally being defiant?"

"It's no big deal," I say, freezing at the feeling of being caged in by him. "I-I got held up after class, and then I saw Daniel while walking here. I stopped to talk to him. I'm not being defiant."

Tristian goes eerily still. "Did anyone give you permission to talk to him?" Although his breath is warm on my ear, his tone is ice cold.

Bewildered, I ask, "He's my stepfather. I need permission to talk to my family?"

"You need permission for almost everything, Story." He shifts behind me, pressing the lean, solid length of his body against mine. "You know, I took the day off from classes to keep an eye on you. Followed you from class to class."

My heart stutters in my chest, remembering the feeling of eyes watching me. "That was you?"

"Of course, it was me. There are a few things you need to understand. We're not like the other frats here. For the Lords, bringing some random girl into our home is a risk. You're always being watched. We'll always know where you are and what you're doing. And if you fail—if you step out of line—there will be consequences. It's not because we enjoy it." He adds with a smirk in his voice, "Well, not *just* because we enjoy it. We also have to protect our interests."

He removes a hand from the railing, the soft pads of his fingertips trailing down my cheek. I squirm against him, feeling bile rush up the back of my throat at the touch. He either doesn't notice my discomfort or doesn't care, instead running his fingers over my shoulder, brushing my arm, and then caressing the side of my breast.

"It's important that you're fully aware of how this relationship works. I don't want any misunderstandings."

"I understand." Although it's a little difficult to focus on rules and regulations at the moment. My brain is fixated on Tristian's fingers and how very close he is to discovering the point of my nipple. "You own me. At school and at the house. All the time."

"Good girl." His fingers go off course, moving down to the hem of my skirt.

And then they dip underneath.

Stiffening, I peer nervously around the balcony. We're in a fairly isolated area, but it's still public. I try to jerk away, but even with only one hand, he effortlessly holds me in place between his body and the balcony's edge.

"What are you doing?" I gasp.

"Whatever I want." His fingers push underneath the lace of my panties and immediately brush against my clit. I rear back, but he just crushes me against him, thrusting his cock against my backside.

My throat clicks with a swallow. "We can't do this here," I say, feeling my heart thunder.

"Sure we can," he argues in a low voice. "Why do you think I picked out this skirt? And those panties. Easy access."

Any coherent reply is caught in my throat. I'm almost sure any protest will just encourage him more, or even worse, alert someone to where we are and what he's doing.

"What I want to do right now," he whispers, running his nose along my neck, "is to find out if you really get as wet as Rath says you do."

Heat pools, both in my cheeks and between my legs. "Rath?"

He chuckles as he swirls his thumb around in a lazy circle. "You think he didn't tell us about how turned on you were that night? How much you enjoyed having my cock in your mouth?"

That's exactly what I'd thought, though I have no idea why I would. So I have some leverage on Rath. So what? He's not trustworthy. He's loyal to the Lords over everything.

I grind my teeth against the way Tristian's fingers are making me feel. "He's lying. I didn't like it. I hated it. I get wet like that because that's just how my body is. N-not because I'm into it."

"Oh, Sweet Cherry, you're always trying to break my heart." His finger pushes between my folds, pressing into my core. "That's okay. If you want it to be a secret, we can pretend." He inserts one finger and groans into my ear. "God, your pussy is tight. You really are a virgin, aren't you?"

I squeeze my eyes closed, trying to block out the sensations. Every man in my life has put a price on my virginity. Killian, Tristian, Rath. Ted. The other Sugar Daddies. I'd briefly thought it to be a source of power as well as vulnerability. But more and more, it seems like a single-edged sword.

More and more, I just want to fall on it.

I should toss it all away. Just get it over with so that they'll all leave me alone. Maybe I should find some guy to fuck and take it off the table. I won't be so special then.

Voices echo off the marble staircase and I go rigid as a group of students climb to our floor. I push aside any and all thoughts but self-preservation. "Tristian," I whisper, "please let me go."

"Come for me, sweetheart. And then you can go." He slides in a second finger, stretching me from the inside, making me both wince and shudder. "Just do this one little thing and I'm happy to walk you home."

I swallow, every nerve on alert. "I can't. Not like this. Not with people… around."

"I think you can," he replies, pumping his fingers in and out. My knees catch and he slides his other arm around my waist. "You know you want it. Jesus, just look at you. So fucking close, you're shaking."

I bite back a gasp. "That's fear. You're scaring me. Someone may catch us."

"That's not fear. It's want, Cherry. It's on the inside. Your pussy is quivering for me." His thumb brushes over my clit and a jolt shoots through me. "You want this over? Then come for me."

I want to tell him that he's wrong, that he doesn't know my body, can't possibly understand it. But once again, my body shamefully revolts. With every thrust of his fingers, my hips begin chasing them, wanting them closer. Every time the heel of his hand presses into my clit, I buck against it, seeking the friction. My heartbeat bangs against my chest, blood growing hotter with every step that brings the students closer. Suddenly, the thought of him stopping seems more unbearable than being caught. Spurred on like some mindless thing, a wave of electric, greedy adrenaline courses through my body.

"Come for me, Story," he demands, voice quiet but hard like stone. It's like a switch flips. My body turns hot, skin prickling with an aching rawness. Sweat begins building, and when I hear the footsteps right behind us, I can't hold back any longer. The orgasm ricochets through me like an explosion, spreading sweet and sharp from the center of my body. I swallow my voice, biting down hard on my bottom lip to hold my cries inside. It washes over me like a wicked wave, pulling me beneath the surface. Tristian, large body draped calmly over mine, holds onto me as I ride his hand and shatter into pieces.

"That's a good, good girl," he purrs, slowing his movements.

I grab onto the railing with both hands to hold myself upright. Glancing behind me, I'm convinced the other students will all be there, gawking at us. But they've already passed by, none of them the wiser.

Even with that reassurance, I step away from Tristian and smooth out my skirt, pretending that I don't still feel the ghost of his fingers inside of me, or the warm afterglow of an incredible orgasm.

In this moment, I hate myself.

I hate my body, and his skilled fingers. I hate it as much as I did back then, that night in the laundry room. I hate this library. I hate all three of them, for being so cold and callous, but somehow still managing to make me feel this sparking heat.

This heat that won't stop. My neck prickles with sweat and the edges of my vision go dark, tunneling. I feel myself sway, but am powerless to stop it. I shoot a hand out to catch myself, but everything goes black.

I don't even feel the fall.

I ROUSE IN INCREMENTS. It's the smell that hits me first—a strong, floral perfume. After that I begin receiving snatches of sound. Shoes shuffling on the floor, indistinct voices, whispers.

My name. "Story? Wake up now."

Tristian.

Feeling a hand on my forehead, I squirm away, slowly opening my eyes. It takes me a long moment to remember. Tristian. The orgasm. Everything fading to black.

Now, there are people standing over me. Not just Tristian. There's a group of guys, but also a gorgeous girl about my own age, with dark, curly hair and smooth skin.

Her hazel eyes bore into mine. "Do you know what day it is?"

I blink at her, trying to orient myself. "First day. Monday. The eleventh."

The girl—woman—nods. "It looks like you passed out. Do you have any medical conditions?" When I shake my head, she hums. "When was the last time you've eaten?"

"Last night," I croak, gently levering myself up onto my elbows. "But before that..." I trail off, suddenly feeling mortified.

She glances back at the group of guys. "She's probably just got low blood sugar or something." Looking at me, she gives a rueful grin. "I'm Sutton, the Countess. I'm pre-med, but that mostly just means a bunch of impossibly hard science classes they make us take to weed out the weak."

"Oh."

She throws Tristian a sharp look. "Is it LDZ tradition to starve their Lady, or are you just particularly negligent?"

Oh, god. Tristian.

He's standing stiffly beside me with those cold eyes glaring daggers at the group. "I don't see how it's any of your business. She's our Lady. We'll take it from here."

Sutton scoffs, standing. She offers me a hand to help me up, and I take it without thinking. "Easy there, Lady. You good?" I nod, carefully avoiding Tristian's gaze as I steady myself.

One of other guys—a Count—chuckles. "Should have known. I wouldn't put a puppy in the Lords' care, let alone a whole-ass woman."

Another Count meets my gaze, mouth curving into a grin. "Hey, Lady. Blink twice if you're being held against your will. We'll feed you something." He grabs his crotch in emphasis.

Tristian smoothly steps between us. "That's kind of sad, actually. A girl would have to be pretty desperate to think your dick was worth putting in her mouth."

The Counts all laugh. One says, "At least the Countess is still standing. At this rate, you'll be Lady-less by Friday."

Another Count pipes in, "Jesus, they can't even feed her. Times must be pretty rough over there. Maybe we should send them a care package. Girl's looking a bit too thin anyway."

Sutton meets my gaze, lips pressed into a tight, unhappy line. But like me, she remains silent.

Tristian grabs my hand. My hackles are already raised at the sight of his stony, expressionless face, but it's even worse at the sound of his voice. Flawlessly even, and still somehow cutting. "Being a Count must be difficult. Always second from the top, but never quite able to achieve glory." He shakes his head, giving them a look someone else might mistake for sympathy. We can all see the lack of sincerity in it, though. "I'll let this pass on account of feeling sorry for you. Well, and because your Cuntess seemed so helpful."

With that, he tugs me away from the group, down the marble staircase, and out of the library.

I try to keep up.

His jaw is rigid when he finally breaks the silence. "Do you have any idea how that made us look?" He doesn't wait for me to answer. "Fucking ridiculous. How did you not eat breakfast? Lunch?"

He's not really looking for an answer, his narrow eyes fixed straight ahead, flashing with ire.

I give him an answer anyway. "If you recall, none of you would let me eat breakfast." Paying no mind to the way my voice sounds—curt, scathing—I add, "And I had things to do during lunch. I was in the student center working out my course schedule."

"Fantastic," he mutters snidely. "Killian and his fucking temper. *You* and your fucking willful disobedience. I can see now that I'm going to have to make myself in charge of these things."

Swallowing nervously, I ask, "What things?"

His eyes cut to mine and he pauses, some of that sharp tension draining from his features. He lifts my chin with a finger and grins. "Taking care of you, Sweet Cherry."

THE RESTAURANT WE WALK TO isn't what I'm expecting. It's a formal type of place, with mood lighting. The staff are in suits. As Tristian talks in low, smooth tones to the host at the front, I shift awkwardly, looking down at my absurd outfit. I'd feel less out of place if I'd just come in naked.

"This way," the man says, leading me and Tristian to a table in the back.

For his part, Tristian blends in perfectly, even being dressed in a casual button-down and jeans. "Sit," he orders, and then to the man, "We'll start with two glasses of water and some bread. And not that processed crap you send out for free. I want your bakery's special. If I see even a hint of bleached flour at this table, I'll be very unhappy."

The man doesn't skip a beat, giving a nod before loping off.

Tristian opens the menu, not bothering to spare me a glance. "You need a good protein. Something fresh. Organic, if we can manage it. Do you eat meat?" Despite the question, he doesn't even leer at me.

I still wait a moment, just in case I'm walking into a trap. "...yes?"

He sighs. "That's disappointing. Being vegan makes it a lot easier." Just then, a waiter arrives with the water and a basket of bread. Tristian asks, "Is your chicken antibiotic-free?" While he and the waiter go over which meats are 'poisoned with unnatural chemicals and hormones'—Tristian's words—I mull over his question.

When the waiter has left, I ask, "Being vegan makes *what* a lot easier?"

"Eating fresh and clean." He tosses the menu aside, nudging the basket of bread toward me. "Well? Go on. Can't have you fainting like some Victorian handmaid again."

He doesn't look angry anymore. The soft light from the centerpiece's candle casts his features in a warm, deceptive glow, even as his cool eyes watch me. I get the startling, unwelcome realization that this is what Tristian might look like on a date.

The thought all at once disgusts and fascinates me.

Reluctantly, I pluck a roll from the basket, tearing off a bite. Hoping to break some of the strange atmosphere, I wonder, "Are you vegan?"

"Sometimes," he answers, perfectly still. The flickering candle reflects in his eyes. "You do know what happened back there, don't you? At the library, before you got acquainted with the floor."

The bread is suddenly like swallowing sandpaper. "It was a lesson," I guess.

He raises an eyebrow. "And? What did you learn?"

My brain combs through the fog for the answer. "That you can do what you want to me, whenever and wherever."

"Yes, that's right." He gives me a patronizing smile. "And?"

"And I need to be where I'm supposed to be, and only speak to men with your permission."

"Yes. Exactly." He reaches out and pushes a sweaty piece of hair off my cheek. "And this, what we're doing right now? You realize this is a reward, don't you?"

Reward.

The word travels sourly down my esophagus with the bread. "A reward for what?"

He lowers his hand and it lands on my wrist, right over the cuff I'd fastened this morning. "You didn't speak to the Counts. You wouldn't even look them in the eye. That's loyalty." He lifts my wrist, pressing a soft, lingering kiss to the back of my hand.

His eyes pin mine as he does it, an oddly sweet gesture, gently returning my hand to the table afterward.

The way it makes me feel inside is foreign and unsettling. It's a soft, wistful sort of feeling, offset by something strangely wounded, as if the better half of me has just realized how very fake it all must be.

I think I prefer punishments.

KILLIAN PAYNE

10

OPPOSITIONAL

Every muscle in my body aches by the time I finally get home from practice. I park my truck in the garage and wince from the soreness. Our first game is Saturday and Coach decided to put us through the gauntlet to make sure we're prepared. I collect my bag from the back of the truck and approach the house, knowing what's waiting for me inside.

Not that I care.

I don't. But the awareness of her presence is a hard thing to shake, like being fucking haunted. It's an annoying thing to reconcile, the half of me that wishes Story hadn't ever come back, and the half of me that's salivating at the thought of owning her.

I hang my gear on a hook by the back door, feeling my aching muscles strain. The truth is, I don't mind a little pain—especially when it's the result of a hard practice or a well-played game. Each hit, each blow gives me somewhere to channel all this pent-up energy I have swelling inside. It's something concrete to fight.

That's another reason I agreed to have Story as our Lady.

Especially after dominating so hard last year, I need a challenge. Shit here's gotten too lax. It'd be easy to fall into the complacency of it. To stagnate. To become less powerful in the process.

Ms. Crane is hunched over the stove when I enter the kitchen. She gives me a sidelong look. "Still alive, I see."

"Why wouldn't I be?" I ask, shrugging off my jacket. The scent of her cooking slams into me like a freight train. "What's for dinner?"

"Lasagna," she answers. "And I better not hear any lip from Satan's right testicle in there. Damn sick of hearing his big blond bellyaching."

"Tristian?" I ask, peering back to see into the dining room. "You know how he is." Tristian's hateboner for Ms. Crane is a thing of legend, and it's completely mutual. They were doomed from start, since he has to have his special fucking organic, non-GMO, locally-sourced yadda yadda bullshit, and I'm not sure Ms. Crane knows how to cook anything that doesn't come frozen or in a jar.

Pausing, I give her a look. "Right testicle? Which one of us is the left?"

She pulls a knife from the drawer and I have to actively stop myself from stepping back. Ms. Crane can be a scary bitch sometimes. "Oh, the other one."

I quirk an eyebrow at her. "What exactly does that make me?"

Her grin bares a row of stained teeth. "You're the foreskin, kid."

I glower at her. "I don't think paid help is supposed to be quite this insolent."

"I don't think I give a fuck," she responds, glowering right back. "I'm not one of your little bimbo bitches. Now shut your damn face hole and get the plates down. You're not too old to put over my blade, boy."

I roll my eyes. I know better than anyone that Ms. Crane has the cred to back up her threats, but if she really wanted to off me, she would have done it when I was a rowdy, pissed off kid, taking refuge in her squat little office on the off weekends. And God knows Tristian would have been dead forever ago. Her soft spot for me is understandable. She's practically family—like a cranky, old, gin-drinking, chain-smoking, ex-felon aunt. But she has a soft spot for the others, too, I guess. After all, we did pretty much rescue her from South Side.

While she's puttering around in the pantry, she says, "I met your little toy today."

I peek back in the dining room, not seeing her. Clenching my jaw, I voice the question that's been kicking around in my head since I pulled in the driveway, "Where is she?"

"How the hell should I know?" Ms. Crane answers, emerging from the cupboard with a bottle of grated parmesan. "Fed her a snack and sent her on her way. She didn't seem inclined to attend dinner with the sentient manifestations of Satan's genitalia. Can't say I blame her. You've got the personalities of an anal itch. Don't know how I stand it."

"You're really on a tear today, Ms. Crane." I narrow my eyes. "What the hell crawled up your ass and died?"

She waves the knife at me. "That girl? Whatever you think she is, she's the opposite. I know the look. She's gonna fuck you up, kid. Can't say I won't laugh when she does."

"You don't know anything about her," I grind out, snatching a plate from the cabinet.

"Oh, I know her better than you ever will." Hobbling past me, she sends me a raspy chuckle. "Birds of a feather. Don't matter if we only just met. Me and her go way back. You'll see."

Fucking cryptic old crime widows.

"You cannot be fucking serious," Tristian says, sneering at the food she sets on the table. There's a vein popping out of his forehead and Rath and I share a look at the building tantrum. "Do you have any idea what's in this cheese? It's not cheese. It's shelf-stable saw dust! The pasta…this can't even be legally referred to as pasta! This bread is full of preservatives and chemicals, and I don't even want to know where you got the meat in there." He rubs his temples like he's grasping for his last shred of control. "I can't eat this garbage, Ms. Crane!"

Ms. Crane stabs a serving spoon into the middle of the lasagna and says, "You can eat this or you can *eat shit*. I don't give a damn either way, you putrid lump of horseshit."

Tristian's eye twitches as he watches her leave the room. "I'm getting sick of her crap! Why is she our housekeeper *and* cook? She shouldn't be getting paid for two jobs if she can only do one and a half."

Rath shoots him a glare. "Leave Ms. Crane alone. It's not her fault you've got some kind of food-related mental illness."

"Caring about my body isn't a mental illness," he responds, standing. "And I'll get the last laugh when you're both eaten up with cancer and have failing organs." Rath and I roll our eyes as Tristian storms from the room.

"I swear he gets worse when he's not getting any," Rath says, serving himself a helping. "Shit's about to get really tense around here. What do you think that's about anyway? The fidelity clause?"

I can't imagine how many calories I burned at practice. It must have been thousands. I heap three big spoonfuls of pasta onto my plate, trying not to think too hard about the clause my bitch stepsister added to the contract. "Trying to piss us off."

Rath looks doubtful. "Nah, there has to be something tactical there. A whole academic year with the three of us, and she knowingly bars us from fucking anyone else? That's just asking to get railroaded at every turn."

"She thinks we can't do it," I explain, chewing my food blankly. "She thinks we'll fold, and then the whole contract will be null and void."

Tristian returns then, plate in hand. "Luckily, I still have leftovers from my little date with Sweet-ass Cherry."

I stop chewing. "Your what?"

Instead of answering, he says, "I've put myself in charge of her general wellbeing now. Any withholding of meals needs to go through me first."

Now, I set down my fork. "How the fuck do you figure?"

"I figure," he begins, chomping into a piece of bread, "since she fainted in the library. In front of the Counts. Because she hadn't fucking eaten today. It made us look like bad Lords. You're too pissed off to look after her, and Rath isn't reliable enough to look after himself most days."

"Hey!" Rath protests, but then instantly nods. "Actually, that's fair."

Tristian tips his drink to him. "Obviously, it needs to be me. Good thing too, considering I'm the only one who gives a shit about nutrition around here." Rolling the tension from his shoulders, he tosses us a grin. "Took her to that nice place on Market Street. A little reward."

I scowl at him. "A reward for what?"

Tristian shrugs. "She came face to face with the Barons and the Counts and she didn't speak to them. Didn't even look at them."

I stare at him hotly. "What were you doing that she fainted in the library?"

Tristian gives a casual shrug. "Fingerbanging the fuck out of her sweet, wet cunt." He chuckles, like he's remembering. "Not what I really wanted to do. Taking her cherry in the library today would have been epic. Instead, I had to settle for a little public exhibitionism."

"Public exhibition?" Rath groans. "Fuck, that's worth—"

"More points than you have," Tristian confirms, smiling like the cat who got the cream.

I feel the anger rise up, swelling and pulsing. It's bad enough that I've only got a measly two points for my punishment that morning. But now they've both had more of her than I have. Figures. Always knew she was a slut. I don't know why hearing about it makes me want to pick up this plate and slam it into their fucking faces.

"How long has she been holed up in there?" I tuck all the volatility away, even though these two can probably see through it. It's never easy hiding stuff from them.

"Pretty much since we got home," Rath says. "She was quiet when she and Tristian got in. Ate a snack in her room."

"She's licking her wounds," Tristian says, grimacing at something on his plate. "She might have gotten a reward, but she still disobeyed several rules today. I had to correct her with that fingerbang."

"I was right, wasn't I?" Rath asks, and Tristian nods back.

"She gets fucking *sopping* wet," he agrees, ignoring the way I'm strangling my fork. "And tight as fuck. I completely believe she's a virgin. I'm not even convinced she's ever had an orgasm that didn't come from the two of us."

Disgusting. These assholes look about two seconds from high-fiving over the table like the shitheads they are.

Tristian continues, "She's just so fucking oppositional, though. Not texting, arriving late…oh, and do you know why she was late to the library?" He doesn't wait for us to answer. "Because she was talking to your dad."

My voice comes out in a low, dangerous hiss. "She was fucking *what*?"

Rath and Tristian both shoot me similar sympathetic looks. They know all about what happened back then, up to and including the spiral it sent me down that year.

Tristian scoffs in derision. "They had a happy little family reunion, right in the middle of campus. Had to nip that shit quick."

Goddamn it.

Motherfucker.

I slam my glass down and lurch from my chair, snatching my plate up. Is that why she really came back here? To be close to my father again? The bitterness that settles in the back of my throat makes food unappealing at the moment.

"This doesn't need to be a situation," Rath says in a sorry attempt at calming me down.

Tristian agrees, "I already punished her for it. She won't be going near him without our say-so again, trust me. She heard that shit loud and clear."

"You know we've got your back."

Since they're both used to my temper, neither looks surprised when I leave the room.

I know it's not fair. These two have been ride-or-die by my side since elementary school. Like me, they've been through some serious shit, but they keep that close and know how to present themselves on the outside. There's no whining. No sniveling. They're tough, loyal, and deep down, maybe more depraved than I am.

But a small, resentful part of me thinks: *You have your own backs.* They want Story. They want her in the same way I want her. Absolute possession. But how could it be absolute if it's three people?

This is a competition. The Game will have a victor. One of us will take her, fuck her, own a part of her that no one else can ever lay claim to. She's mine *by rights*. We all know it. And somehow, these two have pulled ahead of me in the race to have her. It's not fucking fair.

Well, I think as I wrap my plate up, *I've never played fair a day in my life.*

I'm not about to start now.

IT'S LATE WHEN I slip into her room.

I'd picked out the sheer curtains myself, making sure the light from the streetlamps would reach her bed, but nowhere else. It takes my eyes a moment to adjust, but once they do, I see her. Sleeping.

The first time I saw her, that night at dinner when my dad announced his engagement to her gold-digging mother, I thought she was…fine. Cute. Sort of nervous and awkward, but perfectly fuckable. Better still was the knowledge— the intuition—that my dad was gifting her to me.

It made perfect sense. My dad got a toy, and so did I. He never came out and said it, but he never had to. I'd practically grown up on his porn collection, learned the right way to treat a girl, to *fuck* a girl, to put her in her place. The fact that I was still a kid, that he was my dad, made it difficult to share our interests. But he knew. I knew.

Story and her mom were his way of bridging the gap.

So I sat there at dinner and tried to play at being polite, even though I was buzzing with anticipation. I texted the guys the second we hit the parking lot, bragging about my shiny new girl, all mine, no one else's.

What a fucking joke.

What none of them know, however, is that Story is prettiest when she's sleeping. I look at her now, drinking in her milky skin, a lock of dark hair falling over her cheek. Her mouth is always parted in sleep, those plush lips of hers looking wet and ready.

It gets my dick rock hard, just like it always did back then. Sure, I made her life a living hell and the guys happily followed my lead. She was easy to pick on back in high school. Fun. All small and weak. I made it clear we weren't family and never would be. I made sure she had no social clout at school. That she was never to speak or acknowledge me in public. Ever.

That didn't mean I didn't know about her. No. I kept a close eye on the girl in the next bedroom, especially as she got closer and closer to my father. It seemed that, briefly, Daniel Payne suddenly loved playing the savior who swept in and plucked these two unfortunate souls out of abject poverty. I knew it was fake, but they didn't.

Keeping tabs on Story was like an addiction back then. First, because I was fixated on my new plaything. I wanted to know what she smelled like, what she sounded like, what she looked like under the clothes. It was easy enough and it consumed me. I had to share a bathroom with her, giving me access to her things, her scent, her presence. I knew what kind of shampoo she liked, and that she preferred white toothpaste to the blue gels. That her fucking long hair clogged up everything. I knew when I saw the crumpled-up papers in the trash that she was on the rag. I knew everything and it drove me mad, because it just made me want to know more.

The shared bathroom provided something else—something unintentional: access to her room, to her secrets. To *her*. I spent hours sitting with my back against the cool tiled walls, listening as her voice carried through the vent from her bedroom. That's how I found out about her and Mary conning old guys out of gift cards and money by showing them their tits or whatever.

I didn't stop there. Night after night—even after I found out the truth—I snuck into her room and stood by her bed, thinking of all the things I could do to her. At first, these thoughts were all about that soft-looking mouth of hers. The skin that disappeared underneath her little boyshorts. The dark outline of her nipples beneath a tank top. The way her hair might look, wrapped tight around my fist as I *pulled*...

I left her little gifts in the form of my jizz on her lips, on the shiny tip of her tongue. Not enough that she'd notice. Just enough that I'd know she was marked—that she carried a part of me inside her.

But that was *before*.

Before the night I walked past my dad's study and saw them. Story in his lap. His hand up her shirt. Touching her tits. The tits that were supposed to be *mine*.

Dad was clearly drunk, and there she was, just sitting on his knee, staring blankly at nothing as his fingers toyed with her nipple. I know he whispered something into her ear, but I couldn't hear it. I could only see the minute, reluctant shake of her head before I stormed away.

After that, the things I imagined doing to her at night grew into these evil, acrid things. I could smother her with a pillow. I could steal the data on her computer. I could gag her, hold her down, and fuck her hard and fast and brutal.

Right now, she's curled up in the middle of the bed, arms wrapped around a pillow protectively. What is Story afraid of? Me? The guys? Something else?

Whatever it is, she's foolish enough to think that a pillow will be enough. I lower myself in the chair and focus on the girl in the bed—on the rise and fall of her breath and how very, very vulnerable she is right now.

I'd held off the night before, telling myself that all I was going to do was watch. But here I am again, my cock getting harder and harder under the thin fabric of my sweatpants. My hands fist the edge of the cushion. Story's legs shift, moving under the blanket and I freeze, watching silently as she rolls over, facing me. I don't move for a long, treacherous heartbeat, waiting to see if she'll wake up like she had the night before, peering around the room like she was looking for a monster.

Her eyes never open, but in the dim light I see her mouth slack, lips parting once again. Story's lips have always been so red—so plump. It's the first thing Tristian said to me about her when he met her. "I bet those lips would look amazing wrapped around a cock."

I'd played around with it, before I realized that Story was never meant for me—that she'd probably flirted and slutted her way into my father's designer trousers. I used to pull my dick out and slot the head of it between her lips, just the littlest bit. She never knew.

It wasn't enough, though. It was a dissatisfying tease, just like Story herself.

But Tristian had finally done it that night in the laundry room—forced his cock past those red, pretty lips, and *fuck it all*, he'd been right. They did look amazing. I grimace at the memory, my heart pushing blood between my legs. Leaning my head back, I finally relent, shoving my hand into my pants and pulling out my length. The cool air feels good against the overheated skin. I run my hand down my length and conjure the fantasy I've perfected over the years. We're back in the house and I've snuck through the adjoining bathroom and into her room. I'm standing by her bed while she sleeps, and it's some truly kinky combination of motivating factors: fucking and hurting.

In the fantasy, the blanket is down around her waist and she's wearing a tight tank top. I can see her nipples visible through the fabric. Even though I know it's nothing but trouble—she's my stepsister and a dirty whore—I reach out and touch one, feeling the smooth surface instantly pebble. She doesn't wake, and it just spurs me on. I lift the blanket and carefully, quietly, slide into the bed behind her. Her back is pressed against mine, but her breath continues in even, controlled inhalations. When I push my hips forward, I suddenly realize she's not wearing any panties. The feel of my hard cock pressing insistently between her thighs doesn't stir her. I nudge the outside of her hip forward, giving me

access to the warm heat between her legs. I wrap her hair around my fist, and there's no stopping it. There's no controlling the urge to *take*. My cock slides between her legs, pushing at her pussy. I grip her hip and hold her still, forcing my cock inside with a hard, unforgiving shove.

She cries out in the fantasy, always the same sharp, wounded sound that fades into a sleepy, confused whimper.

Now, my hand angrily strips my cock. This fantasy—this old, reliable, never-fails fantasy—takes on a new intensity with her only a few steps away. My balls tighten, the pit of my stomach burning with the need to finally have her. I know the truth, that this fantasy is tied up in the perversion of wanting to hurt Story, humiliate her, defile her. But much stronger than that is something else. It's what releases the trigger of my orgasm, time and time again.

I want to fuck my stepsister.

I want to claim her.

Own her.

I want her to finally be *mine*.

That's what I think about, staring at her sleeping form as I come, the spunk oozing warm and thick down my hand. I exhale silently, chest heaving from exertion, cognizant of one other thing.

I let someone else take her away once.

I won't do it again.

STORY

11

EXHIBITIONISM

As much as I bristle while doing it, I take the time the next morning to dress 'appropriately'. The last thing I want is another correction—aka: strip tease—in front of the guys at breakfast.

I flip through the clothes in my closet, fingering the short, perky skirts that I know Tristian would prefer. There are a few outfits that I assume Rath picked out; faux leather leggings, shirts with strategic rips and tears, a little edgy. It makes me wonder what kind of outfit Killian would like to see me in, but as I pick through the rack of clothing, there's nothing that stands out. Maybe, like he always said, I'm just trash to him, repulsive and embarrassing.

It's a strange comfort, the idea that he doesn't want me, but it makes it that much harder to navigate.

I decide on a mishmash of options. There's a pair of tight, black pants for Rath. A pink top with a swooping low neckline and short, puffy shoulders is for Tristian. I choose a pair of Mary Janes that don't exactly look comfortable, but seem to complete my 'oh so innocent' ensemble. *Innocent.* I shift my shoulders, looking in the mirror. *Yeah, right.* Tristian could have my breasts out in a second flat.

I even open the jewelry box on my dresser, intending to choose something to go with it. I all but laugh at what's inside. A few different, sweet-looking pieces. Earrings. Hair clips. Bracelets.

It's the chain with a small, delicate crucifix hanging from it that makes me slam it closed.

Give me a break.

Martin's inspection goes flawlessly. "Very good, Lady," he says, nodding in approval. I almost expect him to pass me a doggy treat. "I've been asked by Lord Tristian to explain the breakfast standards, so know that unless you're asked to attend in the dining room, you'll eat in the kitchen." At my nod, he adds, "Today, the Lords would like their Lady to eat with them."

After that, I'm sent to the kitchen to get their drinks. I hear the guys in the dining room already, their deep voices and loud movements.

Ms. Crane pours a cup of coffee, eyes sliding to me. "Good plan, girl."

"Plan?" I ask, pouring some kind of ultra-organic orange juice, likely for Tristian.

"The outfit," she says in her raspy voice, gesturing to my chest. "You picked it out yourself, didn't ya? 'Course you did. You're starting to learn."

I feel my jaw tighten at her words. "Yeah, I know my place."

But Ms. Crane scoffs. "I meant you're starting to learn what you can control. Haven't got much. People like us never do. That makes the things we can control that much more important."

I disagree, "I don't have any control. They bought all these clothes for me."

"Open your fucking ears, girl," she hisses, eyes pinning me. "You can't control the year, but you can control the day. You could have worn something else. You chose not to disobey. You chose to do the opposite." Rattling the jar of sugar, she concludes, "You set the tone of the day. Eventually, you might learn to use that thing between your legs, but this is a nice start."

I look at her skeptically, not quite seeing her point, but also a little too scared of making her angry to say so. She's an older lady, and I know from meeting her last night that she seems really cranky a lot. Apparently, my lot in life is handling prickly, unpredictable people.

"I see," I lie.

Ms. Crane nods approvingly. "Yeah, you will. People don't realize how small a life can get. My husband could have made mine fit into a breadbox, if he could."

I look at her curiously. "You're married?"

She barks a harsh, rough laugh. "Hell no, girl. Not anymore." Casually, without any expression whatsoever, she explains, "Stabbed that fucker in the neck. Seven times, too."

I wait a second, half-convinced she's joking. She isn't. I take a step back. "You…stabbed him?"

Without sparing me a glance, she answers, "Damn right, I did. You don't need to worry, girl. He had it coming. My old man would've made those three in there look like goddamn boy scouts." The thought makes me shudder.

I look around the room, wondering if anyone can hear. "Should you be telling me this?"

But Ms. Crane just flaps a wrinkled hand. "I've already been convicted and sentenced. No one can do anything to me. If you want my advice, go for the quiet boy first. He's the best at handling the other two."

Stunned, I enter the dining room behind her, thoughts swirling with what Ms. Crane's life must have been like. Worse than these three? Like Ted levels of worse? Or even worse than that?

I fight down my shiver and begin carefully placing their mugs and glasses around their plates. Ms. Crane puts a plate in front of Killian and Rath, but I notice that Tristian already has a bowl of something gross-looking in front of him.

Killian gives me a curt glance, like just looking at me pisses him off.

I venture a small, quiet, "Good morning," to him.

He ignores me.

Tristian's eyes are following me, though, taking in my appearance slowly, appreciatively.

Rath lets out a low hum. "Don't you look sexy this morning," he says, leaned back lazily in his chair.

Ducking my head, I run my hands nervously down my sides. "Thank you."

"Actually, I was talking to Ms. Crane." He gives her a wink and the old woman sneers back.

"Don't you get fresh with me, you failed abortion."

I stiffen, certain that I can't stomach watching this woman get punished. My panic is short-lived, though.

Rath just shrugs. "Your loss, old hag."

"I've lost dirty socks I wanted more than you," she replies, hobbling out of the room.

"Sit," Tristian tells me, pointing to the seat at his side. "We have some things to go over."

Hesitantly, I do as I'm told, sliding my chair in as I survey the setting in front of me. There's whatever Tristian is eating, just a smaller bowl of it, and an egg with two sausages.

"It's oatmeal," Tristian says of the bowl, "with fresh fruit and granola. You're a woman, though. You need iron." I guess that explains the sausages. Leaning closer, he whispers in my ear, "And you don't just look sexy, Sweet Cherry. You look downright fuckable."

Butterflies whirl in my stomach. "A-are you going to be following me today?"

He shrugs. "You never know when one of us is watching."

"You're here," Killian starts, voice firm, "because we need to discuss appearances."

Rath says, "Tristian told us about your little *incident* yesterday." The way his lip turns up on the word tells me exactly what he thinks of fainting spells.

As if it were a ball for me.

Before I can do something as idiotic as apologizing for them *not feeding*

me, Tristian adds, "We talked about it and decided that you've had enough time to acclimate. People need to know our Lady serves us, respects us, *wants* us."

"Especially after yesterday," Rath agrees.

Tristian explains, "We can't have people thinking we mistreat you. So we'll need to start incorporating some PDA into our daily appearances on campus."

Frowning, I ask, "PDA? Like…holding hands? Didn't we kind of do that yesterday?"

Killian rolls his eyes. "Holding hands is only PDA if you're in fifth fucking grade."

Tristian's voice is gentler, but I can still see the gleam of amusement in his eyes. "Sweetheart, when a girl serves, respects, and wants a man, what does she do?"

I stare back at him, confused. "Well, she….uh…" God, what do these guys want. More than I want to give.

"She embraces him," Tristian finishes for me, looking slightly annoyed at needing to. "She kisses him."

I freeze, staring at them with wide eyes. "Kissing?"

"In case it needs to be said," Rath adds, dark eyes boring into mine, "we're looking for something in the 'tongues and necking' department. Not little gradeschool cheek-pecks."

I feel my face pale. "Like…*French* kissing?"

Killian gives me a disgusted look. "Are you really this stunted? No one over the age of twelve calls it that. It's just *kissing*."

I touch my cheeks, beginning to feel the heat pool into them. "No."

That word gets a reaction. Three reactions. Pissed, amused, and curious.

"'No' isn't part of a Lady's vocabulary," Tristian clarifies. "But why the strong reaction? It's a kiss, Cherry. The easiest way to show affection."

For him, it's easy. But for me...

I swallow. "I'm just not comfortable kissing you guys."

"What's the big deal?" Rath asks, between bites.

The big deal is that it's too personal. Too affectionate. Too intimate.

The big deal is that it's not something they're doing to me or I'm forced to do to them. It's something, I assume, we do together.

The biggest deal is that after all the abuse and manipulation, I've never actually been kissed. My virginity is something I'm willing to barter with—I already expect it to be terrible. First times always are, right? But a kiss, it's the thing you wait for. Girls dream about it. It's a rite of passage and I want it to be right, not taken by an abusive asshole.

I say none of this. Just swallowing the whole rant back, but one glance at Rath and he says, "Tell us why, Sweet Cherry."

It's a command, one with a punishment on the other side, and I can tell by the glint in his eye it will involve more than a strip tease.

"I don't know how!" I blurt. It's completely involuntary, just a lack of brain-to-mouth filter. Of course, it's true. But I know instantly, just from the way they're all staring at me, that I should have faked it.

Tristian lifts an eyebrow. "Excuse me?"

Face flaming, I slowly, reluctantly admit, "I've never done that before. Kissing." There's a long, tense silence around the table while I wring my hands. The guys only take their blank stares from me to share a look with one another.

It's Rath who speaks first, voice flat, "Now I know you're bullshitting us."

Killian adds, "I told you she was full of shit. Probably something she tells to those old geezers she's bleeding dry."

"It's true!" I insist, indignation rising in my chest. "Why would I lie about that?" It's even more embarrassing than being a virgin, because on some level, Killian is right. I *am* stunted.

"I'll bite," Tristian jumps in, wiping his mouth on a napkin before turning to me. "Tell me how it is that you've had a dick in your mouth, but you've never kissed a guy before."

I glare into my bowl of oatmeal, feeling a thread of anger surging beneath my skin. How dare they. "I don't know, *Lord Tristian*, why don't you tell me?

Because it seems like the kinds of guys who are into me would rather force me to my knees and jam their disgusting dicks down my throat." I give him a falsely sweet smile. "It's the only use my mouth ever seems to have for them."

"Careful about that tone," Tristian says, plucking my spoon from the table. He thrusts it into my hand, forcing me to take it. "That might have something to do with it." His smile is sharp and mean, and the threat comes through loud and clear.

Nevertheless, as we eat, Rath keeps throwing me these long, calculating looks. I do my best to tune them out as I force down the oatmeal, inwardly twisting myself into knots at the thought of kissing them.

Kissing.

I never really felt like I was missing out on anything. I'm not *so* old. I still have time to find someone soft and sweet to teach me. Or at least, I thought I did.

Afterward, when we're all collecting our bags for school, Rath gestures for me to follow them. "We're driving today," he explains, hand landing on the small of the back as he ushers me down the hall. "You can ride in the back, with me." He punctuates this by bending down to lick a stripe up the side of my neck.

I only just barely manage to stop myself from flinching away, but it's one more reminder that these men are anything but soft and sweet.

In the garage, there's a huge white truck taking up most of the space— although a motorcycle is parked on the other side. Killian is already in the front seat of the cab. It isn't a surprise this is his vehicle. He'd always wanted a massive, intimidating truck. He'd badgered his dad for one for graduation. Guess he finally got his way.

Rath is already in the back, earbuds plugged in. Tristian opens the back door for me and offers his hand to help me up the big step in my clunky shoes. I climb in next to Rath, ignoring the way my skin prickles just being near him. Tristian gets in the passenger seat, and I glance at the rearview mirror.

Killian's staring back at me.

No, not at me.

At my mouth.

He looks away instantly, cranking the loud, rumbling engine.

Being in close quarters with the guys like this is an assault on my senses. All their scents swirl around me and my awareness of their presences reaches a fever pitch, almost like I'm carrying around an extra, tangible appendage.

Even from back here, I can feel the anger rolling off Killian, the smug cockiness from Tristian, the low-key indifference from Rath. Without my bidding, I start thinking about it.

About kissing them.

Will it be awful? Will they make it hurt? What if I'm bad at it? And that's really the crux of the matter, that they're expecting me to be this girl who can believably, effortlessly do these things. Checking in a few minutes late or speaking to Daniel is one thing. Making them look bad in front of the whole campus is something else altogether. It's not about the rules. It's about appearances.

I'm wholly inadequate.

I stare down at my lap, hands clasped so tightly that my knuckles have gone white, and wonder if I can just fake it. Let go of my fairytale ideals and just do it. How hard can it be? I've seen it done before. My heart pounds hard in my chest and sweat beads on my neck. The car feels warm—hot, stifling—and my hands pluck idly at my clingy pants. There's a pressure in my chest, something wild and heavy, almost painful to breathe against. None of them are aware that I'm on the verge of panic, but suddenly, all I can think about is tongues and lips, the biting pressure of teeth, the sting and taste of blood.

"Stop the truck," Rath says, yanking his earbuds out. Killian keeps driving but Rath leans forward and repeats, "Stop, Kill."

Killian jerks the car over and idles at the side of the road.

"What the fuck?" he asks. "Did you forget something? You know I'm not a fucking shuttle."

Tristian turns around and his eyes dart from Rath to me, curiosity flickering in the blue. I turn to Rath, and he says, "I'm not going out there and just kissing her cold. Not after what you said happened yesterday."

"So what? You just want to go home?" Killian asks.

"You know as well as I do that the best way to get better at something is to practice."

"Practice," Tristian repeats. "We're halfway to school."

Rath snorts. "You're telling me you've never made out in a car with five minutes to spare?" I notice Rath's shifting a second too late. My head turns toward his as his fingers wind into my hair, he pulls me to him.

"Wait—" I start, but he doesn't. His mouth finds mine too fast for me to really think about it. I stiffen, locking up against the soft feel of his lips on mine, the cool shock of his lip rings, but Rath doesn't seem to care that I'm frozen. Even though all of this was fast—*too* fast—his lips pluck gently at mine in slow, coaxing movements. He's not rough. I look at him wide-eyed, even though his closed eyes are blurring into one.

"Relax," he says against my mouth, hand coming up to cradle my jaw. His next kiss is more of a surge than anything, like he's putting his whole body into it. There's something inherently and curiously sexual about the way he moves, the way his tongue just barely peeks out to greet my lips. The hard metal of his piercings are a stark contrast to the softness of our lips meeting.

I will myself to copy him, feeling my face grow hot when our noses bump awkwardly. Rath doesn't miss a beat though, guiding the kiss, tilting my head back.

When he parts his lips, I follow suit.

The feel of his tongue against mine sends a hot, sharp spark of electricity through my veins. It's not quite like I expected. Wetter. Warmer. Rath licks into my mouth as if he's tasting something he likes, but is savoring it with long, quick dips between my lips, massaging my tongue with his. His thumb finds the edge of my jaw and tilts my head back, giving him the access he needs to deepen the kiss.

He swallows my gasp, tilting his head to lick deeper, longer, slower. It isn't until he drops his hand to my thigh that I realize I'm pressing them together in pursuit of a friction that I only barely understand.

He makes a rough, guttural sound that sends a spike of something white-hot shooting right down into my core.

"Rath."

I rear back, breaking the kiss, but Rath remains suspended there for a moment, eyes dark and heavy.

Tristian's twisted around in his seat, staring at his friend. There's a glimmer of annoyance in his eyes, even if his expression is artfully neutral.

Rath seems to shake out of his daze, sending Tristian a red-lipped smirk. "Just figured I'd make sure she doesn't embarrass us all. Is that a problem?"

Tristian doesn't react, though. Why would he? Tristian is calm and collected all the time. Even while fingerbanging me in the library. Reactions are obviously for the weak, and here I am, once again, proving exactly how weak I am.

Rath slowly moves his hand from my thigh as Tristian speaks.

"No," he says, but it's obvious that there is. "She needs to be ready. Not just for school but for the party at the house tonight." His gaze flicks back to me but is settled on my lips, which feel hot and swollen. "We have one every week during football season. Kind of a pregame event. Obviously, you're expected to be there and expected to uphold your duties. Martin can fill you in on the details."

I nod obediently, ducking my head to hide the redness of my cheeks. Killian restarts the truck and the drive to campus isn't long, especially when I spend most of it pressing my fingers to my mouth, trying to process what just happened with Rath. All I can hear in my head is the rush of my heartbeat and Ms. Crane's words.

Go for the quiet boy first.

If that's the kissing they're looking for, then…

Well.

I guess I'll live.

When we park, Tristian gives instructions for the day. "Same rules as yesterday. Keep your GPS on. Text on the hour—*every* hour. No excuses."

"Do I need to meet you in the library again?" I ask.

"Sorry, Sweet Cherry, not today." He pouts like he's sad about it. "You'll meet up with Rath in the music building."

"I'll be in studio A4." I stare, transfixed as Rath's tongue peeks out to prod at one of his lip rings. "I have an oral presentation in my Lit class that might run over, though." It doesn't take much searching to see that he's unhappy about it.

I don't need to ask why.

I nod, pretty sure I know where the music building is. "Anything else I need to know about?"

"Behave yourself," Killian says suddenly. "You're a representative of the Lords now. People are watching you. Do *not* speak to other men who aren't your professors." His gaze hardens. "Including my father."

Bristling, I argue, "He came to see me, Killian. I'm just supposed to ignore him? That's insane."

His chiseled jaw clenches. "Fine, Story, disobey me and see what happens."

The threat behind his words is clear. I don't want to see what happens.

Killian's out of the vehicle before I can respond, door slamming behind him. Tristian follows suit, his expression unreadable, and then Rath, who offers me a hand down from the cab.

Much like yesterday, they all lead me to the fountain in the middle of campus as everyone watches. It's an uncomfortable, oppressive feeling, being watched all the time. Despite Killian's earlier disdain of handholding, I still take the chance of slipping my hand into Rath's.

PDA is PDA.

Rath doesn't seem to mind, barely sparing me a glance as we approach our destination.

When we do, I'm almost knocked off my feet by the shock of strong hands whirling me around. Tristian's mouth is on mine in an instant, more aggressive than Rath's had been. More demanding.

It takes me a frozen moment to recover, opening my mouth to him, taking Tristian's forceful tongue into my mouth. He makes a rough sound, hands tightening on my hips as he pulls me to him. It's difficult to think when this is happening—when Tristian is consuming me, possessing me—but I try. I lift my arms to loop around his neck, hoping that it looks more natural than it feels.

Tristian responds by lowering his hands to my backside, taking two large handfuls of it and *squeezing*.

His voice is low and rough against my lips. "That's my good girl." His hands are still massaging my backside when he leans down to whisper into my ear, "Shame I couldn't have been your first." He pulls away, sending me a smirk. "Not for that, at least."

Swallowing against the lingering sensations, I watch him disappear into a crowd that parts for him like the red sea.

I turn reluctantly to Killian, teeth bearing down into my lip. His gaze is fixed to the action, but his eyes are full of angry fire, face set into a stony stillness. Cautiously, I shuffle toward him, hearing the whoosh of my blood in my ears at the idea of my mouth on his. The thought of throwing my arms around his neck feels akin to touching a red-hot coal. Every particle of my body rails against it instinctively, knowing there's only pain to be had there, but this is the deal. Slighting Killian in public would have consequences. I rise up onto my toes and tilt my face, bracing for impact.

He turns and storms away.

I stumble forward in surprise, only just managing not to fall into the empty space he's left. A rush of mortification washes over me at the thought of everyone watching. At everyone knowing I've just been outright rejected.

Rath smoothly intercepts, throwing his arm over my shoulder and leading me around the fountain. "They're just pissy I got there first."

I pull a face, not really able to doubt him. In my experience, that's all guys seem to care about. They're like the living embodiment of people who comment 'first!' on videos. It's useless and completely without value, but for some reason...

Eager to change the subject, I say, "Can I...ask you a question?"

"You can try," Rath says, his vacant expression making it clear that he doesn't feel obligated to answer.

I try anyway. "If you have so much trouble with...well, you know. Then why are you taking Lit?"

I watch as the hand hanging from my shoulder curls into a fist. "I don't know what you mean."

Jesus, this again. "Sure, you don't."

He comes to a stop, jerking me with him. "Did you just roll your eyes at me?" His gaze is full of thinly-veiled anger. "For your fucking information—not that you're entitled to it—all degrees have required credits. This is one of mine."

"Oh," I blink back at him, understanding. "Then how do you...?"

"Pass?" he asks, eyes narrowed. "The same way I always pass."

I guess, "Bribes. Payments. Threats."

He gives me a hostile smirk. "You're just full of observations, aren't you, Sweet Cherry?"

Intuitively, I realize he's about to strike back. Probably with something that's meant to embarrass me as much as it's meant to scare me. I don't give him the chance. "You're really good at playing piano. I saw you before, the way you were so focused. It looked effortless. It must have taken you a lot of time and practice to get to that level of proficiency. I bet you could pick up...*other things*, in no time."

"Don't you think I've tried?" he snaps. "It's different now that I'm a Lord."

I pause and let a group of girls pass by. Several turn to get another look, most likely of Rath, who's dark, handsome face is the kind that draws a second glance. Secretly—guiltily—I've caught myself doing it, too. "How?"

He looks at me like I'm stupid. "We're the top of the heap at Forsyth—actually, beyond that. Lords don't have weaknesses. Ever. People are always looking to exploit one."

I cut him a look. "It isn't weakness, Dimitri."

Something flutters behind his eyes when I use his real name. "It is when you want to be the best at what you're doing." He sweeps his dark hair from his eyes, scowling. "If people want to think I'm lazy and entitled for making others do my work, then I don't give a fuck." I hear what he doesn't say. That it isn't even a lie. "It's easier this way."

"I think it sounds a lot more complicated, actually." I chance a look up at him, meeting his gaze. "I meant what I said before. I can teach you." I wither at his stare, but force myself to explain. "Look, I'm under contract to keep quiet. And it's not like I don't already know. You might as well get something useful out of the two, right?"

"I can't afford to shake shit up. Don't you understand that?" He stares at me spitefully, cheeks turning a faint pink, but before I can respond he mutters, "Of course you don't. You're nothing but a dumb, worthless bitch, anyway. Like you could teach *me* anything. Seven minutes of making out in the car, and you still kissed like a dead fish."

He storms off, leaving me in his angry wake. I gape after him, stunned and wounded in an odd, surprising way. Something inside me cringes and curls up, feeling dumb for thinking I could get close to him. That I could get through to him.

Ms. Crane is wrong. Rath—Dimitri—is just as hard and cruel as the others. Trying to have a civil conversation with one of the Lords is like stabbing yourself in the eye. Clearly they aren't capable of that or any other functional emotion except anger and hostility. If I'm going to survive being their Lady,

I'm going to remember not to let my guard down.

Ever.

I MANAGE TO GET through the morning without any infractions. At least, I hope so. I texted at the correct times. I didn't speak to any of my male classmates, which is harder than anticipated. The sexy-yet-coy clothing is like a beacon to college men, but I don't fall for it. I suspect wearing these outfits is probably just another trick to come up with justifications to 'correct' my behavior.

When I change classes, I stick to the edge of the quad, ever alert so that I don't run into someone again or accidentally do something wrong. I'm determined not to miss lunch today, so I get in line at one of the takeout places in the student union. I work my way through the queue, heart rate elevated. I know it's crazy, but I can't help but feel the heat of eyes on me. I know I came to Forsyth for a reason—to protect myself and others—but the paranoia may break me before Ted does.

The server calls my name and I flinch, grabbing the bag quickly. The common area is crowded—loud. Too many people to talk to, too much trouble to get into. I've only been in this arrangement for two days, and already my brain is taking hold, seeing every little thing as an instinctual danger. It's frightening to think what kind of person I'll be once it ends.

I take the stairs to the second floor, ignoring the signs that say '*Wet Floors-No Admittance*' and see a grouping of unoccupied leather chairs outside one of the conference rooms. I rush to a seat, drop my backpack and coat on the empty cushion next to mine, and open the bag. I have the sandwich halfway unwrapped when someone moves my backpack and sits next to me.

"Sweet Cherry," Tristian drawls, "did you go get lunch without offering to get me something?"

My stomach sinks as I gaze back at him. "I'm sorry. I didn't know you wanted anything."

"Did you ask?"

His tone is gentle, but I know better. He caught me in a vulnerable, compromised position. His favorite thing. I take a deep breath and hold out the sandwich. "I can go get you something. Or," I swallow back the annoyance, "would you like mine?"

His nose wrinkles, while his stone cold blue eyes hold mine. "As if I'd eat that garbage. Anyway, you're too late. I'm not hungry anymore. At least, not for food." I frown, trying to follow him, but then his hand rests on my thigh. "You didn't wear a skirt for me."

"It was in the closet, but I—" Heat burns in my cheeks and I shift uncomfortably in my seat.

"You dressed for Rath today." The corners of his eyes tighten with a brittle smile. "No worries," he says, as though he anticipated a kink in his plans. He lifts my black coat off the chair next to ours and spreads it over his lap. "As much as I like putting my fingers on—or inside—you, I've been dreaming about yours being on me for a long time now."

He reaches under the coat and I hear the unmistakable sound of his zipper parting. My eyes widen, stomach plummeting. "You want me to…" I can't say it. "…*here?*"

His hand takes mine, cool and large and soft, and slides it under the coat, placing it forcibly on his already erect cock. I can't see it, but I can feel it. The skin is hot, taut, and smooth. I look around, panicked, but we're completely alone. I'd been so worried about not being around other people, about staying out of trouble, that I'd led him straight to the perfect secluded spot to fulfill his obvious need for exhibitionism.

He leans back and exhales, the column of his throat rippling with his groan. "I know you don't have a lot of experience with this, but first off, you're going to need to move your hand a little."

"I can't do this," I whisper, desperate to yank my hand away, but knowing

that I can't. "This is…this is wrong. We'll get in trouble."

"Maybe we will." His lips quirk, like he's almost hoping we will. "This is what happens when you selfishly don't consider your Lord's needs." He settles back and closes his eyes. "The sooner you get started, the sooner you can go."

For a blink, I consider running, bolting out of the building, away from Tristian, the job, and every stupid, *stupid*, decision I've made since I was sixteen. But then his cock twitches under my hand, pressing into my palm, and a different kind of feeling settles deep in my belly. It's the sensation I've struggled with since that night in the laundry room. The bitter conflict of fear and want.

I take another look around, making sure no one is watching us, and then slowly stroke up his cock, toward the tip.

"There you go," he says, cracking one eye to look at me. "Keep it up."

I run my hand back down to the base, touching the soft sack at the bottom. I get a feel for him, the size and girth. He's thick, filling my fist. I shift my position, trying for something more casual, natural-looking. I reach for the bag with my lunch, placing it on the couch between us so that it looks like I'm doing something other than…what I'm actually doing.

What the heck am I doing?!

His voice a low, resonant murmur. "That's it, sweetheart. A little harder, if you don't mind." Tristian, to his credit, looks completely serene, like a college student taking a nap during his break. As I stroke up and down, his face remains impassive, utterly blank, but as I build a rhythm, I begin noticing tells. When I reach the base, his nose wrinkles just a little. When I stroke up his length, his neck muscles tense. And when I get to the top, rolling my thumb over the tip, his tongue darts out and he licks his lips.

I watch him without really thinking about it, finding myself curious. Playing with the reactions. Anticipating them. Creating them.

Controlling them.

"Does that feel good?" I ask. I didn't mean to, but it slips out. I hate that I even want to know.

"It does," he breathes, head lolling to the side so he can look at me. His eyes dart down and he grins lazily. "Your nipples are hard. You little freak." My nipples *are* hard, and the spot between my legs burns. I like the way he feels in my hands. I like that, even though he's in control, I have a little bit over him, too. "Are you wet?"

"Maybe. Just a little," I stiltedly confess, squeezing my thighs together. I hastily divert, "But this isn't about me. It's about you."

The door of the conference room pushes open and suddenly we're no longer alone. Dozens of people pour out of the room. Men, women, students. I look at the sign on the door and see that it says 'Orientation Meeting'. *Fuck.* Those meetings hold a hundred prospective students and their families. My hand freezes, but Tristian's comes down on mine. "Don't stop," he says, his voice a warning.

Stiffly, reluctantly, I continue. Surrounded by the building crowd, I sense Tristian coming closer to the edge. I lean into him, like we're talking quietly, my body curled innocently around his. His jaw tenses. "Jesus Christ," he mutters.

I look up and see a woman watching us, her eyes narrowed suspiciously. Part of me wants her to go tell on us, to make this stop, for someone to tell Tristian this is *not okay*. But there's the other part. The one I battle every day. The dirty, fucked-up, guilty idiot who got myself into this. Sometimes that part overpowers the other.

This is one of those times.

"People are watching," I say, "so unless we both want to get expelled, you need to finish up."

I bend down and press my lips to Tristian's, swallowing up any response. His lips part in surprise, eyes flying open. After a moment, his hand reaches around my neck and crushes me to him. His tongue pushes into my mouth, hips bucking into my fist, and then hot, sticky fluid begins filling my palm. I do my best to catch it all.

The next minutes pass in a blur. I break away from the moment only to find myself flustered, hands and knees shaking, body lit on fire, convinced we're going to get caught. Somehow, though, he gets my hand clean and his cock back in his pants. He leads me through the crowd as I fumble with my coat and backpack. No one would ever know what just happened between us. What he forced me to do.

At the doors, the sun bears down on him, alighting his blond hair in a halo of light. From this vantage, someone might mistake him as god-like.

"See you this afternoon," he says, smirking. No thank you, no apology, nothing a guy should probably normally say to a girl after something like that. I watch him go, fingers sticky with residue, cheeks aflame with humiliation, and my belly warm with want.

Two girls pass me by, eyes sweeping jealously between me and his retreating figure. I feel pity for them, knowing that they saw the façade. The lie. The deceit.

There is nothing god-like about Tristian Mercer. If anything, he's a demon.

IT TAKES ALL afternoon to slow the adrenaline from my lunchtime encounter with Tristian. I half expect campus security to bust through the door and drag me out for inappropriate behavior. I don't hear half of what my professors say and, once classes end, I'm mostly just glad for the escape—even if it does mean going home to the Lords.

The music building is cool and quiet when I enter, and I check the information board to get directions to the practice room. Room A4 is up one flight of stairs, and I peek into the windows of the different practice rooms in search of his. The rooms are sound-proofed, but I can see people playing various instruments, some individually, like cellos and violins, others in small ensembles. When I get to the right room, I pause to peer through the window.

Rath is walking up to the piano and places his sheet music on the stand. He sits, face determined, jaw set in concentration. He's not alone in the room. A small group of students sit in the observation seats. It makes sense. He needs to practice in front of people, I suppose.

As much as I hate to admit it, it hurt when he called me a dumb, worthless, bitch that morning. It hurt when he said I was a bad kisser. Mostly, it hurt that it hurt at all. As if I don't know him. As if he hasn't already hurt me worse than that, and for less. It shouldn't have been a surprise. I knew him being nice to me was nothing more than a trick. The last thing I want to do is sit in the room with him and wait for more abuse. But I know if I don't, the consequences could be worse.

Carefully, I open the door and step inside, trying to be as quiet as possible as he begins to play.

Music fills the room and he doesn't look up as I enter. I take a seat in the back, wanting to stay invisible.

A guy in the front row clears his throat loudly—so loudly that Rath stops playing, shooting him a glare. "That's Prelude in C Major," the guy says, and some of the others laugh quietly in their seats. "The board says you're playing Solfeggietto?"

Rath stares at him unblinkingly, not responding.

The guy shifts in obvious discomfort. "It's in there. In the folder."

After a moment of Rath's dark stare, he gets up from the bench, snatching the folder from the piano. He thrusts it at the man's chest. "If you're so fucking smart, then why don't you pull it out for me, fuckwit."

Forehead creased in a frown, the guy flips the folder open, leafs through the pages, and plucks one out.

Rath snatches it from his hand. "Congratulations, you're capable of something a trained monkey can do. Now if you don't *mind*, I was warming up with Prelude, you shining testament to dead dicks."

The others laugh louder now as the guy shrinks down into his seat. Taking the bench once again, Rath unfolds the paper and begins playing.

If I close my eyes, I can almost imagine it's being played by someone with actual, real-life feelings. Feelings that aren't anger. Feelings that don't only want to hurt. I can almost forget the fact he just effortlessly manipulated someone into doing work for him.

I can almost forget that it's not okay to like those fingers flying across the keys.

His playing sounds magnificent, rich notes reverberating through the room. His fingers move quickly, fast like lightning, and I can't imagine Rath not being able to do *anything*, let alone read. But even though the notes feel flowing and serene, when I open my eyes, I see his shoulders are tense, his jaw tight, a lock of hair falling into his eyes as he reads the music.

Dimitri is troubled.

But the expression on his face, when he stands and bows to the audience, says otherwise.

His eyes flick to the back of the room, to *me*, and a chill runs down my spine. Ms. Crane had been right about one thing. Rath had never been the meanest of the guys—Killian holds that position—and Tristian is just mindfuckingly cruel. Rath is aloof. Dismissive. Indifferent, until he wants something. Like seeing me cry. Wanting to hear me beg. Loving that we share a dirty secret.

He steps off the stage, collecting his things with jerky, hostile movements. Storming down the row toward me, he doesn't stop when he reaches me. He just grabs me by my arm and drags me outside. I stumble in my clunky shoes, twisting my ankle, but swallow back the cry of pain.

"I failed my fucking oral report, thanks to you," he growls, eyes ablaze. "It was worth thirty percent of my fucking grade."

"Me? I didn't do anything!"

"Yes, you did!" he spits, getting in my face. "You got in my head this morning! All that bullshit about trying. You made me think I had something to prove. You fucking played me!"

I gape at him, bending back to put some distance between us. "That's crazy, Rath. You're crazy! I just wanted to put the offer out there, in case—" I swallow. "Your problem is that you're so used to being around assholes that you don't even know what it's like to have someone be nice to you," I tell him, taking a step back. "Because that's all I was being—nice. Just like I thought you were being nice by kissing me before."

His hands move lightning fast, slamming hard into my shoulder. In a blink, I'm pressed into the wall, being crushed against the stone.

He openly sneers at my whimper. "Shut up."

"You're hurting me."

"Good," he replies, applying more pressure, jaw clenching at my wince. "I'll do more than that if you tell anyone what I said this morning. If you tell anyone *anything*."

"I can't, remember? I signed a contract."

"Just don't fucking forget it." He releases me and I rub my shoulder, watching him storm off. I grab my bag and trail after him, knowing that if he shows up without me, there will be hell to pay.

On the way to the truck, I simmer in what I know to be true. Rath is freaking out because I touched something personal. A weakness. Something a Lord shouldn't have. Proof that a failure isn't just laziness or entitlement. It's an inability to do something.

An inferiority.

And I'm going to be the one to pay for it.

DIMITRI
RATHBONE

12
FAMILY

As soon as we get home, I realize the pledges have already arrived to help set up the party. Not in the mood to deal with the toadies, I go right out back to meet Ms. Crane for a cigarette. My blood is pumping with something black and hot. Fucking bullshit, failing my report. I could have worked my way out of it, but no, I had to go up there and make a fucking effort.

What a goddamn joke.

Ms. Crane is in a mood of her own, barely sparing me a grunt as she sucks down her own cigarette. You know we're both over the day when we don't even bother insulting each other.

Once again, I curse myself for letting Story get to me. For allowing her to creep under my skin. Inferiority isn't something I've ever copped to, and it's especially not something I ever want to air out to other people—unlike Story, whose entire persona screams weakness. She's a walking billboard advertising her vulnerability. She always has been. It's a part of what makes fucking with her so enjoyable. It's also like watching a train wreck.

By nature, I'm an empath. Not one of those touchy-feely soulful types. No. I can assess strong emotions and quickly determine how to capitalize on them—how to dominate. On the soccer field, I knew within moments how a player would react. It's like having another sense that could hone in on my opponent. Were they nervous, intimidated, filled with adrenaline, high on ego? I reacted accordingly. Successfully. Winningly. In music, it's even better. It's the knowledge of how to evoke feelings, where to lead people, how to coax them.

There's no one easier to read than Sweet Cherry. It was obvious the first time I saw her, anxiously hiding in the shadows of Killian's house. A mouse afraid of being exposed. She was terrified of him, but that wasn't all. She wanted something from her stepbrother. Approval? Acceptance? Whatever it was, it was cloaked under the heavy musk of fear and impossible to achieve.

I was the one who sensed her up in the laundry room that night. It's like I could smell her all the way down in the basement, taste her special brand of defiance, fear, and want. I couldn't resist tracking her down for Tristian, whose slut of a girlfriend had fucked his head all around. Considering how Story had done the same to Killian's head by choosing his dad over him, it seemed like the perfect little game.

Things escalated faster than I expected, all of us high on the way she tried so hard to bluster her way through it. Killian's easy agreement had come as a surprise, but he was always good at hiding any emotion other than rage. That night, we all revealed a little bit more about ourselves. Especially Story. When I realized how wet she was—how fucking *into it* she was—it was like a whole other side of my mind opened up.

When it comes to Story, every twitch, every gasp and every stare practically screams 'break me'. Underneath all that flimsy bravado is a girl who needs to be put in her place. It was no different back then. If anything, it was more potent. A little more fear, a little less artful in her attempt at hiding it. She was younger than most of the girls we fucked with *and* Killian's stepsister. But that didn't stop us. It just made it more exciting. Something we'd been thinking about for so long that we wanted to savor it. But we didn't get to—not that night.

Not until now.

Those same emotions followed her into the interview, then later into my bedroom. The stink is on her all the time. Defiance, fear, want. But this morning in the truck, it was different. I felt the panic rolling up her spine. It was in her badly hidden gasps, the way she held onto the door like she was looking for an escape. I knew exactly how to handle it. How to handle *her*.

I'd wanted to claim her first kiss as my own, but almost as strongly was the urge to be the one who took that panic away. The one who controlled it. And that's exactly what I did.

But the problem is that she knows about me.

She has a piece of control of her own, and that's not fucking acceptable.

When Ms. Crane and I head back inside, Tristian and the toadies are in the kitchen, setting up stacks of cups.

"We need some snacks," Lahey says. He's a twiggy little fuckface, entirely void of charm, but he's a legacy. "Are these for the party?"

Tristian makes a snide glance at the tray of food Ms. Crane has already prepared. "Only if you want to eat garbage. What the hell are these? They're barely a step up from chips!"

Ms. Crane sneers right back. "You have arms and legs. Cook something yourself if you don't like it."

Tristian's nostrils flare and Killer and I share a glance at the impending bitchfest. "I said I wanted a vegetable tray!"

Ms. Crane goes to the fridge and pulls out a bag of half-thawed baby carrots. "There," she says, dumping them on the counter with a loud 'thud'. "Go fucking wild, you useless rabbit disguised as a man."

Tristian instantly tosses them in the garbage. "*I'm* useless?!"

Lahey laughs, looking between them. "Yeah, you stupid hag. How hard is a vegetable tray, anyway? A trained poodle could do a better job than this."

The kitchen goes silent.

Big mistake.

All our eyes shift to him, but he's too busy arranging beers inside a cooler to notice the absolute mountain of shit he's just dug himself into.

In a low, even voice, Tristian asks, "What did you just say to her?"

A lot of people think Tristian hates Ms. Crane. And he does, in his own way. But it's a petty sort of hate. The kind of hate that's more like a game than anything. Above all that, Tristian might respect her more than anyone ever has.

He was the one to suggest we pull her out of South Side.

Lahey looks up and then does a double-take at the expression on my face. "What?" He jostles when Killian's hand lands on the back of his neck, body stiffening at what I'm guessing is a bruising grip.

"What the *fuck* did you just say to her?" Killian growls, face hard with fury.

Lahey's gulp can probably be heard all the way upstairs. Idly, I glance toward the hall, and then unexpectedly make eye contact with Story. My eyes narrow and she flinches out of sight. Little fucking mouse.

"I was just agreeing with Lord Tristian, that's all!"

Killian looks about five seconds from just taking his head off at the neck. If he doesn't, I might. "That's not your place, *Pledge*."

"We're allowed to talk to Ms. Crane like that. Do you know why?" Tristian's smile is all sharp malice. "It's because Ms. Crane is a part of us. She's family. What exactly are you? You're nothing."

I take my place beside Ms. Crane. The look on her face, eyes cast down, makes me fold my arms to stop myself from punching this fucker in the face. Ms. Crane should never look like that. Cowed. Less than. Pissed off, but too smart to act on it.

She's spent too much of her life looking like that, and at the hands of worse people than some pampered little college pledge fuck.

I ask, "You think the help is beneath you, Lahey?"

His wide eyes ping around us. "Wha—no! No, she's not beneath me."

Tristian slaps a hard, heavy hand down onto his shoulder. "No, she's not. And I think you owe her an apology."

I stress, "I think it'd better sound sincere as *fuck*."

Lahey swallows, finally meeting Ms. Crane's gaze. "Sorry." I scoff and Killian gives him a jostle that results in a wince. "I—I was wrong. The food looks fine. Good, even! You probably worked hard on it, so I'm really sorry."

Tristian prompts, "You're sorry, *what*?"

It still takes Lahey a moment to stutter out a hasty, "Ma'am! I'm sorry, *ma'am*." He stumbles forward when Killian lets him go.

"You're not invited tonight," Killian says, throwing him his messenger bag. It hits Lahey's chest hard enough to almost topple him over. "You can sit out front, in a car, and be the fucking DD. If you even step foot in the house, you're done. And if you want to be invited next time, you'd better come up with a gesture to show Ms. Crane exactly how sorry you are."

Lahey skitters out of the house without so much as a peep.

"Come on," I say to Ms. Crane, gently placing her hand in the crook of my arm. "I'll light your cigarette for you and say something fresh."

She snorts. "Nothing fresh about you, Lord Fuckface."

I pat her hand. "That's our cranky old bitch."

"Don't you fuckers forget it."

13

THE MAKEOVER

I DON'T BREATHE with ease until I'm locked behind my bedroom door. I'm not sure how Ms. Crane earned the luxury of them jumping to her defense like that, but it doesn't extend to me.

Rath is *pissed*.

Even so, I almost expected it out of him. He seems to get along with Ms. Crane the most out of the three of them. Killian sticking up for anyone is a surprise, but Tristian? He quite obviously can't stand Ms. Crane. His words pulse back at me like an acidic whisper.

Ms. Crane is a part of us. She's family. What exactly are you? You're nothing.

Now that I'm alone, I kick off the painful shoes and rub my sore ankle. After all that tension, the last thing I want to do is go to this party tonight. God only knows what I'll be expected to do. Serve food? Rub their shoulders? Grovel at their feet? Considering Tristian's penchant for public displays, maybe even worse.

A knock on the door draws my attention, and I brace myself for whatever Lord is on the other side. "Come in."

The door opens to reveal Martin, who sweeps in without reservation.

"Lady, I wanted to talk to you about the party. As you've been informed, there's a gathering tonight—a pregame ritual. There will be food and drinks and—"

"I know what a party is, Martin." I rub my temples. "What exactly am I expected to do?"

He smiles. "Of course. Well, your role as Lady is to be available to the Lords as they need you. Typically, they would want you by their sides, refilling their drinks and looking—"

"Like arm candy. Got it." I tilt my head. "But there's a problem. They hate me. Well, at least two of them do. I know Killian doesn't want me doting on him all night. Rath, either. So how am I supposed to approach this?"

He shakes his head disapprovingly. "Regardless of what they feel, they have chosen you as their Lady. You need to be available to their every need while guests are in the house. It's how these things are done."

"Fine," I grind out, hearing what he's not saying. If the Lords want to reject me, humiliate me, then I'm meant to just take it. Even though I'm pretty sure they'd rather me be in the kitchen with Ms. Crane. "Anything else?"

"One thing," he says, shifting on his feet. "Killian has some very specific pregame rituals. They are very important to him since—as you may know—Lord Killian is quite superstitious. This season is vital to his career. The NFL will be watching his every move. His rituals can't be disrupted in any way."

"And I need to assist him with those rituals," I guess.

He releases a clipped laugh. "God, no. I actually think it's in everyone's best interest that you stay completely clear of him for the evening."

I can't control the smile that splits my face. "That sounds perfect." A weight lifts off my shoulders. Staying away from my stepbrother is my number one priority on any given day. But during a party with alcohol and drugs? I don't want to be anywhere around him. "Well, do you have suggestions on what to wear?"

His lips form a tight line. "That's not really my area of expertise. I'm sure there's something suitable in the closet."

I cast a skeptical glance at the wardrobe. "I'm not sure what they'd like." I'm not even sure which Lord I should be appealing to tonight. Should I be slutty? Should I be cute and coy? Walking over to the closet, I assess the clothes. In truth, dressing up has never been in my wheelhouse. Back in high school, whenever I needed help I would...

Well, I'd call a girl friend.

But I don't have any of those.

"Martin," I begin, voice reluctant. "I know there are rules about who I can speak to and—"

"No men," Martin emphasizes.

I nod. "Obviously. But I was wondering about other women. Other... students? Like the Countess or the Baroness?"

Martin's face screws up. "Not if it can be helped. Girls are meant to be loyal to their houses. They can't be trusted."

I deflate, remembering how kind Sutton—the Countess—had been to me. Loyal to our houses? Yeah, right. These guys are all deluded. "So basically, I can't have any friends."

Martin frowns, forehead creased in thought. "Well, I suppose...there are other girls loyal to our house. Prior Ladies."

I perk. "A prior Lady?" That's not just companionship or camaraderie. That's actual intel. "Like who?"

Martin pulls his phone from his pocket. "I'll call Charlene. She was our last Lady. Perhaps she can be of more assistance."

As soon as she enters my room, I realize that any hopes I might have had of forming a friendship with this woman were misplaced.

She greets me with a smile that doesn't reach her eyes, cherry red lips pursed into something forced and rigid. "You must be the new Lady."

Charlene is gorgeous in that totally predictable sort of way. Every blonde strand of hair is perfectly curled and styled, tumbling down her back in elegant, platinum waves. She's wearing a little black dress, breasts sloping from the top, accentuating her tiny waist and full hips into the perfect hourglass figure. I bet her list of rules was only half as long as mine. Clearly, Lady Charlene has never had to be told to remain waxed and sexy at all times.

Instantly, I regret asking for her. "Charlene, right?"

She gives me a slow look, eyes taking me in from top to bottom. It's subtle, the way her lip curls, but it's obvious that her expectations haven't been met. "I see we have some work to do." She dumps a bag by the door and walks, high heels clacking, to the closet. "Undress. I don't have all night."

I glare at her back, wishing now that I could send her away without upsetting whatever idiotic ecosystem is running this house. Instead, I do as she asks, pulling my top over my head. "There's a couple black dresses in there," I start, but she raises a hand.

"Black? Please. You're the Lady to our star player." She says this as if that makes any sense, pulling out a few different dresses, assessing them. "You should be in our spirit colors, *obviously*." The sneer in her voice isn't even thinly veiled, and she pulls something from the rack, turning to me. "Colors like this?"

I stare at the oversized jersey—orange and purple—and when she flips it around, I see the number 36 emblazoned on the back. 'PAYNE' is spread across the shoulders. "Looks like one of Killian's jerseys must have gotten in there by mistake." I laugh anxiously. "But I think if I walked out in that, Killian may actually murder me."

She rolls her eyes, putting it back. "You have no imagination. Lord Killian, bending you over any flat surface, nothing but his own name and number staring back at him?" She scoffs. "Probably the best sex he'll ever have."

I clamp a hand over my mouth to muffle my surprised bark of laughter. Maybe this girl isn't *so* bad. "Yeah, he is pretty full of himself, isn't he?"

"Wear this," she says, ignoring my question to fling a hanger at me. The dress is a deep, dark purple. Its short skirt flares at the hips, but the bodice is tight and more revealing than I'm used to. Nevertheless, I do as I'm told, dragging it over my head. "You need a bra with that," she says.

But I just shake my head. "I'm not allowed."

She raises an eyebrow. "You're not allowed to wear a bra?"

"Not in the house," I explain, feeling my cheeks heat. I guess I'd been right before. Charlene clearly didn't have as many rules.

Thankfully, she doesn't question it. "Whatever. We need to do something with your hair next." She starts pulling various instruments from her bag, gesturing to the vanity.

I take a seat and try, "Thanks for helping."

She just hums. "Do you want it up or down?"

"I don't know, really." I look in the mirror, twirling a lock of hair around my finger. "What do you think?"

She pops a hip, resting her fist on it. "Rath and Killian will like it down, Tristian will like it up."

Nodding at my reflection, I answer, "Okay. Let's shave it off."

She doesn't even crack a smile at the joke, gathering my hair to run a brush through it. "You have no idea how good you have it, do you?"

"Good?!" I gape at her through the mirror. "Yeah, it's so good being forced into servicing them, knowing that I can be punished for exercising even the smallest morsel of autonomy. What a blast!"

The brush catches on a knot and she yanks, ignoring my sound of protest. "What's *fun* is being able to have anything you want. You only need to ask. This whole campus will be at your every whim. Boo hoo, you're having sex with the three hottest, most powerful guys here. No one is coming to your pity party."

When the brush hits another snag, I flinch away, glaring as I take the brush from her. "You're acting like they aren't the biggest assholes you've ever met."

She rolls her eyes, watching me gingerly run the brush through my hair.

"Of course they're assholes. They're selfish and greedy and spoiled. So what? They're also good at what they do. Don't act like they haven't made you feel good." She sniffs, raising her chin. "If I were Lady again—*their* Lady—I'd be on my knees for them without even having to be asked."

"The only thing they've made me feel is a deep desire to hurt them back."

"Then honey," she says, bending low to meet my gaze, "why the hell don't you?"

I pause, frowning. "Because I can't."

"Says who?"

"The rules, for one," I reply, setting the brush aside.

She spreads her arms. "Show me where it says in these 'rules' of yours that you can't strike back?" At the look on my face, she grins. "You have a lot to learn. There's a time for compliance and subservience. But selfish, greedy, spoiled boys love it when girls fight back. Everything comes easy to a Lord. Makes it hard to flex their power when there's nothing to test it, don't you think?"

I'm still thinking of this as Charlene curls my hair, pinning it up. She does have a point. Nowhere in the contract did it say I couldn't fight back. That I couldn't hurt them. That I couldn't defend myself. Could she be right? Would they like it if I fought them? Not disobedience or defiance, but a real, physical opposition. Would it make them like me more?

Should I care?

"Did you like it?" I eventually find the courage to ask. Despite that, I still keep my eyes averted. "When they hurt you, did you enjoy it?"

She doesn't miss a beat. "Yes."

Puzzled, I meet her gaze and ask, "Why?"

Her eyes narrow. "It's not black and white. I don't know where you come from, Pollyanna, but pain and pleasure can coexist." She puts her hands on the vanity, leveling me with a look. "The rougher they are, the more they like it. If it hurts—if it *really* hurts—tell me who actually has the power there, honey.

Then tell me how good it feels to know."

I swallow nervously, knowing that I've not had a shred of power since the day Killian and I met. What I can't admit to Charlene is that, in some deep, dark way, I understand that spark in her eyes when she talks about pleasure and pain. It'd be easier to say—*to know*—that I don't like what they do to me. That the pain is so great, it removes the possibility of pleasure.

But it's a lie.

And from the way Charlene looks at me, she knows it.

14

RITUALS

Two hours later, the party is in full swing. I've taken a position near the doorway, watching the parade of pretty people stream into the house. Handsome men. Beautiful women. Money and entitlement ooze off each and every one. The walls of the brownstone shake from the music Rath has pumping through the speakers. Head ducked down, headphone pressed to his ear, he's completely entrenched in the role of DJ, shifting quickly from tortured classical music to energetic pop, bass-heavy hip-hop, and crazy electronica.

Tristian's parked himself near the door, taking on the role of host. Apparently this requires giving every attractive girl who enters a kiss on the mouth before making some comment on their hair, outfits, or tits. They giggle and whisper into his ear, hands resting on his bicep, visibly pleased that he's paying them attention.

Killian's sitting in a soft leather chair in the den, two blondes perched on the arms. They're dressed in FU orange and purple, doting on him like royalty. One is playing with the hair at the base of his neck while the other massages his thigh.

It makes me wonder about my clause in the contract. The fidelity clause. No doubt any Lord could have their pick of girls here tonight. But they can't. Because of me. Briefly, I wonder if I should consider the flirting to be crossing some line. It's a laughable thought, anyway. None of them care about following the spirit of the clause, only about the technicality. And the spirit behind it isn't something I'm willing to cop to.

The spirit being that, secretly—stupidly—the thought of them owning me while fucking other girls struck me as insulting.

I laugh bitterly into my half-empty cup. As if anything about this arrangement isn't insulting.

Now that I'm watching the sorority girls draped over Killian, my stomach twists anxiously. Killian wanting something that he can't have? There's a price to pay for that, and I'm not so sure it'll be worth it, in the end.

The Lords, *my* Lords, are on the highest rung of the social ladder. Just like in high school. They move fluidly together, commanding the room, dictating the music, passing out drinks and ultimately creating social order in a room full of wannabes and chasers.

I have no idea where this leaves me. On the bottom with the slaves and servants? Charlene and the other girls from the interview all seem to believe otherwise, but I've yet to see all these privileges they all think so highly of.

I can only be certain of one thing; there will be hell to pay if the Lords think I'm shirking my duties. I slip back to the kitchen, weaving around boisterous dancers, bellowing football players, and make-out sessions that are getting graphic enough to make my cheeks bloom with heat.

The Lords' personal stash of beer is well-stocked in the refrigerator, so I grab a bottle for Tristian. I pause, thinking of Killian with those blondes, and then of Rath, who's still probably mad at me. With a steeling sigh, I grab one for each.

Entering the hall, I'm forced to squeeze through a group of guys.

"Excuse me," I say, holding the bottles close to my chest.

"Hey, look. This one's got the good stuff," one guy says, pushing off the wall and eyeing the bottles. Or my tits. Maybe both. "You need some help with

14

RITUALS

Two hours later, the party is in full swing. I've taken a position near the doorway, watching the parade of pretty people stream into the house. Handsome men. Beautiful women. Money and entitlement ooze off each and every one. The walls of the brownstone shake from the music Rath has pumping through the speakers. Head ducked down, headphone pressed to his ear, he's completely entrenched in the role of DJ, shifting quickly from tortured classical music to energetic pop, bass-heavy hip-hop, and crazy electronica.

Tristian's parked himself near the door, taking on the role of host. Apparently this requires giving every attractive girl who enters a kiss on the mouth before making some comment on their hair, outfits, or tits. They giggle and whisper into his ear, hands resting on his bicep, visibly pleased that he's paying them attention.

Killian's sitting in a soft leather chair in the den, two blondes perched on the arms. They're dressed in FU orange and purple, doting on him like royalty. One is playing with the hair at the base of his neck while the other massages his thigh.

It makes me wonder about my clause in the contract. The fidelity clause. No doubt any Lord could have their pick of girls here tonight. But they can't. Because of me. Briefly, I wonder if I should consider the flirting to be crossing some line. It's a laughable thought, anyway. None of them care about following the spirit of the clause, only about the technicality. And the spirit behind it isn't something I'm willing to cop to.

The spirit being that, secretly—stupidly—the thought of them owning me while fucking other girls struck me as insulting.

I laugh bitterly into my half-empty cup. As if anything about this arrangement isn't insulting.

Now that I'm watching the sorority girls draped over Killian, my stomach twists anxiously. Killian wanting something that he can't have? There's a price to pay for that, and I'm not so sure it'll be worth it, in the end.

The Lords, *my* Lords, are on the highest rung of the social ladder. Just like in high school. They move fluidly together, commanding the room, dictating the music, passing out drinks and ultimately creating social order in a room full of wannabes and chasers.

I have no idea where this leaves me. On the bottom with the slaves and servants? Charlene and the other girls from the interview all seem to believe otherwise, but I've yet to see all these privileges they all think so highly of.

I can only be certain of one thing; there will be hell to pay if the Lords think I'm shirking my duties. I slip back to the kitchen, weaving around boisterous dancers, bellowing football players, and make-out sessions that are getting graphic enough to make my cheeks bloom with heat.

The Lords' personal stash of beer is well-stocked in the refrigerator, so I grab a bottle for Tristian. I pause, thinking of Killian with those blondes, and then of Rath, who's still probably mad at me. With a steeling sigh, I grab one for each.

Entering the hall, I'm forced to squeeze through a group of guys.

"Excuse me," I say, holding the bottles close to my chest.

"Hey, look. This one's got the good stuff," one guy says, pushing off the wall and eyeing the bottles. Or my tits. Maybe both. "You need some help with those, baby?"

I duck my head evasively. "I'm fine. Thanks."

Another voice pipes up, this time from behind me. "That's a lot of beer for one little girl. Sure you don't want to share?" His heavy hands land on my hips, followed by the sour scent of warm, beer-tinged breath at my temple. "How about the three of us take those somewhere private and get to know one another better?"

It's easy to shoot off a clipped, "How about you fuck off and let me go on my way."

The guys look at one another, their expressions at first stunned, then amused. They laugh, their voices bouncing off the narrow hallway walls.

"You're a little spitfire, huh? Don't you know who we are?" He tilts his head and touches my jaw, eyes tracking his fingertip as it ascends to my bottom lip. Bile rises in my throat. I've seen the look in his dark eyes before. I know what he wants. They have me caged in, towering over me in a way that makes me tremble with the memory of Tristian and Rath forcing me to my knees. He thumbs my lip, trying to force the tip inside. "We're royalty around here. I'm thinking we need to take you out back and teach you some manners—put this smart little mouth to good use. What do you think, Beck?"

"Tucker! Beckwith!" a voice cuts through my panic. The guy touching my mouth looks down the hall to where Tristian is standing. "Can you tell me why your hands are on my property?"

It's taken me some time to learn to read Tristian. It's only now that I realize how much better I'm getting, because his voice is perfectly even. His expression is serene, almost polite. But there's something about those eyes, the way they're able to chill you from the inside out with one look, that tells me just how pissed off he is.

Tucker and Beckwith must sense this.

The one behind me flinches away, while the one in front of me jumps back, dropping his hand like my lips are on fire.

He follows Tristian's gaze to the leather cuff on my wrist and stutters out a hasty, "Hey, man, I didn't recognize her with the hair and the makeup and—"

The other guy shifts further away. "Wait, she's…?"

"Mine," Tristian says, pushing through the crowd. His eyes skim over me like he's checking for injuries or flaws. In one quick movement his arm is over my shoulder and a beer is in his hand. He lifts it to his mouth and swallows. "It looks like you were trying to delay my Lady from bringing me my drink."

"I-I didn't know."

"I'm sure you the fuck didn't, Beckwith," he says, then cuts his eyes toward the other guy, who I assume is Tucker, "because if you were touching my girl, my drink, or any other piece of my property, I'd have to do something about it. Wouldn't be pretty."

"It was a misunderstanding. We were just offering to help her carry those drinks." He gives me a pleading, simpering look. "Right?"

Tristian shifts his gaze to mine, waiting for an answer. Part of me just wants to lie and make it all go away. Another, much angrier part of me is remembering the look in Tucker's eyes as he tried to force his thumb past my lips.

I take a breath and meet Tristian's gaze. "They said they were going to take me out back and make me suck them off because I have a smart mouth. They wanted to teach me some manners."

Tristian's jaw ticks. "Interesting."

"That one there," I point to Tucker, "tried to shove his fingers into my mouth. They wouldn't let me get past." Even though he's palming my shoulder soothingly, those icy eyes of his fix Tucker with an evil glint.

Tucker gives a tense laugh. "Bro, Tristian, that's a complete lie. Come on, you know me. I wouldn't—I mean, not here. She must have misunderstood or maybe she's been drinking, I don't—"

"My lipstick's on his thumb."

Tristian swiftly grabs for his hand, easily confirming this. Once he does, everything seems to happen in a blink. He has Tucker pinned against the wall,

Tristian's big hand digging into his chest. "So not only did you touch my property and upset our Lady, but you also lied to me."

Tucker stammers, "I-I was just—"

"Racking up debt," Tristian finishes. "The fair thing would be to take the two of you out back and teach *you* some manners." By now, the confrontation is drawing stares and whispers. Tristian doesn't seem to mind. If anything, it just makes him press harder. "I'm trying to think how we'd do that. Any ideas, Lady?"

I look on wide-eyed, my heartbeat ratcheting up. "Um…"

But Tristian just shakes his head. "Lucky for you two, we're all just trying to have a good time tonight. I can't bother the others about this, so it'll have to wait." He releases Tucker with one final shove into the wall. "It'll give our girl some time to think of something creative. In the meantime, I think you're going to call it a night and leave the party."

Tucker and Beckwith both nod, still looking like they might piss their pants when they scurry away.

When Tristian turns back to me, I see there's still a hard look in his eye. "Once you're finished delivering those, come find me."

He walks off and a flurry of nerves rises in my stomach when I realize that I fucked up, too. I was talking to other guys. I'd broken a rule. Shit. Shit. Shit. I'm completely screwed. Blood rushes to my ears as I search for Rath and Killian. The best thing I can do is try to make up for my mistake.

Rath is still by the stereo, talking to a group of people about music. I stand behind him and try to discreetly swap out his empty beer bottle with the fresh one. He looks down at me with that same hardness in his expression from this afternoon. Guess he's still holding on to that one. "Do you need anything?" I ask as sweetly as possible. "Something to eat?"

"I'm fine," he says, taking a swallow of beer before turning back to his friends.

I exhale and face the room. Killian is no longer on his throne, but I spot him headed upstairs with the two girls from before. Martin specifically told me not to interfere with his pregame 'ritual'. But I can't think of any ritual that includes going upstairs with two sexy blondes that doesn't involve having sex with them. Not that it matters. What am I going to do? Follow him up there and tell him no?

The thought alone makes me shudder.

Still holding the extra beer, I make my way back to Tristian, who I eventually discover is out on the back deck. He's standing alone, leaning against the railing. He spots me and a small smile curves on his lips. I know the best thing to do is to admit what I'd done upfront. Maybe if I do it out here, he won't embarrass me in front of the whole party.

"There you are," he says, glancing at the bottle in my hands. "Is that for me?"

"It was for Killian, but…he just went upstairs."

"Ah, the pregame ritual." Tristian laughs, using the deck rail and a strong fist to dislodge the beer cap. "I've never met someone so superstitious in my life. Once he does something that he thinks is lucky, he'll add it in. In ninth grade, he wore two pairs of socks and won a game. Now he does that every game." He takes a long swig of the beer. "Junior year of high school, he hooked up with two girls—blondes—before the homecoming game. He scored three touchdowns. He's insisted on doing that ever since." Tristian casually confirms what I already suspected.

"So he's up there right now, violating the contract."

Tristian glances up, either at my words or the flatness of my voice. "Are you jealous?"

I pull a face. "Of what? I don't want to have sex with him any more than he wants to have sex with me. I just think if he's not going to respect the contract, then why should any of us? Why should I?"

He raises an eyebrow, setting his beer down. "First of all, if you wanted to fuck Killer as much as he wanted to fuck you, you'd be up there right now riding him like your life depended on it. Secondly, I'm beginning to think you haven't even read the contract."

I bristle equally at both those assertions. "I've read the contract a hundred times!"

"Then you know that Killer's pregame rituals supersede any other clauses."

I freeze, remembering that section of the contract. "But..." How was I supposed to know his pregame ritual involved fucking other girls? *Stupid.* Deflating, I realize that I've been outplayed. I sullenly wonder, "Do you think it works?"

"The ritual?" Tristian asks, humor dancing in his blue eyes. "I think Killer wants to fuck two girls at once, and there are plenty of blondes willing to help Forsyth have a winning season."

Nodding, I take a deep breath and say, "About earlier. I wasn't talking to those guys on purpose. They cornered me and I was just trying to get away. I promise I wasn't disobeying the rules."

He reaches out, pausing at my flinch, to tuck a wayward curl behind my ear. "Oh, Sweet Cherry, I'm not blaming you for that. Those two are absolute fuckwits. New pledges. There are always a few that don't get the rules. And there's always a few that intentionally twist them."

The feel of his warm fingertip against the shell of my ear makes me shiver. "They do?"

"Well, we sure as fuck did." He takes a sip of his drink and leans his elbows on the railing. "Freshman year, all three of us made a run at the Lady who was serving here at the time."

I hadn't even though of that. I thought being here would keep a girl safe from things like that. "Did it work?"

He laughs, and like this, in the dark without all the artifice and posturing, he looks devastatingly handsome. "Hell no. We got our asses beat. Like, literally thrown through the gauntlet by the upper classmen." He points to his butt. "I still have a scar from the paddling."

I breathe a sigh of relief. "So the Ladies really are off limits to anyone but the Lords."

"Technically, yes." He gives me an assessing look, then asks, "Can you keep a secret?" Before I can answer, he laughs. "Of course you can. You signed a contract. Well, we didn't manage to get the Lady freshman year, but we did sophomore. It was a challenge, and she put up a fight, but in the end, we proved who deserved to live in the house."

It occurs to me that he's talking about Charlene.

It's my understanding that the privilege of living in the house is for seniors only. I wasn't sure how the guys managed to get in the house their junior year, but I guess I'm not surprised. They've always been incredibly competitive and ruthless. The story he just told confirms it. They take what they want. They get more than they deserve. The rest of us are just pawns in their lives.

He rests his bottle on the railing and shifts so that his hand is on my hip and we're facing one another. "If someone ever tries to bother you, come find one of us. Male or female, we don't care. You belong to us, Story. No one should ever lay a hand on you, do you understand that?"

I shiver at both the cool air and the sincerity behind that threat. "I do."

He presses the back of his warm hand against my cheek. "Are you cold?" It's startling, the way he's looking down at me like…

Like he cares?

More startling than that is how, for a long moment, all I can think about is him bending down to kiss me.

All I can think about is how much I want him to.

Swallowing, I quietly admit, "A little."

He doesn't kiss me, though. "You have my permission to go get a sweater from your room, if you'd like."

"Oh." Even with the not-so-subtle reminder that I have no control here, it's still possibly the sweetest gesture he's made since I moved in. "Um. Thank you. Do you…need anything? From upstairs?"

"No, not now," he says, winking, "but hurry back, I may think of something later."

Even though we're probably having whatever in this house constitutes as a pleasant moment, I'm relieved to go back inside.

Squeezing through the crowd, I climb the stairs to the second floor. Both bedroom doors are closed, but as I approach mine, I can hear voices in Killian's. I pause, too curious for my own good. Sure enough, it's obvious that he's in there with at least two girls. I can hear one of them panting in breathy moans. They're almost as loud as the *bang, bang, bang* of his headboard and the unmistakable sound of Killian's angry, guttural grunts. I close my eyes and think about Killian having sex with someone. Those fiery eyes glaring down at her as his powerful hips punch into hers. Tingles run down my body and I can't help but wonder…does he treat them like he treats me? Does he hate them? Does he want to hurt them? Maybe he's different with other girls. Maybe he likes them. Maybe he touches them the way Tristian had just touched me. Maybe he holds them after.

Yeah, right.

My question is answered a moment later when I hear him roar, "Jesus Christ. Are you always this dry? It's like sticking my dick in sandpaper."

"Here," a girl replies, her voice anxious. "Stick it in my ass. It should be good and tight."

"No, let me suck you off first," the other girl says. "I'll get you ready. Fuck my mouth, baby, you know you like that." A moment later, "Oh god, you're so big. I can barely take it. Mmmmmm…"

The hallway fills with sounds of sex; loud and fake, porn star quality moans and squeaks. I can't blame the girls for trying. Killian seems like the kind of guy who would want it that way. But I know better. Silly to think I'd wondered what Killian might be like with other girls. I know him. This is too easy. They like it too much.

That thought is confirmed when he shouts, "Fuck this! I'm done. Get the fuck out of here."

"What?" one of the girls cries. "Why? Come on, baby, give us another chance. You can watch while Sadie eats me out."

"If you don't get the fuck out of my motherfucking room right now, I swear to god, I'll show you what I really want to do to you!"

Even as I hear them scrambling behind the closed door, I'm still frozen in my spot from the sound of his voice, low and furious. I finally jolt when the door swings open and they rush out like the devil is on their tail. I jump, reaching for my door, but he's there in a heartbeat, all big and angry.

Also *completely naked*.

"What the hell are you looking at!" he roars.

"N-nothing," I say. "I swear, nothing." Still, my eyes descend his body. His rippling, tattooed arms. His muscular, heaving chest. His hard washboard abs. He's like a statue chiseled out of marble by one of the ancient masters. And below it all is his thick cock, hanging heavy between his legs. Even limp, it's huge and intimidating, difficult to tear my gaze from. "I-I was just—"

"Just what?" he says, suddenly in front of me. He flings out a hand, clamping it around my upper arm, ignoring my flinch. "Snooping around? Spying? Digging up dirt on me?"

"What? No! I was just going to my room for a sweater. I was cold and Tristian…h-he said I could." His eyes dart over my head to my bedroom door like he's only just remembering it's there. "I didn't hear anything," I hurriedly add.

I instantly regret it.

"Which means you heard everything," he snarls, bruising my arm with his grip. "It's not my goddamn fault. Those sluts with their fake tits and phony moans. It's like a fucking low-budget porn show in there. Do you know how annoying it is to never have a single honest fuck?"

I'm not sure if he's being rhetorical but he's still holding onto me, and the anger's rolling off of him like a warning. I shake my head, offering a meek,

"No."

"It's pathetic," he says through clenched teeth. "They've been fucked and manhandled by half the guys in this school. All I want is a good lay before the game. To settle some of this pent-up energy so that I can focus on the field instead of my cock for ninety fucking minutes." His eyes narrow and pin to mine. "Tell me, why can't I do that?"

"I don't know," I whisper, holding back a wince as he grips my arm harder.

"Yes, you fucking do!" he shouts. "Else, you wouldn't have tried to cut me off with that stupid fucking clause of yours. So tell me. I want to hear you say it."

I look in his eyes, always so full of hatred for me, and I know what he wants me to say. He wants me to take the blame. He wants me to roll over. He wants to hurt me because he knows I can't hurt him back.

Charlene's words come back to me, and suddenly it's like a toxic fog has been lifted.

I strike back. "I said I don't know, Killian. I don't know why it's so hard for you to find a vagina to screw that meets your very special needs. But I can take a guess, if that's what you want." All the disgust and anger I've been carrying for the last three years rushes out. "Maybe you're so fucked up in the head, so evil and spiteful, that fucking someone who's willing just isn't good enough for you. Maybe your dick is just as broken as your head. Maybe, deep down, you know there's nothing appealing about you. Nothing special. Nothing worth wanting. So yeah, every time they moan—every time they beg for it—you know it's fake. It can never be anything else." His expression goes momentarily slack, eyes flooding with a darkness that I know I'm going to pay for. For a split second, I don't care. I think it'll be worth it. "Maybe you only want to fuck people who act just as disgusted by you as they feel. Because at least that's genuine, you sick fuck."

My back meets the wall faster than I can process the collision. "Oh, Story," he says, mouth curling into a sharp, malicious grin. His gaze darts down, and I don't know why, but I look too. His cock is no longer droopy and lifeless. It's sprung to life, growing two sizes in the time it took me to mouth off to him. "I think you might be onto something. Tell me more."

Shit.

"I-I—"

"No? Cat suddenly got your tongue?" I know better to reply, but he's not done. He casually says, "Get on the floor."

My eyes widen. "What?"

"Get on the floor," he says, releasing me and shoving me down on the hallway carpet. I move to my knees, eye to eye with his bobbing cock. I try to wade through the rising panic to find acceptance in this. I knew this would come eventually. I force back the nausea roiling in my gut, but before I can settle it, he moves again, dropping in front of me. "Lay down."

I lock up, gaping at him. "Killian…please…"

His hand shoots forward to take a handful of my hair. "You know that begging makes it hotter, Sweet Cherry. So beg all you want. Do you see what happens to my cock every fucking time you open your mouth? It gets bigger. Harder. The blood is pumping straight through me." He grips it and runs his hand up and down the shaft. "I'm harder right now than I've been in years. It must be the fucking sound of your voice. It's like a goddamn trigger."

I bite the inside of my mouth, forcing myself to be quiet as I stare down at it, at his hand running up and down the pink, taut skin of his erection. It's swollen and crazy big. Terrifyingly so. I think of the girl telling him to stick it in her ass. *God.*

"Lay down," he says again, voice deceptively even.

"No." A blow job is one thing. I've survived that before, and while I know at some point one of the guys will take my virginity, it can't be like this. I won't let him. "This is *not* happening."

His laugh is a brittle, rough thing. "Want to bet?"

He doesn't wait for my compliance, using the hand in my hair to shove me back. I grab his wrist, kicking out with my leg, but he uses every part of his body to force me into submission. It's like I'm the ball wobbling down the football field and he's determined to catch me.

It's hardly a struggle.

He gets me flat on the ground in no time, one hand planted into my shoulder as the other swats mine away. The muscles in his chest hardly shift as he climbs on top of me, using his forearms, his knees, his legs to pin me there like a bug, completely unconcerned by my flailing limbs.

His eyes are alight like this, and even though they're still full of anger, they're also full of something else. Impatience? Excitement? He rips the straps of my dress away like they're nothing, taking both my wrists in one big hand as he yanks it down my body, swiftly exposing me. His cock glides against my stomach, accidentally or intentionally, I don't know. It's smooth and hot and the tip leaves a sticky residue on my belly.

Breathing heavily, he looks down at my chest, greedily staring at my breasts. "Perfect," he mutters, rubbing his thumbs over my peaked nipples. "Fucking perfect."

Trying to stop my own chest from heaving, I let out a string of panicked appeals. "Killian, you can't do this. You can't fuck me, you can't, you can't, you're my stepbrother, you don't…you don't want me. You hate me."

The look in his eyes stops my voice cold. He shifts to pin my legs down with his feet, while his knees press into my arms. "I'm not going to fuck you, Sweet Cherry," he says, his tone implying that he's held off on adding a 'not yet' to his statement. "At least, not your pussy."

He leans over and for a second I think he's going to kiss me, my lips quivering at the thought, but he ducks his head and licks the valley between my breasts instead. He sits back up, his thick cock bobbing over my wet chest. His hands knead my breasts, squeezing and pushing them together before pulling them apart. I clamp my mouth shut, afraid that he's going to force it between my lips, but he lines it up with my tits and pushes it between them instead.

"Yeah, that's fucking good," he groans, slowly pulling in and out. The points of his knees, the weight of his body holding me down, *hurts*. There's nothing I can do. Nowhere I can go. I'm trapped, staring at Killian as his jaw clenches tight and his eyes shut, falling into a rhythm. His thumbs keep pressing down on my nipples, my *very* sensitive nipples. It awakens me, sending gradual jolts of unwelcome pleasure though my body. Every time he thrusts, his ass brushes back and forth across my lower belly, teasingly just above my pelvis. Warm, traitorous heat builds between my legs as I watch, powerless. He has no fucking idea what he's doing to me.

Or at least that's what I think, until he slows down, pushing the tip of his cock closer and closer to my face. He opens his eyes, and growls, "Kiss it."

I turn my head away. "No." The heat in my belly builds with every thrust, every tug and toy of my nipples.

"You will, Sweet Cherry," he says, breath and movements slowing. He's in control here. Always in control. "Kiss it."

I spit, "Fuck you." But saying things like that is now confusing. Am I saying it to make him stop? Or am I saying it to encourage him more? A fog has lowered over my brain, one that combines with the rhythmic push and pull of Killian's cock as it slowly moves closer and closer to my mouth. Push, pull, push, pull. The most confusing thing about it is that, despite the way he's pinning me here—despite the hurt—it doesn't even feel aggressive. It feels like my body is suddenly on fire, like I have to put all my willpower into not raising my hips in tandem with his.

So much willpower that it's impossible to fight the impulse to taste him.

He pushes forward again, his eyebrows pinching together. When he's close enough, I flick out my tongue and lick the salty tip.

"Fuuuuck, *Christ*," he shudders, a tremor running through his body. He does it again and this time I open my mouth, taking him inside. He's slippery and salty, blistering hot. His breath grows ragged along with my own. I squeeze my legs together, seeking friction between my thighs, but the dark truth is that

I don't even need it. I feel like the winding ball of tension building in my belly is fit to explode just from the way he's playing with my tits, from tasting him in my mouth, from feeling the weight of his body bearing down on me. "Tell me how much you hate me," he says, nose flaring wide as he pistons his hips. "Tell me how much you fucking hate my guts, you dirty little white-trash whore."

"I hate you," I cry, feeling the spiral in my belly tightening. "You're evil, and mean, and you let your friends hurt me. You're the reason I ran away. You ruined my fucking life. I hate you so fucking much, Killian Payne!"

He opens his eyes and they hold mine for a long beat before he thrusts forward one last time, grabbing his cock in his hand. His body seizes, bold and beautiful, and warm come shoots out from the tip, coating my chest and neck.

He falls forward, hands landing next to my head, face inches from mine. I'm still trapped under his weight, semen pooled on my chest. He looks down at me, forehead sweaty, cheeks red. He's disturbingly calm now, all that dark hatred and bright loathing seemingly erased from his stony features.

My own breathing is ragged, still coiled tight from being denied an orgasm I didn't even want, caught in a whirlwind of emotions. What I'd experienced wasn't exactly pleasure, but it wasn't entirely pain, either. It was that place caught in the middle, the one Charlene must have been talking about. It's dangerous. Sinister.

Killian blinks, like he's slowly coming back to reality. He sits up, which forces his body to press down on mine. I cry out in pain. Without even looking, I know I'm going to have bruises from the way he pinned me down. He doesn't seem to give a damn.

He exhales, releasing my arms and legs, and then climbs back to his feet. Fully aware that I can move now, I don't. I stay exactly where he's left me, sprawled out, breathless, aching, *used*.

"That," he says quietly, "was your fault. You forced me to do that to you. Just like you always force guys to hurt you. You came up here and got in my business, and then you knowingly provoked me into this. That's what you do, Story. That's what you always fucking do." His eyes travel over me, lips curling in disgust. "You think I'm the one who's broken? Look at you. You can get away, but you won't. Whenever you try, you just come right back. So what the fuck does that make you?" He shakes his head like I'm pathetic. Like he's not the one who just defiled me. He bends and grabs a handful of the dress he'd pooled around my waist, yanking it over his spunk on my chest. "Clean yourself up and go to bed. You're a fucking embarrassment."

He steps over me and walks back into his room, slamming the door behind him. I'm left on the floor, half naked, covered in semen, while the sounds of the party travel up the stairs. A sob rises in my throat as I finally sit up. I don't even try to stand, my arms and legs weak and wobbly from being pinned for so long. I crawl out of the hall and into my room, closing and locking everyone and everything out.

15
FALSE COMFORT

After Story goes in to get her sweater, I head back to the den, keeping an eye out for the pledges, Tucker and Beckwith. It was difficult, going easy on them in front of Story, but I did. Because I know she's jumpy as fuck. But they've got some serious payback coming their way for laying hands on our Lady, and once Killer and Rath find out, it's going to be even worse for them.

"Jesus," I overhear a girl say. She's on the other side of a decorative plant, sitting on the edge of the fireplace. "What the hell do you think is his problem?"

"I don't know," replies the other, "but my vagina isn't dry like sandpaper, that's bullshit."

"It is. He's the one that can't get it up. He needs to stop blaming that shit on us and go see a fucking doctor."

Curiosity gets the best of me and I peer around the plant. It's the two girls that went upstairs with Killian earlier.

"You know something's wrong when he wouldn't stick it up my ass. All guys want that. Every. Single. One of them."

She's right about that, but this isn't the kind of gossip that needs to be going around about any of the Lords. Once a rumor gets going, it doesn't stop, and we have more than just the usual South Side business to keep secret. The parameters of our contract are private. Killian having some kind of problem is a sure signal that something is up, which will only make people sniff around harder. If any one of the other frats founds out that Story's virginity is part of our game, they'd do their best to fuck it up. The last thing we need is anyone suspicious. I stroll over and try to get a handle on what's happening.

Up close, I can tell these girls aren't exactly Killian's type. They're perfectly packaged, with bottle blonde hair, and big, most likely fake tits. Their waists are unnaturally narrow, legs thin with an inch-wide thigh-gap. The only flaw is the red around their noses, the tiny tell of a coke habit that is mandatory if you're a Kappa.

"Ladies," I say, giving them my best panty-dropping grin.

Beverly looks up, and when she recognizes me, she straightens, pushing her shoulders back. "Oh, Tristian. Hi!"

"Hey, cutie." I glance over at Cami, who smiles back, but it doesn't reach her eyes. They're as red as her nose. "What's got you two so upset on a night like tonight?"

"It's nothing," Beverly says, adjusting her top and making her tits bounce around in the process.

I squat before them, making eye contact. "I thought I saw you two go upstairs with Killian earlier."

"We did," Cami says, sniffing. "He just—"

"He acted like an asshole," Beverly blurts, then looks repentant. No one wants to cross the Lords. "It's my fault. I just…I wasn't what he wanted."

I reach out and rub my thumb against the corner of her puffy lips. "Killian's been stressed lately. The NFL's been watching him. We've been getting settled into the house. This rivalry between us and the Counts is heating up, and we've been breaking in our new Lady. There's a lot on the line with the game. You know how he gets."

How he 'gets' is an understatement. Killian's mean streak is legendary. Everyone knows it.

15
FALSE COMFORT

AFTER STORY GOES IN TO GET her sweater, I head back to the den, keeping an eye out for the pledges, Tucker and Beckwith. It was difficult, going easy on them in front of Story, but I did. Because I know she's jumpy as fuck. But they've got some serious payback coming their way for laying hands on our Lady, and once Killer and Rath find out, it's going to be even worse for them.

"Jesus," I overhear a girl say. She's on the other side of a decorative plant, sitting on the edge of the fireplace. "What the hell do you think is his problem?"

"I don't know," replies the other, "but my vagina isn't dry like sandpaper, that's bullshit."

"It is. He's the one that can't get it up. He needs to stop blaming that shit on us and go see a fucking doctor."

Curiosity gets the best of me and I peer around the plant. It's the two girls that went upstairs with Killian earlier.

"You know something's wrong when he wouldn't stick it up my ass. All guys want that. Every. Single. One of them."

She's right about that, but this isn't the kind of gossip that needs to be going around about any of the Lords. Once a rumor gets going, it doesn't stop, and we have more than just the usual South Side business to keep secret. The parameters of our contract are private. Killian having some kind of problem is a sure signal that something is up, which will only make people sniff around harder. If any one of the other frats founds out that Story's virginity is part of our game, they'd do their best to fuck it up. The last thing we need is anyone suspicious. I stroll over and try to get a handle on what's happening.

Up close, I can tell these girls aren't exactly Killian's type. They're perfectly packaged, with bottle blonde hair, and big, most likely fake tits. Their waists are unnaturally narrow, legs thin with an inch-wide thigh-gap. The only flaw is the red around their noses, the tiny tell of a coke habit that is mandatory if you're a Kappa.

"Ladies," I say, giving them my best panty-dropping grin.

Beverly looks up, and when she recognizes me, she straightens, pushing her shoulders back. "Oh, Tristian. Hi!"

"Hey, cutie." I glance over at Cami, who smiles back, but it doesn't reach her eyes. They're as red as her nose. "What's got you two so upset on a night like tonight?"

"It's nothing," Beverly says, adjusting her top and making her tits bounce around in the process.

I squat before them, making eye contact. "I thought I saw you two go upstairs with Killian earlier."

"We did," Cami says, sniffing. "He just—"

"He acted like an asshole," Beverly blurts, then looks repentant. No one wants to cross the Lords. "It's my fault. I just...I wasn't what he wanted."

I reach out and rub my thumb against the corner of her puffy lips. "Killian's been stressed lately. The NFL's been watching him. We've been getting settled into the house. This rivalry between us and the Counts is heating up, and we've been breaking in our new Lady. There's a lot on the line with the game. You know how he gets."

How he 'gets' is an understatement. Killian's mean streak is legendary. Everyone knows it.

"We didn't mean to upset him. We tried to make him happy." Beverly wipes a tear off her face. "I even offered him anal."

"I know, sugar, and that's just a testament to the amount of pressure he's under. I don't know anyone here who wouldn't jump on the chance to pound that fine ass."

"Right?" she says appreciatively.

That seems to mollify her, because ultimately, she's not upset that he was a jerk to her. She's upset that he rejected her. I stroke her hair. "How about this? You two forget any of this happened and the hot tub out back is open to you, any time."

They share a look, smiles spreading across both their faces. Cami says, "Yeah, that sounds great."

When they walk off, I feel confident that they won't go sharing all over social media that Killian's got a limp dick. Jesus. Fucking embarrassing. I suggest they go find a skinny margarita over at the bar and then I search the room for either of my brothers. Rath is still wallowing in his moody, emo bullshit by commandeering the music, but I do see Killian has emerged, shoulders at ease and a big shit-eating grin on his face.

That's not the look of a guy who just struck out limp-dicked with two of the sweetest pieces at his own damn party.

In fact, he looks completely satisfied.

A thought—no, a worry—niggles at the back of my mind. Furtively, I scan the room for Story. It hasn't escaped my attention that she never made it back down with her sweater. I look back over at Killian, eyes narrowing when our gazes meet.

He winks, jerking his shoulder in a rueful shrug.

Fucking hell.

No one sees my tension as I cross the room and climb up the stairs to the second floor. My poker face is my best attribute. It's what makes professors and parents love me. It's what gets girls to undress for me, and it's what allows me to move easily, pretending like everything is fine, even though I know it isn't.

Hopefully it's what helps me clean up whatever mess Killian's left up there.

We call him Killer for a reason. He's a mean, vindictive shit. He's also petty and almost as vain as me. If he really couldn't get it up with those girls—if something broke his ritual—there would have been hell to pay. And if Story crossed his path at that very moment, we may be out of a Lady.

The second floor looks undisturbed, both Story and Killian's bedroom doors closed. I go to hers first, checking the knob. It's locked. "Story?" I call, tapping my knuckles against the wood. "Sweet Cherry, you in there?" I hear a small thud against the base of the door and try the knob again. "I'm going to need you to unlock the door."

"Go away," I hear. There's no bite to it.

"Story," I say, raising my voice. "Open the door. That's a fucking order."

My heart pounds as I wait for the sound of movement, for her hands to reach the knob on the other side of the door. When she finally opens it and I see her, face splotchy and red, I exhale. I don't know what I thought Killian did to her, but at least she's in one piece. When my eyes lower, I see that her dress is hanging off her shoulders, the top stretched and torn. Something shiny and slick is stuck to her neck. I glance behind me and step in the room, taking her with me.

"What happened?"

She laughs. "Like you fucking care." The words are harsh and bitter—deserved. Sort of.

"Hey," I say, cupping her elbow as I lead her into the room. "Didn't I get Tucker and Beckwith off your back tonight? I care."

She yanks her arm away. "Because I'm your property."

I blink. "You say that like it's a bad thing." I don't see why it should be. It is what it is. Story belongs to us. We all signed off on it. Sure, we might get rough with her—might *correct* her—but I took on the role of making sure her needs are met. I don't take my jobs anything but seriously. I study her more closely now, noticing her eyes are red from crying. Her upper arms have dark, reddish marks in a round shape.

Gently, I touch them. "Who did this?" Stupid question, of course. I know the answer. And she knows I know, because she doesn't even bother replying. She walks into the bathroom, turns on the hot water as far as it will go, and listlessly grabs a washcloth off the hook.

I watch, more transfixed than I'd like to admit at the sight of her like this, all debauched and vulnerable. Her hair has completely escaped its pins, tumbling down her shoulders in loose curls. I'd liked it up, the way it accentuated the column of her throat, the feminine slope of her neck. I've always liked girls' necks. The way they feel under my grip. For a moment there on the back deck, I'd wondered if she'd worn it like that for me.

I take a deep breath and start, "Did he…?"

"Rape me?" she bluntly asks, voice dull. "Sometimes I wish he just would. Then he'd lose interest, right?"

I purse my lips, watching her. He definitely has a major hard-on over her virginity. Fuck, we all do. But it's more than that, for Killer. The way he is about Story is something unique. Obsessive. "If he didn't fuck you, then why are you so upset?"

She dunks the cloth under the steaming water, and then holds it up so that it drips down her arms. Her eyes meet mine in the mirror, and I'm not so sure I like what I see. They're lifeless, dark, completely void of that flicker I'd seen earlier. Once again, she doesn't bother replying—I'm not sure I like that either—choosing to scrub at her neck and chest some more.

I don't need to ask what she's washing off. "He's just under a lot of pressure," I start, repeating the lines I told the girls downstairs. "When things aren't going his way, he…well, you know how he gets. Didn't you live with him for a year? I'm sure you remember."

Finally, a flicker. Whatever angrily contorts her face also makes her fling the wet rag at my head. "I remember! You know what I remember most? *You* doing the raping!" She makes a deep sound of disgust at my baffled expression. "What, you think you didn't rape me just because your dick didn't enter my vagina?"

I raise a finger. "It's interesting actually, the legal definition of rape varies on—" I pause. Possibly, it's not the best time to recite my vast knowledge of sexual assault law. Instead, I opt for, "Come on, Story. Let's not be obtuse here. You had a choice that night."

Her eyes start welling again—oh god, oh fuck—right before fat tears start rolling down her cheeks. "Why?" she cries, sobbing. "Why did you do that to me?!" Christ, I fucking hate it when girls cry like this. There's snot and blubbering, all kinds of fluids, and none of the sexy kind. She leaps forward, ramming a fist into my chest. "Answer me!"

It's easy to swat her hand away, taking her wrist in my palm. "You're hysterical." Roughly, I grab her arms and turn her around. "Stand still," I tell her, ducking the washcloth under the water again. I pump a little soap on it and rub it around with my thumb. She watches me with watery eyes, following my every move. I ignore her, tilting up her chin to where I see a shiny, half-dried spot of semen just under her jaw. Gently, I wash it off, explaining, "Hot water and jizz are a bad combo. Soap and cool water are key. There, see? All gone."

I hand her a towel, watching as she mechanically blots her red-raw chest with it, tears having thankfully stopped. Shimmying the dress down her chest, she covers herself quickly, but not fast enough for me to miss the bruises forming on the pale sides of her breasts. Those, along with the ones on her arms, are disturbing.

I jerk my chin. "Take off your dress."

"What?" she whispers, voice rough from crying. "Why?"

"I want to see if there are any other bruises." She strips stiltedly, hands shaking, eyes averted in such an intense show of shyness that I almost laugh. "I've already seen it all," I remind her, raising an eyebrow. Even still, it takes her several moments to finally step out of the dress and drop the towel, head ducked as I look my fill.

The tops of her thighs have bigger, purpling marks. Same on her shins. A picture starts to form in my mind. Killian, possibly a hundred pounds heavier than the tiny wisp in front of me, pinned her to the ground using his elbows, knees and feet. His hands squeezed her tits so hard, I can almost see the points of his fingertips bruised into her flesh.

Fucker.

Motherfucking *fucker*.

It's one thing to use our Lady. It's another to mark her up like this. This shit isn't kosher. It could get us all in trouble, and maybe Story hasn't realized it yet, but it's a violation of the contract, too.

It makes my fist curl at the sight of it—of *him*, pressed into her skin. What gives him the right? She belongs to all of us. And now she's standing here, tattooed all over by one of his stupid fucking tantrums.

I love Killian like a brother. I trust him with my life. My career. My family.

But I don't trust him with our Lady.

Not one fucking bit.

When I realize she's made no effort to move, I look away. "You can get dressed." Like a zombie, she walks over to the dresser, finding a T-shirt and shorts. She struggles to get the shirt over her head, so I move closer and help her into it, giving in to the impulse to graze the bruised sides of her breasts as I do. "Get into bed," I tell her, turning down the covers. Wordlessly, she crawls onto the mattress and leans against the pillow. "Did you do something to set him off?"

She scoffs, moving her eyes to mine. "Do you make it a habit of blaming all your victims, or am I just special?"

"I just want to know the truth."

"No, you don't." She reaches for the comforter and tugs it toward her waist. "That's exactly what caused this. Me, telling the truth." She turns her head away, looking out the window. "I told him exactly what I felt. That he was repulsive and broken. That his dick didn't work because he was a sick fuck." Her eyelids look heavy and swollen from the tears. It's not attractive.

I think.

It shouldn't be.

Softly, I explain, "If you want to survive this job, you're going to have to keep that mouth shut. You know that, right?"

"How am I going to suck you off with my mouth shut?"

Even though she says it bitterly, sharp like knives, it still makes my dick twitch. I chuckle at the way she's looking at me, like she knows it. "I like that sexy mouth, but Killian can't always handle it. I'm not sure Rath can, either. Every time you fight back, you make it harder on yourself."

"It's not in my nature to be submissive," she admits.

"Then why the fuck did you take this job?"

A strange expression crosses her face, and she shrugs. "I needed somewhere to stay. I didn't want to be reliant on Daniel again."

It's bullshit and we both know it. There are plenty of possible living situations that aren't *this*. Story Austin is hiding something, and one day I'm going to find out what it is. "You know that saying, 'you get more flies with honey than vinegar'? You may want to try that. Look at me, Story. I'm easy. But the other two are mean as snakes. Unless you really do want them to make your life miserable, or get kicked out, you're going to have to play the game a little."

She shakes her head, looking away. "There's no winning with the three of you. If I lie—if I act like a perfect little simpering puppet—then I'll be boring, just like those two blonde girls. If I fight back like I did earlier with Killian, then this happens. You all hurt me because you want to hurt me. There's nothing I can do to stop it."

That's a copout of the highest order. Instead of saying so, I sigh, sitting next to her. "You want to know what happened that night? Why I did it?" I shrug, not having really thought about it much, if I'm being honest. "You pushed me."

Her gaze swings to mine, full of fiery rage. Before she can argue, I explain, "Genevieve didn't just dump me. She fucked around on me. She got the best of me. She made me…*feel* something for her, and then she…" Well, she broke my fucking heart. But Story can't know about that. No one can. Love is weakness. I might have forgotten that, back then. But I won't do it again. "And there you were, pushing salt into the wound. Rath, too. He thinks we don't know about his little problem, but we do. You do, too. And you held it against him."

Her forehead wrinkles when I reach out to push her hair behind her ear, but she doesn't flinch back.

"Fight back, Cherry. Be interesting. But if you want to survive this job, you should realize that every time you poke at a weakness, it just makes us feel like we've got something to prove." Chuckling, I think of the look on Killian's face earlier. "I mean, damn, babe. A limp dick is like the number one nightmare for a guy's ego. You didn't even need to pour gas on that fire."

"What about you?" she asks, eying me doubtfully. "I know you, Tristian. I know you're not just coming in here because you're a good guy."

I snort. "No. I'll never pretend to be that. But I don't like anyone—even Killian—damaging our girl. As long as you're in this house, I want you to be safe. Understand?"

"Do you mean that?" she asks, something scared but hopeful shining in her eyes. "You'd really—you wouldn't let something hurt me?"

I look at her pensively, considering. "We'll punish you, if we have to. We'll use your body, enjoy you. But no, I wouldn't let anyone hurt you. Not if I could help it. Maybe even sometimes if I couldn't."

She nods, and I sense a touch of tension falling away. "Good."

I gesture for her to lie back and she hesitantly follows, eyes tracking me as I bend to press a kiss to her forehead. Then I walk away from a half-dressed, vulnerable girl for the first time in my life.

Almost, at least.

"Wait," she whispers, stilling me. When I turn, she's shifting beneath the blankets, squirming. She doesn't meet my gaze. "I can't…uh, you know. Because of the contract, so—"

"Can't what?"

She grimaces, fixing her eyes to the ceiling. "I can't…*you know*…"

Losing my patience, I demand, "Spit it out, Cherry." There's a party going on downstairs. I can't spend the whole night coddling her.

With a tight huff, she gives a terse, "*Masturbate*."

My face falls slack for a moment before I get it under control. Fuck *me*. Could Sweet Cherry be horny? I fight down my smirk. "You have my permission," I offer, continuing for the door.

But then she makes this little noise of protest. "I'm not very…uh, good at it."

I pause, watching her. "Are you asking me to get you off?" Fuck, *please be asking me*. That might be worth more points than I already *have*. "You need to say the words, Story. I can't do it if you don't ask." She gives me a hot, belligerent glare that makes my dick jump. Obviously, she has a point. I've already gotten her off without her asking. But for the consensual request bonus points, it needs to be explicit.

"Fine," she growls. "Would you *please* get me off."

Just like that, I'm rock hard.

I want to laugh, but I don't. He must have done a number on her to drive our Lady to this, considering how tired and sore and pissed off she must be.

Intuitively, I know exactly how to approach this. "Take off your shorts." I watch as she heaves a brittle sigh, blanket shifting as she obeys. I walk back to the bed and perch on the edge, eyes fixed on the way her chin quivers. Oh yes, she's sacrificing something to ask for this. He must have really gotten her close. Classic Killer, getting a girl right to the edge before leaving her in the lurch. Quietly, I say, "Look at me," and it takes her a moment, but she finally does, those damp eyes boring resentfully into mine.

I know what she needs. I cup her cheek in my palm before taking her lips

15 | TRISTIAN

with mine. I keep the kiss gentle, slow, chaste. Let her loosen up a bit at the feel of it. This is easy, coaxing her into it, letting her be the one to part those plump lips of hers. Killian was mean and rough. A little tenderness will go a long way here, but I never do anything by halves.

By the time I lick into her mouth, she's already sighing, shifting into me like I'm a goddamn port of harbor. The way she kisses is completely artless, unpracticed. Maybe some guys wouldn't like that, but the three of us? Fuck. Every time she mimics my movements, licking against my tongue, it's like I'm shaping her, molding her to everything I like.

It's not long before I'm dipping a hand beneath the covers, trailing my fingers teasingly down her warm arm. When I reach her hand, curling my fingers into her palm, she curls back, clutching me.

I lead it to her bare pussy.

Her mouth goes still, but she doesn't protest, letting me arrange her fingers right over her clit. I press them there, coaxing her back into the kiss, guiding her hand. She's a quick study, making a soft sound into my mouth when I make her press into the nub. Unable to help myself, I leave her fingers there to do a little exploring of my own, dipping lower.

I can't hold back my groan when I feel how wet she is. Holy shit, this girl is fucking *soaked*. What the hell did Killian do? She rips her mouth away to gasp, but I stay close, watching the way her eyes fall closed, pressing soft kisses down her jaw.

I whisper, "Did he get you close, sweetheart?" She whimpers, teeth bearing down into her lip as her hips chase my hand. I can already tell from the way her legs are trembling that it's not going to take much. "Does that feel good?"

I can feel her nod beneath my lips as I shower the column of her neck in gentle kisses. She's getting louder now, mindless in that way being on the edge always makes someone feel. The bed creaks with every shift of her hips—we'd engineered it that way, just for Killian—and she lets out a strained whine.

Unable to help myself, I finally allow my tongue to taste her neck, latching onto the skin right above a taut tendon.

I give a hard, powerful suck, sinking my teeth in.

She goes rigid, crying, "Tristian," and god, I can feel it. She clenches, shuddering under me so delicately. It's even better than that time in the library, feeling her spasm, legs clamping tight around my wrist as I work her through it.

I rise from her throat, groaning from the sight of my mark on her there, all purple against her pale flesh. It feels better like this, knowing that Killian isn't the only one on her. She looks blissed out, eyes glazed, chest heaving. Before she can start to worry about the fact my dick could drill a hole through solid steel right now, I pull the blankets up to her chin.

I don't tell her that she owes me for this—big enough that I plan on collecting in full when she's feeling better. But not tonight, I think, taking one last, lingering kiss from her gasping lips.

After a moment, she looks at me, those dazed eyes clearing enough to land on mine. When she does, her expression shutters, going blank. I don't stop her from rolling over and curling in on herself, shutting me out. She looks small like that. Helpless. Sad.

"If I'm broken," she whispers, rusty voice cutting through the silence, "then you're the one who broke me."

I blink at her, confused. "You look pretty together to me."

Silence.

Well.

I guess it was too much to hope for a 'thank you'.

Fully erect and half-annoyed, I snatch the used rag from the bedside table and step into the hall. Closing the door behind me, I'm instantly aware of Killian's presence down the hall.

"What were you doing in there?" he asks, eyes narrowing.

Ah yes, all the squeaking.

"Cleaning up your mess," I say, wiping my hands on the rag. "Literally and figuratively. Was dousing her like a fire hose really necessary?"

He laughs. "Hell yeah, it was. She's lucky I didn't use it to glue her goddamn mouth shut."

"Did you have to mark her up like that in the process?" I hiss, flinging a hand at the door. "She's absolutely fucking covered in bruises!"

He crosses his big arms over his chest. "So what? The bitch went crying to you about it? Since when do you care about getting rough?"

I know I can't move Killian, so when I shove his shoulder and it jerks back, I know he's letting me. "It's too fucking far, Killer. It's visible. I know we don't play the game the same way. You're all about being physical, and I'm—"

"You're all about the mindfuck." He gives me a look that tells me exactly what he thinks of that. "I mean, if that works for you, fine. But that's the long game, Tristian, and I needed to get off *tonight*."

"And now she hates you even more, which I didn't even realize was possible."

"So." He walks past me to stand in front of his door. "I hate her, too. Always so goddamn nosy, always in my fucking space, flapping that fucking mouth of hers, pushing me. Don't act like you don't know what I mean. Watching her get coated in my spunk was the best damn thing that's happened to me in a long time."

I roll my eyes. "You're an ass, and that temper is going to fuck everything up."

He pokes me in the chest with his finger. "And you're a pussy. I'm going to get the most points. A titty fuck? Coming all over her? That's ten points plus."

I look behind me at her door. "Shut up, or she'll hear you."

"What? Over her tears? Whatever."

I decide to get through to him the only way I know how. "Well, I just gained thirty five."

He freezes, jaw dropping. "Bullshit."

I shrug, knowing that he believes me. He wouldn't look so furious if he didn't. "You left her hurt and angry and horny as fuck. I took care of her. She asked for it. That's what your game is doing—giving the rest of us an in. It's also reckless and stupid. Let the Counts see her walking around all bruised to hell, or even worse, the Princes. You know *their* game."

Jaw clenched, he pushes past me, reaching for his door. Before he can enter, he pauses to say, "I do know one thing. If I have a good game this weekend, I'm adding her to my pregame ritual."

He accentuates his claim by slamming the door in my face.

My eyes sweep between the two rooms, conflicted over Killian's brutality and Story's inability to just submit. Killian's right about one thing. We play this game differently. His power is in his body, and mine is in my mind. But the one thing we all do the same is play to win. And I'm going to have to rein Killian in if I'm going to make that happen.

Else, there won't be a game at all.

STORY

16

TURNING THE TABLES

I DON'T WANT TO WAKE UP.

My phone alarm blares at me, but I ignore it for as long as I can. I know the second I move a muscle, I'm going to find out just how badly I ache. It's probably a full three minutes into the alarm before I give in, wincing when I reach for the phone.

If I ever wanted to know what it felt like to get rammed by a two-hundred and twenty pound college football player, then my curiosity is now satisfied. My body throbs, from my arms all the way down to my shins. It's not just the bruises my stepbrother inflicted on me, but my muscles are also sore from tensing up during the attack.

And Tristian might mince words, but that's exactly what it was.

An attack.

When I get a glimpse of myself in the mirror, it looks even worse. Mottled, purple marks litter my arms and torso. I've always been quick to bruise. When we were closer, when I was young, my mom used to call me her little flower petal. She'd say that I needed to be treated with care, or I'd wilt away. I used to think it was sweet at the time, like an endearment. But now, looking back, I can clearly hear the disappointment it was tinged with. Maybe, somehow, she knew she'd be releasing something so fragile into a harsh world filled with cruel men. Maybe she was hoping I'd be stronger.

Despite how badly I look, a small, sickened part of me has to give Killian credit. All of my exposed parts—my neck, face, and hands—are perfectly undamaged.

It doesn't really flood back until I'm in the shower, standing mechanically below the hot spray. I press my fingertips into a deep blue patch of skin below my hip and remember the sound of his breath—quick and eager. I squeeze my eyes shut against the memory, but it's no use. The sight of his cock pushing between my breasts. The way his hands looked, squeezing them, thumbs flicking over my nipples in hard, aggressive sweeps. The sight of his knuckles flexing, the letters on his fingers stark against my flesh, '*KILL*'. The way he watched, eyes just as rapt as they were angry. The way he tasted, salty and hot and slick.

Most vividly, I remember never being so turned on in my life.

Shamefully, I find myself rearranging it all. Removing the hatred. The aggression. The anger. The hurt. I imagine what it might have been like, without all the badness making it seem so tainted. Would I have liked it more? Would I have gone down willingly, taken him into my mouth and moaned around his hard shaft? Would I have asked him—like I asked Tristian—to touch me back, to make me feel good?

I know the answer.

I'm not sure I like it.

It doesn't matter, anyway. Like I'd said to him; it could never be anything else. Hurting is what Killian does, and he did it with zero remorse. He blamed me for his inadequacies with the other girls, like I was somehow to blame for him not being able to get it up. Like it's my fault he obviously needs to inflict pain to get to the pleasure. I suppose we both learned one thing last night. Those Barbies didn't turn him on. *I* did.

And I know he hates that more than anything.

I turn off the faucet and dry off, getting another view of my battered body in the bathroom mirror. Charlene's advice was clearly shit. Idly, I wonder if she'd meant it to happen like that—if she fed me bad advice hoping they'd hurt me back. She's not loyal to me—she's still loyal to them. I shouldn't be surprised. Charlene's played this game longer than I have. She knows the moves, the strategy. I'm just bumbling around, *reacting*.

But what Tristian said last night might hold more water.

You get more flies with honey than vinegar.

If I'm going to stay here—and I *need* to stay here—then I'm going to have to get my head in this game. I'm going to have to find out what to hold back, and what to give freely. I need to make myself useful—no, irreplaceable—and simply showing up on time and handing out some beers isn't going to cut it. I need to play the part, just for a while. I need to figure out how to be a good Lady to all of them.

Even to Killian, I realize, already dreading it.

With that in mind, I dress for the day, making sure to cover up the bruises while still looking sexy. I choose a soft, pale-pink sweater, dark skinny jeans, and knee-high boots with a heel. I pull my hair up into a sleek ponytail and apply a light coat of makeup. Enough to look good for them, but not too much to attract attention from other men on campus. I'm walking more than one tightrope here, but after last night, I need to learn how to balance better.

Martin smiles at me as I descend the steps, nodding in approval. I look around and realize the house is a mess. It's obvious poor Ms. Crane will have her work cut out for her today, and I resolve to offer her my help—not because it's my job, but just because it's the right thing to do.

With a steeling breath, I decide to stop by the dining room on the way to the kitchen. "Good morning," I greet the boys. "I see everyone survived the party."

Even looking at him makes my heart bang wildly against my chest, but I force myself to do it, to face him. Killian looks the same as always, blank-faced and impassive. He's staring at his phone, fork in hand, and he doesn't even bother acknowledging me. Part of me wishes he would—that he'd look and see how much he hurt me, and that he'd be surprised. That he'd feel sorry. A bigger part of me knows he never would. If anything, seeing my bruises would probably just make him happy. This indifference—pretending like last night never even happened—is most likely the best I could have hoped for.

Business as usual.

I do notice that he doesn't seem as tense and hostile. He chews slowly, and the constant knot that's been in the back of his jaw has magically eased.

I shift my attention to Rath. Unlike Killian, he at least gives me a small nod, even if it's curt and served with a cutting glance. He's obviously still holding his grudge. I can't afford to have both of them hating me like this. I'm going to need to repair our rift soon. I just need to figure out how.

Tristian, on the other hand, greets me like a queen, smiling warmly. "Good morning, Sweet Cherry. You're looking fine today."

"Thank you." Although my entire body aches, I force a smile in return. "I wanted to see if you needed anything before I get my breakfast."

Tristian makes a pensive sound, pushing his chair out a bit. "Just one thing," he replies, patting his knee.

It takes every ounce of willpower to not roll my eyes as I wedge myself between him and the table, perching on his lap. The thing that's getting difficult about Tristian is that his touches aren't mean like Killian's, and they're not greedy, like Rath's.

Tristian gently gathers the hair from my neck, sweeping it back. I know the instant his lips touch my neck exactly what he's kissing—the hickey he'd left there last night. My face heats at the memory of asking him, of taking my pleasure from him, of the way he kissed me so sweetly, his fingers working their magic on me.

He hums into the mark he left. "You smell nice. Too bad these two pissy fuckers are too stubborn to enjoy it. Oh well." Arm winding around my middle, he whispers into my ear, "More for me."

I see the way Rath's looking at him over my shoulder, eyes flashing sharply. It'd be silly to call it jealousy. But it's…something.

Something he wants.

Play the game, I remind myself, turning my head to catch his mouth in a kiss. Tristian makes a surprised sound—surprised, but pleased—and cradles my jaw as he licks into my mouth. His other arm pulls me closer, fingers dipping under the bottom of my sweater to tease the bruised skin there. The sound I make—a soft, quiet moan—is only half fake. The other half is pretty sure I feel Tristian thickening against my bottom.

Bang.

I jolt at the sound, whipping my head around to find Killian glaring at us.

His hand is still fisted on the table from where it must have landed. "We're trying to *eat*," he sneers, and that knot in the back of his jaw makes another appearance.

Swallowing, I grab Tristian's glass. "Why don't I get you some more juice?"

When I stand, his hand possessively runs down my backside. There's no reason he couldn't pour the drink himself, but every interaction is to make a point. I understand that now.

"Anything else?" I ask. Tristian watches me closely, like he's considering asking for a lap dance but he shakes his head. I wait for a beat to see if the other two will give me a little—something—but they don't. Tristian gives me a small, encouraging smile, and I head to the kitchen to get my own plate.

The ride to school isn't any more pleasant. They fall into a conversation about the game the next day, excluding me from the discussion. Once again, I'm accosted by their strong scents—particularly Killian's. Every morning I wake up to that overpowering scent of soap and body wash. It's everywhere. He's everywhere. I close my eyes and see him naked on top of me. I taste him in my mouth, I feel his elbows and knees pinning me down. Somehow, I manage not to have a panic attack. I just take deep breaths and focus out the window, reminding myself that I knew what I was doing when I took this job.

"I won't be done until late. Coach is focused on the game and doesn't want us out partying, so he's making us watch film," Killian says. He tosses the keys to Tristian, who catches them mid-air. "You guys can drive home."

He spins and walks off. Rath watches him go and then shifts his eyes to me, then to Tristian. "Did I miss something? He *never* lets you drive his truck."

"Guess he's having a good day," Tristian says, shrugging.

"Or he had a good night." Rath pushes his hair behind his ear. "Did he turn that threesome into a foursome or something?" His eyes turn to me, assessing, suspicious.

"Yeah, maybe so." Tristian says, perfectly aloof.

I focus on Killian's back as he walks across campus. One of his teammates falls in step next to him and they bump fists. It's weird to think about, this guy—this unutterably enormous, evil presence in my life—doing everyday things like having friends, going to class, and taking orders from a coach, like he's a normal human instead of…

Well.

Killian.

Rath scoffs. "Whatever. I've got a packed schedule. I've booked the studio for practice this afternoon, but I have to meet with a professor right before." His expression darkens. "I'll just meet you at home."

He walks off and once he's out of earshot, I turn to Tristian. "You didn't tell him about what happened with me and Killian last night?"

He looks at me in that innately condescending way of his. "We're close, Story, but we're not a bunch of twelve-year-old girls. I don't tell them everything."

I wrinkle my nose. "Well, he's pissed at me anyway. We had this dumb argument yesterday. I need to find a way to make it up to him."

"Rath is an artist. He's all about the ego. All you have to do is stroke it," he grins, throwing me a sleazy wink, "nice and slow."

I pull a face, "I'm starting to think your answer for everything is sex."

"You think it's not?" he asks incredulously.

"Maybe Rath just needs something else," I say vaguely, fully aware that I'm not supposed to reveal that he's struggling with his reading. "Something personal."

"Believe what you want, Sweet Cherry, but I'm going with sex. Look at Killian," he says, gesturing to where he's disappeared. "He certainly seems a lot better after busting a nut, don't you think?"

I give him a hard look. "I'm glad one of us does, because I look—and feel—like a fucking punching bag today."

Tristian frowns. "We should get you some pain reliever. Maybe some time in the hot tub, relax those muscles a bit."

I shake my head, changing the subject, "Plus, I'm pretty sure that was about power, not sex."

"They go hand in hand." He gives me a sideways glance as we start across campus. His hand slides behind my back, looping around my waist. "Part of your problem is that you haven't embraced your sex appeal. Once you get rid of that pesky virginity, I think you'll see things differently."

What Tristian doesn't understand is that my virginity is the only thing that gives me power with the men in my life. They're just too dumb to know it, too led around by their dicks to see things clearly.

"Do you want me to bring you lunch today?" I ask, coming to a stop at the front steps of the business school. "Or, I could—um, meet you somewhere?"

His eyebrow raises. "Look at you—taking initiative."

Shrugging, I offer, "I figured after last night, I owe you."

It's a lie.

Obviously, I will owe him. I'm not stupid. The Lords aren't here to give me pleasure, and Tristian got me off without—as he so eloquently put it—'busting a nut'. That means I have a debt.

But mostly, I'm thinking of last night and how good it felt to have one perfect moment of bliss without it being all wrapped up in how someone's hurting me in the process. It's dangerous, I know. That's something I could get lost in—addicted to—if I'm not careful.

"Not today," he says.

"No?"

"I have a lunch date," he explains, blue eyes sparkling. "Or rather, two."

Before I can ask who he's meeting, he cups my neck and bends, kissing me softly, slowly, tongue teasing mine. Despite knowing this is all part of his game, it still makes my knees feel weak. "Don't worry," he says, pulling away with a smirk. "I'll figure out a way for you to repay me soon."

He releases me and jogs up the stairs. My lips tingle from the kiss and my heart pounds, the twist of confusion building inside. The tightrope I'm walking is narrow and thin. I know that Tristian's goal is to fuck with my head, that he's probably just lulling me into trusting him. My new goal is to convince them that I'm compliant. That I'm theirs. That they have me under their control.

But sometimes, when he kisses me like that, it makes it hard to know who's controlling whom.

DIMITRI
RATHBONE

17
MANIPULATION

"Dammit," I mutter, slamming my hands down on the keys. The sound that comes from the piano vibrates in my chest. Thankfully, the room is soundproofed and I'm alone. No one else can hear that I've fucked up for the third time in a row. I know the song by heart, every keystroke, every note, but I keep losing focus in the middle.

I take a deep breath and position my fingers, preparing myself for another run through. Annoyingly, my concentration is instantly destroyed by the buzz of my phone. It's the GPS, followed by a text notification.

Story arrived at Meyers Hall.

Story left Meyers Hall.

Story: Checking in.

Story arrived at the Union.

Story, Story, Story.

Growling, I toss the phone aside. "Christ on a goddamn cracker, you two."

I'm not like the other guys. I don't have to control every moment of our Lady's life. Unlike Tristian, who will blow a fucking gasket if she's a minute late, or Killian, who'll freak out if she so much as looks at another guy. Story is a grown ass woman. I'm not here to babysit her. For me, she's more like a box of wonders. Open her up and see all the surprises inside. She may be crying on the outside, but she's hot and fiery beneath the surface. She's like one of those songs that starts off easy and simple, then as each instrument joins in and the notes all join together, you realize you're dealing with something much more complex. Something deeper.

That's Story Austin. At least, to me.

Something definitely went down between her and Killian last night, although no one is talking about it. I saw the guarded look in her eye this morning, the slight limp in her walk. Killian was in far too good a mood. Only one thing makes him happy: inflicting pain.

And something went down between her and Tristian last night, too. According to our shared spreadsheet, that fucker is up thirty five points after last night.

Thirty-fucking-five!

It took me my entire morning to figure out how he could have gained so many points in a single night. It wasn't until their little make-out session in the dining room that it hit me. She had to have wanted it.

No.

She had to have *asked* for it.

And what a smug little fuck he's been about it, too. Throwing her winks, leading her around with his hand on her back like she's his goddamn girlfriend or something. Of course she'd buckle for Tristian first. The guy's all flash, not to mention as smooth a talker as they come. Fucking kills me, but I've got to hand it to him. Aside from that little speed bump in high school with Genevieve, Tristian's got massive game.

What the others do isn't my concern, though. I need to focus on my positioning in the game—my own points. But I also need to pass this make-up exam on Monday. I'd managed to finagle a bit of a do-over on the oral I flunked, but now I have to figure out how to make it by. I've put some calls in, so now I'm sitting here trying to get lost in the music, ignoring the problem. The truth

Quickly losing my patience, I snap, "Spit it out."

She flinches, but recovers quickly. "How did your meeting go? The professor? That was about the exam, wasn't it? Because I was thinking, if you need it—I'm not saying you do—but if you did, I could still…you know. Help."

Before I can answer—not that I'm planning to—the door opens again. Jesus Christ, can't a guy just get some goddamn practice time?

"The room's taken!" I say, glaring around Story's shoulder. My glare turns harder when I realize who it is. *Great.* I stand, rigidly eying the group coming down the aisle. "Do you mind? Some of us are here because we actually have talent."

Perez co-conducts and plays first chair in the jazz band—fucking badly, I might add—and is also the head of a serpent otherwise known as Kappa Nu Theta. The Counts. The Lords' oldest rival. "Not a very gracious way to treat someone who's here to do you a favor." I don't like the way his eyes move to Story, descending to her tits, her legs. "Look at this, boys. The Lady's looking better since the last time we saw her. She's almost cute now. Still very little sex appeal, though."

I step in front of her. "Beats jerking off into whatever sad cum dumpster you've recruited this year." Already tired of this game, I add, "And you can't do me a favor, because you don't have anything I want."

Their Countess glares hotly at me, and despite the insult, I have to admit she's pretty stacked. Dark brown skin. Striking eyes. Legs for days. "This sad cum dumpster begs to differ."

Another Count—Lars, pre-law—hushes her. "Rules, baby."

She sullenly steps back and Perez starts, "In case you haven't noticed, Countess Sutton is in quite the position. TA for Professor Lockwood? Ring any bells?" At my blank stare, he laughs. "Yeah, you know what I'm talking about."

Motherfucker.

Lars jumps in, "You're flunking."

Another Count adds, "And you're panicking."

is that the game is distraction enough. I want to win. I want to prove once and for all that flash and smooth-talking isn't all that. It's temporary. Flimsy.

I take one last look at the GPS, watching the little dot as it bobs across campus, before putting it aside.

Taking a deep breath, I prepare to start again, flexing my fingers and then posing them over the keys. When I'm ready, I dive in with enthusiasm, hitting every note and gaining momentum as the crescendo builds throughout the song. Here, I'm perfect. Flawless. Superior. There's no second-guessing, no thinking, just feeling the music, doing what I'm good at. It's no wonder I'd rather be doing this than facing the inevitability of another failed grade, on another dumb fucking exam, in another goddamn class that's all about *reading*.

I'm lost in the rhythm, the complexities of the music, when movement at the back of the room catches my attention. I see her slim figure and dark hair. My fingers stumble, two keys missed. I stop abruptly, slamming down my fingers, shouting, "Fuck!"

She freezes in the doorway, her hand reaching out like she's about to make a run for it.

"Don't you dare touch that fucking door." I raise my eyebrow. "Do you understand me?"

"Yes." Her voice is barely a whisper.

"What the hell are you doing here? Why are you interrupting me?"

"I was just—" She fidgets with the cup in her hand, looking like the same scared little mouse. "I brought you some coffee? I noticed that you sometimes get one after classes, so…" She shuffles down the aisles toward me, pausing for a long moment before slowly, carefully placing the cup atop the piano.

I stare at her. "Do you usually put hot beverages on instruments that cost six fucking figures?"

Her eyes widen and she darts for the cup, snatching it away. "Sorry." She cradles it close to her chest, casting the piano dubious glances. "I was just wondering…"

Lars pulls a faux-sympathetic face. "Those feelers you were putting out earlier? They weren't very subtle. You're the only person in his class in danger of failing, which is actually pretty funny, if you think about it."

The other guy laughs. "Lockwood's class is a classic coast. You'd basically have to put effort into failing."

Of course Lockwood's class is meant for coasting. There's a fucking reason I paid the Dean to get me into it. If these assholes know I'm failing—if they know I'm looking for ways to pass—then they probably suspect all my past exams are fraudulent, too. I'm good at what I do. I've covered my tracks. I pay well. But if someone starts sniffing too far beneath the surface, it won't take much to see the truth.

I'm massively, unbelievably, infuriatingly *fucked*.

"Yeah, exactly." Perez says, reading my expression. "It's this whole thing where you get kicked out of Forsyth, which is fun, in theory. But that's not how we want to win." Perez runs a hand down the back of her curly hair, doing his best impression of a cartoon villain petting his cat. "So our Countess might be able to help you with your little problem. You know, pull some strings."

I smirk, hiding the panic inside. "And what's attached to them?"

"Not what," Lars says. "But *who*."

I hear Story's sharp intake of breath, but before she can speak, I answer, "She's ours."

Perez snorts. "Don't flatter yourself. We're not the Barons. We don't want LDZ's sloppy seconds."

"The maid," Lars says, eyes rolling. "We want the old battleaxe."

My eyebrows climb my forehead. "You want Ms. Crane?" Now, it's my turn to laugh, and that's exactly what I do. Loudly. When I manage to get my amusement under control, I shrug. "Let me think about it."

"What?! You can't do that!"

I turn to Story, glaring daggers with my eyes. "Keep your goddamn mouth shut."

All she does is lower her voice to a whisper, those big eyes of hers shining back at me. "You'd rather hand Ms. Crane over to these—" she gives them a look, face squishing up into an incensed grimace, "—these *jerks*, than just accept some help from me? You really hate me that much?"

I answer easily. "Yes."

Her face falls. "I thought yesterday…you said she was a part of you. That she was family. You defended her. You protected her!"

God, that fucking look in her eyes, so full of horror and sadness, like someone just stabbed a puppy in front of her or something. What Story doesn't understand is that the Counts wouldn't last a week with Ms. Crane. She'd string all of them up by their balls and be back at our place before we had a chance to miss her scathing insults. Not that we'd ever give Ms. Crane away. That old bat is more valuable than anything in this entire fucking town. And, much like Sweet Cherry, she's *ours*.

But goddamn, let a guy bluff for a minute.

Rolling my eyes, I turn back to Perez. "Sorry, Cunts. Looks like the Lady's attached to her. Can't imagine why."

His eyes narrow. "You realize what you're turning down, right? This is a limited time offer."

I pick up my bag, closing the lid of the piano. "Like I said before. You don't have anything I want."

Lars shakes his head, sizing me up. "Bad move, Rathbone. If the Countess can pass you, she can fail you, too."

"She won't need to," Perez argues, looking pissy. "Someone as dumb as you? You'll fail all on your own, won't you, Rathbone? Either that, or get sloppy trying to cheat. Better believe, we'll be there when you do. I wonder who gets your maid when you've all been kicked out? I wonder," he says, looking at Story, "who gets your Lady."

I don't even hear much beyond the second sentence. My vision goes red, narrowing in on Perez's face. I drop my bag, clenching my fists as I stalk forward. "What did you just fucking call me?"

He almost looks surprised at the shove, even though he recovers instantly, bumping his chest into mine, mouth stretched into an aggressive smirk. "I called you dumb, Rathbone. Too dumb to know what that means? Let me find some synonyms for you. Stupid. Simple. Idiot."

I've given them too much. Rationally, I understand that. But all I can hear is my third grade teacher, standing over my shoulder, saying that I'm too stupid to read. Too dumb to understand words. That I'll end up nothing—no one—because the letters just wouldn't arrange themselves into something understandable for me. I can still hear him. *Dumb. Stupid. Idiot.*

The punch I throw never lands.

Instead, I've got a Count holding me back, while another wrestles Perez from me. "Come on, fellas," Lars grunts, pushing us apart. "None of us can afford to do this here. Eye in the sky, remember?" He nods to the camera in the corner, finally getting Perez loose.

I wrench myself away from them, stepping back into Story, whose eyes are wide and alarmed, one armed extended like she's going to reach for me. She snatches it back at the look in my eyes.

Perez gives a seething laugh, straightening his shirt. "You know how you can tell a Lord from the rest of us?" he asks the Countess. "It's the ineffectual tantrums. Always a dead giveaway."

They leave first, filing out of the practice room, looking far less disappointed than I'd particularly fucking like.

"Son of a bitch," I growl, yanking my bag from the floor. Already halfway across the room before I notice Story hasn't moved a muscle, I snap, "Well? Did your legs stop working?"

She spasms into motion, scampering toward me. It isn't until we're almost at the parking lot that she finally speaks. "We can handle this," she says, sounding out of breath as she struggles to keep pace with me. "We can work on it every day. It won't be so bad, if you just—"

I mostly ignore her as I search the lot, passing trucks and sensible sedans. "Whatever."

"It'll be fine!" she insists. "I actually used to tutor back in high school, before—well, before we moved here. You'll let me do it, right? You'll let me help you?"

Truck. Truck. SUV. Sedan. Distractedly, I answer, "Uh huh."

I hear her footsteps falter before quickening. "Good! It'll be better like this anyway. They can't prove you cheated if you don't cheat. And then you won't have to send Ms. Crane away."

Bingo.

Perez drives a sports car. It's this absurd, flashy fucking red thing with chrome rims that only has the vaguest impression of a trunk. I reach into my pocket as Story babbles fucking on and on.

"Why would they want Ms. Crane, anyway? Not that I don't like her. She's…uh, maybe 'nice' isn't the word. But she's something. Kind? Well, useful. But as far as housekeeping goes, it seems like—" She suddenly squeals, "Oh my god!"

Perez's tire makes a low hiss as I wiggle the knife back and forth, deepening the slash.

Story's hiss is a lot louder. "*What are you doing*?!"

I give her an impassive look. "Eating dinner."

"You're—what?" Her expression is such a perfect mix of distress and confusion that it almost makes me crack a smile.

And then I remember that word.

Stupid.

I yank the knife from the tire and head to another one, punching the blade into the rubber. "I'm eating dinner, Sweet Cherry. At home. With you, and the others. There's no one to say otherwise. Catch my drift?"

Her face screws up in anxiety. "You're slashing those tires!"

Christ, this girl. "Yes, I'm slashing his tires. Why don't you say that a little louder? I haven't been kicked out of this fucking place just yet."

She wrings her hands, eyes jumping around the lot. "That's, like…illegal!"

I pull the blade from the tire, rounding the car to get another. "What, like you've never done anything illegal before?"

She goes to argue, but her mouth snaps shut at the look I give her. Yeah. Underage titty photo distribution isn't exactly kosher, Miss Cherry. "What if you get caught?" she worries.

"How would I get caught," I say, slashing the knife down, "when I'm at home, eating with you?"

She rolls her eyes heavenward, like she's asking for the strength. "Oh my god, just hurry!"

I'm on my way to the fourth tire when I pause, that discussion from before finally sinking in through the fog of me wanting to bury my foot into Perez's face. "You're going to tutor me," I realize.

Right. I agreed to that, for some reason.

She looks at me, and then at the last tire, eyes pinging tensely back and forth. "Come on, we should go!"

Instead, I mull it over, and it's like pulling a tooth. God, how unbearable is that going to be? The Lady, teaching her Lord. Above me. Better than me. Telling me what to do, how to do it. The whole concept is perverse.

Or…

Maybe it's the perfect opportunity.

The plan unraveling in my head is buoying enough that I even manage not to glare when I flip the knife around, offering it to her. "You do this one."

She freezes, eyes bugging out. "No way!"

"I won't let you get caught," I say. "He insulted you, remember? Don't you want to get back at him?"

She clutches her bag to her chest, looking scandalized. "I don't even know him!"

Rolling my eyes, I try, "Fine, whatever. Then imagine its Killer's car." She looks at the tire, expression morphing into something tense and pensive. Ah. I've got you. "He did something to you last night, right? Imagine it's his tire. Better yet, imagine it's him. Come on, it's cathartic."

It also means she won't squeal.

She looks back and forth between the tire and the blade, shifting uncomfortably. "I don't know..."

"Do it, and we can leave," I reason. "The longer we stand here, the better the chances are we get busted."

She bites into her lip, practically vibrating, before finally grabbing the hilt of the knife. I'm expecting to have to coach her through it, but whatever Killian did last night must have been pretty brutal.

She lifts her fist in the air and brings it down in a hard, angry stab, embedding the blade into the tire. It gives a slow hiss that quickens when she pulls it out, only to drive it back in again, and oh...

Oh, *fuck*.

The look on her face is pure art. There's this tendon in her neck that's suddenly taut and twitching. Her face is red, but not in the way I'm used to. Not shy or embarrassed. This is something far more bitter. Stronger. She stabs the knife into the tire again and again, face set, eyes hard as she watches, almost like she's fascinated.

Holy shit, Killer better watch his back.

Before she just completely shreds the goddamn thing, I grab her wrist, stopping the next slash. "Easy there. I think you killed it good and dead."

She blinks, looking between me and the deflated tire, chest heaving. "Oh. Oops." After a beat, "Can we run now?"

I give her a smirk, pocketing my knife and offering her my hand. "Ms. Crane would be proud."

18

VULNERABLE

Friday is my early day, no late classes. I'm surprised when Tristian meets me outside the building, leaned back against the wall of the open corridor, sunglasses perched on his nose. Other people cast him glances as they pass, and I know it's not just because of his reputation or standing as a Lord. Standing like this, his blond hair shining in the sunlight, throwing the sharp edges of his jaw into relief, he looks like the picture of perfection.

And he's looking right at me. "Lady."

Swallowing, I ask, "Did your lunch get cancelled?" This morning, he'd told me once again that he had a lunch date. With the same two people. It'd been a relief at the time—two whole days without any very public lunchtime 'encounters'—but now I'm mostly curious.

Is there some loophole in the contract around my fidelity clause for him, too?

"Hm," he hums, peering at me over his sunglasses. "That's how you greet your Lord?"

I look around, noticing all the eyes on us. It's different when I'm alone. People see my wrist cuff and seem to give me a wide berth. But when one of the Lords is near, it's like everyone is watching, waiting for a show.

Tristian, I know, likes giving them one.

With that in mind, I go to him, reluctantly winding my arms around his neck. He doesn't dip down to meet me, making me strain up on my toes to press our mouths together. For his part, the kiss is unhurried, one of his hands coming down to land on my backside, giving it a squeeze that probably looks fond. His tongue is hot and lazy against mine, but no less insistent.

"Good girl," he says, giving my ass a light smack, keeping me close. I can feel him against my hip, half-hard and growing harder the more he crushes me to him. "To answer your question, I thought about it and figured you could join us for lunch today."

Us. I don't know who that involves, and I don't ask. It's pointless. I'm beginning to sink into the acceptance that I'll know what comes when they want me to know. It's a sobering realization to have, knowing that this is shaping me, molding me into someone compliant and quiet.

But it's for the best.

The look Tristian gives me as he leads me away—sharp and satisfied—tells me he notices.

I spend most of the drive preparing myself, heavy with dread and restless nerves. He said he had lunch plans with two other people. It's not the guys. I have to assume it's with two women. Maybe this is the loophole he's found in my fidelity clause; bringing me along, making me participate in some way. Maybe he's even going to want me to do something with them. That's completely outside my wheelhouse. Then again, maybe he just wants people to watch the two of us. That's definitely in Tristian's wheelhouse. This could be it. This might be my last drive as a virgin.

Part of me is relieved. All of the Lords are awful in their own way, but if I had to choose…

I could do worse than Tristian.

I'm so anxious that I don't even realize it when the truck stops, let alone the building we're parked in front of.

His hand rests on my thigh, thumb caressing the skin just below my skirt. "You ready?"

"Listen, Tristian," I start, hands wringing in my lap.

I have this whole speech about how I'll be good for him—I'll go along with it, I'll be *compliant* in the agreement we've made—but that I'm begging him for kindness and understanding and—

One glance at the building makes my words die in my throat. "Wait. What are we doing here?"

The sign says we're at the Forsyth Hills Elementary School.

He reaches into the back seat, pulling out a bag from a local deli. "It's Friday. I have a standing lunch date with the two most important women in my life." He gives me that slow, loaded grin of his. "I figured now that you're my Lady, you all should meet."

I seriously have no idea what he's talking about, but at least some of the fear has dissipated. I don't think he'd push me into a threesome at the elementary school.

He rings the bell and the buzzer sounds, unlocking the security door. He then strolls over to the check-in desk and grins at the older woman. "Here I am." *In all my glory*, goes unspoken, but I can still hear it in the tenor of his voice.

She grins broadly when she sees him. "Tristian! Twice in one week, my goodness. The girls will be beside themselves!"

"One lunch just wasn't enough this week, what can I say?" He scribbles his name on the sign-in sheet and adds mine underneath. "How are you today?"

"TGIF, and all that." She hands him two stickers, and he peels off the back of one, placing mine on my chest. It's a circle that sunnily declares, "Forsyth Hills Visitor."

He gestures down the hall and I follow, still trying to get my bearings. Something about seeing Tristian in the narrow hallway feels surreal. He looks so much bigger here, impossibly more imposing. Up ahead, I see the double doors with the word 'cafeteria' on a sign overhead. The strangeness of it all stops me in my tracks.

I grab Tristian by the arm. "Before we walk in there, care to tell me what's going on?"

He pauses, cradling the bag under his arm, and if I didn't know better, I'd almost say the way his face scrunches is *bashful*. "I have ten-year-old twin sisters. Every week, I come and eat lunch with them."

"Oh," I respond, blinking in surprise. The photographs from his room pops in my head. I thought they were of the same girl, but maybe not. Plus, the bad pottery. The knick-knacks. Signs that Tristian cares about someone enough to disregard appearances. "That's, um, really nice of you, I guess." And totally out of character.

He sighs, pulling me aside, hand cradling my elbow. "Look, Rath and Killer are my boys. They know me better than anyone ever could or will. They've both got fucked-up families they have no problem leaving behind, so that's how they see me. Family." There's something in his eyes as he looks toward the doors, solemn yet at ease. This is important. This is a vulnerability. "But these two girls are my real family. However screwed up my parents are, I won't let these two get caught in it. They've been through a lot for ten-year-olds, and they think I'm Captain fucking America. They think I'm a protector." He gives me an intense look, face hardening. "And it's going to stay that way."

I swallow, trying to imagine anyone counting on Tristian to protect them from anything. "Then why bring me here?" I'm probably the last person who can sing his praises.

His mouth forms a tight, tense line. "I don't usually bring in outsiders when I'm dealing with my family. Not even the guys. But we're having a bit of an issue, and I thought maybe you could help."

"Help?"

His jaw clenches. "Some little bitch in their class is causing them grief. Picking on them, bullying them. And I thought…" He makes a vague gesture at my body. "Well, you know."

"That I would know how to handle being bullied?" I give a dark laugh, hardly able to believe it. "You brought your glorified sexual assault victim to teach your little sisters about…what? Standing up to assholes? Bringing them down? Shaking it off?" I shake my head. "Jesus, Tristian, Shakespeare couldn't write this kind of irony."

I can tell it's not lost on him, because Tristian has this way about him. It's this thing where he might have a great poker face, but at the end of the day, he's a complete fucking brat. "I would deal with it myself, but a twenty-year-old man going savage on a fifth grader isn't going to fly." At my incredulous expression, his eyes narrow. "Don't give me that shit. You owe me, Cherry. I figured you'd prefer me cashing in like this. I know you're taking a child development class. Don't you want to go into social work or something? This is more up your alley than mine." He looks away, grimacing. "And, it may make me look weak, but it kills me, not being able to help them." I can tell he means it too. It's in the way he won't meet my gaze after the confession, the subtle tinge of pink on his cheeks.

Tristian is willing to look weak—willing to show me this truly significant vulnerability—if it means protecting his sisters.

I've done my best to keep my heart out of this. It's enough that I've handed over my body to these guys, and honestly, a big chunk of my brain. But my heart? That's mine and I've tucked it away behind barbed-wire and padlocks and solid, metal walls. But hearing Tristian say that about his sisters? Well, fuck. He just knocked a chink in all of my defenses. Even if I wanted to say no to him, I couldn't say no to two little girls going through something difficult.

"Fine," I assent. "I'll do what I can."

Naturally, he doesn't say thank you. He just opens the door, revealing the roar of children's voices and laughter. The cafeteria is busy and large, but he seems to pick out his sisters instantly, waving across the room. My eyes follow, landing on two identical blonde girls excitedly waving back.

He smiles, a grin lighting up his face. It's such a strange thing to see. Where his gaze is usually chilly and hard, here it becomes warm and bright. Just before we reach the table, he leans down, whispering, "If you make me look bad here, you'll be repaying your debt another way, got it?"

Bristling, I offer a curt, "Got it."

"Tristian!" they squeal, hopping up and giving him a hug. He places the bag on the table and draws them both into a tight embrace. He hugs them like he means it, planting two loud, exaggerated kisses on their cheeks.

"How are the two prettiest girls in the world?"

They both giggle, even though their curious gazes jump to me. When he releases them, he looks up at me and says, "Girls, this is Story. Story, meet Izzy and Lizzy. The two prettiest girls in the world."

The Mercer genes sure are something. Izzy and Lizzy really are just as pretty as their brother. Their blonde hair is just as fine, styled flawlessly into matching French-braided pigtails, blue eyes staring guilelessly back at me. They're the picture of little girlhood—a palette of pinks and cuteness, right down to the little purple flowers embroidered on their cardigans.

"Hi," I say, a smile coming easy. "It's nice to meet you."

Izzy seems shy, reaching up to pat at the bag Tristian's carrying. "What did you bring for lunch?"

Lizzy adds, "We're hungry."

Tristian takes a seat and the three of us follow suit. "Sandwiches on whole wheat. Tuna, avocado, and pickled onions for Izzy. Lots of good omega-3 in here," he tells her, giving it a tap. "Apple, turkey, and Brussels sprouts for Liz, because you need more vitamin C." He takes a third sandwich out, placing it in front of me. "A bahn mi burger for Story. Plenty of nutrients for energy."

I look at the burger dubiously. "Energy?"

He casually explains, "You start the day with a lot of energy, but you crash at noon." He says this like it's the most obvious thing in the world. "I can tell because you get cold and stop fidgeting with everything." He nods to where I'm

hugging my middle, even though I'm wearing a sweater. "You could avoid it if you skipped the coffee and got more B-12 with your breakfast. I'm working you up to it, don't worry."

I stare at him, warring between how creeped out I am, but also…weirdly touched by the thoughtfulness. This whole arrangement is starting to get to me. "Thanks."

I think.

I might not be fidgeting, but Lizzy sure is. She's holding a plastic fork, spinning it around and around. "Is she your girlfriend?"

Tristian freezes, eyes jumping from her to me. "Is she my…?" He clearly didn't see such a question arising, mouth working around a series of aborted replies. "Well, you see…"

I decide to save him. "I'm a friend, who's also a girl. So, I guess I kind of am." Lizzy frowns thoughtfully, but she seems to accept it, nodding along.

Izzy thankfully changes the subject. "Why's your name Story?" she asks.

I laugh, caught off guard by the question. "It's kind of lame, actually. My grandma always used to call my mom her sweet little poem." I don't tell them that this eventually became more of a sarcastic insult than anything. My mom and grandmother never got along. I only ever met her once, and I was too young to remember much except the tension. "So when my mom got pregnant with me, she said she decided to write a story because poems were too short for happy endings." As soon as the words are out of my mouth, I want to stuff them back. Pretty bleak message for two sunny ten-year-old girls.

They watch me pensively, absorbing this. "Some poems have happy endings," Izzy argues.

I nod back. "Yes, some do. My mom eventually got one of her very own." It's still awkward to think about, what with Daniel and Killian, so I hastily divert the topic, unwrapping my sandwich. "What about you? What do Izzy and Lizzy stand for? Izzica and Lizzifer?"

They both laugh, which is a relief. "Isabel and Elisabeth!" they say in such a perfect unison that it's impressive.

Izzy lays out her sandwich, not even scrunching her nose at it. If someone had presented me with either of those monstrosities as a kid, I would have thrown a fit. "Did kids ever make fun of your name because it's not like others'?"

"Sometimes," I say, surprised at the question. "But I liked that it was unique. It didn't bother me."

Lizzy points across the room to a girl with dark, curly hair. "It bothers me. Shelly Baker calls me Lizard Face."

Ah, this must be the bully.

I take a moment to size this Shelly Baker up. She's surrounded by a whole group of other girls, plus a couple boys, laughing and poking at something on her lunch tray. It's hard to hold much against a ten-year-old from this vantage, but Izzy and Lizzy seem sweet—a stark contrast to their brother.

Her voice lowers, eyebrows scrunched moodily together. "She also makes fun of Izzy for being in the slow group for math." It's glaringly obvious that this is the true source of Lizzy's scorn for Shelly Baker. She can handle being made fun of for her name, but someone poking fun at her sister's learning abilities? That's a step too far.

The Mercers are very protective of one another.

Frowning, my mind strays to Rath. Dimitri. I'd spent all of last night thinking up ways of teaching him to read without making it into a whole thing. Defensive is too gentle a word for him when it comes to his reading skills. "That's really mean. Math is hard, and plus, I'm sure Izzy is better than a lot of people at something else."

Izzy immediately straightens. "I'm good at softball!"

Lizzy agrees, "Way better than Shelly."

"See?" I smile at them, picking at my burger, trying to think of something profound to impart. "The thing about bullies is that their main currency is your reaction to them. If you don't give them a reaction, they'll stop bothering." At their skeptical expressions, I nod. "Yeah, that seems pretty hopeless, I know.

Because bullies are also really good at knowing what gets a reaction."

"Are girls mean to you?" Izzy asks, seeming to warm up to the discussion some.

"Sometimes, yes." I think of Charlene, and how to explain to these two innocent children that girls are easy compared to the boys. "In my experience, when a girl is being mean, it means she sees me as competition. It's one of the worst compliments you can get."

"What did you do?" Izzy says, staring up at me with sad eyes.

I take a furtive look at Tristian, who's watching me back. I'm not sure what he's thinking, but I know that this is a complete sham. Because I don't do anything except make it worse for myself. I roll over. I comply. "I can tell you how I wish I handled it," I offer, a white heat blazing in my chest. "I wish I'd fought back harder, even when it felt pointless. I should have not cared so much, and then maybe I wouldn't have been so easily hurt. I should have asked for help, from someone worth trusting. Someone who cared." It's an idle, wistful thing. No one's ever cared. Not about me. But maybe about these girls.

"You should have a big brother," Izzy decides, nodding with such confidence that it almost makes me laugh despite the black thing gripping my heart. "Big brothers make everything better."

I give her a smile that feels rusty and wrong, thinking of the tapestry of bruises currently occupying my skin. "Not all big brothers are as good as Tristian is to the two of you. You're very lucky to have each other."

Tristian suddenly clears his throat, voice deceptively cheery. "Hey, we better get started on these sandwiches." I watch as the three of them begin eating, but my appetite is long gone, snuffed out by the lump that's settled in my throat. Tristian must notice that I'm not eating, because he nudges me with his elbow, voice low. "Eat what you can."

Mechanically, I raise the burger, determined to only bite off as much as I can chew.

For once.

Lunch is nice after that. Even if I'm still lost in a fog of self-pity, I still do my best to put on a good face for Tristian. But the truth is that I'm worried for them—for the life they'll have in this world. Right now, they're so sweet and open, laughing with their big brother about some mobile game they're all competing in.

It's interesting to watch Tristian with them, so absent of the cold artifice I'm used to. He's relaxed here, just as confident but far less intimidating. He's attentive, asking about their homework, interrogating them on the state of their bedrooms at home, making sure they eat enough. I can see little girls all around the lunch room, eying him dreamily, and I know that plenty of them are jealous of the sisters for having such a cool, handsome, and sweet brother.

It doesn't begin really smarting until the ride back to town.

"What will you do later?" I wonder, breaking an abnormally solemn silence. He hasn't said more than three words to me since we left.

"Later?" he asks, sparing me the barest glance as he accelerates through a yellow light.

"Later," I flatly confirm, staring out at the scenery. "When some asshole forces one of them to their knees and shoves his—"

The truck jolts sharply. "Don't you fucking dare finish that sentence!" he barks, knuckles white around the steering wheel. "They are *ten*!"

I shrug, unaffected. "They won't be forever. Those things happen."

"Not all girls are like you," he answers, giving me a hard look. Quieter, he adds, "Not all guys are like me."

"More than you think," I argue. "Ask any woman. Most have had some kind of experience at some point in their lives. Hell, I'm only nineteen and I've yet to meet a guy who didn't..." I trail off, snapping back to reality enough to feel uncomfortable.

"That'll never happen," he says, jaw tight. "I'll fucking kill every guy on Earth if I have to."

I look at him, searching his face, but he mostly just seems annoyed. I want to know, though. I want to know how he reconciles protecting one girl as he's hurting another. I want to know what he tells himself to make it feel okay.

He flips on the stereo, drowning me out, before I can gather enough courage to ask.

THE BROWNSTONE IS SCRUBBED clean when we arrive home.

It's taken all of yesterday and the whole morning to get it back together following the party. The stink of beer and cigarettes have vanished under a fresh lemony scent. Everything is back in its place.

I enter the kitchen and find Ms. Crane sliding a casserole dish into the oven.

"Is there anything I can do?" I ask, eager to take my mind off the lunch. "I know I wasn't much help yesterday with the party clean-up."

Ms. Crane flaps a hand at me. "I'm used to picking up after pigs, girl. These little frat fucks are barely house-trained. But I have a secret to making it all go by quick." She reaches into the pocket of her knitted cardigan, revealing the top of a flask. "My little helper."

Blinking, I awkwardly offer, "Well, the house looks great. You'd never know there were a hundred people in here." I wrap my hand around my backpack strap. "If you don't need anything, I'll head upstairs. I'm supposed to help Rath with something tonight."

"No," she says, halting me. "That maggot-faced asshole's jacket came back from the cleaners today. Take it to his room. Sick of hearing him bitch and moan about the way I hang his stuff. These three are fussier than a house of toddlers."

"Of course," I say, happy to do anything productive and helpful that doesn't involve opening all my wounds in front of the person who helped give them. It doesn't hurt that I know Killian isn't home right now. I carry the jacket, still wrapped in the cleaner bag, up the stairs to the second floor.

I stop in front of Killian's door and gently knock, my pulse ratcheting up at the possibility of him answering. I'm paranoid enough to consider that Ms. Crane is in on the mind games the boys are playing, and not too foolish to barge in on him unannounced. The ache in my arms and legs is warning enough. As I suspect, though, he's truly not home. It doesn't stop my heart from pounding as I carry the jacket over to the closet and, after deciphering his system, hang it carefully inside. As always, I'm struck by the tidiness of everything, all wrapped up in the way his warm, distinct scent lingers in the air.

I close the closet door and face the room, eyes landing on the mahogany desk against the far wall. The surface is neat—books stacked by size, notebooks and folders organized upright. It's the exact opposite of his rage-fueled assault on me the night before. His laptop sits in the middle, screen open, but dark. Blood rushes to my ears as I walk over to it and run my shaky fingers over the keys. The screen lights up and the prompt appears for his password. Curiosity gets the best of me and I start typing.

Lords

Incorrect password.

ForsythU

Incorrect password.

After trying every variation of the school mascot I can think of, I swallow and add in four letters.

Story.

Nope.

Glancing around the room, I suddenly spot the framed photo on the dresser. What was his mother's name? Debra? Darla. I type the name in and press return.

Password accepted.

My heart lurches when it opens, spreading out the icons on his desktop. Like everything else in his room, it's painstakingly organized.

Curiously, I go to his folders and skim the files, but the only thing I find are papers and essays written for school. Scrolling down further I find a folder labeled 'LDZ' and click the mouse. There are dozens of other files, including one named 'Lady Applicants', and 'GAME POINTS'. Game?

Ugh.

Football crap.

There's another folder, though, interesting only because of the name—'South Side'—and the fact that clicking on it gives yet another password prompt.

Before I can start trying more passwords, footsteps echo on the staircase.

"Shit," I mutter, exiting out of the tabs. I make sure the laptop is exactly the way I found it before darting to the door. Peering into the hallway, I hear the quick pace of footfalls continue up to the third floor. I step out of the room, shut the door, and don't breathe again until I'm behind the locked door of my room across the hall.

I catch my reflection in the mirror across the room and push up my sweater sleeve to look at the bruise on my arm. It's twice as bad as it was that morning. If Killian caught me snooping around his room…I shiver and pull down my sweater. I don't even want to think about the consequences.

Later, I run into Rath and Tristian on the stairs. They're both out of breath, shirtless, clad in only loose gym shorts and sneakers. Their chests are shiny with sweat and I pause a moment on the landing, caught off guard by the sight of their muscles, all slick and bulging. Rath has a dark line of hair below his belly button, disappearing behind the obscenely low-hanging shorts, and my gazes fixes to it like glue.

I jerk my eyes away, face heating. "Uh, hi."

Tristian's rolling a basketball in his hands, a thread of amusement in his voice. "My, my. Look at her blush."

Rath pitches forward to speak near my ear. "My eyes are up here, Story."

I clutch the books I'm holding to my stomach. "You guys coming or going?" I'd told Rath we'd spend the night working on his upcoming oral exam, but maybe he's bailing. Part of me hopes that's the case.

"Just finishing up." Tristian says. "Rath owed me a rematch."

"Too bad you lost again," Rath says, grabbing the ball from Tristian and deftly spinning it on top of one finger. "You'd think you'd learn."

"You would," Tristian says, "but I'm a notorious glutton for punishment."

He winks at me and continues up the stairs. Dimitri starts after him, but I grab his sweaty arm, holding him back. "Are we still meeting tonight?"

He brushes the hair out of his eyes. "I don't see the point."

"You said you'd let me try."

He looks like he wants to argue, but instead bites out a terse, "Fine. But I need to shower first. You can wait in my room."

It's not exactly the stamp of approval, but I don't let that discourage me. If he can't pass this test—or worse, if he tries to find some way to cheat—the Counts might hold it over him, and then poor Ms. Crane might become forfeit. Even without what I'd overheard the afternoon of the party, I've been watching enough to know that Ms. Crane is treated well. Sure, the guys throw barbs at her, but no harsher than the ones she lobs back. Tristian's are as close as they ever get to having actual heat behind them, and even he'd jumped to her defense.

Something tells me the Counts won't treat her as kindly.

I follow him, carrying the books up to his room. It's still as messy as it was the last time I was here, books and instruments, record albums and music sheets piled haphazardly. The black piano is the focal point of the room.

"I'm just going to lay out a few things, okay?"

"Whatever," he says, walking into the bathroom. The door shuts and a moment later the shower turns on. I shift anxiously before the leather sofa, flipping through the books apprehensively.

I don't know what level he's at, which is a problem. Most of the books and flash cards for teaching this stuff are aimed at children. Rath would blow a damn gasket.

We just need to get him through his oral exam, is all. After that, we can take things into a more legitimate direction. He'd told me he read the material—through an audiobook—so at least he knows it. He needs to write the report, and then present it thoroughly, if not verbatim.

As I'm pondering Rath's skills of memorization, the shower turns off. When the door to the bathroom opens, the room fills with a warm, steamy, soapy scent. Dimitri walks into the room, drying his hair with a towel, shirtless once again, clad in only black skinny jeans that hang low on his narrow hips.

Jesus. He's beautiful, with those dark eyes and angular features, damp hair falling unkempt around his face. His lips are a dark pink, adorned with those two shiny rings, and in this moment, when he's not looking at me like I'm a toy to play with, body loose and relaxed, I really can understand why women are attracted to him.

He hangs the towel on a hook on the back of the bathroom door and grabs a black T-shirt out of his dresser. "So," he says with no enthusiasm, "how do you want to do this?"

"Well," I say. "I brought up some snacks. Would you like something?" I've noticed he has a bit of a sweet tooth—the heaps of syrup he pours on his pancakes and the bottles of soda he carries around all day are a good tell. Ms. Crane keeps the pantry well stocked with baked goods and treats, so I'd thought to bring some up with me, along with some drinks.

He glances at the spread I've arranged by the couch, face blank. "A beer, I guess."

I grab one and pop off the top. Handing it to him, I begin, "Okay, let's get started."

He takes a seat on the bed across from me, tipping the bottle back as I talk. The lighting in here is different from any of the other bedrooms. Rath keeps it low and moody, a lamp illuminating him into a dark silhouette against the chaos of his room.

I'm about ten minutes into explaining a carefully crafted set of mnemonic devices when he suddenly speaks.

"Where'd you get that sweater?" His eyes have drifted somewhere below my neck, glued there, heavy-lidded.

I pause, confused. "It was just in my closet." When he takes a slow drag from his bottle of beer, I slowly begin again, "So you can memorize the paper we write, which isn't exactly learning, but it'll get you—"

"Are you wearing a bra?"

Startled, I take a glance down at my chest. "Of course not." That's against the rules. He knows that. I fan the book open in my lap, struggling to keep myself from squirming. "Like I was saying…" As I talk, he gulps down the rest of his beer, Adam's apple bobbing as it goes down, and this time his eyes are *definitely* fixed to my boobs.

He interrupts me again. "I should put on some music."

Fed up, I fling the book aside. "What you should be doing is paying attention! Come on, Dimitri, I know you can memorize this stuff if you just got your head in the game."

That makes his gaze harden. "Get my head in the game. Right." Scoffing, he leans over to grab another beer. "This is all your fault."

"What?" I glare at him. "How is any of this my fault?!"

He rakes a hand through his hair, expression flustered. "You come in here in that sweater," he explains, gesturing to me. "You expect me to pay attention when your nipples are pointing at me?"

Blushing, I stutter, "That's not my fault!"

"Yes, it is." He rises to his feet, pacing, shoulders tense. "You put that stupid fucking fidelity clause into the contract, and now I can't get any goddamn action! I haven't had a good nut in forever. I'm a *guy*, Story. My brain doesn't have any clarity until I've come my brains out nice and proper."

I gawk at him, at a complete loss for words. "Uh…"

"Killian has his pregame rituals, and god knows Tristian probably busts one every time he looks in the mirror. But me? I'm going fucking crazy here. I'm round-the-goddamn-clock horny."

Stiltedly, I wonder, "Can't you just…uh, *you know*?" He looks almost fascinated by the lewd gesture I make, stopping in his tracks to watch my fist go up and down.

"What do you think I was doing in the shower?" He rolls his eyes. "It's not the same."

"Oh." I deflate, watching him warily.

"But you're right," he adds, dropping back onto the bed, flopped out on his back. He scrubs his palms over his face. "I have to pass this fucking exam. I just can't focus."

Fiddling with the corner of the page, I can't help but bitterly wonder, "Why haven't you made me do something about it yet?" It hasn't escaped my attention. Killian and Tristian have taken their pleasure from me.

But not Rath.

He drags his hands down his face, turning to curl a lip at me. "*Please.* Tristian and Killian might get off on all that, but I can get it from girls who actually want me. Why bother struggling with someone who doesn't?" Shifting his gaze to the ceiling, he adds in a quieter voice, "It's not the same if they don't want it. It's basically like jacking off, except maybe even worse."

I watch him, taken off guard by the confession. That's nothing like the Rath I remember from back in high school—the guy who definitely got off on me doing something I very vocally didn't want to do.

Maybe he's changed, though. Maybe being in college with new girls—more girls—has shifted his views on it. Maybe Dimitri Rathbone is actually turning into someone who's not a monster.

Suddenly, he perks, levering himself to his elbows. "Maybe we could have Martin alter the contract. Only once or twice. Just so I can concentrate when I need it. Like how Killer has his pregame fucks, right?"

I stare at him owlishly, pointedly *not* saying how terribly that ritual had gone for Killian—and me—last time. "I…I don't know?"

He groans, head lolling back. "Shit, they'd never go for it. This whole thing is useless." I frown as I watch the defeated curve of his shoulders. "Maybe everyone is right. Maybe I'm just fucking stupid."

"You aren't stupid, Dimitri!" I insist, feeling suddenly angry at the word. "You play music like nothing I've ever heard. You're beyond good, you're practically a genius! You just need to get through this." But I can see that I'm not getting through. He's already given up, attention clearly fixed on the piano across the room, fingers fidgeting as if he could feel the keys beneath them.

"What if I," swallowing, I try to work up the courage to voice the thought running through my head, "*wanted* to."

His forehead puckers, eyes finally meeting mine. "Wanted to what?"

I know my face must be beet red. It feels so hot that I press my palms to my cheeks, stomach flip-flopping. Shakily, I offer, "I could…suck you."

He raises a slow eyebrow. "You expect me to believe you *want* to give me head?"

Grimacing, I look away, embarrassed. In many ways, he's right. The thought of doing it makes me vaguely queasy.

It also makes me feel hotter.

It makes me curious.

"I don't…*not* want to. I want to do what it takes for you to pass this class," I try, ignoring the way he's looking at me—baffled and slightly annoyed. "If you're this distracted all the time, we'll never get anything accomplished."

"I don't know…"

"You're cute and everything," I continue, talking myself into it, "and who knows. If I'm not being forced to do it, maybe it'll be different," I wager, sounding far more even than I feel. "Maybe I'll like it."

Or, at the very least, not have nightmares about it three years later.

From my periphery, I think I see him smirk, but when I turn, his face is just as passive as ever. "You want to suck my dick?"

Mashing my lips together, I give a single, uncertain nod.

He doesn't look impressed. "Begrudging nods aren't really the vibe my dick's going for. Thanks anyway."

I pull in a burning lungful of air, willing my stomach to settle at the words I offer. "Dimitri. I want to…suck you off." At his blank stare, I elaborate, "I don't know if I'll be very good at it, so you might have to be patient. But I mean it. I do. Want to. Especially if you think it will help and technically, I am the one that put that no-sex rule in the contract."

He drags his bottom lip between his teeth, eyes straying back down to my chest. "Alright," he decides. "If you want to."

Still, it takes my body a moment to actually get into motion, standing from the sofa and rounding to the foot of the bed where he's sitting, legs spread, dark eyes tracking me from beneath his long lashes.

I rub my palms nervously against one another before slowly sinking to my knees. His thighs are warm and firm beneath my hands when I reach for him, uncertain, but he doesn't move. Doesn't blink. Doesn't tell me to do something else.

So I run my palms up and down, stomach fluttering with nerves when I feel his muscles flex beneath the denim. I can't tell if it's impatience or just his way of moving with me, into me. Taking my time, I ascend to his waist, avoiding the obvious bulge right in front of me, and reach for the button of his jeans, popping them open. The sound of his zipper lowering sends a strange, sudden spark of electricity into the pit of my belly. I watch the teeth separate, curious about this flash of…anticipation? Is that what this is?

It isn't until I reach forward to hook my fingers into the waistband, giving the jeans a tug, that Dimitri responds at all, lifting his hips for me.

I lean back on my heels at the sight of him uncovered, finally following that line of dark hair beneath his bellybutton to the thick, hard cock waiting below. My exhale escapes in a slow gust, and for a moment, I have no idea what to do.

Then it twitches.

I reach out slowly, hesitantly, running my fingertips along the taut, velvety shaft. Dimitri makes a noise, deep in his chest, gritty and low. That's what gives me the courage to finally wrap my palm around it, just like I'd done for Tristian the other day.

"That's it," he sighs, reaching forward to touch my hair. His fingers weave into it, curling around to the back of my head, and I make the mistake of meeting his gaze, seeing how dark they've gotten, how soft his lips look. My own mouth parts on an exhale and his eyes dart down to watch. "You want to suck me, baby?"

I edge closer, giving a small nod. "Yes."

His hand tightens in my hair, pushing me toward where it's fisted in my hand. "Go on. Give it a little taste."

Closing my eyes, I open my mouth and give the tip an experimental lick. It's not much. I barely even have the taste of him on my tongue. But his thigh tenses beneath my hand. Waiting. I go a step further, pushing the tip all the way in my mouth. I give it a slow, gentle suck before releasing him, testing the waters. His hips buck slightly, chasing the warmth of my lips. I can tell from the growing weight of his hand on my head that he's getting impatient and eager, so I finally sink my mouth onto him.

"Fuck yeah," he sighs, fingers kneading my head. I can feel the heat of his eyes on me, watching, voice low and rough. "That's it, baby, make it nice and wet. You like that?" I hum in response and he groans, hips surging up. "You can take it deeper. Come on, I know you can."

I'm still reeling from the taste of him, salt and flesh, and the shape of him against my tongue. I want to explore it, find out what it is about this that's sending a parade of tingles right into my core.

As if reading my mind, he asks in a coarse whisper, "Making you wet, isn't it?" He gives a shaky chuckle, hand pressing me down a little harder. "You're such a squirmy little thing when you're horny. I bet you'd look so good all tied down, wriggling all over the place, so fucking hungry for a dick that you wouldn't even feel embarrassed about the way you look."

His words bring a renewed heat to my face, but they do even more for him. He swells in my mouth, hand pressing harder and harder. I'm no blow job queen. The only one I've ever given was to Tristian that night, but in my sugar baby days I read and watched a lot of videos. I do my best to emulate, using my tongue and lips, sucking and teasing the salty head when his hand lets me rise.

He probably sets the rhythm more than I do, but I'm secretly grateful for it—this gentle instruction, free of violence and spite and greed. The more he does it, the more I want to show that it's working. That I'm good. That I can *be* good, if I just had a little damn kindness about it.

Dimitri seems to understand, giving me praise in low, ragged, bitten-off curses. "Fuck, just like that. Your mouth is so fucking hot. I'm going to fill it up, make you choke on me. You'd like that, wouldn't you? Swallowing my come, tasting me all night."

I know that's what he wants, and I know because of that I'm going to do it—swallow him down. But it's almost like he's asking. It's almost like he cares what I want.

"I'd give you permission," he says, voice sounding more breathless. "And you'll use it, won't you? You'll go to bed tonight and finger yourself thinking of this."

I suck him with vigor, humming along to his filthy sentences, uncaring of the spit dripping down my chin. I know it's coming when he gets bigger, harder, surging in my mouth. I knee forward in anticipation, willing myself not to panic when his hand pushes me down, driving his dick in deep.

He comes with a long, tremulous groan, hand fisted tight into my hair. It's different from that time with Tristian. This time, I can taste him, the heat and the tanginess of his semen. I can appreciate that quiver in his abs as they flex, hips jerking up as his shoulders give a single, hard shudder. I can hear his gasp, and know it's over, know that it's okay to slip away and give a hard gulp, swiping a hand over my mouth. This time, I can see him flopped out on his bed and feel something other than nauseous at the sight of his satisfied expression.

This time, I have a purpose, and I feel less like a toy and more like a Lady.

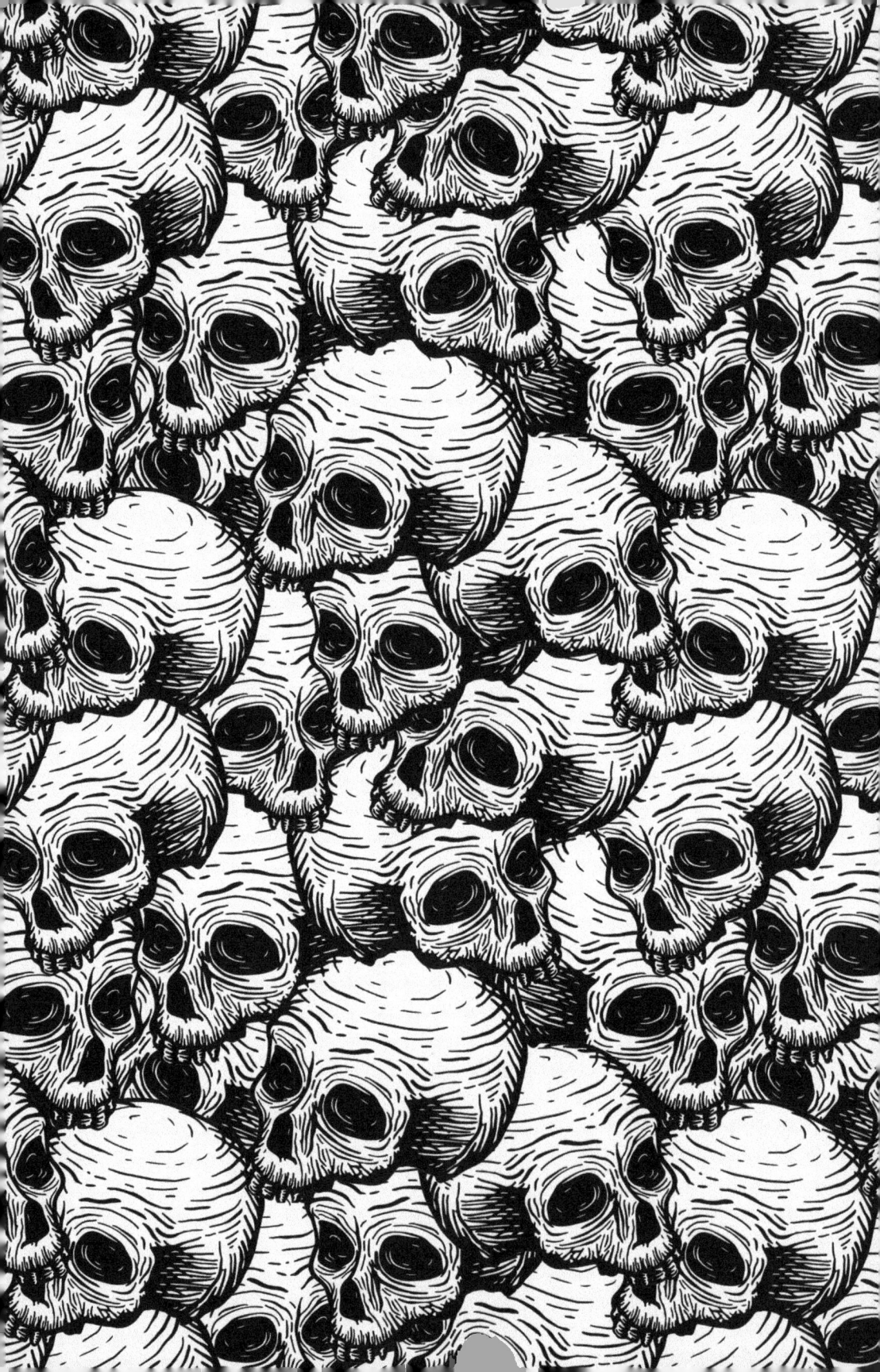

STORY

19

SUSPECTS

I don't know what it is between Dimitri and Tristian the following day, but things are notably antagonistic.

At breakfast, which Killian happens to be absent from on account of game-day matters, they're both sitting at the table—talking about me, I suspect. I can tell, because the instant I enter the room, they both go conspicuously silent.

Dimitri is kicked back casually in his chair, watching me with bright, interested eyes. "Sweet Cherry," he says, eyeing me up and down.

Tristian frowns. "You aren't dressed yet."

Embarrassed, I pull at the sleeves of my sweater. "I wasn't sure what to wear today. For our plans, I mean." It's a Saturday, which means no school. But there is the FU game. People have been talking about it all week. Football is a very big deal at Forsyth.

"We have plenty of time. More than *seventy-four minutes*." Confused about the odd emphasis, I look at him in confusion as Dimitri pats his thigh. "You can sit right here this morning."

"No. She has to eat," Tristian argues, pulling out the chair beside him. "I got you bagels with chia and flax today. Plus, a wheatgrass smoothie." He gestures to what he's prepared for me as if it's a special attraction. Maybe in his own way, it is.

Dimitri gives me a look. "I've got greasy bacon, cheesy hash browns, and chocolate chip pancakes. Your call."

Tristian clucks his tongue. "She doesn't want to eat that garbage. It's all fat and sugar and processed preservative bullshit. Come on, Story. I added some cinnamon to the wheatgrass, so you'll like it this time."

Knowing I definitely won't, I'm paralyzed for a moment, surprised at being given a choice.

I almost think I see Tristian's face fall when I round the table to reluctantly perch on Dimitri's lap.

He laughs. "Look at it this way: more wheatgrass for you. How many sips is that glass? Less than seventy-four?"

I duck my head at Tristian's icy stare. "Sorry." Defensive, I add, "I like bacon." It's going to take a lot more than cinnamon to make that radioactive green goo appetizing.

Dimitri slides his plate closer to me, his other arm winding around my waist. "Don't worry about him," he says, lip grazing the shell of my ear. "If you want to put something in your mouth, then you should be able to."

My face heats at the innuendo, eyes jerking up to catch Tristian's eyes on us, narrowed.

All of breakfast is like that. Dimitri will say something flirtatious and Tristian will look anywhere on a scale of disapproving to outright agitated. I'm not stupid enough to think it's a jealousy thing, but there's clearly some sort of pissing match going on that I'd rather not be involved in.

It's because of this that, when I go upstairs to change, I pick a short denim skirt to wear. Tristian will like it, and he's already called me out on dressing for Dimitri in the past, so he'll see it for the gesture it's meant to be.

After a long, dreadful moment of consideration, I pull Killian's jersey from the rack and slip it on.

Then, I take it off.

Groaning, I put it back on again.

I do this three more times before I finally bite down on my annoyance and follow through. It's more like a dress than a shirt, but I knot it at the waist and slip into some heeled boots, and it's good enough. I nod at myself in the mirror, oddly proud at having dressed for each of them, while also being appropriate for the occasion.

Later, I stand in the foyer and listen to them bicker about who's going to drive. *Definitely* a pissing match. Dimitri might have won the one at breakfast, but this one goes to Tristian, who struts to the garage with a smirk on his face.

I slip into the back seat.

Dimitri does, too.

Tristian adjusts the rearview mirror until he's looking right at us. "What the fuck are you doing." It's said in a carefully even voice, and not pitched as a question.

"You always get shotgun with Killer drives." He rubs a hand over the back of the seat, stretching until it's around my shoulders. "What can I say? I got used to being back here."

If Tristian wants to argue, then he exercises some self-restraint by just pulling in a deep breath and cranking the engine. "Fine."

The whole drive is awkward. Dimitri keeps walking his fingers up my bare thigh, chuckling every time I squirm, and Tristian keeps shooting us cold glances from the front.

It's taken me some time, but I eventually realize there really are perks to being the Lords' Lady. Privileges, outside my primary goal of being safe—of keeping *others* safe—from Ted. There's the gorgeous home, obviously. Plus, having a housekeeper who prepares my meals and keeps my bathroom spotless. But all of that pales when we arrive. The three of us stroll right past the tailgaters outside and enter Mercer Field through a special entry. Right. The stadium is named after Tristian's family. It explains *a lot* about his level of entitlement.

"I thought you'd want to be down in the fray," I say to him as we're ushered by security to what I'm told are special box seats. A plaque by the door shows the name 'Mercer'. Underneath are smaller Greek letters. LDZ.

"It's fun down there," Tristian admits, sweeping his blonde hair back, "but up here we can eat and drink to our hearts' content. And not that shitty junk food they're slinging in concessions, either. I hand-picked the caterer and approved the menu myself." The door to the suite opens and I see that there are already a fair number of people here. I'm struck by the spicy scent of the delicious-looking spread arranged across a long, linen-covered buffet-style table. Tristian's right. It's not shitty stadium food but instead, a gourmet meal.

There's also a fully stocked bar, comfortable seats, and enormous TVs scattered around the room for a better view.

Tristian pulls me close. "More opportunities for privacy, too."

A shiver runs down my spine, but it's not out of fear of Tristian. Well, not completely. Things between us have been a little stilted since the lunch with his sisters. More accurately, since the ride home following the lunch. He didn't take too well to being called out.

I'm just about to play into it a little bit—to pander, to mend whatever needs patched in order to make things run smoothly with our arrangement—when I see *him*.

My blood turns to stinging, sharp ice.

He's across the room, piling his plate with Buffalo wings, and I watch on, horrified as he places one last drumstick on top and licks his fingers.

At first, it's like all the air has been wrung from my lungs, too constricted to take in more. Then, it's like I can't pull in enough, gulping in a hard, shuddering gasp.

"Oh my god!" I whirl around to them, ducking my head to shield my face with my hair. My heartbeat turns to a thick staccato in my ears, drowning everything out.

Tristian immediately lifts up my chin and continues, "Well, if you'd rather not have privacy, I can manage that too. It may be a bit awkward with my mom in the room, though."

Dimitri snorts, but I'm not really listening to either of them. For once, there's someone else in the room that I fear more than the Lords.

Tristian slowly picks up on this, frowning as he ducks down to meet my gaze. "Hey, what's going on?"

Frantically, I shake my head. "Nothing! It's nothing."

"You're shaking," Dimitri says, his fingers grazing mine. He looks up and around the room. "What are you afraid of?"

I glance back over my shoulder at the man. He's moved over to one of the big TVs with a few other men, watching a pregame show. He's not a bad-looking guy. Dark hair with streaks of silver at the temple. Straight but casual posture. Strong, aristocratic features and expensive clothes. I knew he had money—it'd been on his profile.

His Sugar Daddy profile.

"Do you know that guy?" Dimitri's fingers curl around my wrist, tugging. "Story, how do you know Saul Cartwright?"

Saul is not the name I know him by, although it's vaguely familiar. He went by DaddysAlwaysWright on the app, but if I've learned anything about online activities, it's that people hide under many personas. I've considered more than once that DaddysAlwaysWright could even be Ted. That theory shakes me to my core now that I realize he's at the University, standing in the same room. Can this be a coincidence?

Quietly, Dimitri demands, "Cherry, answer the fucking question."

I take a deep breath. "That...guy. He was one of the men on the Sugar Daddy app. I sent him a few pictures and video chatted with him a few times."

The image of him jerking off on the other side of the screen is burned into my memory. His fancy Rolex, jiggling up and down on his wrist, the deep navy of his slacks, opened wide at the zipper, the sounds he made.

"For money," Dimitri says, dropping my wrist. The disgust on his face is clear.

"Or gift cards," I clarify, feeling oddly stung by the rejection, "but yes."

Lip curled, he makes it very obvious how he feels about the whole thing. "That guy's in his fifties. I can't believe you got off on that."

I gape at him, chest swelling in indignation. It's not fair that I should feel ashamed. These two have done far worse things, for far worse reasons. "What makes you think I…" lowering my voice, I hiss, "*got off* on it?!"

It's Tristian who answers, and although his face is schooled into a perfectly passive expression, I can still see the distaste in his eyes. "Why else would you bother? You lived in a fucking mansion as the newest little pampered Payne. Killian does tell us shit, you realize. His dad would have bought you anything you wanted." I'm not sure why he says it like that, all dripping with disdain.

But I know one thing. "You're wrong." So wrong, in fact, that I'm no longer shaking from fear, but anger. "I needed money. Money I couldn't ask Daniel for. Money that I couldn't earn fast enough doing anything else!"

Dimitri still looks doubtful. "Daniel probably wipes his ass with Benjamins. There isn't anything you couldn't ask for."

I take a calming breath before my head explodes, looking around to make sure no one's close enough to overhear my next words. "I was trying to run away."

Tristian smiles indulgently. "Sure. You were trying to run away from a cushy new life of luxury and privilege."

I glare at him so hard that his smile actually disappears. "Yeah, what a great life it was, with a stepbrother who tormented me every fucking day. I don't know why anyone would want to get away from that!" It's not the whole truth, but it's more than enough justification. "I was in a rough spot and I did something stupid, but only because I was desperate. And if living with me for this long hasn't given you even that much insight into my character, then you're both a lot blinder than I thought."

"And what? Now you're scared of him?" Dimitri asks, nodding toward Cartwright. "What's he going to do, take the money back?"

The sad fact of the matter is that my brief time being a sugar baby was the only time I've been able to use my body, my way, for my own gain. It was never something I was proud of, but it did have a way about it. A way of making me feel empowered. Coveted. In charge.

It was all fake. I know that now, seeing Cartwright, knowing that he could be the man who's terrorized me for so long. There were consequences that I couldn't have possibly have expected. Dimitri and Tristian have no idea. But now is definitely not the time to tell them about Ted, if ever.

I deflate, still hiding my face. "Seeing him like this, out here, it's…" Softly, I confess, "It's weird and uncomfortable. What if he tries to talk to me or something?" The 'or something' is intentionally loaded, just not in the way they probably read into it.

Tristian watches me, his blue eyes searching mine, contemplative. I'm not sure what he finds in them, but he seems to come to a decision, putting his drink down on the table. "Well, we can't have that, can we? The good news for you is that Saul Cartwright definitely has more reason to be afraid of you than you do of him."

I frown. "Why do you say that?"

"Because he's the head of Forsyth's Athletic Department. If it got out that he was soliciting sex from a minor," Tristian laughs wickedly, "his whole fucking career would be over. He's the highest paid man on campus, and you've got his balls in a vice, Sweet Cherry."

Smirking, Dimitri adds, "And now, so do we."

That's why I've heard the name before. I just didn't connect the dots. Nothing Tristian just said makes me feel any better. If anything, I could be in more danger. DaddysAlwaysWright—Saul Cartwright—is more powerful than I realized.

"I should go," I say, panic rising once again at the thought of him so close. "Upsetting this party isn't fitting behavior for your Lady."

Tristian gives Dimitri a look before saying, "What isn't fitting is for you not to be here, with us, *your* Lords, supporting another Lord who is about to kick some serious ass on the field. This is my box seat, Story. No one will shame our woman out of here. He's the pervert." His arm loops over my shoulder. "Plus, that dirty old man may need to understand exactly who you belong to now."

"But—" I try, but Tristian heads across the room with an easy, confident swagger. I start after him, trembling in terror at the thought of a confrontation, but Dimitri's hand lands heavy and strong on my shoulder.

"Stand down, Story. He's got this."

My stomach flip flops, sweat prickling at the base of my neck. Everything could blow up in this moment. If Cartwright is really Ted, then he's about to find out everything—where I live, who I'm with, *everything*. I'll need to get back to the house and…what, pack? Leave?

No.

Then I'll not only have a stalker chasing me, but also the three pissed-off Lords I'd made a contract with.

Tristian approaches Saul Cartwright, resting a hand on his shoulder. It's hard to watch, but my eyes are peeled, like watching a car crash. His head tilts forward and he says something quietly in his ear. Everything goes still and silent, and then, a moment later, they're shaking hands like old pals who just finished a business transaction.

Cartwright turns abruptly, heading straight toward the door. I turn as he passes, cringing into the lean wall of Dimitri's body. His hand comes up to cup the back of my head, pressing me closer. I hear the door open, and then shut.

Gently, Dimitri says, "He's gone."

Tristian walks back over, hands in his pockets, smug grin on his face.

"What did you say to him?" I wonder, heart still tripping over itself.

He shrugs. "I made it clear pedophiles aren't welcome in the Mercer suite, and if he didn't want to be exposed and lose his job, he should leave immediately."

Relief floods through me—at least for the moment. I give Tristian a grateful,

"Thank you," but he shakes his head.

"It's not necessary to thank me. You belong to us now. We protect our own. You know that."

The weird thing is, I kind of do. It's what I wanted when I agreed to this position, but I didn't realize then how far that loyalty would extend to me.

"Tristian!" a woman calls, interrupting us. A blonde woman dressed in orange and purple has just entered the room. She's not wearing the tacky stuff you buy down from the vendors outside the stadium. Everything looks very expensive, like she purchased her checkerboard scarf at some fancy Forsyth U boutique for rich ladies. "I wasn't sure if you'd show up."

"Hello, Mother," he says, giving her a hug. Mother? Eager to shake off the tension of encountering Cartwright, I embrace the curiosity about the woman who spawned a demon like Tristian. Did she find the mark of the beast on his forehead at birth? Did she have to cover up cloven hooves? "Just running a little late. You know how it is."

"Partying late this week, I assume." Her gaze shifts past me to Dimitri. "Oh Dimitri, you're looking as handsome as ever. How's the music?"

"Mrs. Mercer," Dimitri greets, pushing his hair out of his eyes. "Everything's going well. My classes are a bit more complicated this year, but I think I had a bit of a breakthrough last night." His lips curve into a grin. Despite our little spat, I find that it's actually quite nice to see him smile, especially knowing that my lesson had something to do with it.

Mrs. Mercer pats him on the shoulder, her gold bangles clicking together. "Pushing through an artistic block is part of the process. I know the program is very challenging. Tristian's father gives generously to the music school every year."

"Mother," Tristian says, placing a hand on my lower back. "I'm sure you remember Killian's stepsister, Story."

She finally settles her gaze on me. "Oh, Story! Yes, I'd heard you were back in town. I figured you might be another one of Tristian's…friends."

Her smile is pleasant but tight, and I can't help but shift uneasily as she assesses my outfit. No one told me we were going to a fancy suite. If they had, I probably would have chosen something a little more dressy and a little less bleacher-friendly. "I've actually invited your mother and Daniel to the box today. I didn't realize you'd be available, or I would have extended an invitation personally, of course."

"Oh really?" I ask, fighting down a wince at the thought of seeing my mom. My mom and Daniel. This box is a certifiable circle of hell. "I haven't had much of a chance to see them since I got back."

"That's right. You spent some time…away, didn't you?"

"Boarding school," I explain, but her tone makes me wonder if she knows about my disappearing act, too. The suspicious way she keeps looking at me makes me uneasy.

"It's about time for kickoff," Tristian says, hand pressing into my lower back. "I'm going to get a drink before the game starts. Anyone want something?"

"Count me in," Dimitri says, heading to the bar.

"Nice to meet you, Mrs. Mercer," I say, ready to make my escape.

"Same, dear." She spins off, scarf fluttering behind her, and joins some other women her age.

When I catch up to the guys at the bar, Tristian shoves a glass in my hand. "Drink this."

"Why?"

"Because you look one step past freaking out."

"Why would I freak out?" I ask in a whisper, inspecting the brown liquid. "Because I almost ran into someone who probably still has naked pictures of me as a teenager? Or because I just got ambushed by your mom, who probably thought I was one of the tacky whores you sleep around with, but then realized I'm just Killian's fucked-up little sister?" I toss the glass back, letting the cool liquor coat my throat in one big swallow. "Or is it the fact my mom and stepfather are coming, and I have no idea how to be your Lady in front of them?"

"Chill out, Sweet Cherry," Dimitri says. "We're not animals. We can behave in polite society."

Maybe they can, but I'm not sure I'm able to. What I do in that house, with these guys…it's something I've had to compartmentalize while I focus on staying safe. But around all these other people, I keep thinking about what Tristian and I have done all over campus, and what I did to Dimitri last night. Can people tell? Do they know?

Mostly they ignore me because the game starts, and everyone is focused on Forsyth U's golden boy, Killian "Killer" Payne. Seeing his broad shoulders and confident stride as he commands the field triggers the memory of what he did to me on the hallway floor. I can feel his hot breath on me, the pain in my arms and legs, his scent, how red his face looked when he grew closer to—

"Story! Oh my goodness, I can't believe you're here, too!" Spinning, I see my mother and Daniel have arrived. I push back all the thoughts and plaster a smile on my face.

"Mom! Hi!" I give her a hug. She's still elegant and thin, although she's cut her hair shorter than I've ever seen it, curling around her ears in a tidy bob. She's dressed in similar clothes as Mrs. Mercer. She's no longer the hard-working single mom that had two jobs just to keep the lights on. She's a fancy real estate magnate's wife, from head to toe. "Tristian invited me."

"What a wonderful surprise." She takes in my jersey, eyes bugging out. "Daniel! Look, Story is wearing Killian's jersey!"

"Well, look at that," Daniel says, grinning. "Never thought I'd see the day."

I tug at the knot, working around the fist in my throat. "Just trying to show my team spirit."

"You look good," Daniel says softly, "like things are going well?"

"They are. Really well." I bob my head reassuringly, even though I want nothing more than to go hide in a closet somewhere.

Mom grabs my hand, gushing, "I'm just so glad to see you! I want to hear everything about college so far. How are your classes?" Her voice lowers. "Have you met any handsome boys?"

"Blair!" Mrs. Mercer calls, diverting her attention. My mother squeals and they hug like two teenagers. A moment later, her interest in my academic and social lives has been overtaken by a discussion about a fundraiser. Thankfully, Daniel seems bored of me too, leaving to find a seat with a good view of the field. The other men clap him on the back, obviously impressed with how his son dominates the field. The distraction is a relief. The last thing I need is her seeming like the doting mother, probing into my life. Even if Ted isn't Cartwright, he's still out there. Watching, waiting.

"Who knew our parents were such close friends?" Tristian says, sidling up to me. The smirk on his face tells me that he definitely knew.

"Yeah, who knew?" I suppose I should have. Tristian and Killian are so close. Why wouldn't they be? "Isn't it a little weird that we're here together?"

He waves it off. "Don't be so high school, Sweet Cherry. No one carries those old grudges into college. Plus, no one could blame us. Who knew little Story Austin would grow up to be such a fox?"

I shy away from his compliments, feeling uncertain and out of place. Everyone else here fits in, but I know I stick out like a sore thumb. Do they all know I'm the Lady? Do they know what a Lady is forced to do? If so, no one mentions it. Maybe this is just how things operate in their world, because I do notice a few other young women in the room. One is sitting next to Mr. Mercer and is acting particularly friendly.

"Who is that?" I ask Dimitri.

His dark eyes take in the blonde. She could've been one of the girls Killian tossed out of his room at the party. "Oh, that's Ruthie Jones. She's Mercer's side-piece."

"Side piece? Here?"

I have so many questions.

He shrugs. "Things operate differently with rich people, you know that.

Mistresses, lovers, sugar babies," his eyebrow lifts, "it's part of the lifestyle."

"But what about his wife?" She's right there!

"I'm sure she'll get back at him by getting railed by her tennis coach tomorrow."

"Jesus."

"Story, we live in a mansion with a housekeeper, personal lawyer, and a sexually indentured servant. You're just now figuring out things operate differently around here?" He gives me an incredulous look and then heads back over to the bar for another drink.

I try to adjust to the new normal of my life. Does my mom know about all of this? Does Daniel? I think back to Killian's threat that he had leverage on my mom. God only knows.

Despite everything, spirits continue to rise as the game proceeds, and then bubbles right over when Forsyth wins. Mr. Mercer has the staff pass around champagne, toasting Killian's leadership. Even after the field and stadium clear, there's no sign of this little party ending. I'm starting to feel a little tipsy from all the drinks and more than once rely on Tristian to keep me standing upright.

"How about you and I go score a touchdown of our own," he whispers in my ear. "You can show me your pom-poms."

I roll my eyes, buzzed enough to feel okay about saying, "You're ridiculous. Don't you think someone would notice if we suddenly went missing?"

"Do you think I care?" I know he doesn't, and when he snakes his hand up under my shirt while my mother—Jesus, and *his* mother—are two feet away, he proves it. "I know you wore this for me," he says, nosing into the space behind my ear.

Before I have a chance to decide if I'm going to fight him off or not, the door opens and Killian enters the room.

Now, it's *definitely* a certifiable circle of hell.

He's cleaned up, wearing an FU sweatshirt and jogging pants. His hair is damp from the shower. Even with my family here, I feel uncomfortable—like

I don't belong. These are his people, not mine, and I know he doesn't want me anywhere around him. He never has. Unfortunately, as he steps into the suite, mine seem to be the first eyes he meets. I shift anxiously under the weight of it, especially when it drops down, taking in the jersey I'm wearing.

Killian stares.

And stares.

And stares.

A moment later, he's swarmed—first by his dad, then the other adults, congratulating him on a good win. Someone presses a beer in his hand while a large, older man claps him on the shoulder. I take the opportunity to escape, but before I can, my mom grabs my arm and pulls me over. In what I have to consider an orchestrated move, Daniel has done the same with Killian.

"I'm so glad to see you two getting along better now," Daniel says once we're in a tight circle. "I know things were rocky for you two back in high school, but a little space and some maturing has probably helped you both."

Killian doesn't answer, but even though he looks at me, it's without the aggression and open hostility I'm used to. Instead, he just looks tired and hard and massively confused.

"I have a great idea," she says, eyes lighting up, "how about the two of you come to dinner tomorrow night?"

"Dinner?" I ask. An image of the four of us, gathered around a table in stiflingly uncomfortable silence comes to mine. And that's a best-case scenario. "At the house? Together?"

Killian rubs the back of his neck. "I actually think I have a—"

"No excuses," Daniel says, holding up his hands. "We finally have our family back in one place. I think it's time to celebrate."

It's a terrible idea, Killian and I, back at home together after all these years. He didn't behave himself then, and he doesn't behave himself now. Just accepting the invitation would be putting myself at risk for personal harm. At least back in the Lords' house, I have Dimitri and Tristian as buffers.

Killian is the greater of three evils.

'No,' is on the tip of my tongue, but my mom is looking at me with such hope. It'd need to be a really good and convincing excuse. Stupidly, I look to Killian for a life raft.

He just stares back at me.

Biting back a sigh that's sure to be full of misery, I say, "Sure. I think that sounds great."

My mom gives me a tight hug around the neck and everyone looks at Killian for his response. He glances at his father, mouth pressed into a tight, unhappy line, and grunts out a curt, "Fine." He turns to me, eyes boring into mine, and adds, "How about I give you a ride tomorrow, Story? We can catch up on the way."

"Perfect," my mother cheers, hands clasped together, unaware that Killian's offer to drive me has nothing to do with generosity. It's just another opportunity for him to torture me.

And there's no way out.

KILLIAN
PAYNE

20
BIG BROTHER REVEALED

"Not so fast," I say, catching up to Story as she makes a beeline toward her room. She and the guys were hanging out in the downstairs living room when I got home, but she bolted as soon as she saw me. We're in the upstairs hall and I can feel the tension rolling off of her, those big eyes of hers darting frantically around, as if searching for an escape route, just in case. It's reasonable. Two days ago, I pinned her to the floor beneath our feet and fucked her tits. But she doesn't need to worry. I'm not here to hurt her.

I just have a question. "Why the hell are you wearing my jersey?"

She ducks her head, her wide eyes taking in the orange shirt, my number emblazoned across the chest. "It was in my closet," she stutters, lifting her chin. "I was trying to be supportive. Isn't that a Lady's job?"

I narrow my eyes at her tone—sulky and a touch insolent. Seeing her up in the suite wearing my jersey…it sent a tremor of warm heat, deep in my lower belly, that still flickers like a burning ember. For a moment there, I'd looked at her in the jersey, my name and number plastered all over her, and thought that maybe…

Maybe she was letting herself be mine.

Just a little.

I should have known it'd be like this—nothing more than a little malicious compliance. "Whatever," I sneer, pretending that I'm not disappointed. "This is about tomorrow—"

"Jesus, my mom," she groans, rolling her eyes. "Don't worry, I don't plan on telling them I'm working here—or for you. There would be way too many questions."

"I know you won't." I level her with a look. "I was going to tell you to be ready by six. I don't want to be there all night."

"Oh," she says, clearly taken off-guard. She rubs her palms on her thighs, gaze jumping to the knob of her door. "Sure, fine. Six, it is."

She shuts her door and I hear the lock turn with a snap. I'm left with her clinging, cloying scent. That, plus one glance down at the floor, floods my mind with images of her down there. Trapped beneath me. Squirming. Begging. She'd been scared, sure. But more than that, she'd been seriously pissed off.

Well, so was I. The girls I'd brought up to my room hadn't done the trick. If anything, they'd made it worse. Sure, they'd bounced on my dick, sucked it, offered up their asses, but none of that worked like it usually did. If I were being honest with myself, I'd admit that it's been a gradual thing. The usual shit's been doing it for me less and less. What happened the night of the party was just a culmination of three years' worth of lousy lays.

My eyes flick to her door and I let the truth pass through my head.

Only one thing gets me hard lately.

This is the same shit that happened in high school. The same thing I told myself over and over again that I wouldn't let happen. When I wake up, I hear her, moving around in her room, doing her hair, dressing. When I eat breakfast, there she is. At school, I see her, walking in the courtyard, roaming the halls. When I get home, she's there. When I eat dinner, she's there. At night, the one time I actually let myself look and want and *have*, she fills my nose with her scent, my eyes with the pale porcelain of her delicate skin, my mind with thoughts of everything I want to do.

She's all I can think about. It feels like I'm fucking choking on her, begging for a single gulp of fresh air, but never able to find it. Everything is Story. The only moment of freedom I've managed to carve out are the minutes I'm on the field, too busy focusing on the game to be obsessed about the way my bruises look peeking out from the hem of her skirt; my mark on her, my claim made flesh.

Now even that's tainted, the sight of her in my jersey already perverting it. I can see it now, being out on the field, thinking of all the people who'd seen her wearing my name, claiming me back.

I'm the guy who always gets what I want. I have money, looks, athletic ability. I don't *have* to kill myself on the football field—I do it because my goal isn't just to just be good, it's to be great. I've accomplished that with a winning record, trophies, and an incredible scholarship that I didn't even need. But it's not all about sports. Academics comes almost as easily and so does being at the top socially. From high school to college, people just fell in line, allowing my social stature to rise. It didn't hurt that I had two loyal, equally impressive best friends. And girls? Girls have always been easy. Always so, so insipidly easy.

Except my stepsister. Story is the one person who gets in the way of my life being exactly the way I want it. I shouldn't need to have her. I've got everything going for me. Story Austin is *nothing.* So why can't I stop thinking about the way she smells? The way her shiny fucking hair sways when she walks? The cut of her hips when she rolls over in bed? The way my fingertips look, digging into her skin? Her tight, fuckable tits?

Why can't I be around her without being consumed by it all?

The rest of the team is partying right now, while I'm at home obsessing over our Lady. I have no choice. The last thing I need is to have to turn down more girls. The other night was a loophole in the contract—my pregame ritual. Otherwise, I'm not allowed to be with any other women, which I'm starting to think was a really stupid deal to make. Especially since popping Story's cherry relies on who wins the game. All of this is just one giant cockblock designed to make me obsess over her harder. I'm horny all the goddamn time now. I've got girls, I'm pumped up on adrenaline, yet my dick wants one thing. *One.*

This is exactly the frame of mind that's going to get me into trouble. All I need is to go out to some bar and take all this energy out on the wrong thing—the wrong person.

I go into my room and change, pulling on loose shorts and an FU T-shirt. I should be worn out after the game, but I'm more keyed up than ever. I open my laptop, intent on finding some porn—the one thing that does seem to work for me lately—but instead see a message pop up about the weekly points tally.

Shit. The points.

I open the spreadsheet and do a double-take.

No fucking way.

The guys are both relaxed when I storm downstairs, and why shouldn't they be? "How in the hell," I growl, snatching Rath's tumbler of whiskey right out of his hands, "are you scoring so goddamn high?!"

Rath looks momentarily pissed that I'd taken his drink, but it's gone in a flash, replaced with something smug. "By having so much game that she's begging for it. Sucks to be the two of you."

"I'm seven points behind. I could dust your ass in a single lunch." Tristian rolls his eyes, but adds in a begrudging tone, "That said, the tutoring mindfuck was genius. You and I," he points to me, "are going to have to up our game."

"How?" I ask again, distantly surprised that this glass isn't shattering in my grip. "How the fuck do you get so many points? I spend ten minutes with her and I want to put my fist through a wall, but you expect me to believe the two of you—"

Rath holds up a hand, eyebrows climbing his forehead. "Are you doubting us?"

"Every point can be backed up," Tristian agrees, sipping from his own tumbler. "I watched Rath's video myself. She *asked* to suck his dick. She swallowed. She didn't run away after." He's ticking off point modifiers on his fingers. "Look, I know you don't think much of the long game, but Story isn't like you think, Killer. The path of least resistance works with her. She's, like... just a normal girl."

Rath leans forward to pry his glass back. "She's putty, dude. The punishments don't pay off, but you know what does? Being *nice*." He chuckles at this, like he's tickled fucking pink at the idea. "Tristian bought her one of those paper flowers after the game. You know, the ones they sell to fundraise? You should have seen the look on her face."

"She was blushing and tripping all over herself," Tristian explains. "It doesn't even take much."

"Prince tactics," I sneer, but Tristian shakes his head.

"Not at all. You see, you're so fucking terrible to her that she latches onto the smallest gesture of kindness like Velcro. So hey, I guess here's to you." He raises his glass toward me before tipping it back.

"This is fucking bullshit," I seethe, planting my feet to stop myself from pacing around like an irate tiger. "Kindness? Niceness? Since when do you fuckers play the game like that?"

"Since I'm going to be breaking in that pussy with my fat cock in a few months." Rath laughs, grabbing his crotch. "Sorry, bro. All's fair."

Tristian must sense that I'm about to blow because he puts his glass down, lacing his fingers together. "Killian. *Killer*. You need to chill out. Story does what she's told. She's a good Lady. You just have to give her something to work with."

I burst, "Like fucking *what*?!"

He raises a palm, like he's giving me something. "Like a compliment. A gift. A reward for being good. Positive reinforcement. Be nice to her for five fucking minutes. You'll see what we mean. The Princes are pussies, but there's some merit there."

Rath adds, "Might help if you at least tried to kiss her."

"Why would I want to kiss her?" I give them a disgusted look, even though the thought of her mouth is already making my cock stir. "And anyway, she doesn't want anything 'nice' from me, and even if she did, why should I? She's the bane of my fucking existence. Every day I don't barge into that room and strangle her ass is enough of a gift."

Tristian shakes his head, lounging back in his chair. "Fine. Do it your way. Keep upsetting her and making her feel horrible, and we'll be there to rack up the points. Your move."

I swear I can still hear them laughing when I leave, climbing the stairs. What fucking jokes. Be nice. Gifts. Rewards. Positive reinforcement.

I bet she wouldn't think they were so nice if she realized they're treating her like a dog.

Stopping outside her door, I've decided I've waited long enough. It's been a long day and I'm pissed off, imagining her asking Rath for it, on her knees for him, swallowing him down. I wonder if she liked it. She didn't—not when it was Tristian. But Rath's had time to get into her head. Maybe she was into it.

The thought makes my fist curl around the key, and a moment later, I'm slipping through the door. The lights are off and she has a fan going on the dresser, pointed at her bed. She's always been a pretty deep sleeper, but I know—I remember—that she wakes up if it gets too hot. I'd put the fan in the closet before she moved in, knowing she'd find it and use it. How's that for fucking nice.

I creep inside, closing the door quietly behind me. The room is dark, but I can make out her body in the bed. Each time I come in here, I get a little braver—going from sitting on the couch to inching closer to the bed. Tonight, I stand over her, inhaling her sweet scent, and look down at her sleeping body. It takes my eyes a moment to acclimate but when they do, every single nerve in my body fires off in shocked awareness.

She's still wearing my jersey.

For the briefest moment, I wonder if she knows I'm coming in here—if she wanted me to find her like this, all splayed out in her bed, swimming in this shirt. *My* shirt. It's basically a goddamn invitation. One I can't refuse.

Silently, I suck in a breath and reach for the blanket covering her lower body. I pull the cover down, slowly, revealing the soft flesh of her thighs and her smooth calves. From here, I can just barely make out the fading bruises. Maybe it's sick, but it gets to me almost as much as the jersey, knowing that I've pressed myself into her flesh. That she's wearing me. Being owned by me.

She's not wearing shorts under my jersey and my fingers itch to lift it up and see what she has on underneath. Something lacy? Nothing? My cock twitches, growing harder. If only I could crawl in next to her.

No. That's too far, too soon.

I've had the fantasy forever—ever since I crept into her room all those years ago. It was before I'd found her with my dad, back when I still thought she was meant for me—mine.

I was seventeen, and after realizing she was a complete chicken for horror movies, I wanted to scare the fuck out of her. But when I got to her room, my body had other plans. Spontaneous boners were something I was totally used to; in the shower, at breakfast, in math class, sometimes even at dinner. But seeing Story all vulnerable in that bed, no fucking clue that I was in there or what I could do to her…it was a whole new level. My mind started to churn, thinking of the things I could do, the pain and humiliation I could inflict—but one wouldn't get out of my head.

I wanted to crawl in the bed and explore her body, run my cock between her thighs. I didn't care that she was sleeping. That made it better. I didn't want her to know how she made me feel.

Night after night, I'd go in her room and fantasize about it, all the different ways it could go. In most of them, she'd never wake up. I'd just fuck her senseless and go. But sometimes there were other fantasies. Ones where she wakes up and cries out in fear, begging me to stop. Or the one where her body instantly arches back into me and she moans in satisfaction, so turned on by my cock that she doesn't even care. Whatever way, I crept into her room, and jerked off to whatever conjured-up sex fantasy I had, night after night.

Or I did, until she ran away.

I've just run my hand down my length, feeling the familiar stirrings, when she rolls over and faces me. I freeze. I'm so close to the bed—closer than I've ever gotten—close enough to reach out and touch her. Her eyes are still shut, but her lips part, expelling a soft, gentle sigh. A flash of her licking the tip of my cock comes to mind, forcing me to stifle a groan. My eyes dart from her lips to the curves of breasts, down to where I know a flat, smooth belly is hiding beneath my jersey. If that wasn't enough to get my dick *completely* hard, her hips shift against the mattress and her hand presses between her legs.

I stop breathing.

In all my nights of watching Story, she's never touched herself. As far as I know, she's never had a sex dream or anything close. A few nightmares maybe, where she jolts up and looks around the room like she's searching for a monster, but this is different. There's no urgency, no fear, just her slow, squirming restlessness against the sheets. The way I'd always imagined.

There's no fucking way I'm leaving now.

I take a step back until my calves hit the couch and I sit, pulling my cock out of my pants. I can still see her, hear her, as she slowly bucks against her hand. It's a sleepy movement, lacking in finesse. This is something mindless and primal, meant to be private. All of her squirming makes the jersey ride up, finally revealing what's beneath.

A lacy pair of pink panties.

I stroke my length, thumbing the tip and gliding back down, putting pressure on my balls. It's so much more intense though, watching her like this. I don't have to work nearly as hard. I follow the rhythm of her short breaths, the sound of her rustled shifting against the sheets. I don't know if it's just the sight of Story pleasuring herself or if it's the scent of her in the air, but it doesn't take long to lead myself to the edge, cock growing so hard that it throbs painfully against my restrained pace. My jaw falls slack and I stare at her face, transfixed. I've fantasized more than once about feeding my spunk to her. Sometimes, back then, I used to smear a little on her lips and imagine her licking it off later. I used to watch at the table during breakfast, knowing that she'd taken it in, even unknowingly, and I'd spend the whole day half-hard and impatient for bedtime.

I came even closer to achieving it a couple of nights ago when I sprayed her chest. My balls tighten at the memory and I close my eyes, trying to remember every detail about it. The burn inside is so good, it feels so right, and the wispy little moan coming from the bed only makes it sharper and more acute. It draws my eyes back open and I look at her.

Her big, sleepy eyes are staring back.

Fuckfuckfuck

I freeze, heart pounding, balls aching, orgasm tickling at the edges of my awareness. I wait for the freak-out, the terror, the screams. What do I do? Run? Hide? Deep in my heart, I know that I won't do either of those things. I'll shut her the fuck up and finally fulfill that fantasy that's been running in my veins for the last four years. I'll make her pay for finding me here. I'll make her beg me to stop.

No.

I'll make her beg me *not* to stop.

We're both quiet for a long moment as I assess my next move, but then it dawns on me that she's not even reacting. She stares back at me, mouth softly parted, hand pressing between her thighs, and says…nothing. My boner is still hard as rock, sticking straight out. If she really is awake there's no way, even in the dark, that she can't see it. I run my hand down the length, feeding the urge, which hasn't abated in the least. Her hand keeps moving between her legs, pressing and pushing, and I realize what's really going on here.

Sweet Cherry knows I'm in the room and whatever little dream she was having has made her horny as fuck. We sit, feet apart, and quietly fulfill our needs. Her fingers dip under her panties and mine push and tug my cock. Soon the room is filled with the sounds of our erratic breathing and working hands. The twist and tightening of my orgasm doesn't take long—not under these circumstances—not with Story riding her hand so close by.

Watching her come is the sweetest fucking ache. Her shoulders quiver with it, mouth open in a tiny, gentle cry. Blood thrums in my ears, and for a moment, I'm lost in the swell of euphoria. Sticky cum drips down my fist as her breathing and motions slow.

It's the first time we've ever been equals—shared a moment instead of stealing one. She watches me take off my shirt and wipe down my cock, and I watch her right back. I only look away for a second, just to tuck myself back into my pants, but when I glance back, her eyes have fluttered shut, breathing slowed and even like she was never awake. Like this never happened.

Briefly, I wonder if I fell asleep and made the whole goddamn thing up. Was it just a sex dream? No. I don't believe it. Even in the dark, I can tell her cheeks are flushed and her lips are red from biting down on them. Standing, I lurk over her bed for a long moment, watching her, wondering if I'm crazy for coming in here every night—for choosing to be this close to her but never letting myself have her.

After tonight, I know one thing is for sure.

There's no way I can make myself stop.

STORY

21

TRUE CONFESSIONS

LEANING BACK ON MY HEELS, I wipe my mouth, watching the quick rise and fall of Dimitri's chest. It was even better than last time, sucking him. Easier. Faster. *Hotter*...

"Shit," he gasps, sprawled on his back. "You're getting good at that." Listlessly, he reaches down to tug his pants back up, lifting his hips with a groan.

After taking a drink from the soda I'd brought up with me, I climb to my feet, feeling restless and antsy. It's even harder, looking at him like this. More than once, the thought has struck me.

Specifically, the thought that a repeat of what he'd done to me my first night here wouldn't be unwelcome.

But like last time, he's given me permission to touch myself tonight, to get myself off, and I already know I will. I *have* been. I did last night.

Swiftly distracting myself from that very complicated and super-confusing memory, I say, "Okay," and open the laptop I'd left on his sofa. "Let's get started."

Dimitri really does do better after I've sucked him off. He rolls toward me, loose-limbed and clear-eyed, and then reaches out to sweep my hair over my shoulder. It's an idle gesture, hardly intimate, but still takes me by surprise. If he notices, he doesn't make it known.

It's completely forgotten once we're focused on the work, me typing out his thoughts, making him repeat them back and memorize them verbatim.

He focuses better.

Me? Not so much.

My blood feels a little too electric, my skin a bit too tight to properly concentrate. It doesn't help that my gaze can't stop drifting to his eyes. He has such long, dark lashes. They brush against his cheek when he looks down. His eyes are soulful, but strangely shuttered, like he's hiding multitudes just beneath the surface. It makes me want to ask him things, like why did he just touch my hair like that?

It takes two hours, but we finally manage to bang out a workable draft. As I'm packing up my things, I say, "I'll probably head down. Killian and I have dinner with our parents tonight and I should get ready."

He rises from the bed, stretching his arms high into the air. My eyes dart to the patch of skin exposed by his shirt hiking up his torso. When they ascend once again, he's smirking, having caught me. "Sure. 'Get ready'. Consider yourself excused."

"Thanks," I reply, pointedly ignoring the implications.

Before I go, however, he stops me. "You should wear something cute."

I pause, turning. "Cute?"

"For Killian," he clarifies, quirking an eyebrow when I stiffen. "He likes those cute little dresses you wear sometimes. Girly stuff. All sweet and innocent, you know?"

"Oh." I blink, confused. Am I expected to dress for Killian? I hadn't really planned on it. I've been avoiding thinking of him at all. "Uh, right. Thanks for the tip."

As I walk from the room, I see him open a small book on the piano. He plucks up a pen and makes a few quick marks before closing it again. He did that the last time I was here too, but I didn't think much of it then. Now I wonder if he's taking notes after our sessions, and if so, what they say. Is it good? Can it help me help him? Going through the guys' personal stuff makes me queasy. Even checking the computer in Killian's room felt like a huge, scary risk. I'm still half-convinced he's going to jump out of a corner at any moment to punish me for it.

Downstairs in my room, I quickly shower and dress for the night. After Dimitri's comment, I find myself looking at the dresses. They *are* cute. Truthfully, they're the sort of thing I'd wear freely, without being told to. There's a peach-colored sundress in the closet that ties on the shoulders. It stops a few inches above my knees and isn't racy in the least. After slipping it on, I spin, watching myself in the mirror.

Would Killian like this?

It's a dumb thought. Killian doesn't like anything about me, and I'm not sure why I should make the effort. He doesn't deserve anything more than the bare minimum. I live under his roof and take his punishments. That's enough.

Still, I wear the dress. What was that Ms. Crane had said about Dimitri?

"He's the best at handling the other two."

If Dimitri thinks this is the best way of handling him, then it's worth a try. God knows I've never been good at it. Either way, it doesn't matter. Tonight isn't about him. Not in the least. It's about suffering through a family dinner together. We're going to our parents' house, and over there, I'm just Story. His stepsister. Not his Lady.

Unluckily, I step into the hallway at the same time he does, coming face to face with his large frame. His scent wafts over me and I reach back, holding onto the door to steady myself. Without bidding, I'm assaulted by the memory of Killian in my room, cock out, stroking himself in the dark. The way he looked, shadowed but still clear, and the sound of his quick breaths are burned into my memory like a brand. A sparking heat runs up my spine from my own enjoyment. The memory is so whole, so real, that I know in my heart it wasn't just a dream, no matter how much I wish that were the case.

"What?" he asks, watching me.

"N-nothing."

His face is infuriatingly expressionless, even when he looks at me up and down, taking in my dress. The dress I'd worn for *him*. He clears his throat and I'm not sure what this is, the way he stands, still and stiff, but he asks, "Are you ready?"

I swallow. "Yes."

I try to process my thoughts—my feelings—as I climb into the front seat of his truck. Killian isn't acting mean and hostile like usual, but there's also nothing on his face that speaks of what happened last night. Maybe I'm wrong. Maybe it really was just a dream. Maybe I can just pretend.

Maybe he'll even let me.

The truck's powerful engine rumbles to life as Killian backs it out of the garage. I feel ridiculous sitting here. If he wanted to, he could reach out and snap my neck with a single blow. But even though his hands are wrapped around the steering wheel, gripping so tight his knuckles are white, he doesn't regard me at all. I keep my mouth shut. What would I say? *I know who you are and what you do. I know somewhere, deep down, you want me the same way I want you.*

But I can barely admit that to myself, much less him.

We're about halfway there when he suddenly reaches over. I flinch, but it's unnecessary. He just pulls a bag of M&Ms from the center console, ripping it open at the next stoplight. I remember now that he always hated my mom's cooking—on the rare occasions that she had to put in the effort.

I watch from the corner of my eye as he tips the bag back, catching them in his mouth and chomping down. I'm so stiff in my seat that my bones are beginning to ache. I look out the window at the passing scenery—buildings, residential homes, parking lots—and wish I were anywhere but here.

Killian clears his throat, drawing my attention. He holds the bag out, giving it a shake. When I just stare at it, confused, he shifts his shoulders and offers,

"Want some?" I gape at the bag, because I must be losing my damn mind. Killian offering me something? What the hell is this? He throws me a quick look, jaw tightening. "Well?"

I look at them, suspicious. Maybe they're poisoned or something. Worse, maybe this is a test. Reluctantly, I extend my hand, half expecting him to smack it away. He doesn't.

He dumps a handful into my palm.

If I inspect them closely before slowly putting one into my mouth, it's only because I'm not stupid. "Thanks," I mutter, still baffled. "Don't tell Tristian."

His only response is a quiet grunt as he pours more into his mouth.

"I NEVER THOUGHT I'D SEE THE DAY COME," my mother says, pouring her third glass of wine, "when we had the whole family back at home again. Did you, dear?"

"No, not really," I say, stuffing an olive from the charcuterie tray into my mouth. It's bitter and salty, which reminds me of the taste of Dimitri's cock.

"Sure you don't want some wine? You're old enough to have some with dinner now."

"No, thank you." God, the last thing I need to do is drink in this house. I have my eye on the back deck, where Killian and Daniel are caught up in the manliness of grilling steaks. I'm not letting my guard down for a second. Killian's strangely cool behavior, the M&M stunt, the quiet drive over...

These things are loaded.

I just don't know what they're loaded *with*.

My mother follows my gaze. "I'm just glad to see you two are able to get along better now. You and Killian really had a hard time adjusting to one another back in high school." She takes another long swallow. "Of course, you struggled to get along with anyone back then. Most girls would have been ecstatic to have such a popular older brother, but you had that way of always making things difficult."

Yes, Mom, getting felt up by my stepdad and then assaulted by my stepbrother and his friends really was all about me being difficult.

Maybe I do need some of that wine. Instead, I pick up a marinated artichoke and cram it in my mouth.

She reaches out and pushes my hair out of my eyes. "I'm just glad that after all the worry and expense, you finally seem to be on the right path."

"Yep. I've got it all together," I say, ready to take the attention off of me. I point to the living room. "Did you redecorate?"

"Oh! You noticed!" This leads to thirty minutes of stories about all the work she did to get the room just right, and how Daniel wanted this feature or that new technology, or the TV that slides out of the ceiling. The entire time she speaks, I can't help but wonder if this is always who my mother has been, or if she changed along the way. I know she worked hard when I was younger, and marrying Daniel had been like a gift from heaven. I don't blame her for not looking too deep under the surface. Having shiny new toys and a seemingly devoted husband isn't something you want to mess with.

The back door opens and Daniel pokes his head in. "Five minutes, ladies," he says, then gives me a wink before ducking back outside. *Jesus Christ.*

"Story," my mother says, reaching into the cabinet, "can you take your stepfather the platter?"

I'd rather stab myself in the eye with the corkscrew, actually.

Dealing with Daniel is one thing. He's not stupid enough to do anything overt in front of my mother—plus, I'm not even sure he'll bother me anymore. He doesn't even treat me the same. Maybe girls over the age of sixteen don't even do it for him. But Killian is another thing altogether. He's both my stepbrother and my Lord. I don't know how to balance the two.

Thankfully, when I step out on the deck, Killian is off to the side talking on the phone. Daniel smiles appreciatively, takes the plate with one hand, and squeezes my shoulder with the other. The scent of his cologne makes me want to gag.

"I'm so glad you came tonight," he says, picking up a two-pronged fork and stabbing into the sizzling meat. "I want you to know that this will always be your home. If you ever need a place to decompress or just have a little time away from your hectic school schedule, you're more than welcome."

"Thanks," I say tightly, glancing over at Killian. He's still talking but his eyes are on me, watching closely. "I don't think it'll be necessary, though. Things on campus are good."

"I'm glad to hear that," he says, flipping the other steak. "Have you made any friends? Are you dating anyone?"

"Dating? Story?" Daniel looks over my head. Killian's heavy hand lands on my shoulder. "Little Miss Perfect 4.0 is too busy to date now, just like she was in high school. I can't even get her to come over to the frat house for a party. I keep telling her, all work and no play makes for a boring-ass life."

Daniel's eyes flick from Killian's hand on my shoulder to my face. "It takes strong conviction not to get caught up in the distraction of college life. I'm impressed. Your brother has never known the meaning of the word 'no'."

A bit of spittle gets lodged in my windpipe and I cough.

Tell me about it.

"I should go wash my hands," I say, abruptly turning back inside. The nearest bathroom is adjacent to the laundry room. There's no way in hell I'm reliving that little nightmare while we're here, so I head out the other door and escape upstairs. When I reach the landing, I automatically turn into my old bedroom and flip on the light.

Those stories about parents keeping their kids' bedrooms like a shrine after they leave home does *not* apply here. I have no idea how long I was gone before my mother called her decorator, but I suspect I was still on the bus. Other than the bed frame and the antique oak desk against the wall, nothing is the same. As alienating as it feels to be erased, I'm not sure I mind.

I enter the Jack-and-Jill bathroom and scrub the oily marinade off my fingers. After drying them off on a towel, I decide to take a quick, curious peek into Killian's room.

Ah, and here's the shrine.

Trophies, team photos, football pennants, and banners decorate the tidy room that smells just like the one across from my own at the Lords'. There's a framed picture of his signing day for Forsyth, hung with prominence right above his chest of drawers. In it, he's flanked by his father—hand resting proudly on his shoulder—and his high school coach. Killian Payne; star quarterback, devoted son, abusive asshole.

I'm just about to head back through the bathroom when the door opens, Killian striding through. "What are you doing?" He looks suspicious and annoyed, narrowed eyes taking in the room.

"Looking around. Seeing what's changed." I shrug, because it's easy to fall back into the old dynamic here. "My old room isn't anything like it used to be."

His eyes land on me and remain there, and that same weird energy from the truck returns. "You left." It's said accusingly, but there's no real bite. If anything, he just looks uncertain and impatient, oddly jittery.

Treading carefully, I decide not to take the bait. An argument here, tonight, would just make the whole dinner impossibly more awful. Instead, I duck my head, heading back to the connected bathroom.

When I pass him, his hand shoots out, grabbing my arm.

I stiffen, bracing for the pinch, the squeeze, the hurt. When it doesn't immediately come, I look up, meeting his gaze. Killian is staring down at me, mouth half-parted like he was just about to say something but got distracted.

His eyes are glued to my lips.

I get that same tingle of awareness from that day he'd come to offer me the position of Lady. His pupils dilate, weight shifting, and I know I must be crazy. I must be. Because Killian is not about to kiss me.

I'm only half right.

He does dart forward to take my mouth with his, but it'd be absurd to call it a kiss. Almost instantly, his hands come up to grab my arms, spinning to slam me up against the wall. My mouth opens on a surprised gasp and he pushes his tongue inside, strong and unyielding.

My response is all Dimitri's fault. It *is*. He'd gotten me all worked up before and I didn't have time to do anything about it. Now Killian is licking into my mouth, the hard length of his body pinning me against the wall, and all I want to do is follow the current.

That's exactly what I do, mindlessly taking a fistful of his shirt and surging into him. He growls, deep in his chest, and there's a sting of pain when his teeth bear down into my lip. He doesn't give me time to process it. He rushes back, his whole body folding around mine. Killian kisses like he plays on the field. Hard. Unforgiving. Greedy. There's nothing but sharp edges in this, the way his palm rises to wrap around my throat. He doesn't squeeze—he just holds it there, like he needs me to know he could. I'm trapped by the point of it, although it's not necessary. His broad chest is already holding me there.

Killian's body is physically designed to bring people to heel. The more he tries, the more I want to push back. My heart hammers like crazy, flooding my ears. This is nothing like what I thought kissing him would be like. There's pain in the way his teeth graze my lips, but nothing else. His fingers flex around my throat, but he doesn't press. My hips buck forward, seeking friction, and he smoothly wedges his thigh between them, a rough rumble spilling from his chest.

He's shaking.

It takes me a long moment to work out why. It isn't until he rips his mouth away to press a series of hard, biting kisses down my jaw that I realize he's holding himself back. Maybe he wants to hurt me, after all.

"I should fuck you right here against the wall," he hisses, pressing his thigh harder into my center. I gasp for air, and even though I'll feel ashamed of it later, I grind down into it, chasing, desperate. "Everyone thinks you like it nice, but I know better. You'd rather have me tear you open on my cock." His voice is raw as he grinds back. "That's exactly what you fucking deserve. Maybe then, everyone would know it's *mine*." He sounds vicious and angry, and this must be Dimitri's fault. It has to be. Because it shoots through me like a lightning bolt.

The orgasm is such a sharp surprise that I don't even have time to stifle my cry. The climb was too steep—too fast. It aches in the best of ways, spreading from my center to the tips of my limbs. I'm powerless against it, riding Killian's leg senselessly, relentlessly.

It isn't until I come down that I realize he's covering my mouth, his big palm digging into my face to stifle the sounds.

"Kids? You up here?"

We break apart at the sound of Daniel's voice, so quickly that I stumble, my knees still weak. I catch myself on the dresser, knocking over an old alarm clock in the process. It's only just clattered softly to the carpeted floor when Daniel enters the room, cradling a box in his hands.

"There you are," he says, looking completely oblivious. "The two of you are still having all your mail sent here. Maybe today we'll learn a lesson about change of address, huh?" He dumps the box on the bed and gives Killian a salute before striding from the room. "Enjoy."

My body still feels like it's on fire, singeing me from the inside out. Killian had flung himself across the room and now he's staring at the door, eyes full of the same fire I feel.

Clearing my throat, I reach for the box with unsteady hands. "Probably just a bunch of junk."

His eyes shift to mine, the rise and fall of his chest shallow and rapid. "What?" Shit. That look in his eyes, full of unspent heat and crackling energy. Nothing good has ever come from that.

"The mail," I blurt, trying desperately to distract him before that darkness in his eyes takes over. "Here, I'll separate them." Frantically, I dig through, making two piles on the bed. There's more for me than him, since I'm guessing Killian's been home a lot more recently than I have. I hear him approach, but stay focused on the task, trying not to flinch when he reaches past me to pluck some envelopes from his pile.

I'm right—it's mostly junk. There is one bigger envelope with my name on it and a return address from campus. It must be something from admissions that I'd missed.

Before I can wedge my nail under the flap, it's being ripped out of my hand. By Killian.

He reads the front before pulling a knife from his pocket—the same kind Dimitri had used to slash that guy's tires. It tears through the envelope easily.

"Hey," I protest. "That's for me!"

He doesn't look bothered in the least. "Contract says otherwise."

"That's for mail sent to the brownstone," I bite out, watching him shake the contents out onto the bed, "not for mail sent—"

My words die in my throat.

It's a pair of purple lace panties.

Killian's face twists into something dark and dangerous. "Who the fuck is this from?" He fists the panties. They're new, and although Killian doesn't know it yet, they're also unused. He recognizes them though, and he would. They're part of the set the Lords' bought me. "These are yours."

My whole world shatters around me. This is a message. He found me. He knows where I am, and he knows about the Lords. My mind flashes back to Saul Cartwright and the way Tristian had whispered into his ear. Saul knows. And now Ted does, too.

"They are." There's no point in lying. I already know the punishment for that will be worse. "I have no idea how someone got them or why they would send them to me."

Face eerily blank, he digs through the envelope and extracts a card. It's small, set on thick, embossed paper. I know the card just like I know the panties, because it's the same paper I'd been given instructions on that first morning in the brownstone. Without seeing what's written on the front, I still know it has the letters 'LDZ' printed in the lower-right corner. Words are scribbled on the back and he flips it over and holds it up for me to see.

You're Mine, Whore

His face grows darker. "You're fucking someone in the frat, aren't you? An underclassman? Someone trying to oust us?"

"What? No." I try to reach for the card, but he pulls back violently. "I *am not* sleeping with anyone else. I'm not sleeping with *anyone*! You of all people know that. You fucking checked my hymen!"

"Someone came to you with a better deal, didn't they? What are they giving you to betray us?" His teeth grind. "I knew you were hiding something. I knew there was something more to you showing up on our doorstep that day. Do you think we're fucking stupid?"

I could tell him the truth. That I'm running from Ted—the actual person that sent me this. The person trying to destroy my life for the last two years. A *killer*. But even in my head it sounds like an over-the-top, fantastical lie. No. I need to just calm him down, assure him that someone is fucking with me—us.

"Killian, look," I start, begging him with my eyes to understand. "Someone has been messing with me. Sending me messages, watching me. This is just another—"

He cuts me off, spitting, "Another reason that you're a gold-digging, opportunistic whore, just like your mother!" I rear angrily back, but he reaches out to grab me, clamping his hand back around my throat. His eyes grow wide and crazed as he seethes, "Don't fucking deny it. I always knew this would happen. You play this act, like you're such a sweet, innocent little victim, but I know the truth. You'd trip over your own two feet to give that cunt to the highest bidder. To give away what's mine!"

"It'll never be yours!" I explode. My chest fills with a different sort of fire and I clamp onto his wrist, letting my nails dig divots into the skin. "I would give it away to anyone else. They don't even need money. I'd do it in a heartbeat! I'd rather die than fuck you. There's nothing good about you, Killian. Whenever I'm with you, anyone looks better by comparison. *Anyone.*"

He grows more apoplectic as I speak, that vein in his temple throbbing a rapid tempo. His fingers squeeze around the column of my throat, but his hand is trembling. He's holding himself back.

Just barely.

"Here's what you're going to do," he says, voice low and full of warning. "You're going to go downstairs and get into the truck. You're not going to talk to your slut of a mother. You're not going to even *look* at my father. You're going to just disappear." With that, he shoves me, sending me stumbling back.

The second I gain my footing, I barge out the door.

RAGE ROLLS OFF OF HIM as he cranks the truck with an obnoxiously loud rumble. I should be scared of what's going to happen, but the thing is?

I'm mostly just done with all of it.

I'm done with Ted, always nipping at my heels. I'm done with Tristian's games and Dimitri's sly remarks. I'm done with Daniel, who's trying to act like we're some big happy family, as if he wasn't the main catalyst to this whole miserable existence. And I'm done with Killian, who only wants to take and hurt.

When we arrive at the pub, I don't even have it in me to be confused. I'm just thinking of how to hit them all back—how to take even the smallest nugget of control back for myself.

Killian doesn't say a word to me as he flings his door open and jumps out. He slams it so hard that the truck rocks, but I don't even flinch. I watch him stride up to the doors and angrily yank them open, disappearing inside.

Twenty minutes later, it's clear that this isn't a quick visit.

I get out of the truck and follow him inside. It's darker in here, and even though it's barely seven in the evening, it's already packed. Despite that, I spot him instantly, sitting ramrod straight on a stool at the bar. He's throwing back a tall glass of amber liquid with one hand and doing something on his phone with the other. His whole aura screams 'stay away', and it looks like everyone is heeding it.

He doesn't spare me a glance when I stride up to him. He swallows, banging his glass on the bar to sneer, "Did I say you could come in here?"

"I have to use the bathroom," I sneer back. "Or do you want me to piss in your precious penis euphemism?"

"Go," he barks. "Leave me the fuck alone."

"Gladly!" I turn, finding the restroom and stalking toward it.

It's quieter inside and I choose a sink to turn to full blast. The water is refreshingly cool against my hot face, shocking me back to reality. Bracing my hands on the sink, I stew, thinking of him out there, drinking like he's been jilted in some way. What the hell was all that stuff about my virginity being his to take? Since when?

And how can I make sure that never, *ever* happens?

Just then, someone exits a stall and I stiffen, trying to look more put together than I feel. I look into the mirror and freeze when I realize who it is.

"Oh," I say, blinking the water from my lashes. "Hi."

The Countess watches me back, giving me a small grin. "Hi. It's Story, right?"

I nod. "Yeah, and you're…can I call you Sutton? Or is that something else I'll get yelled at for?"

She laughs, approaching the sink beside me. "Sutton is fine when it's just us." She's a lot prettier than me, with her full lips and elegant posture and smooth, dark skin. But her eyes are also warm and kind. "Are yours out there? The Counts have the billiards room. We might have to keep them distracted so they don't get into another slap fight."

I smile tightly. "Only one of them. He's at the bar. And the only one he wants to fight with tonight is me."

"Ahh, one of those nights. Which one?" she asks, dropping her purse on the counter. "No, wait. Let me guess. Killian Payne."

I laugh darkly. "How did you know?"

"Oh girl," she unzips her bag, "his tantrums are legendary around FU. That boy can't handle things not going his way." She pulls out a shiny silver stick of lip gloss. "Not that I can talk. One of the Counts got so pissed the other day he tore the flatscreen off the wall." She rolls her eyes. "It's like they're children."

I nod. "Overgrown babies."

She bends toward the mirror, assessing a tiny, almost non-existent blemish. "So, what happened? You look at another guy? Bend over too seductively? Talk to the bartender?" It's none of those things, but Sutton seems to understand my situation better than I would expect. She shrugs. "I'm friends with Charlene. I know the drill."

I watch her apply the gloss along her bottom lip. "Charlene told you that? Ladies aren't supposed to share their contract with anyone. Fuck, I'm not supposed to even talk to you."

"Girl, they want it that way to keep us in line, but women talk. We've always talked. We always will." She pops the cap back on the gloss. "Otherwise, how else would we survive?"

She's right about that. I turn and lean against the counter. "There are times when I feel like I'm drowning. Like nothing I do is right, and everything is my fault. Especially with Killian. He's just so angry all the time. I have no idea how to make it better."

Sutton glances at me and smirks. "No idea?"

"Well," I smooth down the front of my dress. "I wore this outfit for him. I think he liked it. And I didn't argue with him once tonight. I thought things were going okay until that—"

Her eyebrow rises. "Until what?"

"Nothing." I exhale. "Nothing I do makes him happy. It never has." Perhaps the worst part is that there's some tiny, deep part of me that's always wanted to. Even after all these years, that stupid, awkward, sad teenager still lives inside me, wishing the handsome boy in the room next door would just *like* me.

"Story, honey," she says, zipping up her bag and resting her hand on my arm, "there's one thing all men want, especially men like Killian: for you to fuck him senseless. For you to let him shove his cock into and up every orifice you have. All these assholes want is to claim their woman. Just go get him, drag him back in here, and let him fuck it out of you, right on this counter. Fog up his brain with an orgasm so good that he can't remember why he's so pissed. And the bonus?" She winks. "Is that you get off too. It's win-win."

She says it so easily. Like it's the easiest thing in the world. Spread your legs and let him fuck you senseless. And she's right. It should be easy, but there are layers upon layers attached to my relationship to these guys, to our past, to Ted, Daniel, and every other man I've encountered. It's the only power I've ever had. The only leverage. Am I ready to give that up?

"I'm a virgin," I blurt, the weight of the secret weighing on me. The deficiency. The 'why' Killian is so pent-up and angry. "It's why they picked me as their Lady. I'm a virgin and they like me that way."

Sutton's lips form a small circle and her eyes grow twice the size as normal. "Holy shit. Are you serious?"

"Yes." I turn away and reach for a paper towel. Just for something to do with my hands. "Pathetic, I know."

"No," she says, a little too quickly. "It's not pathetic. Honestly, it makes *a lot* of sense. You have the one thing the rest of us don't." She laughs and I peek at her face. She looks positively amused. "No wonder he's wound so tight."

"Yeah. See? I told you, it's all my fault, one way or the other."

"No, babe, this isn't your fault. This is...well," her lips curve into a small smirk, "it's a good thing. Really, really good."

"I don't know," I tell her. "They're obsessed with it, like it's some kind of prize. Sometimes I just want to just do it and get it over with. Take the pressure off and find a guy that cares more about me than the hymen between my legs."

"No. Don't think of it like that," Sutton says quickly. "It makes you powerful. They'll protect you no matter what. Me? I've got nothing left to lose."

A fist bangs loudly on the door, making us both jump. "Countess! You still in there?" a guy's voice yells.

"Coming, my Count!" she calls back, then rolls her eyes dramatically. "Guess I took too long."

"Go," I say. "And thanks. Talking to you really helped."

She hitches her purse over her shoulder. "Us royalty need to stick together, you know?"

I smile. "Yes, we really do."

She steps out into the hall, and I wait a few minutes before following, just in case Killian is watching. I shouldn't have told Sutton those things, but the confidentiality rule? It's just more manipulation and bullshit. Another way to control me. I mean, what's the worst that can happen from a little bathroom girl talk?

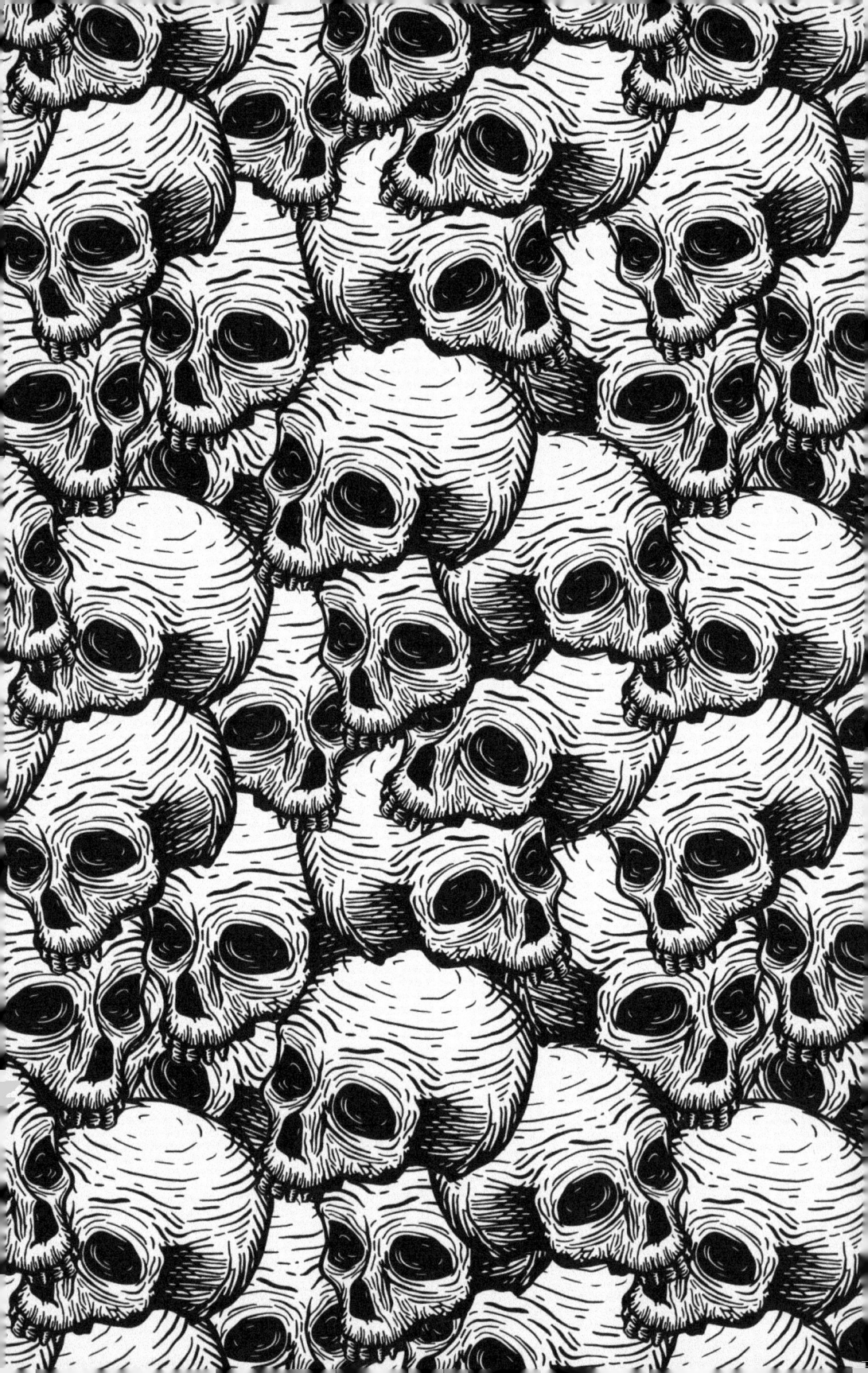

TRISTIAN
MERCER

22

PUNISH

"WE NEED SOMETHING on this guy," I say, reading the name aloud, "Rufus Hammond."

Rath's finger trails down the ledger, trying to find a connection. "Nick isn't giving us shit to go off of here."

I snort. "Ugly Nick, or Pretty Nick?"

Rath sarcastically mutters, "Yes."

Well, he's not wrong. Walking the line between the factions is a fragile thing. Sometimes we have to do things for the Nicks, sometimes the Nicks have to do shit for us. It's a whole harmony deal, which makes it difficult coming back to school after a summer spent working South Side. It's a balance we have to get back in the rhythm of, and it takes time.

Sighing, I begrudgingly admit, "Maybe we should ask Ms. Crane." It's harder to get dirt on people when you have classes and frat duties. South Side informants aren't exactly waltzing onto campus.

"No," he replies, shaking his head. "Today's her wedding anniversary. She won't want to dig anything up. I'm surprised she's even here at all."

"What good is having a living, breathing, cussing database of South Side fuckery if we can't ever approach her about it?" Throwing the folder aside, I rake my fingers through my hair. "You two coddle the shit out of her."

"And you treat her like a living, breathing, cussing database of South Side fuckery." He gives me a hard look. "Delores Crane is more than that. She's a goddamn testament to this whole crooked institution. She's an *icon*."

"She's a relic," I correct, all prepared to give him a tirade about the old ways and how cronies like Crane would never survive in the information age.

And then Killer storms in.

It's obvious that he's furious, even though he doesn't say a word. He just stands there all rigid and still as Story enters behind him, immediately sprinting up the staircase to her room.

Rath closes the laptop. "What now?"

Killian points a finger toward the stairs, snarling, "That fucking bitch is fucking around with someone." And, oh, he's really worked up about it too, pacing now.

"No way," I insist, snorting. "We have that girl locked down twenty-four-seven."

Rath agrees, "She's with us all the time. We track her phone. When would she have the opportunity?"

"Even if she did, she wouldn't," I argue, knowing it in my bones.

Killian stops, glaring at us. "Are you listening to me? I'm telling you she's fucking around! It's someone in LDZ, too. They sent her a pair of panties in the mail, along with this."

I catch the card he flings at me, squinting as I read it.

You're mine, whore.

Rath takes it next, scoffing. "Are you sure *you* didn't send this?"

"Someone's taking a run at her," Killian swears, snatching the note back.

I lean back, thinking. "Underclassman?"

"They have access to the house," he agrees. "Probably someone trying to get a jump on us."

"We have two years left in this house," I say. "We won it."

"That didn't stop us." We had no respect for the former Lords and their Lady. We set our sights on Charlene and flipped the game. The problem is that it set a precedent. And if these little snot-nosed fuckers think they can take a run at us and our Lady…

"I don't know," I say, tapping my knee in thought. "Do you really think Story would do that? It doesn—"

He barks, "Don't you fucking dare say it doesn't seem like her! She's a money-grubbing slut. We knew there was a risk of this when she moved in here. All it took was a better deal to come along and she wouldn't give a shit about our reputations."

Rath stands, face blank, looking between us. "Okay, so say it's true. How do you want to handle it?"

Beneath the skepticism, I see the worry in his eyes. I know what he's thinking; that Killian will want to kick Story out for violating the contract. It's valid. There is a strict no-fucking-others clause in there, but even if she had betrayed us like that—and she didn't—I'm not sure I'm ready for her to leave, either.

"We're not kicking her out," I say, squashing that shit now.

"I agree," Killian says.

I look up in surprise. "You do?"

"Whoever did this needs to learn what happens when you fuck with the Lords." His jaw clenches. "And Sweet Cherry? She's going to learn there's no easy way out of this contract."

Shit. "What's that mean?" I ask, apprehensive about giving him too much slack. Killian is as close to a sociopath as I ever expect to meet. Whatever he has planned can't be good.

"Call a meeting. Of the whole frat," he says, not answering my question. "Bring Story to the meeting room. Dumb bitch is probably up there packing as we speak. You know her first instinct is to run."

That, we do know.

Killian starts off and I grab his arm. "What are you going to do to her?"

He looks me in the eye and I don't like what I find there. "I'm going to make sure she, and every other member of this fraternity knows exactly what happens when you try to play with the Lords' favorite toy."

I ONLY KNOCK ONCE BEFORE trying the knob.

It opens, so I let myself in, fully expecting to see Story packing the sad, tattered duffel she'd come here with. Killer was right. She's a runner. She ran from here three years ago, and then again at boarding school, and then again when she returned. When it comes to instinct, she's all flight and zero fight.

Which is why, when I see her standing in front of the bay windows, just staring down at the street, I know I'm right.

Still.

I have to hear it from her.

She doesn't turn her head when I approach. The room's growing dark—she hasn't turned the lamps on yet—but the intense glow of the sunsets illuminates her with a wash of warmth. She's pretty, wearing this simple little dress. I know without asking that she'd chosen it for him—for Killian.

"Story." Her eyes don't move, fixed to nothing in the distance. "Look at me." When she doesn't, I touch her chin, easing it toward me. When she finally meets my gaze, all I see there is anger and exhaustion. "Are you fucking around on us?"

"He wouldn't listen," she grinds out, jaw tight. "He never fucking listens."

"I do," I say, demanding, "answer the question."

She doesn't blink, those big eyes staring right through me. "I'm not."

Story lies, but she's never good at it. Killian has her all wrong. Deception isn't her game—never could be. She lacks the steel in her bones to make it convincing. She's soft inside, elastic. She'd divert my attention, maybe omit some details, and she'd be good at that. But not this—not bald-faced lying.

Holding her gaze to mine, I ask, "Do you know who sent that?" She goes to look away, but I jerk her chin back. "Don't make me ask twice."

She lifts her chin. "Yes."

"Who?"

She drops her gaze, but this isn't insolence. It's dread. "I can't tell you." When she meets my eyes again, they're pleading. "Don't make me lie. I just can't tell you."

"Why not?" I ask, pressing. She shakes her head, exasperated, and I shift gears. "Is it someone on campus? In the frat?"

"No!" She says it with such certain authority that I almost want to go downstairs and slap Killian upside the goddamn head.

"And you haven't fucked him." Before she can answer, I clarify, "Or messed around with him, or—"

"I've never even met him," she insists.

Satisfied with that much, I drop my head, giving her a nod. "He doesn't believe you."

She rolls her eyes, and when they meet mine again, they're shining with unshed tears. "Of course, he doesn't. If he thought I was loyal, he'd have to stop hating me for one godforsaken moment."

Well, she's certainly got his number. "Yeah, he's got some issues. I'm not saying it's fair, but that's a part of this." Sighing, I make sure she understands the weight of my words when I add, "He's going to punish you now."

"I know."

I'm in no place to judge Killer. After Genevieve, it's not like I'm in any hurry to trust any of these bitches, either. All they do is fuck around. Every girl here is doing someone behind someone else's back. It makes me fucking sick.

That's why it has to be Story. Whatever Killian thinks, something is keeping her here. It's the reason I didn't find packed bags when I walked into this room, even though she has every reason to bolt. That's her nature and she's going against it. People don't do that for nothing. It's not the purest form of loyalty. It's not authentic or genuine.

But goddamn.

It'll fucking do.

"Why haven't you done it yet?" she asks, searching my eyes. "I've been here long enough. You could take it, right now. You could have days ago."

I raise an eyebrow, knowing exactly what she's talking about. *Fuck me*. Her virginity. I have to tread very carefully here. "Maybe we're waiting for you to be ready. Your first time should be special."

She immediately replies, "None of you care about that."

Yeah, that was always going to be a hard sell. "Fine. Virgins are bad lays, Cherry. They don't know what to do or how to do it. We're just letting you get some experience under your belt."

Her mouth thins, and I know she buys it. It's perfectly on-brand for us. "Sometimes, I wish—"

Her lips are soft and yielding when I bend down to kiss her, cutting her off. Either I get her off the subject, or I drive her toward the finish line. All I need are the words—an explicit, semantic request—and holy fucking shit.

I could win the game right here, right now.

And from the way she attacks me—there's no other word for it—maybe she wants me to. She plants both palms onto my shoulders and drives me back toward the bed. It only works because I let her, falling when the backs of my legs hit the mattress. She climbs into my lap without even breaking the kiss, winding her arms around my neck.

I reach behind her to grab her ass, groaning when she grinds down into my cock. It's just all so obvious. Her back arches into me. She moans. Her tongue licks into my mouth. She's a woman on a mission, with something to prove.

But she still hasn't asked.

Grabbing her hips, I flip her around, laying her out on the bed. She stares up at me with this startled look on her face. It only grows in confusion when I just stare down at her. I know exactly how to clinch this. Oh, yes. Story Austin would like it gentle and sweet. A kiss to her cheek. Soft touches to her arm. Nuzzles to her neck. All it'd take is some artificial romance, some words about how pretty she is, and she'd ask for it. None of us care about her first time being special. But she will.

I only make it to the soft, tender kisses up her neck before she springs up, spine straight, shoulders tense.

"Um," she mutters, yanking one of her dress straps back up her shoulder. "We should…"

Motherfucker. So close.

"Yeah," I sigh, willing my cock to stand down. We don't have time for this, anyway. Standing, I clear my throat, hoping it comes off more like I'm gathering myself than growling into my fist. "Killian wants to see you downstairs, so yes. We should."

"Do you know what my punishment is going to be?" she asks, voice shaking, either out of fear or from how closed we'd just been.

"No." I tuck a piece of her hair behind her ear. "But it won't be pretty. Or easy. And there's nothing Rath or I can do about it, understand?"

She nods and looks at the ground. "I understand."

I lift her chin with a finger. "Regardless, you're our Lady now and you'll be our Lady after."

That's the truth, I think, leading her out of the room. What I'm unsure about is how broken she'll be when Killian is done with her, and if it'll even be possible to pick up the pieces.

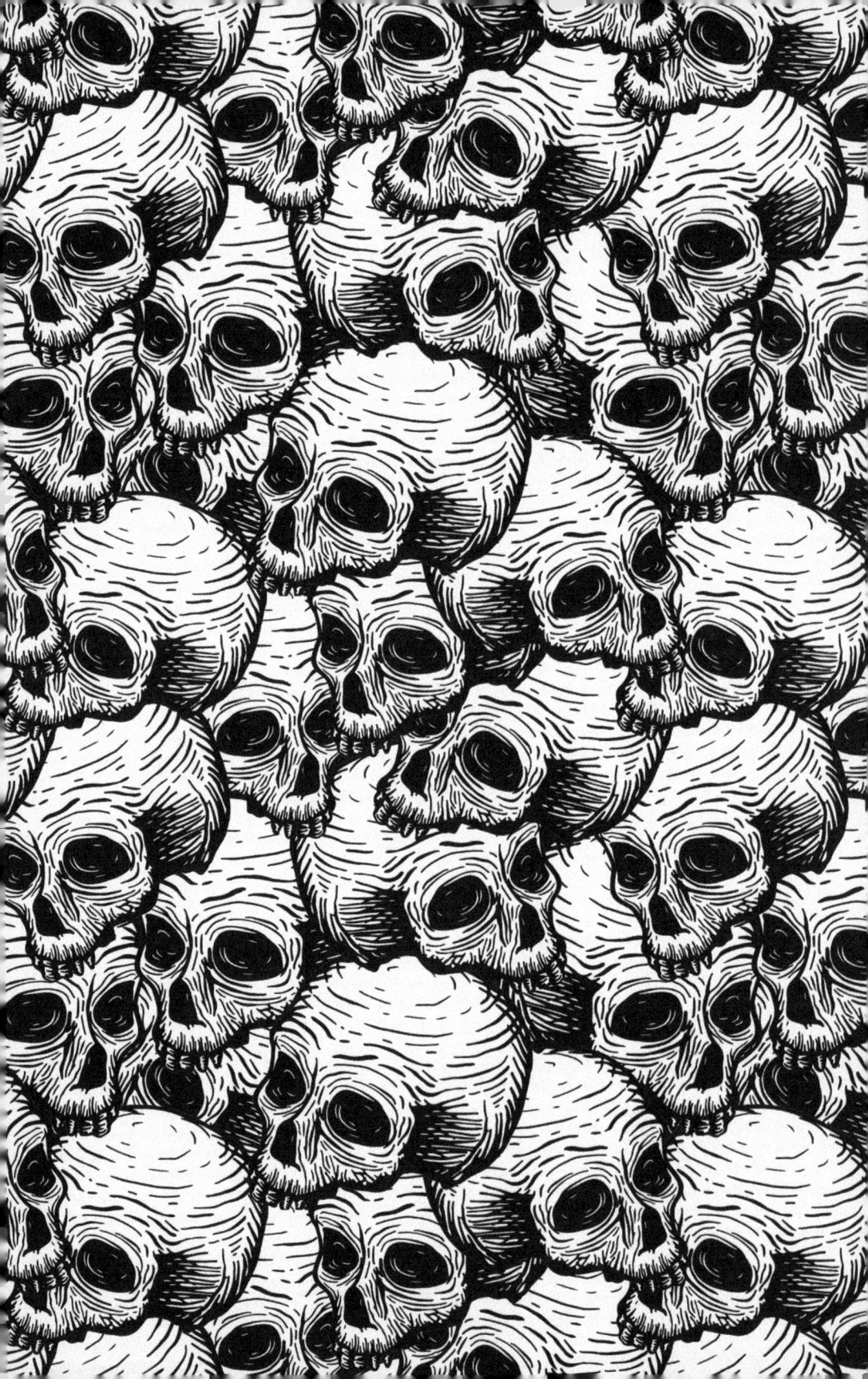

STORY

23

GRATITUDE

I'VE NEVER SEEN THE WHOLE frat before.

There must be forty of them—possibly more. The room Tristian brought me to is in the basement, but it doesn't look like a basement. It's windowless, but lines of sconces illuminate the room in a warm, if eerie glow. It's furnished with rows of upholstered chairs, which are currently being occupied by a group of boisterous men. In the back, near where we enter, there are a dozen of them standing, shifting restlessly from foot to foot, even though there are still a few empty chairs left.

Tristian leans down to whisper, "Those are the pledges."

I catch the eye of the guy who was mean to Ms. Crane that day in the kitchen, and then the two jerks from the party the same night—Tucker and Beckwith. All of them are grinning in a disturbing way. The vibe in the air, curious and full of anticipation, is a stark contrast to what's currently roiling in my gut.

Tristian's got his hand on my lower back, guiding me up the room from the back, whispering at me the whole time. "You can't talk back. If you do, he'll make it worse. He'll have to, do you understand? He can't seem weak to these guys. Don't provoke him any more than he already is. You know how he gets."

I give a tiny nod, but my eyes are on Dimitri now, waiting stoically up front. He catches and holds my stare, and I can't help the shiver that wracks through me at the blankness in his gaze. It's only now I realize how much he's let me see while living here. The boy I used to know—his discomfiting, cold presence—has at some point shifted to that of a man who's quiet and sullen, but also sharp and sly.

That's all gone from his face now.

My heart sinks at the possibility he believes what Killian's been saying. I'm not entirely sure why it should.

Killian is at the center of it all, and if I thought he looked like a gangster on that first day I walked into this brownstone, then I was wrong. *This* is the gangster. He doesn't even look at me, but I can tell the malice in his eyes from earlier is gone, replaced with something hard and shuttered.

Until now, it's always been pretty easy to reconcile this new version of Killian with the one I remember from high school. He might have all those tattoos and look broader, a little harsher, but he acts exactly the same. Only now I'm wondering if I might be wrong, because he commands the room with nothing more than a nod.

A nod.

The room instantly goes silent.

This is a version of Killian with power. A version who commands respect and gets it, without question.

Before he even opens his mouth, I feel the alarm of being powerless here. Briefly, I consider that I should have followed through upstairs, with Tristian. It all feels silly now, the way I'd felt when he kissed me so gently, chest aching from the tenderness he'd shown. I'd had this moment—this flash of clarity— that it's possible I don't hate him anymore. I'd thought about Ted, who no doubt knows about the three of them now, and I'd felt worried. For *him.*

The realization was startling and confusing, and I'd balked. Tristian has hurt me and humiliated me, and has never taken any of the blame. He's the same selfish, entitled monster as ever. A few kind moments of comfort—a few sweet kisses—shouldn't be enough to change that. It was a weak, frightening moment that made it clear just how ready I'm *not*. It'd be too easy to fall into the lie, to let my heart grasp onto something it wants so badly, that it stops listening to my head.

Still, if he'd taken my virginity, Killian might have two people to divvy all this hatred between. This? The way his cold eyes take me in? It's too intense, too undiluted.

"One of you is a traitor," Killian says, finally breaking the silence. The way the light hits his face from the sides digs two pools of shadow where his eyes should be. He looks out over the antsy crowd, jaw sharp and tense. "Someone is trying to take a run at our Lady, which is unfortunate, because it's not even going to work. We have every inch of her ass locked the fuck down. Now we have to spend our week finding out which one of you is a disloyal, disrespectful piece of shit. That's time better spent actually enjoying our Lady."

He laces his hands behind his back, pacing the front of the room, projecting his voice. "I figure some of you are new here and haven't had the opportunity to appreciate what it means to be in the presence of a Lord. Our *Lady*," he sneers, eyes narrowing on me, "doesn't seem to, either. Every single person in this fucking room needs a lesson in keeping their hands off of what belongs to me—her included."

He stops, and even though he turns to face the room, I know he's addressing me when he says, "Come here." The words, low and dangerous, send my stomach churning.

I'd already decided upstairs with Tristian that I wasn't going to take this 'punishment' the way Killian wants me to; cowed, scared, trembling and weak. I lift my chin and march myself right to him, schooling my features into something hard and blank. In another time, I might have cowered or run.

Those days are over.

If Killian wants to see me shrunken and hurt and begging for his mercy, then he's about to be wholly disappointed.

He looks bigger when I'm standing in front of him, waiting, face growing stony when his eyes lock on mine. It's a useless thought, but for a second, I wonder when Killian became this hard. Was he born this selfish and insecure, or did something happen to make him this way? Are monsters born, or are they made?

It doesn't matter. This is the only version of him I'll ever know, and it's etched into my bones. This thought is solidified with five harshly whispered words.

"Get on your fucking knees."

My stomach drops, eyes falling closed in dread. I think I'd known the second I walked into the basement what he planned to do. Maybe even the second he found the panties. This is how Killian works. He finds the deepest wound and works it open until it's a gaping, ugly thing. And this is a wound he's always known about. He helped make it, after all.

He'd hurt me less if he took that knife out of his pocket and buried it into my gut.

A week ago, I might have begged. I would have said 'please' and tried to reason with him. I would have cried and lashed out.

Now, I lower myself to my knees in front of him.

There's a long moment of silence, the sounds of guys shifting in their seats behind me, impatient and expectant. I wonder if they know what he's about to say—what he's about to make me do.

"Take it out," he says, voice deceptively even. "Make it hard."

The room erupts into whispers and impressed laughter, like they just realized what kind of show they're in for. Like they all think this is some fun game. The three of them really found their tribe here.

I stare forward at Killian's crotch, but it takes me a moment to push my arms into motion. Robotically, I reach up to raise the hem of his shirt, revealing his button and zipper. Without bidding, I think about those times with Dimitri, up in his warm, comfortable room. Down here, it's cold and hard and too quiet, and the sound of this zipper lowering just makes my blood run cold in anticipation.

He's already half-hard when I ease his pants down the tops of his thighs, his cock jutting out. I try to shut out the sounds of the men behind me, but I can't help but wonder if they like it. Will they pleasure themselves? Will they get off to this? Will Tristian? Dimitri?

He's warm in my hand when I wrap it around him and it can't be too appealing, the way I mechanically squeeze and work my fist. He still grows harder, though, thickening in my hand faster than I'm expecting.

There's something black and breakable swelling in my chest, but I shove it down, watching the way he looks in my hand, sickly fascinated by how fast his cock fills.

Then come the words I've been expecting. They're spoken quietly enough that most of the guys behind me probably don't hear, but the hiss is caustic and cutting.

"Now suck it."

I think I hear Tristian say something—a floating, distant whisper—but I can't hear it over the crowd behind me. They're laughing. Some of it has an edge of nervousness, like they're surprised and not sure how to take it. Some of it just sounds jubilant and jeering.

If I'm ashamed of anything, it's the way their laughter makes me feel: alone. Like I'm trash. Like I'm nothing, no one. Just a toy. Something to be used and thrown away. A punchline instead of a living, breathing human being.

Sitting back on my heels, I let him slip from my hand, resting my palms on top of my thighs. Killian's staring down at me when I look up, meeting his gaze. Any argument would be futile. I know that, even without seeing the steel in his eyes. I could run away, but it never works. I understand that now. I don't want to run for the rest of my life. I just want to look back on this and know that I have nothing to regret.

"You're wrong about all of this," I tell him. It's not a plea. It's just a bare fact. "I haven't done anything with anyone else."

"Now, Story," he orders, eyes flashing.

Undaunted by the angry flare of his nostrils, I quietly confess, "I actually used to like you, you know. In the beginning, when things were…better. I wanted you to like me back. I wanted you to see me. I thought maybe we could…" It's so old and flimsy a notion that I can barely grasp the substance of it. It doesn't matter. He's watching me with this look on his face, which has suddenly gone slack, eyebrows puckered. "I never wanted to admit it to myself, but even after everything you've done to me, I think it's still been there. Just a little, like this residue I could never get rid of, even though it hurt *so much* to have it." I hope my smile is as watery and cruel as it feels. "This won't be a punishment, Killian. It'll be the only kind thing you've ever done for me. Because after this, there's no part of me—no fucking cell in my body—that'll feel anything but disgust for you." I look into his startled eyes and tell him, from the bottom of my heart, "Thank you."

I pitch forward, sinking my mouth onto him.

The room erupts into a scandalized cheer behind me, but I block them out. It's nothing like it was with Dimitri, and I'm grateful. Those moments with him in his room were like a balm to an old, smarting burn.

It's also not like it was with Tristian, though. That had been all hurt and fear and shame. All of that's still present now, but there's also resolve and something unshakable—something that's being created within me with every rise and fall of my head. I don't really understand it—not yet—but I think it might be armor.

I think it might protect me.

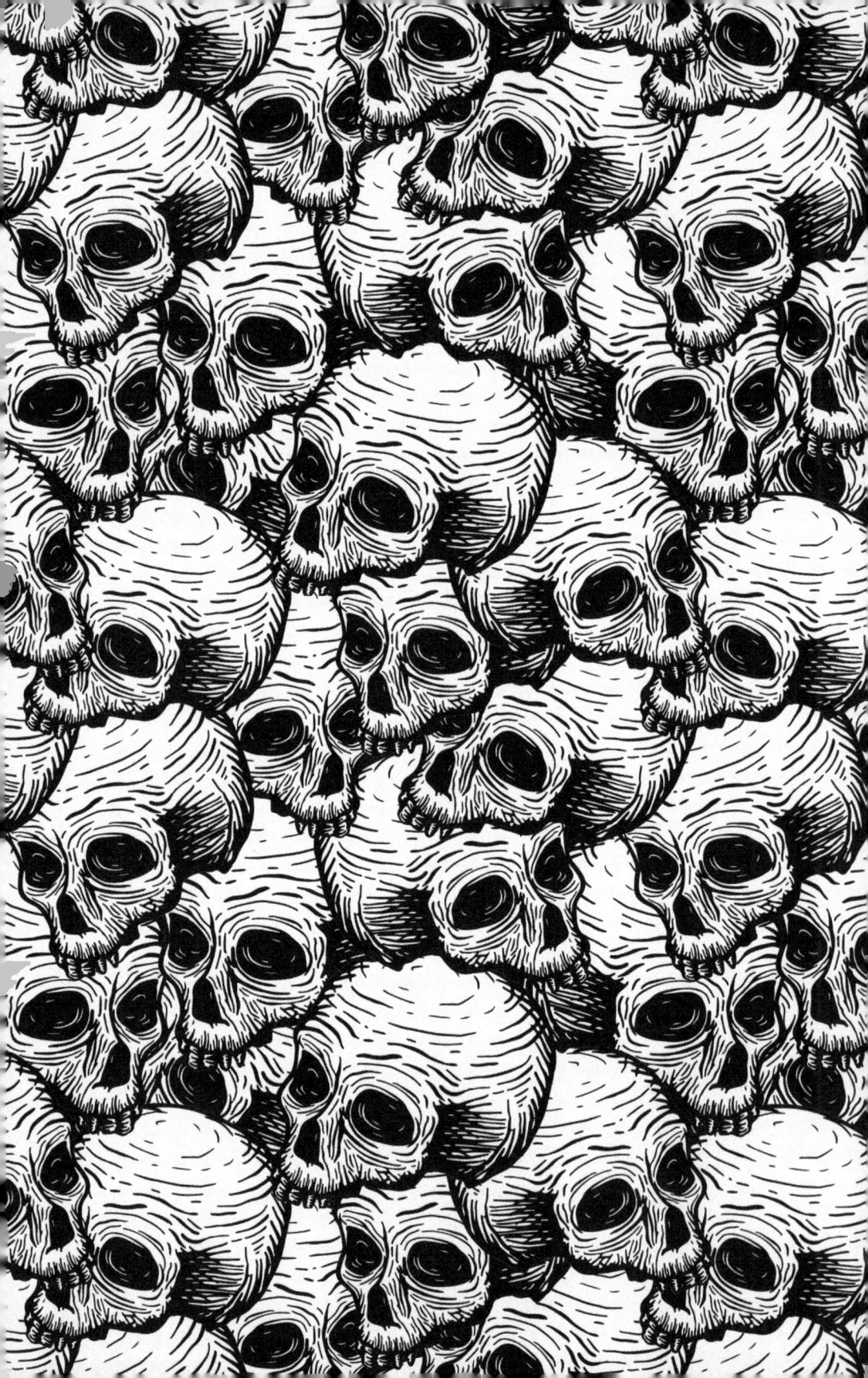

24

PAIN

…Thank you…

Her words keep ricocheting around in my head, so I shut them out, focusing on nothing but the feel of her hot, wet mouth around me. I watch her instead of all the guys in the room, the way a lock of her hair catches on her lips, the fan of her eyelashes as she works, eyes closed. It's all at once the best and worst.

It's the best because it feels even better than I imagined. The sight of my dick disappearing between those lips is the culmination of years of fantasizing. And fuck, she's actually good at what she's doing. Even if every motion is stiff and detached, it's still the perfect tempo, the right amount of suction, never any teeth. Her tongue works against me as she bobs her head. For years, I've been thinking back on that night with the others, feeling envious of Tristian for having the balls to actually go through with it. Wondering how good it felt. Wishing I'd been the one in front of her, feeding her my come. Now I don't have to wonder, and more than that, I know for a fact I'm getting it better than he did—better skills, more drive, harder purpose. It's a battle to remain stony and aloof when all I want to do is grab her hair and throw my head back, basking in this victory.

…Because after this …

It's the worst because it doesn't feel like a victory at all. It feels more like defeat than anything else. The head is good, but she's only got skills because she's been sucking Rath's dick and *liking it*. She doesn't like this. She looks bored and rigid, like she just wants to get it over with. There's no heat there. No desire. Nothing. And the whole time, all I can think about is what she said about liking me. About maybe wanting…something. With me. Back then.

I can tell myself over and over that it's probably a lie and it wouldn't matter. The confession still catches on something inside of me—this sick sense of satisfaction I thought I'd given up on chasing years ago.

Carter, this dickwad Philosophy major who'd pledged with the three of us freshman year, belts out a crude, "Make her choke on it, Payne!" and the others rally behind it with gleeful taunts. He's too close to Rath to be saying shit like that, and Rath makes sure he knows it. The sound of his slap against Carter's head reverberates through the room with a sharp crack.

"Show some fucking respect," he snaps.

…there's no part of me…

Even though I'm not planning on it—this isn't a fucking porn show for them—she pushes down until I hit the back of her throat and hangs there, breathing roughly. The whole move is spiteful and insolent, like it's a fucking *challenge*.

I can't help myself then, biting back a groan as I reach down to grab a handful of her shiny dark hair. I have to pull her back, and the sound she makes—this long, raspy inhale—shoots straight to my balls.

…no fucking cell in my body…

I'm used to everyone watching me, cheering me on the second I step onto the field. I've always thrived on having an audience. But while the frat is watching Story, my friends aren't. I can feel Tristian and Rath's eyes on me instead as I fuck her mouth, using my grip on her hair to set a punishing rhythm. Story might have been sucking Rath off for a few days now, but I can tell this is her first time taking it hard and deep. The awareness makes my stomach tighten, knowing I'm the only one who's fucked her mouth like this. I clutch onto it like a man possessed, and why the fuck shouldn't I? It's clear now that nothing else of hers can be mine. *Nothing.*

…that'll feel anything…

This is it, right here. This is all I'll ever have of her. A forced blow job in a dimly-lit basement in front of forty-five other men.

It hits me like a boulder, right in the chest.

Curling my fingers into a fist in her hair, I grab the base of my dick and yank her off, jacking it fast and hard. She gasps in a breath before clamping her mouth closed, but I roughly demand, "Open your mouth."

She fixes her eyes to my stomach and obeys.

…but disgust for you…

The orgasm hits me like a punch, seizing my balls tight. I tip her head up, shooting my thick ribbons of come onto her outstretched tongue. It fogs me up so entirely that I can hardly keep focus on it—this fantasy I've been so goddamn desperate for.

The reality is such a fucking disappointment.

I don't even want to watch her swallow me down. Catching my breath, I hike up my pants and thrust my chin toward the door. "Go."

Even now, she doesn't run. She rises to her feet, smoothes down the skirt of that pretty peach dress, spins on her heel, and strides silently away.

Tucker, who's sitting near the back, cups his hands around his mouth to bellow, "Make another deposit!"

"Shut your fucking mouth," Tristian barks, springing forward to grab a thick handful of his shirt. "Say one more word to her and I'll cut your goddamn tongue out."

I stare in shock for so long that I miss her exit. Tristian is always composed and there's good reason for it. It's taken him years to perfect a façade. He's got skin that flushes up at the smallest bit of anger, and he's always hated it. I haven't actually seen it in years, but there it is now. Glowing fucking red.

Tucker raises his hands defensively. "Sorry, just chasing the vibe."

I dismiss them before this can turn any worse than it already is. Tristian and Rath follow them all out, probably to make sure everyone actually leaves. If I'm right—if one of them is using access to the house—then we'll need to be more careful about who comes and goes.

When the room is empty, I stand there, trying to get my bearings. I let the quiet sink into me, but it doesn't stay—not with her words bouncing around in my head, unwanted but incessant. That boulder in my chest is still heavy, driving me fucking insane. Only one thing could fix that.

The guys are nowhere to be found when I make my way upstairs, pouring myself a glass of whiskey. I throw it back and savor the burn, but now it's worse. Now I'm remembering that kiss from before, back in my old bedroom. I'm remembering the way she kissed me back, those hands pulling me closer. She'd tasted bitter but somehow still sweet. I know she got off riding my thigh. I had to clamp my hand over her mouth just to quiet her sharp, surprised cry. But I could still hear it, trapped in her mouth. I could still see the way her face collapsed in pleasure, eyes squeezing shut, and *fuck*.

How the hell did I go from such great heights to...*this*.

Huffing, I throw back another glass before searching for the guys. They're not on the first floor, so I check the second, then the third. As I pass Story's room, I linger, trying to hear something behind the door.

There's nothing.

Clenching my fists, I descend the stairs and go out back, but the garden and hot tub are empty. It isn't until I round the side of the house that I find them, standing in the shadow of the basketball court, sharing a cigarette like two goddamn degenerates.

Tristian shakes his head as soon as he sees me. "You don't want to be near me right now, Killer."

I hold my arms out. "Got something to say? Say it."

"It was too much, dude." It's Rath who steps up, handing the cigarette over to Tristian. "There's a reason you didn't tell us what the hell you were doing. You knew we'd say no."

"This isn't a fucking democracy," I snap, feeling the anger swell up in my chest. It's good. Better than the weight of that goddamn boulder. "I don't remember either of you asking me permission for jack shit. She got what she deserved. She's been fucking cheating on us!"

"You don't know that!" Rath argues, thrusting a finger into the center of my chest. "You suspect it, but you don't know anything. She's done everything we've ever asked of her. Jesus Christ, she even did *that*! If you can't look at the facts and see that she's loyal, then you're just too fucking hot-headed to think objectively."

"He's right," Tristian says, tossing the cigarette aside. "I know you've got issues, but ever since she walked through that door, you've been losing your grip."

"My grip is just fucking fine," I growl.

"Bullshit," Tristian disagrees, eyeing me with displeasure. "It's one thing that you leave us to take care of South Side business while you go off to your bogus family dinner, but taking our Lady down there and doing that to her? She's not just yours!"

"I let you two go unchecked on her every goddamn day, but the second I do something, you're up my ass about it!" Ticking off on my fingers, I say, "I can't withhold meals, I can't leave marks, I can't make her blow me. I'm getting sick and tired—"

"We don't break her," Rath says, interrupting me with another one of those chest pokes. This guy's about to fucking get it. "Neither of us has ever corrected her out of anger. But that's all you fucking do. You don't even pick up the pieces after—you leave that to us."

"She isn't your goddamn punching bag, Killer." Tristian runs his fingers through his hair, visibly trying to calm himself down. "It's fucked up."

I raise an eyebrow, feeling my blood boil. "Oh, it's fucked up now, is it?

That's rich, coming from you."

His eyes narrow dangerously. "What the hell is that supposed to mean?"

"Maybe you're so high on that horse that you can't see it, so let me spell it out for you." Lifting my chin, I look down my nose at him, seething. "Making her suck a dick in front of our brothers wasn't a concept you had a problem with three years ago."

His face contorts, voice lowering. "That was different."

"No, it fucking wasn't, and you know it."

He points at the house, eyes flashing hotly. "You humiliated her in front of forty-five people in there!"

"Yeah, and she's still here." I shrug, even though there's a little voice in my head telling me to stop. To salvage this. Like always when I hear it, I barrel forward. "But you fucked her up so bad, she ran away."

His laugh is cold and mocking. "No, I didn't. The more I get to know her, the more I see the truth. She could have handled what me and Rath did to her, however fucked up it might have been." He steps up to me, chest puffed out. "It's you, Killer. You're the reason she ran. You drove her away on a daily fucking basis, because you're so messed up that you can't even fall in love with someone without sabotaging yourself." He gives my fuming expression a cold smirk. "Don't deny it. All three of us know the truth. You didn't just want to own her. You got attached. You fell for her, and you couldn't handle it. So, you let every man in your life get a piece of that ass first, and you want to know why?" Closer—quieter—he hisses, "It's because you're a pussy."

The shove sends him to the ground instantly, sprawled on his back. He doesn't stay down long, jumping to his feet to throw the first punch. Tristian is faster than me, but I'm bigger—stronger. I can't dodge his punch, but I hit him back twice as hard, sending his head whipping to the side.

Before I can get in another, I feel a hit to my jaw, cracking up through my temple. Rath. *These motherfuckers.*

I tackle him next, getting him to the ground easily. Rath is even slower than

I am, but he's also a malicious little shit. His knee catches me right in the balls, sending sparks through my vision for a moment.

But then Tristian is there, dragging me off of him. I plant a hard elbow into his side, but he barely reacts, burying a knee right into my kidney. I grunt, kicking Rath before he can lever himself up. It's all a crazed whir, taking one out just to swat at another. Fucking gnats. That's all these two are.

With a big burst of power, I shake Tristian off of me and regain my footing.

But so have they.

The two of them stand there under the light of the court, breathing hard, stares sharp like daggers, and suddenly I'm just done with it all.

I spit, my blood splattering on the pavement. "She's a liar and a whore and she's got you two so pussy-whipped you've forgotten that this is a game. That's all it is, a game!" I take a step back, spreading my arms wide, knowing what I have to do. "But if you want her so bad, then you can fucking have her."

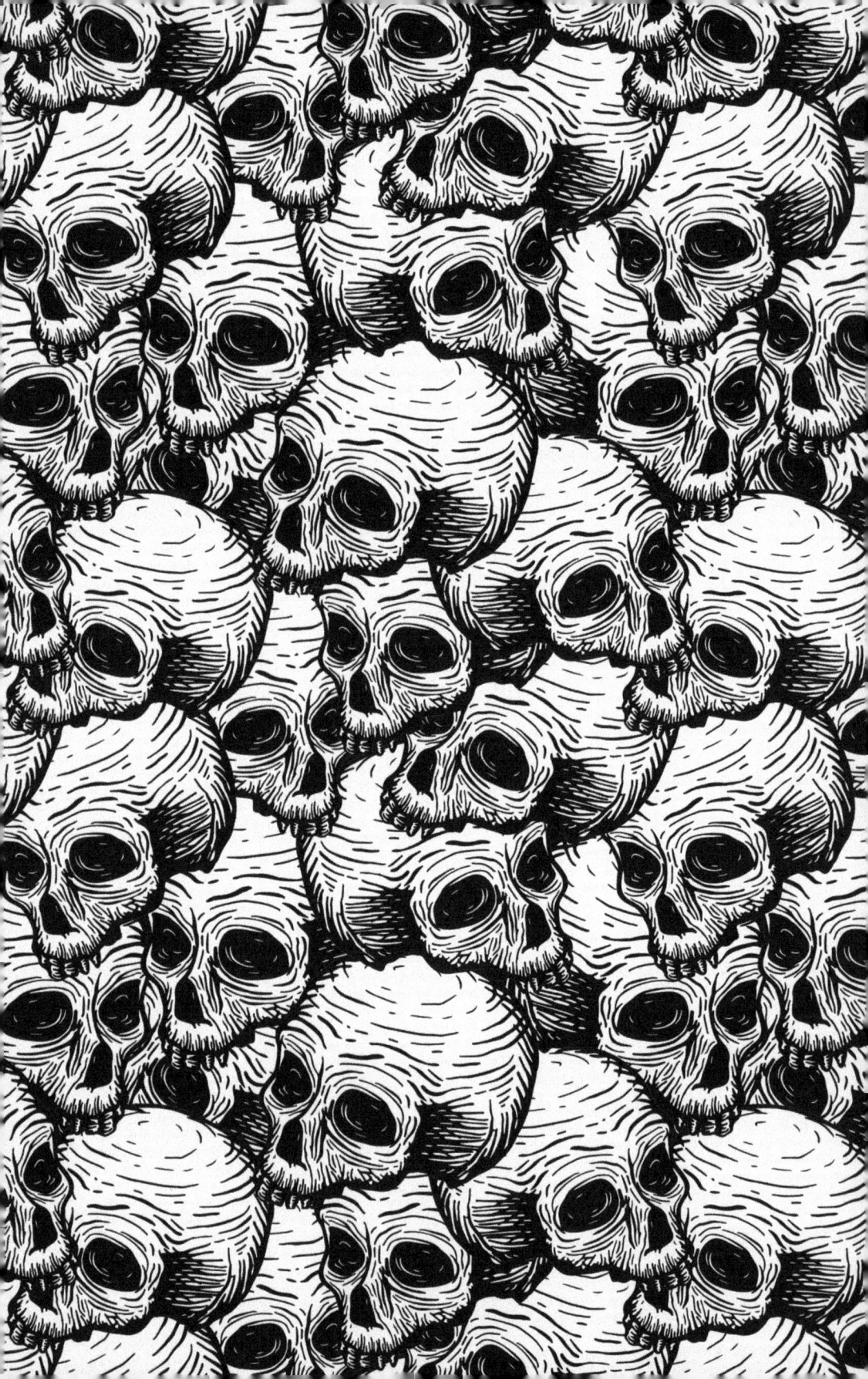

STORY

25

MOURNING LIGHT

EIGHT.

That's how many dresses I find in the closet that are like the one I'm wearing. Cute. Pretty. Perfectly innocent.

Chosen by Killian.

I lay them out on the bed and look at them, but something isn't quite right. I reach down, fingering the dress I'm wearing. It's wet down the front. When I got into my room, I vomited into the toilet and then brushed my teeth for ten minutes. It didn't really make me feel any cleaner—not until I take this fucking dress off.

Ripping it off, I stand there in nothing but my underwear, throwing the dress with the others. That feels better, seeing them all lined up like that. I don't need these anymore—if I ever did at all. Today was the first and last time I dressed to please him.

I only use the scissors to get me started, cutting a notch into the skirt of one of the dresses. After that, I grip it in my hands and pull, ripping it until I can't anymore. One isn't enough, so I do it again and again, until the first dress is a pile of sad, limp shreds.

I work my way through the dresses methodically, thinking about what

I overheard earlier. The basketball court is right outside my window, and if I crack it the smallest bit, I can hear everything. It's especially easy to hear when there's yelling and fighting.

I grunt against a particularly stubborn seam, arms trembling with the struggle. Eventually, it gives, making a satisfying sound as it tears all the way to the neck.

There's a soft knock at the door before Tristian's voice comes through. "Story?" He tries the knob, but even if it were unlocked, he wouldn't be able to get through. The knob goes still. There's a suspended moment of silence before he adds, "Fine. You don't need to open the door. Just say something so we know you're good."

Good?

I pick up another dress, ripping it down the side. "Something."

There's another beat of silence before he answers, "Do you…need anything?" The words sound uncertain and stilted, like he's testing them out, and maybe he is. His sisters aside, he must not have much experience with things like concern.

I'm just about to tell him to go away when a thought hits me. Clenching my teeth, I rip my blanket from the bed to cover myself with. The desk, which I'd wedged in front of the door, scrapes loudly against the floor when I push it out a few inches—just enough to crack the door.

"There's something you can do for me," I answer, peering out the crack at him.

Tristian looks back at me, half startled, half apprehensive. He's sporting a split lip. "We didn't know he was going to do that."

Ignoring that, I continue, "You can get me something to wear that isn't skin-tight, see-through, short, or in any way marketable for paid internet porn."

He catches the scraps of dresses I throw at him, unflinching. He looks down at them, inspecting the jagged, frayed fabric, and gives a slow, sure nod. "I'll see what we can scare up."

When he turns, heading toward the stairs, I notice that Dimitri is here, too. He's leaning up against Killian's closed door, holding an ice pack to his jaw. When he sees me watching, he shoots me a roguish grin. "Should see the other guy, baby."

I prop myself against the door jamb, knowing my eyes are red. I didn't let myself cry for long, and it wasn't like last time. These were bitter, exhausted tears—the remnants of whatever this hard thing inside of me are driving out. "The whole point of *this*," I say, kicking the desk in front of the door, "is to avoid that."

His lips purse. "Finally worked out that he's got a key, huh?"

"I assume you all do."

He lowers the ice pack, revealing a large, angry bruise. "Just him. Sneaking into bedrooms isn't really our style."

Tristian returns then, a bundle of clothes in his arms. "These are going to be big, but maybe you can make do." He feeds them through the crack in the door and I grab hold, clutching them to my chest.

I mumble a small, "Thank you," and step aside, just out of sight. The blanket falls to the floor and I unfold the clothes. Sweatpants, a loose undershirt, and an oversized hooded sweater. Tristian's right—everything is way too big. It's a nice change.

"Will you come downstairs?" Tristian asks, sighing. "Have a drink with us, decompress."

Dimitri adds, "Killer won't be back tonight."

Slipping the sweater over my head, I hug my middle, not feeling any warmer. "How do you know?"

Tristian snorts. "He's doing his own decompressing. Trust me."

Inching closer to the door, I softly wonder, "Are you going to make me… do things?"

"What?" Tristian sounds unjustly offended. "Of course not."

Dimitri jumps in. "Look, we'll be downstairs. If you want to be alone to wallow and stew, fine. If you don't, come chill. Consider yourself off the clock, either way." Quieter, to Tristian, he adds, "Come on. Stop hovering, let her work her shit out."

Their footsteps recede moments later, down the stairs. I peek out of the crack, seeing that I'm alone. Deflating, I try to reconcile two competing forces. Tristian and Dimitri obviously hadn't been okay with what Killian did to me. They sounded really mad about it, actually. They turned on him—someone they've been best friends with since they were just little kids. I didn't think anything could ever come between them. That means something, doesn't it?

On the other hand, they're not blameless. They've dished out their own malice, over and over again.

It takes a moment to move the desk far enough that I can slip out of the room. I leave it close, fully planning on moving it back the next time I'm inside. Mostly, I feel stupid. Thinking a lock makes me safe? When has that ever been enough?

The house is quiet when I descend the stairs, following their low voices to the den. This is where they hang out most of the time, but aside from the interview and the party, I haven't been in here much. It's a den for wolves, waiting to eat me whole.

Tugging the sleeves over my fists, I warily shuffle into the room.

Killian did leave. I heard the whole fight, so I know that he stormed away. I even heard the sound of his truck as it sped out of the garage. Still, a part of me still expects him to be lurking around a corner and my heart builds to a crazed tempo, racing with the possibility that *everyone* is still here. I can still remember the sounds of their laughter and jeers, all those cold, heartless men watching my debasement like it was entertainment.

Luckily, it's just Tristian and Dimitri. They're mirror images of one another, perched on different sofas, speaking in low tones across a bold-looking coffee table, each holding a tumbler of brown liquid.

They both pause when I walk in, curling my fingers into the large, soft sweater. The sweater, like the sweatpants, has 'Varsity Swim' emblazoned on it—a relic from our old high school.

It's Tristian who stands, moving fluidly to where the glasses and liquor await. He pours a glass and refreshes his own before returning to his seat, sliding mine down the table. "Go easy," he says, nodding at the glass.

Reluctantly, I perch on the couch farthest from them both, tucking my limbs in close. The booze smells strong and sharp when I lift it to my nose, sniffing suspiciously. Being anything but stone-cold sober in this house is a mistake. I know that. But maybe it'll help. Maybe it can quiet this chaotic storm that's tearing up my chest.

Still, I wait for Tristian to take a drink of his before following suit.

Instantly, I start hacking, pulling a face at the contents of the glass. "This is worse than the wheatgrass."

Dimitri barks a small laugh, but Tristian gives me a look. "That's fifty-year-old bourbon. It costs more than most people's rent."

Grimacing, I say, "You got ripped off."

"It's an acquired taste," Dimitri assures, swirling his around.

I'm not sure it's a taste I want to acquire, but the burn does begin warming my chest. It spreads outward, a comforting tingle settling in my gut. For a brief moment, I actually feel my muscles relax. Giving it another look, I pinch my nose and throw it back, downing the whole thing in one go.

"I said easy," Tristian chides, sounding all at once distressed and disappointed. "I can't believe you're drinking aged bourbon like it's cheap tequila. Jesus Christ."

I set the glass on the table and shudder at the aftertaste. "You always give me the grossest stuff," I tell Tristian.

He rolls his eyes, taking a much more delicate sip. "If you drank the wheatgrass that enthusiastically, you'd be healthy as a horse."

I swipe at my mouth, looking around the room. It's dimly lit and smells of something sharp and sweet. A stuffed buck's head hangs with prominence over the bar, its bold antlers reaching like skeletal fingers over the room. There's a stuffed bear's head, too. A large fish of some kind, mounted on a huge chunk of driftwood. On the mantel rests a large bronze LDZ skull, just like the one on my wrist cuff. In the corner, there's an enormous vase filled with bare, brittle-looking, vein-like limbs. They reach into the air and spread like a web over the entrance.

This house is full of dead things.

"Do you know anything about Killer's mom?"

Tristian shoots him a hard look, voice full of warning. "Rath."

Dimitri holds up a hand. "I'm just asking. I won't tell her anything."

Everything's a little softer and warmer now, the bourbon making my arms feel heavy. "I never met her," I admit, wading through the comfortable fog to think back to when I lived with him. "They never talked about her much. I know he keeps a picture. She was pretty, I guess."

"Hm." Dimitri finishes his glass, setting it on the table like I had. "Guess it doesn't matter. Killer was out of line."

I'm curious about her, this Darla Payne, but it's clear from the look the two of them share that they won't tell me anything. They might be in a fight with Killian, but they aren't about to spill his secrets. "What's going to happen?" The cuff of the sweater rides up, revealing my wrist band. I pick at it like a scab, shoving a finger underneath to rub the sensitive skin.

Tristian's lips press into a thin line. "Nothing is going to happen. We're going to go to bed in a minute, then wake up and go to classes, just like we always do."

I look up at him, pleading, "Can't I miss a day? Just one?"

He actually looks rueful as he shakes his head. "Things have to stay routine. We can't let everyone think—"

"All those guys have seen me," I lament, pressing my fists into my stomach, feeling sick at the prospect of facing them all. Yet again, their words and laughter drift back to me. Not even the booze is enough to dull the flush of shame and humiliation that washes over me. "I recognized some of them from my classes. Everyone will know." Tears come, unbidden, but I blink them rapidly away.

"It won't be like that." Tristian slides down the couch, reaching to touch my knee, but I recoil. He drops his hand, sighing as he leans back. "People like this—" *Like me,* he doesn't say, "—they smell chum and they get worked into a frenzy. Hiding from them is like blood in the water. The best thing to do is act like it doesn't bother you. Isn't that what you told Izzy and Lizzy?"

I narrow my eyes at him, sniffing back my tears. "That's not even remotely the fucking same."

Dimitri pipes in then, "We'll send everyone a warning. Let them know what's going to happen if they so much as glance at you."

Tristian agrees, "They're assholes, but they're also sheep. They'll do what we say."

I don't feel comforted by this in the least. If they'll listen to Tristian and Dimitri, then they'll listen to Killian, too. "He's going to be mad when he comes back," I realize, panic breaking through the bourbon's haze. "He'll blame me. He'll punish me again. He has a key to my room and he's strong enough to—"

"He's not coming back tonight."

"How do you know?" I ask Tristian, feeling on the verge of hysteria. They didn't know what he was going to do before. Killian is nothing if not unpredictable.

Tristian watches me, those icy blue eyes searching mine. "You can sleep in my room, if you want," he offers, sounding both hopeful and uncertain. "Killian wouldn't try anything if you were with one of us."

The thought makes my stomach churn. It's not a simple feeling. I've always been haunted by that night in the laundry room, but tonight, the memory feels so fresh and raw. Those cold blue eyes might be looking at me differently now—softer, less malicious—but they're the same eyes that held mine as he forced me to take him inside. As he hurt me. As he used me.

Slowly, I shake my head. "No, thank you." Tristian nods, looking unsurprised. Without really needing to think about it, I add, "What about Dimitri's?"

Tristian's mouth snaps closed. "Rath's?"

Nodding, I look to Dimitri. "Please?"

He blinks at me, looking startled. "You want to sleep in my room?" At my nod, he gives Tristian a stunned, anxious look. "I'm probably going to practice some before I go to sleep."

"That's okay," I assure, feeling embarrassed at the request. "I like to hear you play."

Frowning, Tristian says, "I have a couch, too. I can even put on some music for you."

I wrap my arms around my middle, ducking my head. Softly, I confess, "I want Dimitri."

There's a long moment of silence, and I know if I looked up, I'd see them having some sort of conversation with their eyes. Maybe I'll pay for this—for rejecting one in favor of another. Right now, I just can't seem to care.

Tristian releases a long sigh, standing from the couch. His voice is a little too even—a bit too casual—when he says, "Alright. I'll see you both at breakfast," and leaves the room.

I peek up at Dimitri, who's giving me a carefully neutral look. "Is he mad?"

He lifts a shoulder. "Maybe. Nothing he won't get over, though. We're not—" He pauses, eyebrows knitting together as his dark eyes hold mine. "We're not like Killian."

You're not, I don't say. Dimitri's never forced me to my knees for him. He's callous and impulsive and as prone to tempers as any of them, and he isn't blameless in anything. But he's the only one who's ever asked—ever cared if I wanted it.

It's a testament to the sad state of my life that Dimitri is the best guy involved in it.

I follow him up the stairs, passing mine and Killian's room, and then Tristian's. As soon as I step inside, I know I made the right choice. This room had been the place I'd escaped to in my head as Killian used me. The soft, comfortable lighting. The way everything was a little unkempt. The sounds of the music. The way his bed always looks, warm and inviting.

Dimitri pauses in the middle of the room, reaching up to scratch the nape of his neck. "Uh, I guess…do you want me to sleep on the couch?" He phrases this like a question he finds odious.

I suppose this—handing the decision of his comfort over to me—is probably exactly what that's like. "I don't care," I admit, shuffling my way to the bed. "I think I'd like sleeping beside you." It's a difficult thing to give away, but the bourbon has made my tongue a little loose.

Apparently, it did the same for Dimitri. "I had this teacher," he suddenly says, face shadowed. "Third grade. Mr. Yelchin. My mom worked for months to get me into this academy. The teachers were supposed to be real cream-of-the-crop types." His eyes grow hazy, as if lost in a memory. "When I had… issues reading, he'd call me names. Tell me I was stupid. Hit me with the ruler. Make me stand up in front of the class and embarrass myself." His fists clench, jaw tightening. "I still let it get to me sometimes. Pretty fucking stupid, right?" It's asked like he's looking for agreement, but there's something in his eyes—haunted, ashamed—that's asking for the exact opposite.

I happen to have some experience here. "I don't think that's something you can help."

He nods, like he was expecting that answer. "I hope…" he pauses, frowning. "I hope tonight wasn't like that. For you."

Swallowing, I reply, "Me too."

The look we share says that we both know it will be.

Like a switch flipping off, he turns away, shoulders tensing. "I don't fucking cuddle."

I pull the blankets back. "Okay."

"I mean it," he says, voice firm as he takes the piano bench. "Don't be wrapping around me like a goddamn octopus. I need my space."

The notes reverberate through the room before I can agree, slipping between the sheets. His bed is just as comfortable as it looks, and I settle at the edge, making sure to leave him plenty of space. Houses like this one are drafty and cooler than usual, but I instinctively know that I'm going to wake up sweating buckets if I fall asleep in Tristian's clothes. After a long moment of internal struggling, I reluctantly decide to take off the hooded sweater and pants, fishing them out of the blankets once I have. I lay them in a tidy lump on the floor beside me, curling up to listen to the music.

It lulls me instantly to sleep.

I'M STILL HOT.

I don't know what time it is when I surface from a deep, dazed sleep, but the room is dark. All the lamps are off, nothing but the soft glow of a computer screen illuminating the room. One twitch is enough to send my chest into a panicked frenzy.

I can't move.

I squirm against the thing that's pinning me down, breaths coming faster, before I realize it's an arm. Specifically, Dimitri's arm. Confused, I blink down at the dark dusting of hair covering his forearm. I'm still at the edge of the bed, in the exact same position I'd been in when I fell asleep. I've always been a hard sleeper, not prone to tossing and turning, which is why I hadn't been worried when he warned me against taking his space.

And now here he is, engulfing me in his arms, his steady, even breaths tickling the top of my head as he sleeps.

Not a cuddler, my ass.

I come to find that I don't really mind it. So much, in fact, that I wriggle back into him, only feeling a brief spike of anxiety at the way he clutches me closer in response, his arm seeming as immovable as steel. It's a jarring, almost frustrated yank. Apparently, he's just as greedy and irritable in sleep as he is awake.

It doesn't take very long for me to succumb to sleep once again, filled with the scent of him, surrounded by the hardness and warmth of his body.

FOR THE FIRST TIME IN A LONG WHILE, I'm not awoken in the morning by my alarm.

I rise from the fog of sleep slowly, like climbing my way out of a thick cloud. It's made both easier and more difficult by the gentle groan in my ear, something firm and persistent pressing rhythmically into my backside.

Before I even have the presence of mind to stiffen in worry, I realize that Dimitri isn't completely awake, either. He's still curled around me and his movements are slow and uncoordinated, purely instinctual.

I know he's awake when he falters, stilling.

His fist flexes against my belly, a rough sound escaping his throat. "*Ugh*," he croaks, a thread of disappointment present in the sigh that follows. "Sorry. Morning wood." He goes to roll away, stretching his legs, but I reach out, grabbing his arm to stop him.

Pausing, he haltingly sinks back against me, the feel of his cock obscene and obvious against my ass.

He fingers the hem of my shirt, voice still soft with sleep when he whispers a surprised, eager, "Yeah?" into my neck. He presses a gentle, uncertain kiss to the skin there, thrusting against me. "You want it?"

Swallowing, I give him a nod, even though I don't know what I'm agreeing to. I just know that it feels good—that the only time *any of this* has felt good, completely absent of shame or hurt or regret, is in this room, with him. I want to touch someone—be touched *by* someone—who I'm choosing. I want to wash the memory of last night away with something that's not tainted and twisted.

I want to take my body back for one godforsaken moment.

There's a new energy in the way his fingertips dip beneath my shirt, inching up. It may be stupid of me, but his motions seem slow and dubious enough that it fills me with the oddest assurance.

Like maybe he'd stop if I asked him to.

His hand finds my breast, fingertips brushing over the warm flesh before engulfing it in his palm and squeezing. "Fuck," he breathes, driving his hips into mine. His thumb finds my nipple, sending a shockwave of electricity right between my legs. "Like this?" he asks when I gasp, stretching my neck.

I go easily when he rolls me to my back, shucking my shirt up. His eyes are still glazed with sleep when he looks down on me, taking in my exposed breasts. He watches his hand on them, gathering one up into his warm palm before ducking his head to suck at it.

My head digs back into the pillow, body writhing at the sensation. His mouth is an impossible point of fire, tongue flicking lazily at my peaked nipple. Even when it's just his lips, his lip rings rub against me in a novel way, making my back arch in response. The moan I give sends him into motion, frantically shoving the blankets away as his palm rubs down my thigh. He grabs below my knee to hook my leg over his hip, jostling until he's settled in the cradle of my thighs, thrusting his hardness against the cotton of my panties.

It's all a little too fast, rapidly becoming devoid of the slow, sleepy aura it began with. But the sharp zings to my center from the way his cock grinds against me are making me not really care. I scrabble at the warm skin of his shoulders, which I'm realizing now are bare. Dimitri is shirtless, clad in only a pair of loose boxer shorts. His back is warm beneath my hands, muscles rippling with the way he surges into me.

His kiss is impatient and demanding, but strangely comforting. The pointed jerk of his body as he grinds against me, the restless sweeps of his palm on my breasts, the sharp, deep kisses are all proof of his eagerness. For the first time, I finally understand everyone's words. Ms. Crane. Tristian.

Eventually, you might learn to use that thing between your legs…

Your problem is that you haven't embraced your sex appeal…

There's power here, I realize, seeing the pinched, hard look on Dimitri's face when he pulls back. There's weakness in the crush of his brow as his eyes take in my body. When I sweep my hands down his muscled back, he arches against them, chasing the touch, mouth parted as he rocks into my thighs.

"You like that, don't you?" he asks, breaths coming harder. "You like how my dick feels."

He doesn't go beneath my panties, keeping the barrier up. It's surprising he doesn't go further. He could, and the big secret is that I'd probably let him. But I don't need it. Neither does he. I can feel it in the hardness sending my clit into a frenzy. I can feel it in his movements, impatient and hungry.

Nodding, I wet my lips, bucking my hips into him. "Yes."

His eyes flash in a sharp satisfaction. "God, I can't wait to fuck you. I bet you'd get so wet for my dick." He ducks his head to watch our hips moving together.

Unthinkingly, I follow his gaze, belly seizing at what I see. The head of his cock has completely escaped the waistband of his boxers, a bead of clear fluid falling from the tip as it drags against my panties. I grind up into it, desperate for the friction.

Groaning, he adds, "Fuck, sometimes it's all I can think about. Getting my dick inside you. Drives me fucking crazy." I know he's babbling now, lost in the same mindlessness that's driving our hips together. "Want to bend you over and fuck you hard. Make you scream my name." He puts his mouth to mine, hovering there as his jaw clenches. "Say it," he demands, his thrusts growing urgent and a little too hard.

Digging my fingertips into his shoulder blades, I'm momentarily lost in the chase. This ball of electricity building in my belly is so close to exploding that my knees are trembling against his thighs. He's got me pinned to the bed by nothing more than the press of his dick.

"Say it," he growls, hips rolling. "Say my fucking name, Story."

It hits me like a tidal wave as I fall from the precipice. My strained, "Dimitri," is some crooked combination of gasp and yelp, but it makes him grunt hard in response, his hard cock slamming against me. There's no invasion, just two bodies working together. Shifting, rubbing, quivering.

He holds his hips against mine and I can feel it. The twitch. The shift of his flexing muscles. The warmth against my belly as he erupts. It makes the orgasm that much sweeter, the way his palm cups my cheek as he breathes quick and damp into my neck. It feels kind of like gratitude.

Yes.

There is definitely power here.

I LEAVE WHILE DIMITRI SHOWERS, still feeling weak-legged from our…encounter. I'm only halfway out of that dazed headspace when I run into Tristian on the second-floor landing.

His eyes jump down to my chest, the hooded sweatshirt back in place. Something hard and pleased crosses his features before it's erased. "Good morning," he says, shifting his grip on the bags he's carrying. "I was just about to come see if you two were up. I didn't know if you had your phone and Rath is always forgetting to set his alarm." Much like Dimitri's jaw, Tristian's lip looks worse in the light of day—swollen and scabbed.

"We, uh," I can't contain the hot flush that instantly comes over me, "woke up."

"Oh," Tristian says, realization clear in the blink of his eyes. He gives me a look. "Is this something I need to hassle him about, or…"

I shake my head, eyes widening. "No! Not like that."

Not like Killian.

"I see," he answers, face going carefully blank. "Can we get in there?"

I follow his nod to my door, easily slipping through the crack I'd made. Tristian is wide, however. I have to scoot the desk out some more to make space for him to enter.

When he does, he eyes the remaining dress scraps still left on my bed. "I guess we're done with the sun dresses." He moves them aside to dump the bags on my bed in their place. "That's okay. I went out early to pick up some things."

My stomach fills with dread. "Like what?"

To my shock, he begins laying out pairs of jeans. They look snug, but not unbearably so. Then, he produces some shirts. Not halters or tanks or anything ridiculous. Just shirts. There's a cardigan, too. A pullover sweater. Loose pajamas. A pair of comfortable-looking shoes.

He gestures to the choices, reaching up to rub at his neck. "It's not a lot, and you'll still be expected to look a certain way most of the time, but you should have something…else. Sometimes." Turning to smirk at me, he adds, "Not that I don't enjoy seeing you in my clothes, because that's pretty fucking hot, Cherry."

I finger at one of the shirts. "Tristian, this is…" *Nice* is on the tip of my tongue, but I'm not so sure it's merited. Letting me wear clothes I'm comfortable in *sometimes* shouldn't be something to gush about.

He doesn't let me finish anyway. "Oh, and there's more." He reaches into another bag, pulling out a fresh bouquet of daisies and extending them to me.

I eye them suspiciously, confused. "Flowers?"

His smile grows stiff. "Well, I noticed you liked the paper one I got for you, so I thought I'd try the real thing." Slowly, I take them, the plastic wrapping crinkling as I give the bouquet a dubious sniff. "I also got you this," he adds, pulling a smaller paper bag from inside the larger one.

When I open it up, I find a huge cherry Danish waiting within. It's still warm. Warm and full of sugar and processed preservatives and whatever else he hates.

I look up at him—at that stiff smile on his handsome face—and level him with a slow, "Tristian."

His smile flattens. "You're mad at me. I get it. I told you I wouldn't let him hurt you again, but I had to stand there while he did that." Running his fingers through his hair, he looks away, agitated. "I couldn't do anything. We have to project a united front. It's dumb frat-house bullshit, but it's important."

I set the bag and flowers down, dragging in a hard breath. "I was never naïve enough to think you'd stop Killian from hurting me. Dimitri, either."

He raises an eyebrow at me. "You don't seem to be holding it against Rath."

"And I'm not holding it against you." I find that it's true. I've known the score here, ever since I walked in that door. I've never been stupid enough to think otherwise.

"Then why are you so cool with him, but—" He instantly freezes, expressions flattening into something hard. "It's because I did it, too."

I don't bother denying it, reaching down to skim a finger over a daisy's soft petals. "It brought back a lot of memories." I heard what Killian said to him out there.

"Making her suck a dick in front of our brothers wasn't a concept you had a problem with three years ago."

He wasn't wrong.

Tristian is silent for a long moment, standing stiffly in the middle of my room. He shifts, burying his fists in his pockets. "Would it help if I said I was sorry?" Scoffing, he adds, "I guess it wouldn't hurt."

I shove the daisies aside, meeting his gaze with as much steel as I can muster. "You can say you're sorry. You can tell me you regret it. You can ask my forgiveness. Say what you like, it still happened."

He shrugs, saying matter-of-factly, "I don't believe in regret. And I believe in forgiveness even less than that. But I do believe in owning up to my shit." He walks closer, those blue eyes pinning me. "I was in a bad place. I'm not going to bullshit you by saying I've turned a new leaf, or that I didn't enjoy it. I never really thought of you outside of that. I never wondered about what it must have been like for you. How badly I made you feel. To be honest, I just didn't care."

I give an inelegant snort. "What, and now you do?"

"Well…yeah," he says, like this should be obvious. "I'm taking care of you now. I don't want to see you like that."

"Like what?" I press, half-appalled, but half-curious.

His expression turns thoughtful. "Diminished, I suppose. Hurt. Upset."

Blandly, I guess, "Because I'm your property."

"That's a part of it," he admits, unabashed. "But there's also this other part. I'm not really sure I understand it yet, but I know that it's making me say this." He touches my chin, tipping my face up, eyes holding mine. His voice is quiet but firm, completely void of artifice. "I'm sorry, Story."

He pitches forward to press a gentle kiss to my head, walking out of the room before he can see the stunned tears in my eyes.

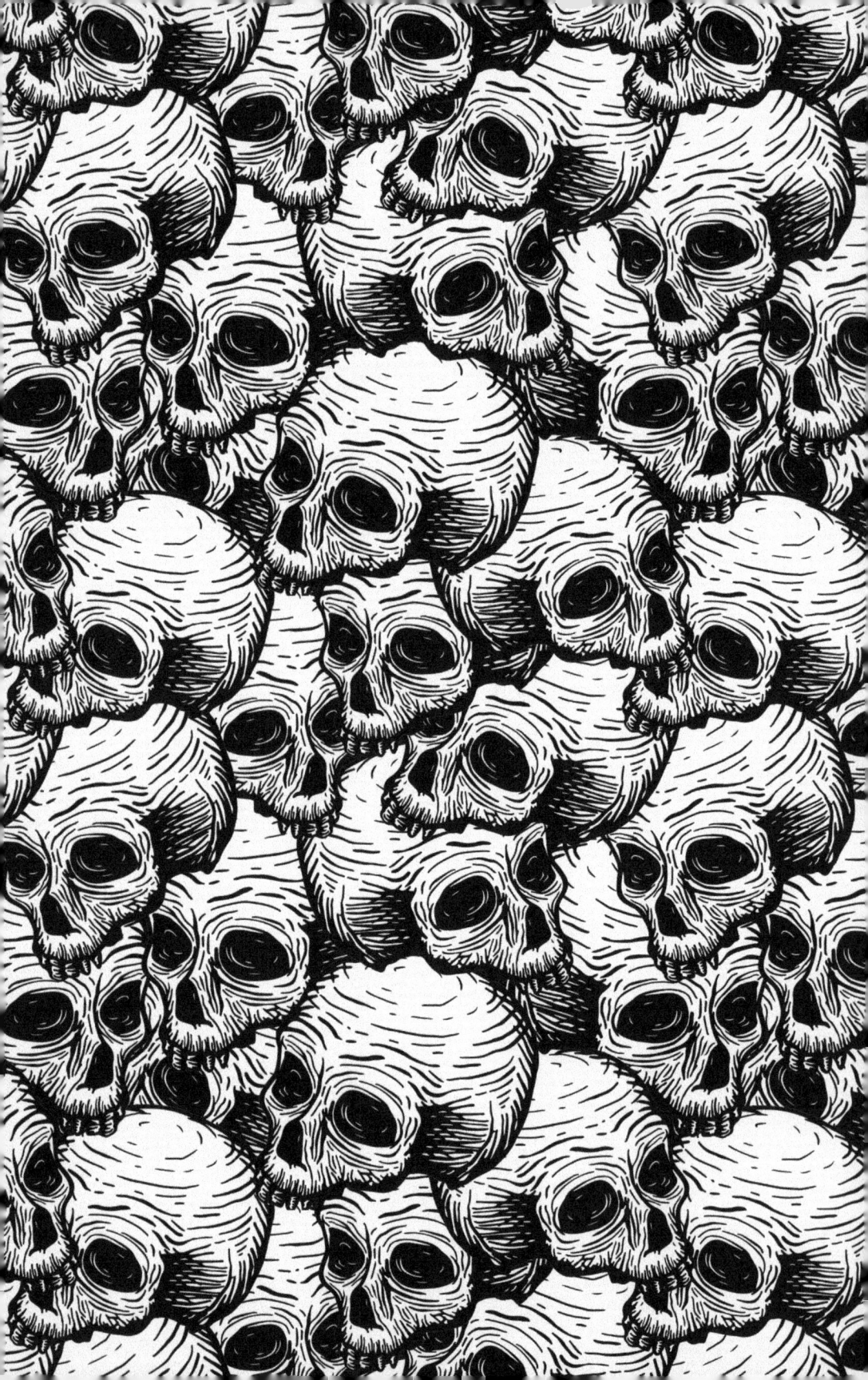

DIMITRI
RATHBONE

26
EVIDENCE

It's been years since my morning shower didn't feature a quick nut to get my day started right. I've always hated the idea of waking up beside a girl. Smelling her morning breath. Having her all over me, telling me to wake up. Being annoyed by her voice.

The reality is a lot fucking better.

I know I must be jonesing for pussy if a quick and embarrassingly juvenile dry hump was *that* good. I haven't rubbed myself off against a girl like that in years. Any other time, I would have pushed for more, maybe just yanked her panties aside and slid right on into home base. But I know better than to think the rules of The Game are flying out the window just because Killian is being a dick.

Turning the knob of the shower, I step out, strutting into my room. I know she's gone—I'd heard her sneak out—but that's okay. She could probably sleep with me again tonight. Tristian is apparently not in the 'guys Story can sleep beside' loyalty club. It's only got one member—me.

I shoot off a group text to the frat before heading downstairs, warning every member and pledge that a single look at, or word about our Lady will call for some serious punishment, if not outright removal.

Downstairs, the two of them have already started breakfast. It doesn't matter that he throws me a nod and looks perfectly normal. Tristian's clearly still sulking over me being the Lady's favorite Lord. He doesn't have me fooled.

It's hard to look at Story and not pitch a tent at the memory of her, just forty minutes ago, laid out beneath me, grinding up against my dick and loving the shit out of it. I stop by her chair to press a kiss to her cheek, stealing a piece of cherry Danish in the process. "Who got Danishes?"

Tristian shoots me a glare. "I got *one*, and it's for her, not you."

My eyebrows hike up my forehead, but I take my seat and refrain from showing how surprised I am. Tristian buying sweets for someone is basically his version of second base. My boy is laying it on pretty thick. He must have really been stung last night.

Story looks a little better this morning than she had last night. Her eyes aren't all red and empty anymore, even if she still looks wary and a bit hunted. There's a yellow flower tucked behind her ear and she glances up at me, cheeks flushing. "I think Ms. Crane made you waffles."

Fuck yeah, she did. I'm Ms. Crane's favorite, too. I decide to cut Tristian some slack this morning. It can't be easy living with someone who keeps scoring all the bitches.

I'm halfway through the aforementioned waffles when I decide to check my phone. "We might need to go in a little early," I say to Tristian. "A couple of the guys haven't checked the group text yet."

Story goes stiff at the mention of the frat, looking between us. I shoot her a wink to let her know it's all good.

Tristian nods, setting down his glass. "Let's roll out, then."

FINDING BECKWITH IS EASY. He's always hanging around the parking lot, showing off his Trans-Am. Putting the fear of God into him is even easier.

But not usually this easy.

"I already told him," he says as I approach, holding his palms out defensively. "I haven't done anything with her!"

I stop, narrowing my eyes. I don't know which 'him' he's referring to, but I decide to play it cool. "Really."

"Really!" he insists, backing up. "I wouldn't lie to Payne, okay? That guy is a fucking psycho. I've never seen that card before, and I've only talked to the Lady once—at the last pregame party. Tristian was there. Ask him for yourself!"

Killian.

Comprehension dawns as I realize Killer's been grilling the guys about that goddamn package. He's like a dog with a bone—won't stop until he can prove it.

I tilt my head, searching his face. "In defiance of the charter that you pledged to, you haven't checked your texts, Beckwith."

His eyes bug out. "Are you serious? One of you takes my phone and smashes it, and then another wants to penalize me for not answering texts? What do you expect me to do, share with someone else? It's only been an hour."

Rolling my eyes, I whip out my phone and repeat the warning I'd sent the others. I'm not cleaning up any more of Killian's messes. If he wants to go around giving everyone the third degree and smashing their phones, then that's on him.

I have to wait outside the admin building for twenty minutes before the second guy appears. I know instantly from the look on his face that Killer's already been here.

"He smash your phone, too?" I ask, deadpan.

Morris is big and broad and epically pissed off. "Yes, and it was brand new."

I wince on the inside. Killer is really burning a path through campus, apparently. I repeat the warning to Morris and move on to the next, but it's exactly the same. Every guy who hasn't checked the group text has had his phone destroyed by Killian Motherfucking Payne.

It takes me the length of my first class to work out why.

Last night had been crazy. I'd like to say that I never doubted Story's loyalty, but there for a moment, Killer had me second-guessing. It wasn't until she walked into that basement, Tristian stone-faced at her side, that I realized just how wrong Killian was.

After that, the whole thing was just hard to watch. I tried focusing on the guys instead, but that made it worse. I kept getting all these flashbacks to third grade—the jeers and taunts and laughter. I kept hearing them say fucked up things about our Lady. *My* Lady. I had to shut one of them up, whopping him hard upside the head. Fucker's lucky he didn't get worse.

But now I'm thinking I wasn't keeping as close a watch as I should have, because every guy I've had to hunt down had one thing in common last night: Their phones were out.

Which means Killian is not only grilling the frat, but he's also destroying any video evidence of what he made our Lady do to him.

She doesn't know it yet, but that's as close to an apology as he'll ever give.

STORY

27

VIPER STRIKE

I'M HALFWAY ACROSS campus when my phone buzzes.

Tristian: Held up in class. Won't make lunch.

Dimitri: (Auto Reply: In Session - Do Not Disturb)

I sit on the edge of the big fountain in front of the administration building and watch the screen for a moment, waiting, wondering if the third Lord will break his silence and reply. Luckily, it never comes, allowing some of the tension to drain from my shoulders.

Some—not all.

After this morning, it's clear what needs to be done. I can't keep them in the dark about Ted—not anymore. Tristian and Dimitri aren't forgiven for what they've done to me, but I don't want to see them get hurt anymore. It no longer feels fair to involve them in my fight with Ted when they're left in the dark about it.

I'm not quite sure how to do it or where to start, but I know that tonight, I'm going to come clean to my Lords.

To two of them, at least.

A burst of laughter catches my attention and I look up. Students are milling around between classes, some alone, others in groups. The outburst drawing my focus belongs to a few girls, sitting on a bench, leaning into one another. I recognize Sutton, the Countess, the Princes' Princess, and the Baroness clustered together. They look like a palette of precious metals—Sutton's warm bronze, the Baroness's cool silver, and the Princess's radiant gold. They look exactly like the royalty they are.

I guess the other frats aren't as picky about their women making friends.

My phone buzzes again.

Tristian: Story, you may go to the Student Center for lunch. We'll meet you at the car at 3.

Lady: Yes, my Lord. Thank you.

It's unusual for both guys to be held up at lunch and it makes me feel at loose ends. Watching Sutton makes it even more so. I guess that's how dependent I've become on them. They tell me where to go, what to eat, who to sit by, when to spread my legs, when to sleep, and when to wake. At first, their control felt more like a leash than anything. But after Ted's surprise and Killian's punishment, the Lords' possessive nature is providing an odd comfort.

I reach for my bag, and when I look up again, Sutton is standing in front of me.

"Hi," she says.

I glance around, paranoid this is some kind of test set up by the guys. Things have been too good today, with the gifts and the apology and no-strings orgasm. I don't see them anywhere, however.

So I smile back, answering, "Hey."

"You meeting your Lords?"

"Actually, no," I say, giving my phone a disappointed glance. "Just heading to the Student Center for lunch, I guess."

She jerks her head toward the other girls. "We're heading off campus to grab salads at that 'make your own' place. Want to join us?"

I look over at the girls, clutching their bags and looking happy. I shake my head, sighing. "I shouldn't."

"You sure?" she asks, frowning. "You know, we'd love to have you. There aren't many other girls on campus with our special circumstances. We should stick together."

"I don't think the guys would like it." I *know* they wouldn't. Tristian would be over the moon about the salad part of it, but that's about it.

"Pssh." She waves me off. "I know they have all those rules but come on. We do too. They know we get together like this. It's like a little open secret." She grins, her curly hair catching the sunlight. "It's not like they don't benefit from it."

Tilting my head, I wonder, "How so?"

"Talking about how to better serve our men is one of our main topics of conversation," she explains, taking a seat at my side, voice lowering. "You know, little tricks that make life as a Royal woman easier and better for them. Autumn is going to tell us the secret to rim jobs. One of her Princes is very into it at the moment."

"I don't know…" Things are finally better with me and the guys—at least the two of them. Tristian had actually apologized and I'm still not sure what to do with it. Does it make it better? Easier? I'm not quite sure yet, but I find myself curious, wanting to find out where we go from here.

Sutton gives me a soft look. "You look lonely all by yourself, Story. You deserve some time for yourself. Time with *friends*. The way we live—the things we do—sometimes it's hard to remember that." She gives me a nudge with her shoulder. "It's just lunch."

The reminder of being alone hits me. I'm a sitting target for Ted, not to mention Killian, who's around here somewhere. Being with these girls is better than putting myself at risk. And plus, Sutton is right.

Everyone needs friends.

I give a reluctant smile, agreeing, "Okay. I have two hours before my next class." Then, I pause. "Oh, shit."

"What?"

"The Lords." God, this is embarrassing. "They actually…track my phone."

Shockingly, she doesn't look surprised or horrified. She just shrugs. "We can drop it in my car and take Autumn's. That way, it'll be here the whole time."

I bite my lip, worry churning in my gut. "You're sure?"

"Yep."

"Okay," I say, feeling anxious, but also embarrassingly excited. "Let's do this."

She waves over the other girls, who grin when they see me. I know what I'm doing is risky, and the guys are strict. But after this morning, I don't think they'd truly terrorize me for anything. I just hope that Killian doesn't find out.

Sutton and the other girls talk the whole way to the parking lot. Clothes, parties, sex, hair. I drink it all in, laughing along, realizing how much I've missed this. I went to an all-girls school, after all. This was part of my daily life.

"Story," the Princess asks, threading her arm through mine. "Who's the best kisser out of your Lords?" She's a beautiful girl, with all the looks of a pageant girl. Heavy eye makeup. Big blue eyes. Hair in perfect curls.

"Oh, um…" I think it over, cheeks heating at the thought of sharing this so easily. "They're all good—just different. Dimitri kisses with his whole body. It's always intense with him, but also…very easy to fall into. Comfortable." I duck my head, biting back a smile as I remember this morning. "Tristian kisses like he's got something to say with it. He's all about the flash. But it has this way of making you feel like you're the only girl in the room."

"Mmmmm," she hums at my description. "What about Payne? God, talk about extreme."

My smile falls as I think about the one time we kissed. It feels uncomfortable to describe, but in the spirit of a newfound sisterhood, I try. "Killian kisses like he's trying to claw his way inside your skin. It's hard and it hurts, but you don't really realize it at the time. Sometimes, with him, the bad stuff seems good. It's confusing."

The Baroness turns to us, perching her sunglasses on her nose as she beams.

"And *that's* why a girl shouldn't settle down with one guy too soon."

We get to the edge of the parking lot, where each spot is filled with a car.

"My car is over here," Sutton says, pointing to the left.

"Okay, we'll drive over to get you," the Princess says. She follows the Baroness as she ducks between two cars. I follow Sutton, squeezing between an oversized SUV and a badly parked van.

"Asshole," Sutton mutters, glaring at the two tires that are clearly crossing the line. "It's too tight to pass through." She lifts her chin. "Go back that way and we'll go down another row."

I turn around and jump in surprise.

There's a man, dressed in all black, mask covering his face, right in front of me.

My heart slams into my throat, paralyzing me for a suspended moment as my eyes climb his chest to the masked face. My backpack drops heavily to the ground, and it's dumb—it's so fucking stupid—but my feet are glued to the ground.

Move, my brain hisses.

The door of the badly-parked van slides open, revealing two more masked men.

Spinning on my heel, I take in a deep breath to cry out for Sutton, but I barely catch a glimpse of her hair before he's on me, roughly shoving a hood over my head and grabbing me around the middle. I inhale instinctively, dragging in a musty breath to scream with, but something bitter hits my nostrils and throat, bringing on a coughing fit instead.

"Help!" I try to scream, kicking out wildly. My foot catches something hard and metal—the side of the van—and I push, forcing my assailant into the side of the SUV. He grunts a sharp, "Come on, bitch," and shoves.

I know I'm in the van by the sense of the jostle and the encroaching quiet. Panicking, I flail, kicking out some more, struggling against the arms holding mine. The chemical scent embedded into the mask is choking me, burning the back of my throat, clenching my lungs in its grasp.

When my foot bashes into something soft, a voice cries out, "Shit!" It's a deep voice—male. "Goddamn it, my fucking nose!"

I struggle harder, hoping to get another hit, but the door to the van slams shut and the engine cranks. In less than three seconds, the wheels are rolling. Now, it feels like my limbs are moving within something viscous and impossible. I strike out, I scream and cough, but everything feels heavy. The smell in the hood is overwhelming, dizzying, and suddenly the most urgent struggle is the one against my drooping eyelids.

Just before the wave of sleep takes me over, I hear a harsh, masculine voice say, "This is gonna be one sweet cherry."

Ted, I think as it drags me under.

All this running. All the fighting. Now he's got me. Now it's done.

It's almost a relief.

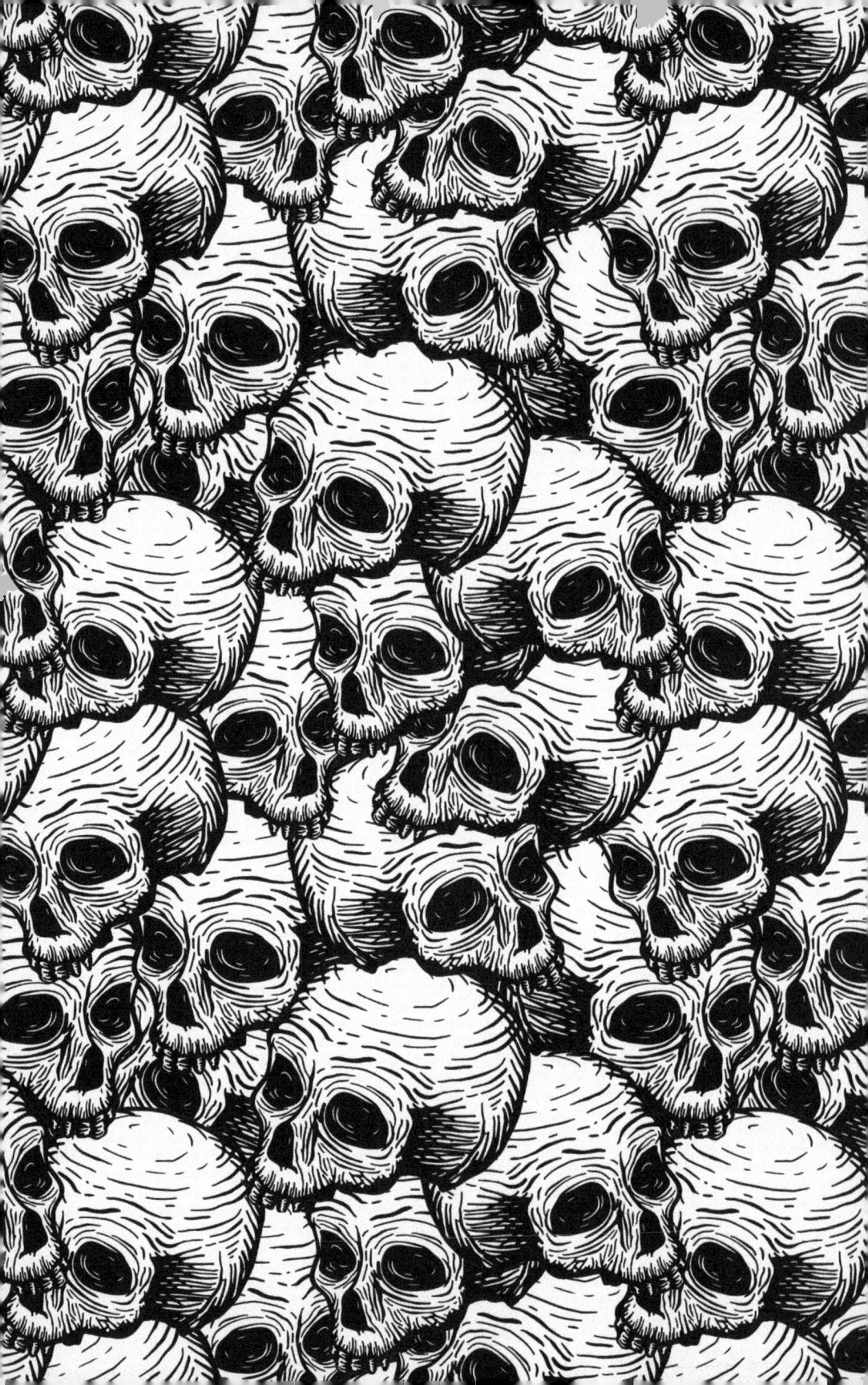

28

POSSESSION

I'm going to prison for murder.

That's all there is to it. Izzy and Lizzy will be disappointed, but once they get to college and find themselves stuck in a group project with two people they hate, they'll get it.

Jason is a low-level Count and looks the part—dark shirt, ratty jeans, and an arrogant slouch. "I just think that we should use a PowerPoint and not a video."

"Dude, no one wants to use a PowerPoint," Mark says, eyes rolling. "Get over it."

"I told you," Jason says, leaning back in his seat like we've got all the damn time in the world, "teachers love PowerPoints. Graphs are like porn to them."

"Yeah, but the video—" Mark starts.

"The video is bullshit," Jason jumps in.

I glance down at my phone for the third time. I've been in this stupid group project meeting for two hours. The first hour was spent arguing over what topic to discuss. The second was on the merits of a PowerPoint or a video. If I didn't already hate Jason because of his affiliation with the Counts, this would put him on my shit list for life. Mark, a mid-level Prince, isn't much better. But at least he's right about the goddamn video.

I have no idea how the professor determined groups, but it's almost like he was trying to stir up shit. A Lord, a Count, and a Prince locked in the same room is a powder keg.

Again, I look down at my phone. It's almost one and Story should be checking in before going to her afternoon class. She's very good at checking in now. Almost depressingly so. Her compliance doesn't give me many opportunities to come up with fun, sexy, ways to correct her behavior anymore. That's the difference between me and Killer. My corrections are all in good, sexy fun. His punishments are always more about his ego than his dick.

The numbers on my phone cross from 1:59 to 2:00 and I open the tracking app. Her little blue dot hovers over the campus. I enlarge the screen, zeroing in on her location. The GPS scales down, pulling the campus into view. She's not in the Student Center, nor en route to her classroom. Her dot is just blinking passively in the parking lot. *What the hell is she doing out there?*

"What do you think, Mercer?"

"I think I don't give a fuck," I say, standing up, eyes glued to the phone. "You guys figure it out and email me my part."

"No way," Jason says, acting all affronted, although I don't know why. There's no way this wasn't going to happen. I should get a medal for having stayed this long. "We have to turn in the project outline today by five."

"Then turn it in." I sling my backpack over my shoulder. The dot hasn't moved at all. I click on it, pulling up the details.

11:00 Story left the social sciences building

11:02-11:08 Story made a short trip to Forsyth Quad (6 min)

11:17 Story made a short trip to Arthur Grant Drive (5 min)

11:17am -2:01pm Near Arthur Grant Drive (1 hr, 46 min)

I blink. According to the tracker Story has been in the parking lot since 11:17 am. Something isn't right. I stalk toward the door.

"Where are you going?" Mark asks, his chair sliding on the floor. "We need to finish this up."

I look back over my shoulder, smirking. "Do what you need to do. If I get an 'F', I'll just have my dad donate a new wing." I turn and bump straight into Jason, who is now blocking the door, his arms crossed over his chest. "Are you fucking serious right now? Get the hell out of my way."

Jason's jaw tics and he glances over my shoulder, like he's considering if Mark will help him if he starts a fight. "I really didn't expect much more out of a Lord, seeing as how you're all lazy, cheating shits. But you're not sticking us with all the work."

I step closer, letting my mouth stretch into a grin. "Move, or I'll make you move." I know he won't call my bluff, but I see his eyes move down to my split lip, narrowing. As much as I'd love to bash this fucker's smug face in, I definitely don't want to waste the time.

"Let him go," Mark says, sounding a little too casual about it. "We're good here."

Jason unfolds his arms and slowly steps out of my way, extending an arm. "Kumbaya, my Lord." I don't like the smarmy grin plastered on his face. They're probably going to fail me.

Oh well.

I push past him out into the hallway, phone already to my ear. Story's cell goes straight to voicemail. "Sweet Cherry," I say, keeping my voice as calm as possible, "you missed your check in. Call me right away."

Next, I dial Rath, whose phone goes straight to his 'Do Not Disturb' response. *Fuck!* Whenever he goes into a session like this, the room basically gets locked down until he's finished, which won't be for another fifteen minutes. No phones. No interruptions.

I stop outside the building and check the tracker again. No change. Something is definitely up. This isn't like her.

My thoughts go straight to Killian. It may not be very charitable of me, but he hasn't earned much of my charity these days. If he made an order to her, she'd follow it. Because it doesn't matter what he thinks—she's loyal like that.

Something is wrong. Moving on instinct now, I jog down the sidewalk, toward the athletic dorms. I push through the door and skip the elevator, rushing up to the third floor. Killian's got a suite of his own, paid for personally by my Dear Old Dad. We spent a lot of time up here last year, partying and plotting South Side jobs. It'd be the only place he'd go to.

I knock twice before opening the door, barging inside.

"Killer!" I stop, gaping at the state of the room. It's an absolute fucking pigsty. Pizza boxes, dirty boxers, sport drink and beer bottles all over the place. There are two game controllers sitting on the laundry-covered couch, while intro music and the glow of the TV screen fill the room.

Killian must be losing it, just like I said. The guy isn't just infamous for being tidy. It's like his whole life hinges on some nebulous concept of order and cleanliness. 'Anal' isn't a strong enough word. I've seen him throw an absolute conniption just because a few binders fell over on his desk. If this is the state of his room, then I don't even want to know where his head's at.

I curse, kicking an empty energy drink bottle out of my way as I exit the suite.

Since it's between here and the parking lot, I double-time it to the music building, eyes only half fixed on where I'm walking. I keep looking at my phone, but that fucking dot never moves.

As expected, Rath is locked in the studio. Looking through the window, I can see him in there, face tense and annoyed as he ignores whoever's speaking. He looks wound up, and I know that look on his face—the way he pinches the bridge of nose, feet shifting restlessly, eyes darkening. He's about to lose his shit. Distantly, I remember him mentioning that he's having a peer review today. They've never gone past noon, though. Rath has his weak points, but music has *never* been one of them.

"Fuck this," I mutter, grabbing the knob and yanking it open. Maybe dad can buy him a wing, too. Everyone's gaze lurches up to me as I enter, including Rath's.

His surprised expression morphs to displeasure, and then confusion. I don't know what he sees on my face, but it makes him immediately spring to his feet, rattling off a quick, "Lewis can't reach the pedals, Willis has shitty timing, and Gregory can suck my big fat balls if he thinks I'm sitting through another twenty-minute Russian piece." He throws them a peace sign. "I'm out, fuckers."

Their angry protests nip at his heels, but Rath strides right up to me. "What now?"

Leading him out of the studio, I explain, "Story isn't checking in."

The look he gives me could peel paint. "That's what this is about? Jesus Christ, you had me thinking one of the Nick's showed up on our doorstep. You know, something actually fucking *important*."

Teeth grinding, I insist, "This is important!"

"I don't get you," he says, gait unhurried at my side. "The whole tracking thing, needing to know her every goddamn move. It's too much work. I don't know why you bother. If the girl wants to blow off for a few hours, I say—"

Grabbing his arm, I yank him to a stop. "Listen to me, Dimitri." His mouth presses into a tense line at my use of his name. I only whip that out when shit is serious. "Her tracker has been in the same spot—the wrong spot—for two fucking hours. Killian's suite in the athletic dorms is trashed, and I can't find him, either."

At least that gets some urgency into his expression. He shifts his eyes around, brow knitting together. "You think he did something?"

Shrugging, I admit, "I don't know, man. But Killer's been on a short fuse lately."

"Fuck." Rath drags in a hard breath, raking his fingers through his hair. The look he gives me is uneasy. "This morning, when I was tracking down everyone who hadn't checked their texts yet, I found out he's been interrogating the frat."

"About what?" I ask, although I instantly realize the answer. "About Story fucking around."

Rath nods, eyes shifty. "He was smashing phones, too. I think maybe a few of the guys were taking video of what happened last night."

Eyes widening, I shove his shoulder. "You didn't take their fucking phones at the door?!"

He swats my hand away, eyes flashing angrily. "How the fuck was I supposed to know he was going to make her suck his cock in front of forty-five pussy-hungry degenerates?"

"Goddamn it." I press my fingertips into my eyes, trying to ease the ache forming behind them. "God-fucking-damn it, Rath."

"He destroyed their phones," he repeats, palms out, hapless. "You know Killian. He's thorough."

I snort bitterly. "Yeah, and he's tearing a warpath through the campus to do it. Meanwhile," I hold up my phone, showing the unmoving dot on the screen, "our Lady is MIA. This doesn't fill me with comfort."

"I'm sure she's just…" He shrugs at the phone, momentarily at a loss for words. He voices another possibility I don't want to hear. "Maybe she bolted. I mean, come on. Could you blame her?"

"No," I admit, looking in the direction of the parking lot "But if she didn't—if Killian's fucking with her somehow, then…"

I have a lot of ground to cover when it comes to making shit right with Story. I apologized this morning, and it doesn't matter that I saw the shocked tears shining in her eyes. It doesn't matter that she let me put that daisy behind her ear before breakfast. It doesn't even really matter that, after breakfast, she let me bend down to kiss her lips, or that she kissed me back, slow and sweet.

Words don't matter here.

The real ground starts with this—keeping a promise. Keeping her safe.

"Rath." I look into his eyes, willing him to understand. "I told her I wouldn't let him hurt her again."

From the set of his shoulders, the way he straightens, I think he gets it. "Okay," he says, jerking his head in the direction of the parking lot. "Let's go find our Lady, then."

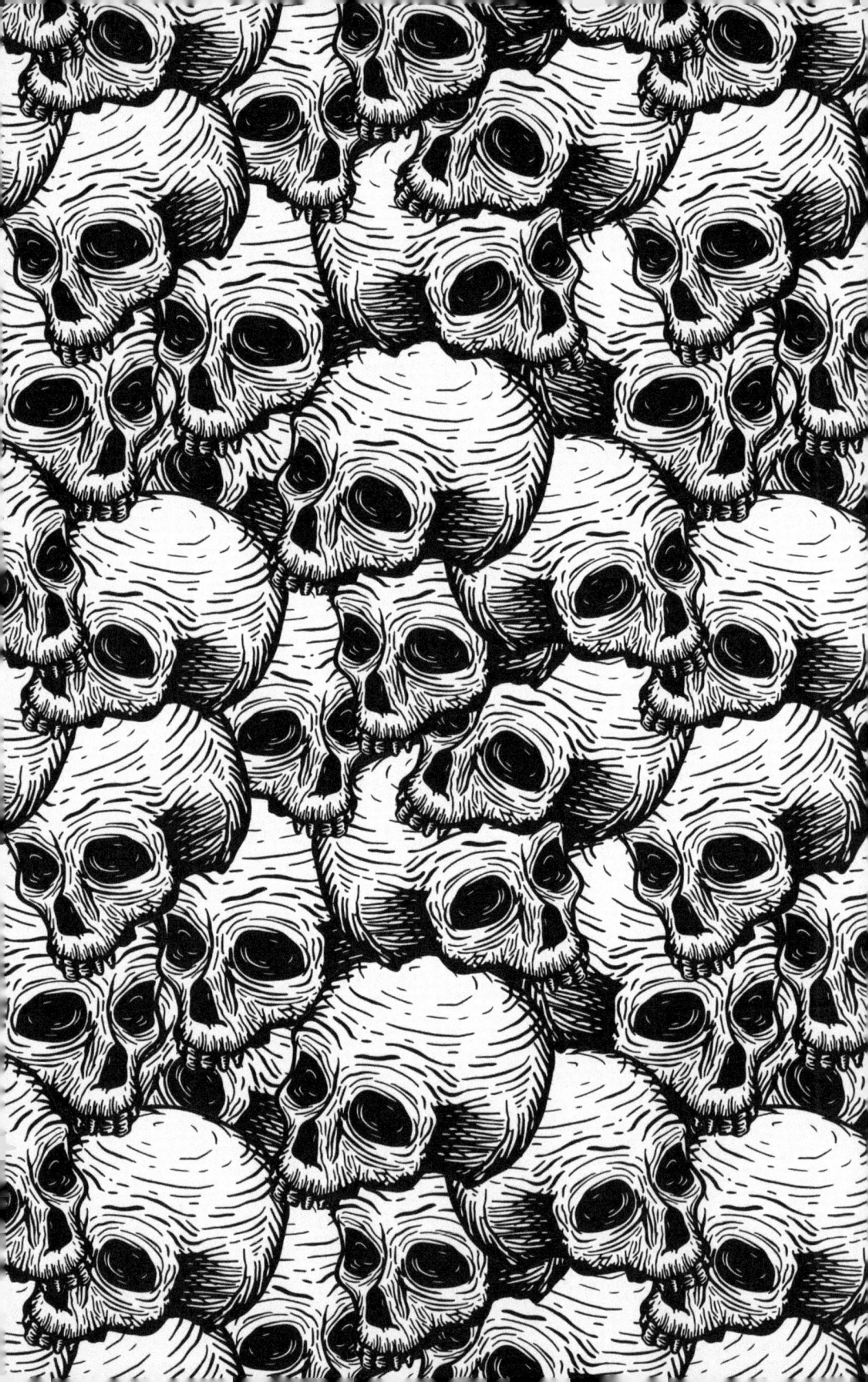

STORY

29

SAVIOR

THERE'S A DREAM AT the frayed edge of my mind. It's fuzzy and indistinct, but I can feel the softness of Dimitri's bed, remember the sleepy morning kisses, the way his arm had felt around my middle. Safe. Warm.

But there's another dream that keeps tainting it. It's filled with flashes of Jack, my old roommate. I've trained myself to skirt away from the memory, flinching somewhere deep in my mind. I've tried not to ask questions. What are his parents like? Did he have siblings? Is he being missed? Was I responsible for ripping a hole in their lives?

I haven't let myself think of Jack in a long time. As I slowly rouse to consciousness, he's all I can think about it. I wonder if it hurt. Did Ted make it quick? Did Jack struggle? Did he understand why it was happening?

It's dark when I try to open my eyes. At first, I think I can't raise my lids, but then I realize it's a blindfold. All of waking up is like that; thinking there's something wrong with my body only to find otherwise. I can't move my arms and legs. They're extended, but tied down to something. I can't open my mouth. It's covered with tape.

The panic comes gradually, in waves. I try to pull against the restraints, but it's feeble. The drugs are still fogging up my mind. My throat still burns with the chemicals and everything feels muddled. Only one thing shines through loud and clear, like a beacon of light cutting through the clouds.

Fight.

The binds are tight on my wrists—less so on my ankles—and they're cutting into the skin, making my tendons ache. It's cold here, where I'm lying on something pliable and soft. When I make a futile attempt at turning, jostling, the squeak of springs gives it away as an old mattress.

Suddenly the mattress dips with a heavy weight at my side. I freeze, heart hammering in terror. Ted, I remember, stomach plummeting as my lungs constrict. I try to scramble away from the dip, but the binds are too tight.

I scream behind the tape when I feel fingertips on my cheek, tossing my head to the side. The fingers follow, however. I tremble, but refuse to cry, curling my hands into fists around the ropes.

"Sorry about this," the man beside me says, caressing a sore spot on my cheekbone. "Hitting girls isn't our style. It's just that we weren't expecting so much of a fight. You broke a guy's nose, sprained a wrist, and gave one a pretty good headache. Got a little messy in the van." His finger runs down my neck. Across my collarbone. "Wouldn't know it by looking at you. You're such a sad-looking, tiny little wisp of a thing. But you're a fighter." His voice sounds pensive and excited. "I shouldn't be surprised."

I shiver at the cold in the room—the terror coursing through my veins—and it makes my nipples peak. The response has nothing to do with his touch on me, but he chuckles into my ear anyway.

"You like that?" he says, trailing his finger around a nipple. "You like it when I touch you like that?" Drawing in the breath, I mumble under the tape. "What's that, darling'?"

"Mwuf Mmew!"

His fingers dig into my cheek before ripping the adhesive off my skin. I yelp in pain and he shushes me. "Tell me what you wanted to say."

"I said," I lick my lips, tasting blood from where the tape pulled the skin off, "*fuck you.*"

He gives a loud, barking laugh, but that's not what sends a chill up my spine. It's the sudden presence of other, distant voices, perhaps in the next room. We're not alone. My head whips back and forth, chasing the sounds, trying to count.

"So fucking feisty," he says, giving my nipple a sharp pinch. "I have no idea how those bastards held off on you. Lords aren't really known for their self-restraint. They have more willpower than I thought. I admit, I'm impressed. No wonder they kept that little detail about you a secret."

My mind spins, brow crushing in confusion. The more he talks, the less convinced I am this is Ted. It doesn't make sense, though. Who else would take me like this? Who would want to hurt me?

"That isn't a surprise though. The Lords keep their shit locked up tight. Do you have any idea the coordination that went into this?" Laughing, he adds, "You made it a lot easier though, trusting the wrong person."

"I don't know what you're talking about," I gasp, twisting away. "I don't trust anyone!"

His fingers trail over the tops of my breasts, then down the sides, before coming back up to flick at my nipple. "Ironic, right? All it takes is one slip. One little detail and the power structure of this whole little system is turned on its head." His breath is hot on my ear. "We never would have known about their prized possession if you hadn't told our Countess."

Sutton.

I think about her earlier that day, asking me to lunch, the look on her face when she told me to turn around, to walk another direction. But I know that's not when it happened. It was that night after dinner with our family, when Killian stopped at the bar. When Sutton approached me in the bathroom. Eased me into gossiping. She found out about my virginity. I told her why the guys picked me as Lady, and she went behind my back and…

His hand remains on my breast, but another digs beneath my head, untying the blindfold. My vision is blurry at the edges as I blink to adjust, chest heaving from the panic.

I don't realize how intensely I'm expecting to see Saul Cartwright's handsome features until I don't. "I remember you." It's Perez, the guy Dimitri had gotten into that argument with. The one who wanted Ms. Crane. Next to Saul Cartwright, this guy looks like…no one. A nobody. A wimpy college guy, nothing more. Stunned, I ask, "Are you kidding me? This is just about some dumb frat rivalry crap?"

"*Dumb?*" he asks, eyes flashing angrily. "The only dumb thing about this is *you*. Do you have any idea how high the stakes are here?" He grabs my breast, squeezing it painfully. "We're all sick of LDZ's bullshit. They control the game, the faculty, the scouts, even fucking South Side. This year is going to be different."

"What do you want from me?" I ask, stomach flinching as his fingers explore my flesh.

Smirking, he says, "You know what we want, Story. It's the same thing *they* want. We just want it for different reasons. Although…" His eyes sweep down my body, two broad hands grabbing the collar of my shirt and ripping it down the middle. I make a startled sound, momentarily so distressed by the loss of the shirt—Tristian had given it to me as an apology—that I don't even think to worry about being exposed. Perez licks his lips at what he sees. "Taking your virginity won't exactly be a burden, if you catch my drift."

My heart stops, catching in my throat. "What?" I worry about being exposed *now*, twisting futilely.

"I'm just saying, I've had worse jobs," he says, watching his hand massage my bare flesh. "In fact, it's the second biggest reason we even decided to team up with the Princes and Barons to begin with. They're beneath us, honestly. Even the prospect of taking down the Lords wasn't quite enough to convince me an alliance was worth it. But you…" He leans down, licking a path between my breasts and emerging with a devious grin. "Popping your cherry really sweetened the pot, Lady." He wedges his fingers under my waistband, working the buttons to my jeans open.

My scream is deafening even to my own ears.

That's how I know this is real. In my dreams, my screams are such feeble, tenuous things. Here, now, they're full of anger and alarm, so loud that it makes my ears ring and my throat ache.

Even though I see his jaw tense, Perez says, "Scream all you want. No one can hear you except the guys in the next room. They're waiting their turn."

I do exactly that, howling as loudly as I can, thrashing against the mattress. Despite his insistence that no one will hear me, he spits a curse and starts fishing around on the bed, producing the strip of tape he'd taken from my mouth. He looks annoyed as he tries to replace it, but my mouth is open too wide, my screams tearing from my throat like a banshee.

He clamps a hand over it instead, ripping my pants open. "I wanted to do this nice and gentle," he hisses into my face, "but now you're really starting to piss me off."

There are three loud bangs on the door before it opens, a rusty-haired man poking his head in. "Hey, we might have some trouble out front."

Perez growls, hand halfway down my pants. "I don't even have her naked yet!"

The guy glares back at him. "It's not my fault you need three hours of foreplay. We need to make sure this location's secure."

"We're in South Side, you moron," he snaps, levering himself up. "Nothing around here is secure. But if you're going to be such massive pussies about everything, then—" The door slams behind him and I'm left alone, breathless and lightheaded.

I know I don't have much time until someone returns. I check my surroundings, noting how derelict everything looks. The house is obviously old—probably even abandoned. There's graffiti on one of the walls and a cloudy window beside the bed with three jaggedly shattered panes.

That's where he appears.

Startled, I almost cry out again, but he puts a finger to his lips, eyes hard and urgent. I obey more out of instinctual fear than anything else, mashing my lips together. I watch as he searches the window frame, fingers running along the bottom. He must find purchase because suddenly the window makes an awful screeching sound.

He pauses, shoulders tense.

Fuck your orders, I think, opening my mouth and releasing another bloodcurdling shriek.

Killian's eyes grow wide and angry—a flash of betrayed discontent—but I nod at him encouragingly. He must finally understand because he shoves the window up in a single, swift, commanding thrust, his muscular shoulders jerking with the motion. The screech of wood on metal is swallowed by my wail. I quiet, panting as he climbs through the window.

When he does, he leans out, looking left and then right, before finally turning to me, plucking the knife from his pocket. I watch in a panicked stupor as the blade slices through the rope. "We have to hurry," he says, face set into a grim expression. "My buddy isn't going to keep them occupied for long."

When my wrists are free, I hastily cover myself, cringing away when Killian reaches out for me. He gives me a look—something both surprised and accepting—and reaches over his shoulder instead. He tugs his shirt over his head, baring his broad, tattooed chest.

"Put this on," he says, moving immediately to my ankles, carving easily through the rope. When he releases the last one, he lingers there for a moment, fingers soothing the red-raw skin. His dark eyes hold mine. "Can you run?"

At first, I nod, but as soon as I sit up to put on the shirt, my head spins. I moan, clutching my forehead, but do my best to power through, shedding the torn shirt and pulling Killian's over my head.

He turns to check the door, and that's when I see it.

There's a pistol tucked into the waist of his jeans.

My first frenzied attempt at standing does not go well. Killian lurches forward to catch me, grunting a curse. "The drugs," I explain, vision swimming in and out of focus. "It's got me all dizzy."

"This is a problem," he grinds out, winding an arm around my waist. "I can't just pitch you out the goddamn window. We're on the second floor. *Fuck*." He holds me there for a moment, arm clutching me against his warm chest. "I really didn't want to do it this way," he mutters, bending down to sweep me up, sending my head into another whirling spin as he cradles me. He gives me a jostle, securing me against him. "I'll have to try to sneak." He sounds really grim about it, which makes sense.

Killian isn't a stealthy kind of guy even when he *isn't* carrying someone down a shabby, creaking staircase.

Every step he takes makes the muscles against me tense more and more. The stairs are squeaky and obviously rotting, but he manages a safe—if not altogether silent—path down to the landing. I train my eyes to his throat, to the pulse jumping beneath the skin, and remember the words he said to me that day I was offered the position.

"I'm not your savior, then or now. You need to get that through your pretty little head."

Everything is muddled and confusing, and I think that if I get out of this, I might have time to sift through it all and untangle the irony of me being constantly shuffled back and forth between greater and lesser evils. But right now, I don't.

So I hold on tighter.

He looks down at me, surprise clear on his face, but just as quickly returns to the task of sneaking us out of here.

It all falls apart feet from the back door.

"Drop the girl, Payne."

I go more rigid than Killian, my heartbeat spiking. When I swing my wide, terrified eyes to his, I notice that he looks more annoyed than afraid.

"Perez." Killian turns slowly, mouth set into a tight, flat line. Perez is joined by two other men, all of them still dressed in the same black clothes as before. "Should have known you were teaming up. Your houses are all too fucking stupid to pull something like this off alone. Not that you've actually managed to now." Gently, he lowers my legs, letting me slide to my feet. "Sending Gonzo to get me drunk last night might have worked, except I had shit to see to this morning."

One of other guys shrugs. "Worked on the others just fine."

Perez scoffs. "You aren't taking all three of us."

"You sound pretty confident for a guy who needed three people to take down one girl."

I clutch at Killian's arm as I watch them go back and forth, and I'm taken by a moment of perfect clarity. It's aided by the angry, wild thing in my chest, desperate to break loose.

Desperate to *fight*.

I speak through clenched teeth, voice as raw as my throat. "I wanted to do this nice and gentle." I reach behind Killian, pulling the gun from his waistband. "But now you're really starting to piss me off."

Perez ducks when I point the gun at him, screeching, "Holy shit!"

The other two are no braver, one diving behind the counter, the other fleeing from the kitchen altogether.

Even Killian flinches back, and really, he should. "Story. Chill, okay."

I keep Perez in the gun's sight. "Go fuck yourself, Killian."

He touches my shoulder and I jerk away. He doesn't seem to care. He doesn't even seem afraid. In a low voice, he says, "I get you want to shoot this asshole, but that brings cops. That's a paper trail. That's exposure and attention, and a whole shitload of drama you don't want."

"No," I snap, not moving the gun, "that's attention *you* don't want. This piece of shit was going to rape me. I don't care anymore!"

"You don't mean that," he says, cupping my elbow. "Do you know what it means to kill someone? Are you a killer, Story? Because I don't think you are."

I shrug one shoulder, not even needing to think about it. I tell Perez, "I feel pretty good about taking out a kneecap. But whatever you guys drugged me with is making me kind of dizzy, so I might miss."

Perez's eyes squeeze shut.

Killian mutters, "Enough of this," and, quicker than I can react, snatches the gun from my hand. "Someday, you and I are going to have a talk about these not being a toy," he says, tucking it back into his waistband. "And also about how guns are a lot less scary when you don't take off the safety."

I deflate, stumbling to the side, but Killian catches me again. *Jesus*. I'd forgotten about the safety.

When Perez jumps back up, face clenched in anger, Killian snaps, "Get down, fuckface! She might not know how to work a safety, but I sure as fuck do. And that whole kneecap plan is sounding pretty goddamn good to me."

Perez doesn't stop us from leaving, grinding out a sharp, "Fucking psychos," as Killian scoops me back up into his arms.

I START HYPERVENTILATING the second the truck is in motion.

My lungs feel like they're on fire and I can't stop shaking. All of the adrenaline, the panic, the terror, comes crashing into me like a freight train. It's not just from this afternoon. It's from all of it. Last night with Killian. The package from Ted. The night of the party. It's all stacked up to a leaning tower of trauma that's finally crashing down inside of my chest.

Killian reaches out to cup the back of my head, pushing me down. "Put your head between your knees."

Like before, I obey instinctually, ducking down to gasp at the floorboard. I don't need Killian, of all people, to talk me through a panic attack.

I spend the whole ride like that. It never goes away—I know that better than anyone. But it gets less enormous. Easier to pick parts from, to be tucked away and never thought about again. By the time he pulls into the garage at the brownstone, I'm already being hit with the numbing exhaustion that always follows.

Killian cuts the ignition and we stay there for a long moment, listening to the clicks of his cooling engine. He clutches the keys, sighing. "You weren't fucking around on us."

I slide my gaze to him slowly, knowing that it's full of everything I can't say. That I hate him. That the only thing he's ever been to me is another abuser. That I know I'll spend the next few days—maybe even weeks or months—concocting fantasy scenarios in my mind of him being on the other side of that gun. That he's not really much better than Perez and those other guys.

He sees it. He sees all of it. He watches me back, expression shuttered, and eventually gives a quiet, "Yeah."

And then he helps me from the truck, leading me inside the brownstone.

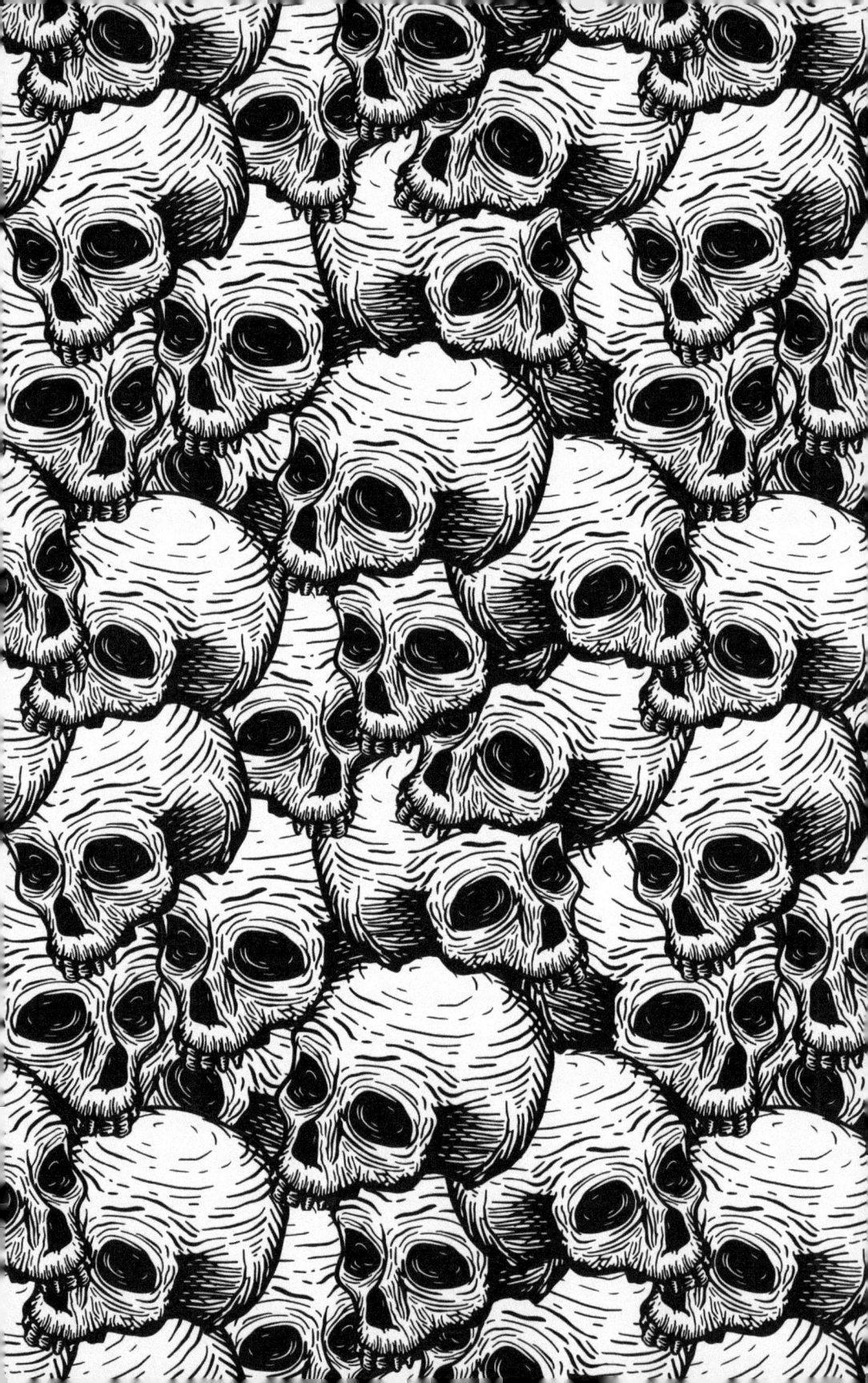

30
THE TALLY

Tristian looks back at me, his jaw flexing like he's gnashing his teeth. "Where is she?"

"Upstairs," I say, jerking my chin toward the staircase. "Ms. Crane's been in and out, but I haven't..." I don't say the truth, even though we all know it. Story doesn't want to see me.

Dimitri doesn't look any less pissed off, pacing the den with slow but hard steps. "Those motherfuckers." He pauses by the fireplace, hand shooting out to grab something off the mantle. He throws it across the room. "Those motherfuckers!"

I don't roll my eyes, but it's a near thing. Wouldn't be fair, anyway. I was trashing the steering wheel the whole way to that abandoned house in South Side. "They didn't get the chance to do anything," I reiterate, sick of watching him pace around. "She was just a little drugged up." I don't tell them about her ripped shirt. I figure the fire is hot enough without gasoline.

Tristian thrusts a finger at me, eyes ablaze. "This is your fault. You threw that goddamn fit about the package, which was obviously from the Counts, and then you punished her for it and stormed off like a fucking toddler." His laugh is completely without humor. "It did exactly what they wanted it to do.

If there'd been a third Lord to watch her while we were tied up in other shit, this never would have happened."

"They planned it like that," I argue, trying to quell the anger rising in my head. "Your group project, Rath's peer review...they were making sure you were both out of the way. They tried it on me too, it just wasn't as effective."

"We need to retaliate," Rath decides, finally coming to a stop. "We can't let them get away with—"

Tristian raises a hand. "Retaliation will come. Right now, we need to clean shit up." He looks at me. "What kind of damage are we talking here? Witnesses? Injuries?"

I shrug, picking listlessly at the label on my beer bottle. "She got a little roughed up, but nothing too bad. Bruise on her cheek. Her wrists and ankles are a little raw. She's probably up there sleeping off whatever they drugged her with." Sighing, I set my bottle on the table. "I paid one of the corner guys to run diversion so I could get in there. Perez and the others caught us just before we escaped, so Story pulled my gun on them and—"

Tristian's head rears back. "I'm sorry, she fucking what?"

"I had it in my pants," I explain, leveling him with a look. "The safety was on; it was never a danger. But you can bet your ass that they shit their pants." For the first time in days, I'm able to crack a smile. "That shit was priceless. You should have seen Perez, cowering like a damn baby."

Tristian isn't smiling. At all. "They know about our contract, which means that this won't stop."

"They'll keep gunning for her," Rath agrees, face grim. "I don't know about you guys, but we're burning a candle at both fucking ends here, between LDZ and South Side. I know the two of you get off on being glorified babysitters, but we don't have time to be bodyguards."

I give a heavy nod. "So what do we do? Release her from the contract?"

Neither of them seem to like that idea.

Tristian props his elbows on the bar, taking a calming breath. "No. We have to end the game. Tally shit up, and get it over with."

Rath pauses, looking between us. "That'd be me, then." At least he has the good grace not to smirk while saying it.

Tristian nods in agreement, but even though he has to be disappointed, he doesn't look it. "You're up by eleven. Give her some time, though. She should take the day off from classes tomorrow. We should get her used to the idea first. She might be a little—"

I down the last of my beer before saying, "Rath wouldn't win. It'd be me."

Rath scoffs. "No, it wouldn't, you're down by almost eighty points."

My stomach churns in displeasure at what I'm about to say—almost as badly as the thought of not being the one to have her first. *Almost.* "Blow job, exhibition, multiplied by forty five." Looking up at Rath, I add, "That's over three hundred."

They stare at me for a tense beat.

It's Tristian who speaks first, his voice a low hiss. "You cannot be fucking serious."

Rath holds my stare, his eyes dark and threatening. "That's the real reason you did it, isn't it?"

I give a firm, certain, "No." Sweeping my hair back, I lock my jaw, remembering. "I did it because the thought of her fucking around with someone else made me fucking crazy. It got in my head. It got me all twisted up, because this is what I do. Are you even surprised? It's like I see red and nothing else—not until it burns itself out. I won't defend it. You were right before," I tell Tristian. "I gave them exactly what they wanted. I see that now. But Story?" I give a harsh laugh, shaking my head. "She's done with me. She's mine by rights, you both know it. But she'll never..." I curl my fist, unable to say the words aloud.

Her voice has been banging around in my head ever since she got to her knees and spoke. They're what I heard when I peeled out of the driveway. They mocked me when I got to my suite in the dorms. They hissed themselves at me as I drank myself into a toxic stupor until two in the morning. They were still there when I woke up, hungover and nauseous. Even when I was breaking into that house to rescue her, all it took was her cringing away from my touch to tell me everything I needed to know.

Story will never be mine.

"I blew it." The words come out simple, matter-of-fact. There's no sugar-coating this shit. I'm the only one to blame. "This is all I'll ever have."

"Let me get this straight," Rath says, voice low and dangerous. "You know she'll never want you, so you're going to *make* her fuck you. That's some pure romance shit, right there. It's a wonder she wasn't falling at your feet years ago, you goddamn lunatic."

I spring to my feet, feeling the red pulsing at the edges of my mind. "Like you're so fucking above it? You think what the two of you have done—have *been* doing—is any better?"

"Yeah, I do," Rath answers, eyes narrowing. "Because she actually fucking likes me. Maybe it's not all based on truth, but at least she can suck my dick without vomiting."

I lurch over the table, fully prepared to shove this asshole into the fireplace, but Tristian suddenly appears between us, pushing me back.

"We're not doing this shit again," he says, giving us both a warning look. "There's only one way to settle this in a way that's fair to everyone here—including Story."

Rath raises a skeptical eyebrow. "And how the hell do we manage that?"

"Easy. The Golden Snitch of the game." Tristian lets go of my shirt, sending me a smirk. "We let her choose."

I SPEND THE WHOLE NIGHT STEWING.

Golden fucking Snitch.

They just as good as counted me out, just like that. It's not like I could argue. It's the best way to handle it. Logically, I understand it. Still pisses me off, though.

The guys are both quiet and focused on other shit for the rest of the night, leaving me at odds. Ms. Crane is, if possible, even colder to me than usual, so I suppose she's heard all about the punishment that went down last night. It's not enough that I spent my whole morning hunting down anyone with the video—and I knew they existed. Maybe Tristian and Rath weren't paying attention to the crowd last night, but I sure as fuck was. I could see every single guy who had their phone out, and I was taking notes.

It's also apparently not enough that all my interrogations were what led me to finding her in the first place. It doesn't matter that I saved her. Everyone thinks I'm the bad guy.

And the worst part is, I'm pretty sure they're right.

The guys both go up to see Story in shifts. I'm not there when they tell her to choose, but I know it's been done by the nod I'm given after one of Tristian's visits. He goes out to buy food, then carries it upstairs to her. He's gone for a long while, probably eating it with her.

The only time I see her is later that night, when she comes downstairs and warily enters the den. Her cheek has the kind of bruise that's more red than blue—sure to heal quickly. She's wearing a pair of loose pajamas that I didn't even think she owned. We'd culled all of her ugly, ratty clothing when we settled her in, replaced it with sexier, more expensive things.

She doesn't even spare me a glance, shoulders tensing up when my head turns her way. "Dimitri?" she says, tucking her hair behind her ear. "Can I sleep in your room again?"

He closes his textbook and stands, not looking surprised by the request. "Sure. You ready now?"

She nods and I don't miss how she doesn't flinch when *he* touches her, reaching out to place a hand on the small of her back, guiding her. If anything, she leans into it.

I give Tristian a look, but he's not giving anything away. She's sleeping in their fucking rooms now? I don't even get the chance to sneak my key into that lock and get a good look at her. Her bedroom stays empty the whole night.

It's almost a relief to go to classes the next day.

At school, I'm still Killer Payne, star quarterback, LDZ royalty, North Side elite. It gets harder to sink into the roles, though. Story hating me is something I've grown used to, but Rath and Tristian are pissed at me, too. Nothing feels right or settled. I spend the whole day trying to fit into my own goddamn skin. We have to get revenge on the other frats, but not until we resolve this. Not until she's safe.

God, that's rich.

When we all meet back at the house, things are just as tense as they were yesterday.

They get a lot tenser when Story enters the den that evening. She meets Tristian and Rath's gazes, giving them a nod. "I've decided."

I put my phone away, already prepared to leave. I almost don't want to know which one of them it is, but I can tell from the vibe between them that it'll be Rath. If I were a little less greedy and jealous, I might even find it in myself to be glad. He'll treat her right.

"You can't get mad, though," she adds, ducking her head to shield her face.

I know she's talking about me. From the looks the other two give me, they know it, too.

"No one will be mad," Tristian insists. "It's not a big deal."

Liar.

Story nods, wringing her hands together. Despite Tristian's assurance, she doesn't look any less tense as she looks up, giving us a name.

"Killian," she says, her voice filled with what has to be false resolve. "I choose Killian."

STORY

31

THE PRIZE

THEY ALL LOOK stunned.

"Seriously?" Tristian asks, pulling a face as he looks between me and Killian.

I just say, "Yes."

Meeting Dimitri's confused gaze is the most difficult. We'd spent last night together again, his music shepherding me into a deep, but restless sleep. Much like the first time, I'd awoken to him wrapped around me, holding me close. He still kissed me in the morning—long, slow, sleepy kisses—but there was no urgency or hunger in them. Dimitri makes me feel safe.

And then there's Tristian, who'd kept coming up to my room and sitting with me. There were no rules or expectations. He just said he didn't have anywhere else to be and pulled up a seat at my desk, emptying a bag of delicious-smelling Thai food. Sometimes, when he smiles at me this certain way, I think I can see the kind of man he might have been, if things had been different. Tristian makes me feel cared for.

And that's the problem.

I have no idea how these two men managed to become people I've come to find solace in or comfort with. They've done terrible, unforgivable things to me, and yet…

And yet sometimes I find myself wondering what that forgiveness would look like.

I'm not so naive that I don't see it for the stupidity it is. Quite the opposite. Killian is a monster in his own right, but he can't touch me—not really. Not on the inside. Not where it matters.

But Tristian and Dimitri…

It would be so easy to fall into that. To have sex with them, to feel them inside of me, to give them this enormous, yet fragile part of myself. It would be *so damn easy* to tear down the barbed wire protecting my heart, to let them in. It's getting more and more difficult to not want it, that's the problem.

That's why it has to be Killian. I'm not at risk of feeling anything but apathy toward him. Sex with him will be painful and maddening, but emotionally sterile. Letting him inside my body will be easy, because I already know he can never get inside my heart. Nothing about sex with him will be confusing.

Even Killian looks at a loss for words. "Why?"

I look away, unable to put voice to my reasoning. None of them would understand what it means to be a woman in a world with cold, hard, selfish men. "That's my decision," I say, tone final.

Without saying a single word, Dimitri stands and storms out of the room.

The pang of worry and regret that follows is proof that I've made the right choice. It's enough that I've come to think of him as a safe harbor, but the thought of wounding Dimitri like this is cutting me up inside. It's how I know that he's already too close.

The way Tristian is looking at me hurts in its own way. It's this spark of disappointment in his eyes—not in my choice, but disappointment in *me*. Like maybe something about me is broken. Like he's realizing he doesn't know me as well as he thought he did. He releases a hard breath, sweeping his hair back. "Are you sure?"

Killian, who's been watching me ever since Dimitri left, cuts his eyes to

Tristian. "It's not because she wants me more," he says, tipping his head in a meaningful nod. "It's because she wants me least." I blink at him, shocked by the perception. Killian isn't someone I'd expect insight from, but he's managed to sum it up in a single sentence.

He doesn't look put off by it.

Tristian shakes his head, and I can tell he doesn't get it. He doesn't understand.

Killian does him one better, explaining, "It's the difference between fucking Charlene and fucking Genevieve."

Tristian's looks at me, lips a tense line. "Jesus Christ, Cherry. Rath would have made it good for you."

Nodding, I say, "I know." *I'm sorry* is on the tip of my tongue, but I refuse to give it. This is mine. I won't apologize for how I choose to use it. "It's complicated."

"Clearly," he says, moving his gaze to Killian. Something sharp and stormy crosses his features. "*One* mark," he raises a forefinger, "and your ass is forfeit, Killer. I fucking mean it. If you bring her back bruised and crying, I'm going to—"

"I won't," Killian cuts in, narrowing his eyes.

"And she gets to decide when it happens," he adds, eyes flashing. "You don't get to browbeat her into following through."

"I want to do it now." At least I can settle this worry for him. "I want to get it over with."

They both look shocked again.

"There's no rush," Tristian says, even though I can hear the lie in his words. The whole point is that doing it will make me safer. Tristian doesn't even realize just how true that concept is. "You're probably still sore from yesterday."

I look down at my wrists, still red, bruising at the edges, and shrug. "I can take it."

He folds his arms, jaw hardening as he gives a single nod. He pushes off the bar and strides forward, but I stop him before he can leave.

"Could you stay close, though?" I whisper, pleading with my eyes. I don't know what to expect, but I know there'll be pain. I know that afterward, the thought of having him near will bring me a sort of peace. "Please?"

His blue eyes hold mine, pinning me there.

And then he's kissing me.

He cradles my face in his hands, licking insistently at the seam of my lips. It's easy to open for him, to walk back when he guides me, pressing me against the wall. The sound I make is small and surprised, but not unwelcome. He's warm and solid against me, an arm coming down to wind around my middle, drawing our pelvises closer.

It's like I told the girls before—before I realized they never wanted to be my friends. Tristian kisses like he's got something to say with it. With this, he's saying that he wants me better than Killian does. He's saying that he'll let me do it anyway. He's saying that he doesn't like it.

With the hard, biting kiss he sucks into my neck, he's saying that I'm still his Lady.

It's hard to resent the comfort that brings.

From the couch, Killian scoffs, but it just makes Tristian suck harder. When he pulls away from my neck, his eyes fix to the mark he's left. He traces it with a fingertip. "I'll stay close," he agrees, tipping up my chin to give me a final chaste kiss.

Then, he leaves.

Killian's leaning forward now, elbows resting on his knees. His knitted hands hang between them, eyes fixed to his restless thumbs. "We can do it in your room."

"No." The thought alone makes me balk. "In yours."

He looks up at the sound of my voice, cold and emotionless. "Okay, fine. Mine." He stands, and for once, he doesn't look murderous. He just looks straight-faced and ready, extending an arm toward the doorway in invitation.

I climb the stairs ahead of him, butterflies whirring in my gut. Truthfully, even though this whole thing is abhorrent, I know I'll be relieved to have it over with. To not be a virgin anymore. To not be someone people want for her innocence. This was never going to be special—not for me. It was always bound to be like this; frightening and painful and just like this fucking house.

Full of dead things.

I can feel his presence behind me the whole way, looming and ominous. When we reach his room, I stand back, wrapping my arms around my middle, letting him enter first. The room still smells of him, a scent that once made my belly flip with a different kind of nerves.

Unbidden, I'm struck by an old memory from high school, back before Killian grew so hostile and aggressive toward me. I'd only been living in the house for a week. Things were different back then—tenuous and uncertain, but there was also an electric curiosity between us. He invited me into his room to hang out one night. Unraveled a game controller. Handed it to me. Taught me how to play by wrapping his arms around me from behind, hands guiding mine on the buttons. I'd been nervous then, too, but it was an excited sort of flutter in my blood. Because this Killian Payne was cute and strong, and he looked at me in a way that would take me years—until *just now*, maybe—to really understand.

He looked at me like I was his.

I didn't understand flirting at the time, either. But there was a tickle in the back of my mind, an awareness that this wasn't the way a guy treated his new sister, and it stuck to me like glue. He's been a flirt, an enemy, a monster. But he's never been a brother.

Now, as I stand in the middle of his room, trying not to tremble, I'm grateful for it. The whole thing seems painfully inevitable now, as if it always had to be this way. Killian was, however briefly, my first sense of wanting someone back.

He watches me as he closes the door, filling the room with a *click* of finality that sends my pulse into a messy spike. He stands there for a moment before crossing to the desk and clicking around on his laptop.

Music suddenly fills the room.

The volume is low, and it's definitely no Dimitri, but at least everything isn't so quiet. I remind myself that Tristian is close as Killian approaches me, doing my best not to flinch away when he reaches out to touch my hip.

His eyes are dark but his face is stone, giving nothing away. This must be why, when he ducks down to kiss me, I rear back in surprise. He blinks at me, easily diverting his path to the side of my neck Tristian hadn't marked. His hair tickles my nose as he opens his mouth against my skin, licking a kiss into the sensitive skin.

My gulp sounds loud to my own ears, and I try not to lean back when his hands grasp my hips, slowly dragging me closer. I turn my head away to breathe in something that isn't his scent, but it just gives his mouth more access to kiss my neck. That's exactly what he does, hands flexing on my hips as he kisses a trail to the edge of my jaw. His teeth scrape gently over the bone and I clamp my eyes shut.

"Take this off," he breathes, giving my shirt a soft tug. He backs away for a moment, shucking his own shirt off first, baring his broad chest.

I comply mechanically, pulling the shirt over my head. I don't bother covering my breasts. He's already seen them, and that's exactly what he's looking at now, those sharp eyes taking me in.

"Lay down."

It isn't until he reaches for the button on his jeans that the panic really sets in. I turn away before he can see it, crawling onto the bed and settling there, flat on my back, staring wide-eyed up at the ceiling.

I don't watch as he takes off his pants, but I can hear it—the shifting of fabric, the steps he takes to the bed as he kicks them loose from his ankles. When he climbs on the mattress, the weight making it dip, I can see in my periphery that he's naked, cock swinging heavily between his thighs.

"Relax," he says, bending down to return his attention to my neck. One of his broad palms rests on my side, sweeping up to catch my breast in his hand. He mutters into my neck, "This doesn't have to be bad, you know. I might not be all mysterious and sensitive like *Rath*," the way he sneers this tells me just how low he thinks of it, "but I know how to make it good for you."

As if to prove this, he descends to my chest, taking one of my nipples into his mouth. My toes curl, but I try to remain passive. It gets a little harder when he wedges his hand between my thighs, rubbing my center as his tongue alternates breasts.

"I don't want it to be good, I just want it to be over with," I grind out, mostly because I already know it *could* be good. Even with all my efforts to approach this indifferently, I can feel my body responding to what he's doing.

He pauses for a second, the curve of his shoulders tensing. It's not like it was with Perez, where every nerve ending rejected the thought of him touching me. With Killian, my mind recoils but springs right back, seeking more. It's a confusing twist of want and shame.

He lets go of my breast, pushing up to look into my eyes. I stiffen as I feel his fingers hook into the waist of my leggings, tugging. "Too bad. Need to get you wet for me, or it'll hurt more." He rears back, taking my leggings and underwear with him, drawing them down my unyielding legs. His nostrils flare wide at my lack of response, but he doesn't say anything.

He tosses the clothing aside and grabs my knee, spreading me open before him. "I'm not going to hurt you." The words come out surly and forceful, but it just makes me scoff. That's a lie. This was always going to hurt. His brows crouch low at the sound, the muscle in the back of his jaw tensing into a tight knot. He gives me an ornery look before shoving my thighs apart and ducking down to lick a hot, wet path up my center.

My legs lock, half in shocked surprise and half because of the bolt of electricity it sends up my spine. His hands hold me open, though, fingers clamped around my thighs as his tongue explores my most private area.

I rise up onto my elbows, but I'm not sure why. I want to get away, but I also want to move closer. The two competing forces pull me in both directions, making me restless. When his tongue finds my clit, I collapse back to the bed, hands fisting in the comforter. I clamp my lips together, refusing to make a sound, but...*oh god.*

It's so warm and good.

His eyes flick up to mine as his tongue works me over, full of a dark, livid determination. He lets one of my thighs free, but before I can even think about clamping my legs shut, his fingers are joining his mouth, exploring my folds, seeking my entrance.

He slips a finger in slow and easy, pausing to watch my reaction.

Mortifyingly, I buck against it, pushing it in deeper.

His eyes flash, filling with fire. "Yeah, you fucking like it."

I shake my head against the pillow, but we both know it's a lie. He pumps his finger in and out, letting a second join. The stretch is a surprise, and I start to protectively close my thighs, but his tongue is back so quick that I can't feel anything else but the shooting sparks in my clit.

He makes a sound, rough and eager against my core, and I can't help it then.

Mouth falling open on a gasp, I grind up into him.

The feel of his fingers slipping free startles me, but his face looks harder now, eyes full of something aggressive and crazed. He spreads my lips wide and slides lower, forcing the pointed tip of his tongue inside me.

Throwing my head back, I grab out blindly, clutching onto a handful of his hair.

It's like nothing I've ever felt before—not even when Rath did this to me. Not even when Tristian uses his fingers on me. It doesn't last long before Killian is lurching up, mouth latching onto my breast as his fingers enter me again.

"Stretching you out," he says, sucking a kiss into the top of my breast. "Your pussy's so goddamn tight. They should have been preparing you for this."

Involuntarily, I wonder what that would look like. Tristian, sliding more fingers into me? Dimitri's head between my legs, assaulting me with his tongue?

I know it's coming when Killian's hips start to twitch in the rhythm of his fingers, his teeth growing more and more present in his kisses across my collarbone. He's getting impatient.

His fingers slide free only to wrap around the base of his cock. When he pulls up, I finally let myself look at it. It looks painfully hard, and when he pumps his fist, I feel myself begin panicking again. How the hell is that thing going to fit?

He pushes my thigh up, spreading me for him, hooded eyes glued to my pussy. "Fuck, you're nice and wet. You ready?" he asks, guiding the tip *right there*, up against my entrance.

My knees tremble, something scared and angry wedged into my throat. "Just fucking do it."

With a forceful punch of his hips, he shoves it inside.

I cry out, going rigid against the sudden, intense burn. Grinding my head back into the pillow, I strike out blindly, grasping onto the first thing I feel. His biceps are tense, holding him above me as he digs deeper inside, hips pushing.

His breathing is ragged. "Relax. Breathe."

But my hands just want to push him back. "*God*, it's too much—too big."

"You can take it," he says, bending to rumble into my ear, "but you need to *let me in*." He punctuates this by pulling his hips back, dragging his cock away, only to push it back inside. My body seizes around him and he groans in a way that seems more frustrated than anything. "You're so goddamn stubborn, would you just—" He shifts his weight to one arm, reaching down to press two fingers into my clit.

Oh.

Fuck.

I embrace the instinct to raise my hips into the touch. Anything to chase that feeling. Anything to make this better. He thrusts again, but it hurts less now, tempered by the point of pressure that's making my blood thrum.

His groan is different now, coarse and raw. "That's right. Let me make it good for you." He cups his hand around the top of my head, using a measured twist of his hips to sink another thick inch of his cock inside. He pauses at the sound I make, breathing hard into my temple. I can feel from the tremble in his arms how much it's costing him to stay still—to restrain himself—until my legs go lax again.

I give an experimental, curious shift of my hips, watching Killian's jaw go sharp-edged in response. It starts feeling less like being torn open and more like a satisfying sense of being full. It's the kind of feeling that makes my chest swoop, like maybe I'm imploding a bit against the flutter of Killian's fingers.

It's not terrible.

It's *really* not terrible.

He eases back before his hips curl forward in a calculated, testing way. This careful slowness wasn't what I was expecting from sex with Killian, and I find myself bracing for the worst, waiting, anticipating.

It never comes.

He's not even touching my clit anymore, but it doesn't feel any less good. Every time our bodies meet, I'm filled with the urge to push back against him. I don't bother fighting it anymore.

"That's it," he mutters, voice tight with a control that sounds shaky. "So good. *Fuck*, you're taking it so good." He watches, eyebrows knitted together. There's the long, slick, tugging sensation of him retreating, and then the controlled, gliding, pushing sensation of him returning. I turn my head away because it's too intense, too confusing, too tangled to look him in the eye as he rocks into my body, commanding it to rock back. But now I'm face to face with this *girl* on the inside of his bicep. A tattoo. Her hair is long, floating about his muscle in elegant tendrils, a tall, black diamond shape painted over each eye like makeup. Who is she? Is she someone Killian's fucked like this?

"Look at me," he says, grabbing my chin and wrenching me back. His eyes are heavy but bright, full of something that I'd call passion on anyone else. Roughly, he demands, "Look at me while I'm fucking you."

The kiss is bruising and takes me by surprise. I whimper against his lips and he rumbles back, reaching down to cup my breast in his wide palm. His hips meet mine in a hard thrust, punching a sharp gasp from my lungs. Killian takes advantage of my parted mouth, licking inside.

I think maybe I can taste myself on him, and I'm so distracted by the electrifying drag of his cock that it doesn't even occur to me to not kiss him back. His kisses are possessive and urgent, and it's just like I'd told the girls. He kisses like he wants to claw his way inside.

Except he's already there.

His movements grow more pointed—hips meeting mine in gradually harder thrusts. It hits me just the right way, the gift of friction yanking a needy moan from my throat. He swallows it down and uses it, finds out just the right pressure and push, until I'm the one shaking.

A part of me doesn't want it, this building climb to a precipice that Killian has no right leading me to. It'd be better to fight against it, to feel nothing, to walk away from this knowing that nothing about it was good or soft or worth ever doing again.

The reality is much more complicated. Because Killian is kissing me, and there's a frightening hunger to it, but there's also a reverence, like he's savoring every push inside me and holding it greedily close. This doesn't feel like anger or the cutting brag of a victory.

It feels like he's making love to me.

My orgasm is sharp and deeper than I'm used to. I thrash my head to the side, not bothering to stifle my cry.

He grabs my hip, yanking me closer as he grunts. I scramble for purchase, digging my fingers into his shoulders, and he pants against my cheek. "Yeah," he breathes through clenched teeth. "Harder. Make it hurt."

It's an easy request to fulfill.

He hisses, eyes fluttering closed as my fingernails dig divots into his flesh. I get a look at him over his shoulder, at the way he's fucking into me, hips pumping forward and back, and the whole thing is shockingly obscene. His muscles shift and ripple beneath his skin, and for a moment, I'm lost in the thought of all the raw, physical power being used to push this one part of him inside of me.

He goes stiff, driving himself deep and hard, and then he growls. I know he's coming because I can feel it, the burning rush of his spunk as it fills me.

He doesn't linger for very long, breathing hard and damp into my skin before rolling off of me. The tug of his softening cock being pulled from my body makes me wince, but then I'm able to close my knees.

Even though he's gone, I can still feel him inside of me.

He mutters a curse, drawing my attention. He's holding his spent cock. I can tell from the way he lunges for his shirt that he's trying to wipe it clean before I see the blood.

"I don't care," I say, moving my gaze to the ceiling.

"Most girls bleed," he's saying, and there's an uncalled-for thread of defensiveness there, as if he's worried I'll think he's torn me up unnecessarily. "It's normal."

"I don't care," I say again, looking him in the eye to make sure he knows it. When it comes to Killian, there's a lot I don't care about.

From the look on his face, I think he can see it.

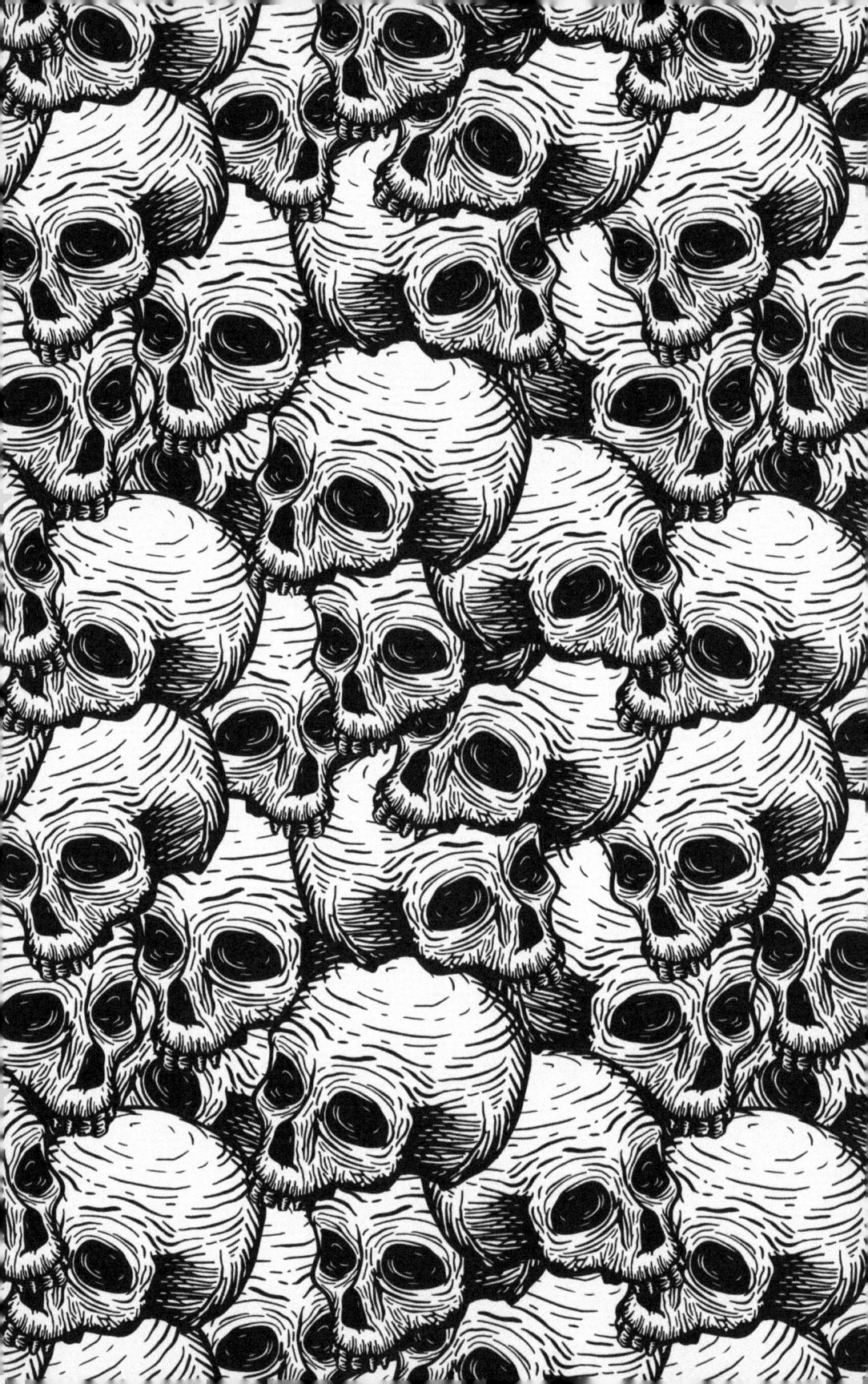

32

EXPOSED

Killian falls asleep before I even have a chance to climb off the bed. I do it now, careful not to wake him. I feel like I'm trapped inside a lion's den, desperate to break free. I think of Tristian, who's waiting for me somewhere. I think of Rath, who's probably still upset with me. Mostly, I think of anything *but* the semen running down my thigh.

There's a spot on the bed where I was laying, stained with blood and Killian's come. I stare at it for a long, tense moment, wishing I could rip the sheets from underneath his sleeping body, and just throw them away.

I settle for pulling on my clothes instead, pausing when he lets out a muffled snore. I wait, not wanting to face him again, staring at the computer screen, and bide my time. As the playlist cycles through, I think of the last time I opened it, recalling the neat little folders. There was one for the other Lady Applicants. For LDZ. For the South Side. But that's not what rings in my head like a faint bell.

That night after Killian punished me in front of the frat, when he and the guys were fighting on the basketball court, he'd said something about this being a game. He was angry. I was traumatized, but now, with my mind numb, I remember where I'd seen it—here, on Killian's laptop.

Cutting my eyes to the figure on the bed, I slowly approach the computer, still unlocked. Finding the folder again is easy, GAME POINTS is in all caps.

It's a spreadsheet.

A spreadsheet with scores.

Oral (give) - 5pts

Oral (rec'v) - 10pts

Exhibition (public) - x5

Exhibition (home) - x2

Fingering - 4

Handjob - 7

Spoken Consent - x2

Spoken Request - x3

The list goes on and on. It looks like some kind of twisted sex game. It's finely detailed to the point of categorization. There are nine variations of hand use, and almost twenty variations of oral.

On the next tab, I find a score sheet.

Beside each score is a date, a description, and a link.

T - 8/30 - 25pts - Fingered Lady in Library

R - 9/6 - 76pts - Lady asked to blow me

K - 9/3 - 36pts - Fucked the Lady's tits

My heartbeat feels like a jet engine in my ears. I click a link without thinking, not knowing what to expect. What appears is a video of Rath's bedroom. He's lounging out on the bed and that's me on the couch, looking uncomfortable.

I press my palms to my cheeks, shakily offering, "I could…suck you."

He raises a slow eyebrow. "You expect me to believe you want to give me head?"

Grimacing, I look away, embarrassed. "I don't…not want to. You're cute and everything, and who knows. If I'm not being forced to do it, maybe it'll be different. Maybe I'll like it."

There's a smirk on his face, but it's gone in a flash when I look his way.

"You want to suck my dick?"

I give a single, uncertain nod.

He doesn't look impressed. "Begrudging nods aren't really the vibe my dick's going for. Thanks anyway."

"Dimitri. I want to...suck you off." At his blank stare, I elaborate, "I don't know if I'll be very good at it, so you might have to be patient. But I mean it. I do. Want to. Especially if you think it will help and technically, I am the one that put that no-sex rule in the contract."

He drags his bottom lip between his teeth, eyes straying back down to my chest. "Alright," he decides. "If you want to."

The whole thing is there, and I don't even care that the audio is coming over the speakers in the room. I watch, eyes glued to the screen as I take Dimitri into my mouth. Minutes later, his head tips back, eyes meeting the camera.

And he fucking *smiles*.

I hastily click out of it, frantically clicking through the others. There are three more with Dimitri, even if the mornings I woke up in his bed aren't included.

Not yet.

There's some with Tristian, and then the time with Killian in the hallway. The one that stabs into my chest the most isn't even attached to any points on the spreadsheet. It's just labeled 'Den – Talking Some Sense Into Killer'.

"I'm seven points behind. I could dust your ass in a single lunch." Tristian rolls his eyes, but adds in a begrudging tone, "That said, the tutoring mindfuck was genius. You and I," he points to Killian, "are going to have to up our game."

"How? How the fuck do you get so many points? I spend ten minutes with her and I want to put my fist through a wall, but you expect me to believe the two of you—"

Rath holds up a hand, eyebrows climbing his forehead. "Are you doubting us?"

"Every point can be backed up," Tristian agrees, sipping from his own tumbler. "I watched Rath's video myself. She wanted to suck his dick. She swallowed. She didn't run away after." He's ticking off point modifiers on his fingers. "Look, I know you don't think much of the long game, but Story isn't like you think, Killer. The path of least resistance works with her. She's, like... just a normal girl."

Rath leans forward to pry his glass back. "She's putty, dude. The punishments don't pay off, but you know what does? Being nice!" He chuckles at this. "Tristian bought her one of those paper flowers after the game. You know, the ones they sell to fundraise? You should have seen the look on her face."

"She was blushing and tripping all over herself," Tristian explains. "It doesn't even take much."

"Prince tactics," Killian sneers, but Tristian shakes his head.

"Not at all. You see, you're so fucking terrible to her that she latches onto the smallest gesture of kindness like Velcro. So hey, I guess here's to you." He raises his glass toward Killian before tipping it back.

Killian seethes, "This is fucking bullshit. Kindness? Niceness? Since when do you fuckers play the game like that?"

"Since I'm going to be breaking in that pussy with my fat cock in a few months." Rath laughs, grabbing his crotch. "Sorry, bro. All's fair."

This.

This is the game.

My trust.

My feelings.

My virginity and who takes it.

Me.

I don't feel the tears rolling down my cheeks until one lands on my hand, trembling over the trackpad. It was all a lie. Every moment of comfort I felt with Dimitri—with *Rath*—was just a joke. Something I was manipulated into feeling. Here I've been, thinking Rath was above all that, but it's a lie. Those times in his bedroom, on my knees for him, was no better than what Tristian and Killian did to me, after all.

Fake.

It was all fucking fake.

Tristian's kindness, probably even the apology. Maybe it even runs deeper. Maybe they were secretly on board with that night in the basement.

"You're so fucking terrible to her that she latches onto the smallest gesture of kindness like Velcro."

It all makes a terrible sense now. They weren't changing. They weren't growing to care for me. They were playing me the whole time.

And I ate it up, like a stupid, naïve, moronic little victim.

The hurt—the grief and humiliation—is so much less then. I gather it up and tuck it away, refusing to feel it. I embrace the fire instead of the cold, letting it heat me from within. I realize now that this is how everything works. There is no comfort, no compassion, no safety. The only warmth in this world comes from blood or fire.

I swat away my useless tears, sniffle back my pathetic snot, and look to the bed once again. My phone slides easily from my pocket, and when I approach the bed, Killian doesn't stir.

Not even when I take a picture of the stain in the middle of it.

I access that ancient email of mine—the one meant for spam. The one Ted had sent me messages to. I compose a message with the title, "It's gone."

Attaching the photo, I type only a single sentence in the body of the email:

What are you going to do about it?

They have my blood, and now they're about to meet my fire.

Because I'm going to burn this motherfucker down.

EPILOGUE

TED

The house sits on a massive lot, right in the middle of the city. There are no rolling hills or manicured lawns here, just the flat, paved surroundings of what used to be a three-block, government-owned housing project.

"This seems a little extravagant for the South Side," I say, getting out of the BMW. I'm hedging, and chances are, she knows it. From the nervous look on her face, she won't call me out on it. Folding my sunglasses, I tuck them into my coat, adjusting my shirt cuffs.

Yes, I know exactly what this property is.

But she plays along. "GussyZ built it for his mother. You know, the rapper? He grew up right here, and after he made it big, his mother refused to move. So he razed the apartment complex he grew up in, and built this monstrosity on top of it." The agent shakes her head, admiring the building. "Too bad about that tax lien. Government seized it and now it's up for auction."

"Too bad for him. Perfect for me." I haven't been keeping an eye on this like I should, so I missed the lien, but the location couldn't be better. Sprawling lot, plenty of rooms, nestled deep in the seedy underbelly of South Side. My territory.

I'd been skeptical when she set the meeting. Not only has Leslie been skimming tens of thousands a month off my rental income, but she's ripe to turn informant, too. She thinks I don't know about the skimming, but I can see in her eyes that she worries. As she should. Given half the opportunity, this woman would bury a blade in my back and smile while doing it. It's often the case with women.

Despite that, she really brought me her best today. Staking a claim in this and moving my venture to the next level is the right step for my enterprise.

When she enters the code in the front door, I can see her hand shaking. It's merely a small tremble, but my eyes don't miss anything. I should put her out of her misery, but I decide to watch her fumble for the time being.

When the lock engages, I swoop in, amused by her frightened flinch, and hold the door open for her, the gold inlay on my ring glinting in the daylight.

She gives me an anxious look and scurries through the entrance.

"How many bedrooms?" I ask, taking in the space. The floor is a bold, inlaid mosaic of a medallion, with marble pillars standing proudly on either side of the staircase. The chandelier hanging above is gold and crystal. Tall, two-story archways invite one to enter a sitting room to our left.

It's tacky and ostentatious.

"Ten," she answers, eyes apprehensive.

In short, it's perfect.

"Baths?"

"Eleven full," she adds, pushing her shoulders back. Yes. You find that spine, sweetheart. "Three half."

I hum, shoes clicking on the marble as I walk the space. "And an in-law suite downstairs?" I turn to her, noting the way her eyes widen.

She realizes I already know, but still answers, "Yes."

"Good." I nod, lacing my fingers behind my back. "I have some property I've been meaning to repossess. The old bat will need living quarters." Turning to her, I add, "Good job, Leslie."

She looks like she might have a heart attack, her shoulders deflating, chest expanding with a relieved gulp of air. Despite that, she smiles at me, so grateful that it almost makes me wish I'd held out a little longer. "Thank you, sir. I knew as soon as I saw it on the wire that you'd want it."

I walk through the main floor, making a few notes on my phone. "We'll need a full bar over here." I gesture to the back wall. "A sitting area out by the pool would be nice. Tell me about the underground garage. My clients require discretion."

She nods obediently. "Yes, sir. It includes a back access from the alley and

EPILOGUE

the doors work on a sensor. With a little rigging, it could—"

The phone chimes in my hand, an email notification popping up on the screen. The moment I see it, I tune Leslie out. I blink, sure I'm reading it wrong.

Email Notification: Sweet Cherry.

I keep my voice calm and calculated. "Excuse me," I say, blood thrumming as I walk from the room and escape outside. My head swims with anticipation, heart pounding an urgent rhythm. Three years since I've heard from this one. Three years since she slipped through my fingers.

I swipe it open and stare at the message title: *It's gone.*

I'm half-convinced it's a prank. Likely, those cocky little bastards she's hiding with found out about me and thought this would be a fun way to fuck around. That's okay. I've been preparing for how to deal with them.

Then I see the message.

What are you going to do about it?

It's a crisp photo, the contents unmistakable. It's a bed with white sheets, pristine if not for the stain sitting stark against the paleness. Blood. From the dark dampness that surrounds it, probably some semen, too. Blood and semen and her arousal.

Oh, Story…

I'm looking at the remnants of her cherry.

There's a man's hand curled up next to it, wrist dark with tattoos. He's wearing a gold ring in the shape of a distinctive skull. I don't need to zoom in to see the 'LDZ' engraved within it.

It's the same ring as my own, after all.

I turn off the phone, knowing who it is and what he's done. I grind my teeth, trying to shove the crazed hurricane of anger back into my chest. Just for now. Just until I can make a move.

But it's hard, imagining those hands on my sweet young Lady. Knowing he's taken what belongs to me. Knowing that he's defiled her, tainted her, forced his dirtiness inside her. I tried to warn her. This world is a machine. The cogs turn, making it spin, and the wheel never stops. It takes a woman and turns her into a whore. Unclean. Polluted. Impure.

If the Lords think I'll let that happen to her, then they are sorely mistaken.

Storming back through the door, my head is still full of the sight of those sheets. I wonder how it happened. Did he tear his way inside? Did he fuck her like an animal? Did he stretch those greedy lips into a smile as he defiled what's rightfully mine?

Leslie turns when I approach, fumbling with her folders, so eager to regale me with more details that she misses the gun I pull from my coat.

I raise the barrel and put three bullets into her head.

As she falls to the floor, the sound of gunshots still ringing against the marble, I draw in a feral, steeling breath, soaking in the silence.

Yes, that's better.

My vengeance has never been swift, but it's always absolute and without mercy.

The Lords are about to discover just how true that is.

ACKNOWLEDGEMENTS

A THANK YOU FROM ANGEL

When we started the Lords' books, we had no idea what to expect. We were both a little nervous about releasing a book that was so dark and probably revealed a little too much about the inner psyche of Samgel. Our author note in that first book is 100% true. We were wary of our friends and family seeing the result of our collaboration.

Sam put a sticky note on her computer that said, "Don't Hold Back!" which is exactly why I had approached her in the first place to help me write these darker books. I had the ideas, but Sam had the execution.

We knew the cover was good—great even. It just clicked. Killian, Dimitri and Tristian? They were terrible, awful, horrible men and, well, they clicked. And Story, omg, well, if you've read through the Dukes of Peril, you understand there's a bigger game afoot. We can't wait to reveal it.

The truth is that Lords released with a, um… not a whimper, but also not a bang. Just kind of a nice, normal release. If you're an author, there's kind of a pattern to releases. Day 1-3 are nice. The preorders drop, the KU reads roll in, the book finds a high spot on the rankings (in our case mid 100-200, which is really great. We were happy! And, like usual, the book started to slowly settle back to 300 or so. It was a good release. We were excited to move forward… and then… three weeks later, Lords of Pain hit the top 100. Guys, I have been doing this for ten years and let me tell you, ranks never go backwards. Never. I was so confused. Little did I know at the time that word of mouth, Y'ALLS' MOUTHS, was buzzing on BookTok (which was new) and Bookstagram, and in readers groups. You guys made Lords of Pain become a best seller, and therefore, ultimately, made this Kickstarter happen.

So, this is just one big giant thank you to everyone that shared, reviewed, posted, commented and helped Lords of Pain take flight. This special edition wouldn't be here without your enthusiasm.

A THANK YOU FROM SAMANTHA

I REALLY DO still have that sticky note, and I try my best to always heed it! Who would have thought that white-knuckling all those long nights of anxiety as we wrote Pain would have brought me here? Certainly not me. To be frank, this book took me a very dark place, and I really wasn't sure I could do it again.

But I'm starting to understand that place better now. I revist it with every new Forsyth book we write. It's not pretty. This is not the sepia-toned, glasses-askew, happy clunking-typewriter montage every author beginning their journey in publishing imagines it will be. Mine is full of night terrors, intrusive thoughts, manic episodes, stacking piles of dirty laundry, and unhinged 4am emails to Angel.

And then something amazing happens, just as it did that first time with Lords of Pain. A ray of light breaks through the shadow, and I'm convinced

ACKNOWLEDGEMENTS

that—for me, at least—nothing beautiful can possibly be created without the triumph of untangling it from the darkness like some precious thing caught in barbed wire.

So I give to you my second beautiful triumph with Lords of Pain: This special edition hardback. I had almost as much turmoil over designing it as I did writing it, and you all deserve nothing less.

So thank you all for being awake with me at 4am without ever realizing it, for pushing me through that shadow without ever knowing, and for being there to greet us with open arms when we finally emerge from it.